Also available from Diana Palmer
and Harlequin HQN

Coming in November 2014

Wyoming Strong

DIANA PALMER

LONG, TALL TEXANS

VOLUME II: *Tyler & Sutton*

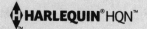

ISBN-13: 978-0-373-77976-5

LONG, TALL TEXANS VOL. II: TYLER & SUTTON

Copyright © 2014 by Harlequin Books S.A.

Recycling programs
for this product may
not exist in your area.

The publisher acknowledges the copyright holder of the individual works as follows:

TYLER
Copyright © 1988 by Diana Palmer

SUTTON'S WAY
Copyright © 1989 by Diana Palmer

This edition published by arrangement with Harlequin Books S.A.

For questions and comments about the quality of this book, please contact us at CustomerService@Harlequin.com.

® and TM are trademarks of Harlequin Enterprises Limited or its corporate affiliates. Trademarks indicated with ® are registered in the United States Patent and Trademark Office, the Canadian Intellectual Property Office and in other countries.

HARLEQUIN®
www.Harlequin.com

Printed in U.S.A.

CONTENTS

TYLER

CHAPTER ONE

To TYLER JACOBS, the hot arid southeastern Arizona landscape still seemed about as welcoming as Mars, even after six weeks of working on the Double R dude ranch near Tombstone.

He was restless and vaguely depressed. He'd taken a day off to fly to Jacobsville for his sister, Shelby's, wedding to Justin Ballenger, a man she'd refused to marry years ago. Tyler was still puzzled by the courtship. They hadn't looked the picture of a happy couple, and he knew that Justin had been bitter toward Shelby for breaking their earlier engagement.

But it wasn't any of his business; he had to keep that in mind. And better to see Shelby married to Justin, who was old-fashioned enough to keep his marriage vows, than to see her mixed up with the local playboy attorney she worked for. Maybe things would work out for them. If the way Shelby had looked at Justin was any indication, they had to work out. She was obviously still deeply in love with him.

Abby and Calhoun had been at the wedding, too, and Tyler was relieved to find that his brief infatuation with Abby was over. He'd been ready to settle down and was unconsciously looking for the right kind of woman. Abby had fit the bill in every respect, but he wasn't nursing a broken heart. His eyes narrowed in thought. He wondered if he was capable of loving a woman. Sometimes he felt that he was impervious to anything more than surface interest. Of course, there was always the woman who could hit a man hard before he knew it. A woman like Nell Regan, with her unexpected vulnerabilities and compassion...

Even as the unwelcome thought touched his mind, his pale green eyes narrowed on a rider approaching from the direction of the ranch house.

He sighed, glaring through the endless creosote bushes. They dominated the landscape all the way to the Dragoon Mountains, one of Cochise's old strongholds back in the mid-1800s. The "monsoon season" had almost passed. Today it was on the verge of a hundred degrees, and damn what they said about the dry heat not being hot. Sweat was pouring down his dark olive complexion from the sweatband of his gray Stetson, soaking his Western-cut chambray shirt. He took his hat from his jet-black hair and drew his forearm over the wetness while he got his bearings. Out here one stretch of valley looked much like any other, and the mountain ranges went on forever. If elbow room was what a man wanted, he could sure get it in Arizona.

He'd been out in the brush trying to round up some stray Hereford calves, while his worn leather chaps were treated to the double jeopardy of cholla and prickly pear cactus where the creosote wasn't so thick. Nothing grew around creosote. Having smelled the green bush, especially in the rain, he could understand why.

Before the rider got much closer, Tyler realized that it was Nell. And something was wrong, because she usu-

ally kept the length of the ranch between them. Their
relationship had become strained unexpectedly, and
that saddened him. It had seemed as though he and
Nell would be friends at their first meeting, when she'd
picked him up at the Tucson airport. But all too soon
something had sent Nell running from him.

Perhaps that was for the best. He was earning a living, but not much more, and all his wealth was gone.
He had nothing to offer a woman like Nell. All the
same, he felt guilty if he'd hurt her, even inadvertently.
She didn't talk about the past, and neither did anyone
else. But Tyler knew that something had happened to
make her wary and distrustful of men. She deliberately
downplayed the few attractions she had, as if she was
determined not to do anything that would catch a man's
eye. Tyler had gotten close to her at first, because he'd
thought of her as a cute little kid. She'd been so anxious
to make him comfortable, sneaking him feather pillows
and all kinds of little things from the house to make
him feel at home. He'd flirted with her gently, teased
her, delighted in her shy company. And then, like light-
ning, the housekeeper had made him see that the child
he was playing with was really a twenty-four-year-old
woman who was misinterpreting his teasing. From that
night on, he and Nell had somehow become strangers.
She avoided him, except at the obligatory square dance
with guests twice a month.

Nell did seem to find him useful in one respect. She
still hid behind him at those every-other-Saturday-night
barn dances. The way she clung to him was the only
crumb left of their easy first acquaintance. But it was
vaguely insulting, too. She didn't consider him a threat

in any sexual way, or she'd have run screaming from his presence. He'd made some hard remarks about Nell to his sister, Shelby, but he hadn't really meant them. He hadn't wanted anyone to realize how Nell was getting to him.

He sighed, watching her approach. Well, she wasn't dressed to fan a man's ardor, in those baggy jeans and blouse and slouch hat, and that was a good thing. He found her shyness and his odd sense of empathy for her disturbing enough without the added complication of an exquisite figure. He frowned, wondering what she looked like under that baggy camouflage. As if he'd ever find out, he thought, laughing bitterly. He'd already scared her off.

He wasn't a conceited man, but he was used to women. His money had always attracted the beautiful ones, and whatever he wanted, he got. And so, being snubbed by the stone girl stung his pride.

"Have you found those strays yet?" Nell asked with faint nervousness as she reined in beside him.

"I've only gone through five thousand miles," he murmured with soft antagonism. "Wherever they are, they're probably enjoying the luxury of enough water to drink. God knows, except in the monsoon season, they'd need a divining rod or second sight in this barren wasteland to find any."

Nell searched his hard face quietly. "You don't like Arizona, do you?"

"It's foreign." He turned his gaze toward the horizon, where jagged mountains seemed to change color as the sun shifted, first dark, then mauve, then orange.

"This takes some getting used to, and I've only been out here a few weeks."

"I grew up here," she remarked. "I love it. It only looks barren. If you see it up close, there's all kinds of life."

"Horny toads, rattlesnakes, Gila monsters..." he agreed dryly.

"Red-winged blackbirds, cactus wrens, roadrunners, owls, deer," she corrected. "Not to mention wildflowers by the score. Even the cacti bloom," she added, and there was a sudden softness in her dark eyes, a warmth in her voice that was usually missing.

He bent his head to light a cigarette. "It looks like desert to me. How's your trail ride coming?"

"I left the guests with Chappy," she said with a sigh. "Mr. Howes looked as if one more bounce would put him on the ground. I hope he makes it back to the ranch."

Tyler smiled slightly as he glanced at her rigid figure in the saddle. "If he falls off, we'll need a crane to get him back on."

Nell grinned without meaning to. He wouldn't know it, but he was the first man in years who'd been able to make her smile. She was a somber, quiet woman most of the time, except when Tyler was around. Then she'd found out what he really thought of her....

"Tyler, could you take over the campout for me?" she asked unexpectedly. "Marguerite and the boys are coming for the weekend, and I have to go into Tucson and get them."

"I can handle it, if you'll persuade Crowbait to

cook," he agreed. "I'm not making biscuits again. I'll quit first."

"Crowbait isn't so bad," she defended. "He's—" her dark eyes narrowed as she searched for a word "—unique."

"He has the temperament of a cougar, the tongue of a cobra and the manners of a bull in heat," Tyler said shortly.

She nodded. "Exactly! He's unique."

He chuckled and took another draw from his cigarette. "Well, boss lady, I'd better get those strays before somebody with an itchy trigger finger has beef for supper. I won't be long."

"The boys want to go looking for Apache arrowheads while they're here," she added hesitantly. "I told them I'd ask you."

"Your nephews are nice kids," he said unexpectedly. "They need a firmer hand than they get, though."

"Marguerite isn't the ideal parent for two high-strung boys," Nell said defensively. "And since Ted died, it's been worse. My brother could handle them."

"Marguerite needs a husband." He smiled at the thought of Marguerite. She was like the life he'd been used to—sophisticated and uncomplicated and pretty. He liked her because she brought back sweet memories. She was, in fact, all the things Nell wasn't. "But a dish like Margie shouldn't have much trouble finding one."

Nell knew her sister-in-law was beautiful, but it hurt somewhere deep inside to hear Tyler acknowledge Margie's good looks. Nell was only too aware of her own limitations, of her round face and big eyes and high cheekbones. She nodded, though, and forced a smile to her unlipsticked mouth. She never wore makeup. She never did anything to draw attention to her…until recently. She'd tried to attract Tyler, but Bella's comments had killed the notion. Tyler's subsequent behavior had buried it.

Now Nell knew better than to make eyes at Tyler. Besides, Margie was just his style, she thought bitterly. And Margie was interested, too.

"I'll go into Tucson, then, if you're sure about the campout. And if you can't find those strays by five, come back in and we'll let your Texas friends look for them in the morning," she added, referring to two of the older hands who shared a Texas background with Tyler and had become fast friends of his in the six weeks he'd been in residence.

"I'll find them," he said carelessly. "All I have to do is look for a puddle of water, and they'll be standing on their heads in it."

"You already know not to sit in any dips or washes," she murmured. "Out here is even worse than in Texas. It can be raining twenty miles away and the sky can be clear, and before you know it, you're in a floodplain."

"We have flash floods where I come from," he reminded her. "I know the dangers."

"I was just reminding you," she said, and hated the concern that she'd unwittingly betrayed.

His eyes narrowed and he smiled unpleasantly, stung by her condescending attitude. "When I need a nursemaid, honey, I'll advertise," he said in a pronounced Texas drawl.

Nell steeled herself not to react to what was blatantly an insult. "If you have a chance tomorrow, I'd like you to speak to Marlowe about his language. One of the guests complained that she was getting tired of hearing him swear every time he saddled a horse for her."

"Why can't you tell him?"

She swallowed. "You're the foreman. Isn't keeping the men in line your job?"

"If you say so, ma'am." He tipped his hat with faint insolence, and she wheeled her mount too quickly, almost unseating herself in the process when she pulled on the bit too hard. She urged the horse into a trot and soothed him, stroking his mane as she apologized. She knew Tyler had seen that betraying action, and she felt even worse. She was the last person on the ranch who'd ever hurt a horse voluntarily, but Tyler had a talent for stoking her temper.

He watched her go, his cigarette smoking, forgotten, in his lean, tanned fingers. Nell was a puzzle. She wasn't like any woman he'd ever known, and she had quirks that intrigued him. He was sorry they'd become antagonists. Even when she was pleasant, there was always the reserve, the bitter holding back. She seemed to become rigid when she had to talk to him.

He sighed. He didn't have time for daydreaming. He had to find six little red-and-white-coated calves before dark. He turned his horse and moved into the thick brush.

Nell dawdled on her way back to the adobe ranch house. She wasn't anxious to have Marguerite around, but she hadn't been able to find an excuse to keep the redhead away. Tyler's remark about her sister-in-law still rankled. He found Marguerite attractive, and it wasn't because of Nell that Marguerite was finding reasons to spend time on the dude ranch. She wanted Tyler. She'd made it obvious with her flirting.

Marguerite was beautiful, all right. She was redheaded, green eyed, and blessed with a figure that looked good in anything. She and Nell got along fairly well, as long as neither of them looked back nine years. It had been Marguerite who'd helped put the scars on Nell's young emotions. Nell had never been able to forget what had happened.

On the other hand, it wasn't until Tyler came that Nell really noticed how often Marguerite used her. She was impulsive and thought nothing of inviting her friends out to the ranch for horseback rides or of leaving her two young sons in Nell's care.

Those actions had never bothered Nell very much until lately. Recently, Nell had been feeling oddly restless and stubborn. She didn't like the idea of Marguerite coming for two weekends in the same month. She should have said so. Giving in to her sister-in-law had become a habit, the way of least resistance. But not anymore. She'd already given Marguerite some unmistakable signals that little Nell wasn't going to be walked over anymore.

Margie only came out to see the Texan, Nell was sure of it. She felt a sense of regret for what she might have felt for Tyler if he hadn't made his lack of interest so apparent. But that was just as well. Margie had made it obvious that she liked Tyler, and Nell knew she was no competition for the older woman. On the other hand, she was pretty tired of letting Margie use her for a doormat. It was time to say so.

HER SISTER-IN-LAW and her nephews, Jess and Curt, were already packed and waiting when Nell parked the Ford Tempo at the steps of their apartment. The boys, red-headed and green-eyed like their mother, made a bee-line for her. At seven, Jess was the oldest. Curt was five and already a contender for a talking marathon.

"Hi, Aunt Nell, how about taking us to hunt lizards?" Curt asked as he clambered into the backseat a jump ahead of his taller brother.

"Never mind lizards, nerd," Jess muttered, "I want to look for arrowheads. Tyler said he'd show me where to look."

"I reminded him," Nell assured the older boy. "I'll go lizard hunting with Curt."

"Lizards make my skin crawl," Marguerite said. She wasn't quite as tall as Nell, but she was equally slender. She was wearing a green-and-white striped dress that looked as expensive as the diamond studs in her ears and the ruby ring on her right hand. She'd stopped wearing her wedding band recently—just since Tyler came to the ranch, in fact.

"Well, if I get a lizard, he can live with me," Curt told his mother belligerently.

Nell laughed, seeing her brother in the small boy's firm jaw and jutting chin. It made her a little sad, but it had been two years since Ted had died, and the worst of the grief had worn off. "Can he, now?"

"Not in my house," Marguerite said firmly. After her husband had died, Margie had taken her share of the ranch in cash and moved to the city. Margie had never really liked ranch life.

"Then he can live with Aunt Nell, so there."

"Stop talking back, you little terror." Marguerite yawned. "I do hope all the air conditioners are working this time, Nell. I hate the heat. And you'd better have Bella stock up on Perrier—there's no way I'm drinking water out of that well."

Nell got in under the wheel without any comment. Marguerite always sounded like a conquering army. It was annoying and sometimes frankly embarrassing to have Margie ordering her around and taking things for granted. Nell had taken it for a long time, out of loyalty to her late brother, and because the boys would suffer if she didn't. But it was hard going, and until just recently she'd taken a lot from Marguerite. It was only when Marguerite began making a dead set at Tyler that Nell had started talking back. And now that she'd gotten the hang of it, she rather liked not being talked down to and told what to do. She stared at her sister-in-law coldly while the boys argued in the backseat about who got the middle and who got a window seat.

"The ranch is mine," she reminded Marguerite quietly. "Uncle Ted is in charge until I turn twenty-five, but after that, I'm sole owner. Remember the terms of my father's will—my brother got half and I got half. Uncle Ted was executor. Then when my brother died, you got his share of the ranch in cash. As executor, Uncle Ted keeps control until I come of age. You don't give orders to me, and you don't get special consideration just because you're an in-law."

Marguerite stared. It wasn't like Nell to fight back so fiercely. "Nell, I didn't mean to sound like that," she began hesitantly.

"I haven't forgotten what happened nine years ago, even if you're trying to," Nell added quietly.

The older woman actually went bloodred. She looked away. "I'm sorry. I know you don't believe that, but I really am. I've had to live with it, too. Ted despised me for it, you know. Things were never the same between us after I had that party. I still miss him, very much," she added in a soft, conciliatory tone, with a glance in Nell's direction.

"Sure you do," Nell agreed as she started the car. "That's why you're dressed to the teeth and finding excuses to suffer the heat at the ranch. Because you miss Ted so much, and you want to console yourself with my hired help."

Marguerite gasped, but Nell ignored the sound. She pulled out into traffic and started telling the boys about the new calves, which kept the older woman quiet during the drive home.

As usual, when Bella saw Marguerite coming in the front door, the buxom housekeeper went out the back door on the pretense of carrying an apple pie over to the bunkhouse. On the way there she ran into Tyler, who looked tired and dusty and half out of humor.

"What are you doing out here?" he asked, grinning at the older woman with her black scowl.

"Hiding out," Bella said grumpily, pushing back strands of salt-and-pepper hair while her black eyes glittered. "She's back," she added icily.

"She?"

"Her Majesty. Lady Leisure." She shifted the pie. "Just what Nell needs, more people to take care of. That lazy redhead hasn't lifted a finger since poor Ted drowned in a dry wash. And if you knew what that flighty ex-model had done to Nell..." She flushed as she remembered who she was talking to. She cleared her throat. "I baked the men a pie."

"You baked me a pie," Nell muttered, glaring at her housekeeper as she came out of the back door. "And now you're giving it away because my sister-in-law is here. The boys like pie, too, you know. And Margie won't spoil her figure with sweets, anyway."

"She'll spoil my day," Bella shot back. "Wanting this, wanting that, make the bed, bring her a towel, cook her an omelet... She can't be bothered to pick up a shoe or carry a cup of coffee, no, not her. She's too good to work."

"Don't air the dirty linen out here," Nell said shortly, glancing at Tyler.

Bella lifted her small chin. "He's not blind," she said. "He knows what goes on here."

"Take my pie back in the house," Nell told her.

Bella glared at her. "She's not getting a bite of it."

"Tell her."

The older woman nodded curtly. "Don't think I won't." She glanced at Tyler and grinned. "You can have a slice, though."

He took off his hat and bowed. "I'll eat every crumb twice."

She laughed gleefully and went back inside.

"Aren't you late for the campout?" Nell asked curiously.

"We canceled it," he replied. "Mr. Curtis fell into a cactus and Mrs. Sims got sick on the chili we had

at lunch and had to go to bed. The rest figured they'd
rather watch television."

Nell smiled faintly. "Oh, well. The best-laid plans...
We'll try it again on the weekend."

Tyler studied her quietly, his eyes narrowed in
thought. "About this afternoon..." he began, holding
Nell's surprised gaze.

But before he could say another word, the door behind Nell swung open.

"Why, Tyler, how nice to see you again," Marguerite
said laughingly, pausing in the doorway.

"Nice to see you again, Mrs. Regan," he replied
dryly, and there was a world of knowledge in the pale
green eyes that swept lazily down her slender body.
Marguerite couldn't take him in with that strategic pose.
He knew too much. But it was amusing to watch her try.

Nell wanted to throw herself down in the dust and
cry, but that wouldn't have done any good. She went
back inside, giving up without a struggle.

Marguerite gave her a curious glance, but Nell didn't
even look at her. If she wanted Tyler, she was welcome
to him, Nell thought miserably. After all, she had nothing to give him herself.

Supper was a quiet affair, except for the boys squab-
bling over everything from milk to beans.

"Tyler is taking me riding tomorrow," Marguerite
said, giving Nell an apprehensive glance. "You'll mind
the boys, won't you?"

Nell looked up. She felt rebellious. Restless. "As a
matter of fact, I can't," she said with a faint smile. "Take
them with you. Tyler's already said he wouldn't mind
helping them find arrowheads."

"Sure!" Jess burst out. "I'd love to go."

"I'll go, too," Curt said.

Marguerite looked annoyed. "I don't want you along."

"You don't love us," Jess wailed.

"You never did," Curt seconded, and he started to cry.

Marguerite threw up her hands. "See what you've done now!" she accused Nell.

"I haven't done anything except refuse to be your doormat." Nell finished her potatoes. "I don't remember inviting you here," she replied coolly. "Don't expect me to entertain you or babysit for you."

"You always have before," Marguerite reminded her.

"That was before," Nell replied. "I'm not doing it anymore. You'll have to take care of yourself."

"Who's been talking to you?" Marguerite asked, fascinated.

"Nobody has," Nell replied. "I'm just tired of holding up the world. Why don't you get a job?"

Marguerite's gasp was audible, but Nell had gotten up and left the table before she had time for any outbursts.

TYLER TOOK MARGUERITE and the boys riding the next morning. Marguerite did look good in a riding habit, Nell had to concede, but the redhead was obviously out of sorts at having the boys along. Tyler hadn't fussed about taking the boys, either. He liked children. Nell smiled. She liked them, too, but it was Marguerite's job to be their mother, not Nell's.

She wandered out to the kitchen and picked up a

biscuit, having refused breakfast because she hadn't wanted to hear Margie raising Cain about the boys going along on her romantic ride.

"And what's eating you, as if I didn't know?" Bella asked.

Nell laughed. "Nothing at all."

"You've got Margie running for cover. Imagine, you talking back to her and refusing to be pushed around. Are you sick or something?" she added, her keen old eyes probing.

Nell bit into the biscuit. "Not at all. I'm just tired of being worked to death, I guess."

"And watching Margie flirt with Tyler, I've no doubt."

Nell glared at the older woman. "Stop that. You know I don't like him."

"You like him. Maybe it's my fault that things never got going between you," Bella confessed gently. "I was trying to spare you more heartache, or I'd never have said anything when you put on that pretty dress...."

Nell turned away. She didn't like being reminded of that day. "He isn't my type," she said gruffly. "He's Margie's type."

"That's what you think," Bella murmured dryly. She put her towel down and stood staring at the other woman. "I've wanted to tell you for years that most men are nice critters. Some of them are even domesticated. All men aren't like Darren McAnders," she added, watching Nell's face go pale. "And he wasn't even that bad except when he was pushed into getting drunk. He loved Margie."

"And I loved him," Nell said coldly. "He flirted with

me and teased me, just like Tyler did at first. And then he did…he did that to me, and it wasn't even because he was attracted to me. It was just to make Margie jealous!"

"It was despicable," Bella agreed. "But it was worse for you because you cared about him, and you felt betrayed and used. It was a good thing I happened upstairs when I did."

"Yes," Nell said tautly. The memories hurt.

"But it wasn't as bad as you've always made it out to be, either," Bella said firmly, ignoring the shocked look she got from Nell. "It wasn't," she added. "If you'd ever gone out with boys or had a date, you'd understand what happened a lot better. You hadn't even been kissed—"

"Stop it," Nell muttered miserably. She stuck her hands in her jeans and shifted. "It doesn't matter, anyway. I'm plain and countrified and no man is ever going to want me, no matter what I do. And I heard what Tyler said that night," she added with a cold glare. "I heard every word. He said he didn't want a 'lovesick tomboy hanging on to his boots.'"

Bella sighed. "So you did hear him. I was afraid that's why he was getting the deep-freeze treatment lately."

"It doesn't matter, you know," Nell said with deliberate carelessness. "It's just as well I found out early that I was annoying him. I've been careful not to bother him since."

Bella started to say something, but obviously thought better of it. "How long is Her Highness here for?"

"Just until tomorrow afternoon, thank God." Nell sighed. "I'd better get cracking. We're going riding, and then this afternoon I've got a busload of shoppers to take into town. I thought I'd run them over to the El Con mall. They might like to get some real Western gear at Cooper's."

"The silversmiths are over near San Xavier," she was reminded. "And they could have some Papago fry bread for refreshments."

"Tohono o'odham," Nell corrected automatically. "That's a real Papago word, meaning 'people of the desert.' They changed it because they got tired of being called 'bean people' in Zuni."

"I can't say that," Bella muttered.

"Sure you can. *Tohono o'odham.* Anyway, the fry bread is a good idea if we have any time left from the shopping."

"Are any of the husbands tagging along?" Bella asked.

Nell pursed her lips. "Do you think I'd look this cheerful if the men were coming with us?"

"Stupid question," Bella said with a sigh. "I'd better get started on chow, or is Chappy laying on a barbecue tonight before the square dance? He never asks me, he just goes ahead with whatever he wants to do."

"Chappy did say something about a barbecue. Why don't you make a bowl of potato salad and some home-made rolls and a few pies to go with it?" She put an arm around Bella's formidable girth. "That will save you some work, too, won't it? Actually, I think Chappy's kind of sweet on you."

Bella flushed and glared at Nell. "He ain't, neither! Now get out of here and let me get busy."

"Yes, ma'am." Nell grinned and curtsied before she darted out the back door.

Nell went down to the stables to check on the mounts for the morning ride. Chappy Staples was alone there, and after all these years, Nell was still a little in awe of him. He was older than most of the men, but he could outride the best of them. He'd never said a thing out of the way to Nell, but she couldn't help her remoteness. It was the same with all the men, except Tyler.

"How is the mare this morning?" she asked the wiry man with the pale blue eyes, referring to a horse with a bad shoe.

"I had the farrier come over and take a look at her. He replaced the shoe, but she's still restless this morning. I wouldn't take her out if I were you."

She sighed. "That will leave us one mount short," she murmured. "Margie's gone riding with Tyler and the boys."

"If you can handle it alone, I'll keep Marlowe here and let him help me work the colt, and one of the guests can have his horse," Chappy said. "How about it?"

"That sounds great." She sighed, thanking her lucky stars that the foulmouthed Marlowe was being kept clear of her guests. If he kept it up, he'd have to go, and that would leave them a man short. Nell didn't like the idea of adding on new men. It had taken her long enough to get used to the ones she already had on the place.

"We'll start at ten," she told Chappy. "And we have to be back in time for lunch. I'm taking the ladies shopping about one-thirty."

"No problem, ma'am." He tipped his hat and returned to work.

Nell wandered back toward the house, deep in thought, almost running head-on into Tyler because she didn't see him until he rounded the corner of the house.

She gasped, stepping back. "Sorry," she said, faltering. "I didn't see you."

He glared down at her. "I was about to head off riding with Margie and the boys when I heard that I'm escorting Margie to the square dance tonight."

"Are you?" she asked, all at sea.

He lifted an eyebrow. "That's what Margie tells me. She said it was your idea," he added in an exaggerated Texas drawl that could have skinned a cactus at close range.

"I guess you wouldn't believe me if I told you I haven't said a word to her about it," she said resignedly.

"You throw her at me every time she comes out here, don't you?" he asked with a mocking smile.

She lowered her eyes and turned away. "I did once or twice, sure. I thought you might enjoy her company," she said in a subdued tone. "She's like you. Sophisticated and classy and upper crust. But if you'd rather she went with someone else, I'll see what I can do."

He caught her arm, noticing the way she tensed and froze. "All right. You don't have to make a federal case out of it. I just don't like having myself volunteered for guest escort services. I like Margie, but I don't need a matchmaker."

"No, you wouldn't," she said more sadly than she realized. "Will you let go of my arm, please?"

"You can't bear to be touched, can you?" he asked speculatively. "That was one of the first things I noticed about you. Why?"

Her heart went wild. He couldn't know that it was his touch lancing through her like white-hot pleasure that made her tremble, not a dislike of being touched by him. And that surprised her. "My private life is none of your business," she said firmly.

"No. You've made that very clear lately," he replied. He let her go as if her arm burned his fingers. "Okay, honey. Have it your own way. As for Margie, I'll work things out with her."

He sounded vaguely exasperated, but Nell was far too nervous to wonder about his tone of voice. A quick getaway was on her mind. When she was alone with him, it took all her willpower not to throw herself into his arms, despite all her inhibitions.

"Okay," she said, and shrugged, as if what he did were of no consequence to her. She went around him and into the house without looking back, unaware of his quiet gaze following her every step of the way.

CHAPTER TWO

NELL AVOIDED TYLER for the rest of the day, and she didn't go to the square dance that night. She excused herself right after the barbecue and went up to her room. She was being a coward, she thought miserably, but at least she wouldn't have to watch Margie flirt with Tyler.

But memories of Tyler wouldn't be put out of her mind. Her thoughts drifted relentlessly back to the very beginning, to his first few days at the ranch. From the moment she'd met him at the airport, he'd been gentle and kind to her, putting her at ease, making himself right at home in her company.

And not only with Nell—he'd won over the men and Bella just as quickly. Nell had warmed to him as she never had to any man, with the exception of Darren McAnders. But even though Darren had left deep scars on her emotions, Nell knew instinctively that Tyler wouldn't harm her. Before she realized what was happening to her, she was following him around like a puppy.

She grimaced, remembering. She'd alternated between sighing over him and trying to find ways to make him more comfortable. She didn't realize how her eagerness to please him might seem to other people...

or even to Tyler. She was in awe of him, the wound of McAnders's long-ago rejection forgotten.

There was a square dance the second week he was in residence. Nell hadn't put on a dress, but she did make sure her long hair was clean and neatly brushed, and she didn't wear her slouch hat. As usual when there were strangers around, especially male ones, she drew into herself. Tyler made a convenient hiding place, and she got behind him and stayed there.

"Scared?" he'd teased gently, not minding her shy company. She was a little sunflower, a child to cosset. He hadn't asked her age, but he assumed she hadn't made it out of her teens yet. She didn't threaten him in any way, and he could afford to be kind to her.

"I don't mix well," she confessed, smiling. "And I don't really trust men very much. Some of the guests… well, they're older men and their wives aren't interested in them. I guess any young woman, even one like me, is fair game to them. I don't want trouble, so mostly I stay away from dances." Her dark eyes sought his. "You don't mind if I stick back here with you?"

"Of course not." He leaned against one of the posts that supported the loft and busied his fingers braiding three strands of rawhide he'd found. "I haven't been to a barn dance in a long time. Is this an ongoing ritual here?"

"Every other Saturday night," she confided. "We even invite the kids, so everybody gets to join in. The band—" she indicated the four-man band "—is a local group. We pay them forty dollars for the evening. They aren't famous, but we think they're pretty good."

"They are," he agreed with a smile. He glanced down

at her, wondering what she'd think of the kind of party he was used to, where the women wore designer gowns and there were full orchestras or at least string quartets and jazz quintets to provide the music.

She twisted a strand of her hair in her fingers nervously, watching the married couples dance. There was a wistful expression in her eyes. He frowned as he watched her.

"Do you want to dance, Nell?" he asked gently.

She blushed. "No. I, well, I don't dance," she confessed, thrilling to the thought of being in his arms. But that might not be a good thing. He might see how attracted she was to him. She felt helpless when his hand accidentally brushed hers. She wasn't sure she could handle a dose of him at close quarters without giving away her growing infatuation for him.

"I could teach you," he volunteered, faintly amused at her reticence.

"No, I'd better not. I don't want to…" She was going to say that she didn't want to have to explain to the male guests why she wouldn't dance with anyone but Tyler. It was too hard to make him understand that her flesh crawled at the thought of being handled by strange hands. But she coveted *his* touch, and that was new.

"Okay, tidbit. No need to worry the point." He smiled. "But I think I'm about to be abducted, so what will you do while I'm away?" he asked, indicating a heavyset middle-aged woman who was heading toward him with a gleeful smile.

"I'll just help out at the refreshment table," she said, and excused herself. She watched him being led onto the dance floor and she sighed, wishing she was the one dancing with the long, tall Texan. But she was uncertain of herself. It was better if she didn't rush things. Much better.

After that evening, he became her port in a storm. If there were business meetings or problems that she had to discuss with the men or male guests, she always made sure Tyler was included. She began to think of him as a buffer between herself and a world that frightened her. But even as she relied on him, she couldn't help feeling an attraction that was making it impossible for her to go on as she had. She wanted him to notice her, to see her as a woman. It was the first time in years that she'd wanted to show off her femininity, to look the way a woman should.

But as she stared at herself in her mirror one morning, she wanted to cry. There wasn't even good raw material to work with. She'd seen photos of movie stars who looked almost as bad as she did without their makeup, but she didn't have the first idea how to make herself look beautiful. Her hair, while long and lustrous, needed shaping. Her eyebrows almost disappeared because they were so sun bleached. She had a good figure, but she was too shy to wear revealing clothes. Maybe it wasn't a good idea to go overboard, anyway, she told herself. It had taken years to get over her bad experience and the brutal honesty of the first man she'd set her cap at.

Finally, she'd braided her hair into two long pigtails and looped Indian beaded holders around them. That didn't look too bad, considering that her paternal grandmother was a full-blooded Apache. She only wished her face looked as good as her hair did. Well, miracles did happen. Maybe someday one would happen for her. And Tyler did actually seem to like her.

She tried a hint of lipstick and put on her newest jeans—the only ones she had that really fit properly— with a pullover knit blouse. She smiled at her reflection. She really didn't look too bad, she thought, except for her face. Maybe she could wear a gunnysack over it....

Then Bella called her to lunch before she had time to worry anymore.

She bounced into the dining room with more energy than she'd had for weeks. She felt reborn, full of new, shy confidence. She was blooming.

The rain had come to the desert, making the guests uncomfortable and ranching dangerous. The men were working overtime keeping cattle and horses out of the dry washes that could kill so suddenly and efficiently when they filled with unexpected rainwater. The past three days had brought a deluge, and two of the guests were giving up and going home. The other eight were going to tough it out. Nell had smiled at their stubbornness and was determined to make life as pleasant as possible for them.

The guests were having their meal half an hour later than Nell, Tyler and Bella in the huge oak-decorated dining room with its heavy chairs and table and comfortable lounge furniture.

Tyler hadn't shown up, but Bella was bustling around putting platters of food on the table when she got a glimpse of the mistress of the house and almost dropped the tray she was carrying.

"That you, Nell?" she asked hesitantly, her gray head cocked sideways.

"Who are you expecting?" Nell asked, laughing. "Well, I won't win any beauty contests, but don't I look better?"

"Too much better," Bella said gently. "Oh, honey, don't do it. Don't set yourself up for such a hard fall."

Nell stopped breathing. "What?" she asked.

"You take him things for the cabin," Bella said. "You sew buttons on his shirts. You make sure he's warm and dry when it rains. You're forever making him special things in the kitchen. And now this transformation. Honey, he's a sophisticated man who was, until just recently, very rich and well traveled." She looked worried. "I don't want to smash any dreams, but he's used to a different kind of woman. He's being kind to you, Nell. But that's all it is. Don't mistake kindness for true love. Not again."

Nell's face went bloodred. She hadn't realized that she was doing those things. She'd liked him and she wanted him to be happy. But it didn't look like that— of course it didn't. And her new appearance was going to put him in a very embarrassing situation.

"I like him," Nell faltered. "But I'm not...not chasing him." She turned and ran upstairs. "I'll change."

"Nell!"

She ignored Bella's remorseful wail and kept going. But she wouldn't come back down for dinner, despite the pleading from the other side of the door. She felt raw and hurt, even though Bella had just meant to be kind. Nell was going to have to watch her step. She couldn't afford to let Tyler think she was chasing him. God forbid that she should invite heartache again.

Downstairs, Tyler and Bella had been sharing a quiet meal. He studied the old woman curiously.

"Something bothering you?" he asked politely.

"Nell." She sighed. "She won't come down. She fixed her hair and changed clothes, and I…" She cleared her throat. "I said something."

"Nell could use a little self-confidence," Tyler said quietly. "That wasn't kind of you to knock her down when she was just getting started."

"I don't want her to get hurt again," Bella moaned. "You just mean to be kind, I know that. But that child has never had any affection, except from me. She doesn't know what it is to be loved and wanted. Her father lived for Ted. Nell was always an afterthought. And the only other time she was interested in a man, she got hurt bad." She sighed again. "So maybe I'm overprotective. But I just didn't want to see her throw herself at you because you pay her a little attention."

"I never thought she was," Tyler said, smiling. "You're wrong. Nell's just being friendly. She's a cute little kid with pretty brown eyes and a nice way about her. I like her and she likes me. But that's all it is. You don't have to worry."

Bella eyed him, wondering if he could be that blind. Maybe he could. "Nell is twenty-four," she said.

His black eyebrows arched. "I beg your pardon?"

"Well, how old did you think she was?" the woman asked.

"Nineteen. Eighteen, maybe." He frowned. "Are you serious?"

"Never more so," Bella told him. "So please don't make the mistake of putting her in patent leather shoes and ruffled pinafores. She's a grown woman who's lived alone and been slighted all her life. She's just ripe to have her heart torn out by the roots. Please don't be the one to do that to her."

Tyler hardly heard her. He'd thought of Nell as a cute kid, but maybe he'd gotten everything wrong. Surely she didn't see him as a potential romantic interest? That was just too far-fetched. Why, she wasn't even his type. He preferred a much more sophisticated, worldly woman.

He picked at his food. "I didn't realize," he began, "that she might be thinking of me in those terms. I'll make sure I don't do anything to encourage her." He smiled at Bella. "I sure as hell don't want a lovesick tomboy grabbing me by the boots every time I walk by. I don't like being chased, even by attractive women. And Nell is a sweet child, but even a blind man couldn't accuse her of being beautiful."

"Have some more beef," Bella said after a minute, grateful that Nell was still up in her room and not likely to hear what he'd said.

Of course, as fate would have it, Nell had started back down the hall and was standing just outside the door. She'd heard every word, and her face was a pasty white. She just barely made it back to her room before the tears that she'd pent-up escaped.

Maybe it had been for the best that she'd found out early what Tyler really thought of her. She'd gone a little crazy because of the attention he'd paid her, but now that she knew what he really felt about her, she'd keep those stupid impulses under better control. Like Bella said, she'd mistaken kindness for interest. And she should have known better. For God's sake, hadn't she learned her lesson already? She had nothing that would attract a man.

So she'd dried her eyes and put back on her comfortable clothes, and later she'd gone down to supper as if nothing at all had happened. Neither Bella nor Tyler realized what she'd overheard, and she hadn't told them.

But after learning how Tyler felt, Nell's attitude toward him changed. She was polite and helpful, but the light that had been in her eyes when she looked at him had gone out. She never looked directly at him and she never sought him out. The little attentions vanished, as did her shy adoration. She treated him like any other ranch hand, and what she really felt, only she knew. She never talked about him again, even to Bella.

But tonight, in the silence of her room, she still ached for what might have been. It seemed very likely that she wasn't cut out for a close relationship with a man, much less with Tyler Jacobs. But that didn't stop her from being hurt by what had happened. It had been the first time in years that she'd made an effort to look like a woman. It would be the last, too, she vowed. She rolled over and closed her eyes. Minutes later, she was asleep.

A COUPLE OF weeks later, the sun was out, thank God, because the recent rains had been catastrophic. Bookings had been canceled and the ranch's finances had suffered. But now they had all eighteen rooms filled, most of them double occupancy. The ranch catered to families with children, and family fun was emphasized, with hayrides and trail rides and barbecues and square dancing. They did a lot of repeat business. Mr. Howes and his wife had been regulars for ten years, and although Mr. Howes spent a great deal of his time falling off his horse, it never seemed to deter him from trying to keep his girth in the saddle. And despite the fact that Mrs. Sims had been infuriating her ulcer with Crowbait's homemade firehouse chili for the past five years, she kept trying to eat it. She was a widow who taught school back East during the year and vacationed for a week at the ranch every summer.

Most of the regulars were like family now, and even the husbands didn't bother Nell because she knew them. But there was always the exception, like the very greasy-looking Mr. Cova who had a plain, loving wife whose affection he seemed determined to abuse. He was always watching Nell, and she looked forward to the day when they left.

"You could have Tyler speak to Mr. Cova, if things get too rough," Bella mentioned as she was setting the buffet table for lunch.

"No, thanks," Nell said quietly. "I can take care of myself."

She turned, almost colliding with Tyler's tall form as he appeared quietly in the doorway. She mumbled an apology and dashed past him without a word. He watched her irritably for a minute before he swung himself into a straddling position over one of the kitchen chairs and tossed his hat onto the table. His lean, dark hands lit a cigarette while he nursed a warm regret for the friendliness he'd once shared with Nell. He felt as if he'd hurt her somehow. Her quiet sensitivity disturbed him. She touched a chord in him that no other woman had ever reached.

"You're brooding again," Bella murmured dryly.

He smiled faintly. "It's just that Nell's changed," he said quietly, lifting the cigarette to his chiseled lips. "I thought we were going to be the best of friends. But now, when I come into a room, she can't leave quick enough. She sends me messages through Chappy. If I need to see the books, she has somebody bring them to me." He shrugged. "I feel like a damned leper."

"She's just nervous around men," Bella soothed. "She always has been—ask Chappy."

Tyler's green eyes shifted and met hers. "It wasn't like this at first. I couldn't turn around without bumping into her. Do you know why things changed?"

Bella shrugged. "If I did," she said, choosing her words carefully, "she wouldn't thank me for saying anything. Although she sure is quiet these days."

"Amen. Well, maybe it's just as well," Tyler murmured absently. He took a draw from his cigarette. "What's for lunch?"

"Open-faced roast beef sandwiches, homemade french fries, salad, homemade banana pudding and iced tea and coffee."

"Sounds delicious. By the way, I've added two new men on the payroll to help do some work on the equipment and renovate the stable and the barn. That's going to have to be done before we finish haying, as I'm sure you know."

Bella whistled through her teeth. "Nell isn't going to like that. She hates having to deal with new men."

He scowled at her. "What happened to her?"

"I can't tell you that. She'll have to."

"I've asked, but all I got was the runaround."

"She's a secretive person. Nell doesn't talk about

herself, and I won't." She smiled to soften the words. "Trusting someone doesn't come easy to that child."

"Trust is difficult for most of us." He tilted his hat over his eyes. "See you."

THE BARN, LIKE every other building on the place, leaked in heavy rain, but when it was sunny like today, it was cozy and plenty warm enough. Nell was kneeling beside a small Hereford calf in a rickety stall filled with green-gold hay, stroking its head.

Tyler stood in the hay-filled aisle watching her for a long moment, his eyes narrowed in thought. She looked like Orphan Annie, and maybe she felt that way. He knew what it was like to live without love, to be alone and alienated. He understood her, but she wouldn't let him close enough to tell her so. He'd made a mistake with Nell. He didn't even know what he'd done to make her back off and treat him with such cool indifference. He missed the way things had been at their first meeting. Her shy adoration had touched him, warmed him. Because of Nell, he felt a kind of emptiness that he didn't even understand.

He moved closer, watching the way she reacted to his approach, the way her dark eyes fell, her quick movements as she got to her feet and moved out into the aisle. As if, he thought irritably, she couldn't bear being in an enclosed space with him.

"I thought I'd better tell you that I've hired two men, temporarily, to help with some repairs," he said. "Don't panic," he added when he saw the flash of fear in her eyes. "They're not ax murderers, and they won't try to rape you."

She blushed furiously and tears burned her eyes. She didn't say a word. She turned and stormed out of the barn, hurting in ways she couldn't have told him about, old memories blazing up like bonfires in the back of her mind.

"Damn it—!" he burst out angrily. He was one step behind her. Even as she reached the barn door, he caught her arm firmly to stop her. The reaction he got shocked him.

She cried out, twisting sharply away from him, her eyes wide and dark and fearful.

He realized belatedly that what had frightened her was the anger in his face, the physical expression of it in his firm hold on her. "I don't hit women," he said quietly, moving back a step. "And I didn't mean to upset you. I shouldn't have made that crack about the new men. Nell…"

She swallowed, stuffing her hands into her jeans while she fought for composure. She hated letting him see the fear his violence had incited. She glanced away from him and her thick black lashes blocked his view of the emotion in her dark eyes.

He moved closer, looming over her. His lean hands slid into the thick coolness of her hair at her ears and tilted her face up to his.

"Stop running," he said curtly. "You've done it for weeks, and I can't take much more. I can't get near you."

"I don't want you near me," she said, choking on the words. "Let go."

Her words stung his pride, but he didn't let her see. "Tell me why, then," he persisted. His gaze was level, unblinking. "Come on."

"I heard what you said to Bella that night," she said, averting her eyes. "You thought I was just a kid, and when she told you how old I really was, you...you said you didn't want a tomboy hanging from your boots," she whispered huskily.

He saw the tears before he felt them sliding onto the backs of his hands. "So that was it." He grimaced. He hadn't realized that Nell might have heard him. His words must have cut her to the quick. "Nell, I never meant for you to hear me," he said gently.

"It was a good thing," she said, lifting her chin proudly as she fought down embarrassment. "I didn't realize how...how silly I was behaving. I won't embarrass you anymore, I promise. I liked you, that was all. I wanted you to be happy here." She laughed huskily. "I know I'm not the kind of girl who would appeal to a man like you, and I wasn't throwing myself at you." Her eyes closed on a wave of pain. "Now, please, will you let me go?"

"Oh, Nell," he groaned. He pulled her close, wrapping her up in his arms, his dark head bent to her honey-brown one under the slouch hat. He rocked her, feeling the pain in her as if it hurt him, too. His eyes closed as he swung her in his arms, the close contact easing the tears, easing the pain. She wept silently at the sweetness of it, even while she knew that she couldn't expect any more than this. A few seconds of pity mingled with guilt. Cold comfort for a lonely life.

She let herself rest against him for one exquisite moment, loving the wiry strength of his tall body, the leather and tobacco smells that clung to his soft cotton shirt, the sound of his heartbeat under her ear. This would be something to dream about when he left. But now, she had to be strong.

She pulled away from him and he let her go. She knew that there was no hope for her in his life. Margie was more like him—she was sophisticated and good-looking and mature. They'd hit it off like a house on fire, and Nell had to keep that in mind and not let her heart get addicted to Tyler. Because Margie wanted him, Nell was sure of it. And Margie always got what she wanted.

She drew in a shaky breath. "Thanks for the comfort," she said. She even forced a smile. "You don't have to worry about me. I won't make things hard for you." She looked up, her brown eyes very soft and dark, shimmering with a hurt that she was trying so hard to keep from him.

Tyler felt something stir in him that knocked him in the knees. She had the most beautiful, sensual eyes he'd ever seen. They made him hungry, but for things that had no physical expression. She made him feel as if he'd been out in the cold all his life, and there was a warm fire waiting for him.

Nell felt that hunger in him, but she was afraid of it. His eyes had become a glittering green, and they were so intent that she flushed and dropped her gaze to his chest. He made her weak all over. If he looked at her like that very often, she'd have to go off into the desert forever. She felt as if he were taking possession of her without a physical move.

She stepped back, nervous, unsure of herself. "I'd better go inside."

"About those new men—they're only temporary. Just

until we get through roundup." His voice sounded oddly strained. He lit a cigarette, surprised to find that his fingers were unsteady. "They'll be here in a few weeks."

She managed a shy smile. "Well, I'll try not to treat them like ax murderers," she promised nervously. "I'm sorry about the square dance. About leaving you to deal with Margie." She lifted her shoulders jerkily.

"I don't mind. But don't make a habit of it, okay?" he asked, smiling to soften the words. He reached out and tugged a lock of her long, unruly hair. "I'm feeling a little raw right now, Nell. I've lost my home, my job...everything that used to matter. I'm still trying to find my feet. There's no place in my life for a woman just yet."

"I'm sorry about what you lost, Tyler," she said with genuine sincerity, gazing up at his hard, dark face. "But you'll get it all back one day. You're that kind of person. I can't see you giving up and settling for weekly wages."

He smiled slowly, surprised at her perception. "Can't you? You're no quitter yourself, little Nell."

She blushed. "I'm not little."

He moved a step closer with a new kind of slowness, a sensual kind of movement that made Nell's heart stop and then skip wildly. She could barely breathe, the manly cologne he wore drifting into her nostrils, seducing her. "You're not very big, either," he mused. He touched the very visible pulse in her soft neck, tracing it with a long, teasing finger that made it jump. "Nervous, honey?" he breathed.

She could hardly find enough breath to answer him. "I...I have to go inside."

His head bent so that his green eyes were looking

straight into her dark ones while that maddening finger traced a hot path down her throat and up to her jaw.
"Do you?" he asked in a husky whisper, and his breath
touched her parted lips like a kiss.

"Tyler…" Odd, how different her voice sounded.
Strained. Almost frantic.

His eyes fell to her mouth, and he wanted it suddenly
and fiercely. His chest rose and fell quickly, his eyes
glittered down at her. He almost bent that scant inch
that would have brought her soft, full mouth under his.
But she was trembling, and he couldn't be sure that it
wasn't from fear. It was too soon. Much too soon.

He forced himself to draw back, but his hand gripped
her shoulder tightly before he let her go. "See you later,"
he said with a slow smile.

She cleared her throat. For one wild second, she'd
thought he meant to kiss her, but that was absurd.
"Sure," she said huskily. "See you."

She turned and went into the house on wobbly legs.
She was going to have to get her imagination under control. Tyler was only teasing, just as he had in the beginning. At least he still liked her. If she could control her
foolish heart, they might yet become friends. She could
hardly hope for anything more, with Margie around.

CHAPTER THREE

A COUPLE OF weekends later, Margie and the boys were back at the ranch. Curt and Jess were up at the crack of dawn Sunday, and Nell noticed with faint humor that they followed Tyler wherever he went. That gave Margie a good excuse to tag along, too, but the woman seemed preoccupied. She'd tried to get a conversation going with Nell earlier, although Nell hadn't been forthcoming. It was hard going, listening to Margie try to order her life for her. Margie apparently hadn't noticed that her sister-in-law was a capable adult. She spent most of her time at the ranch trying to change Nell into the kind of person she wanted her to be. Or so it seemed to Nell.

"I do wish you'd let me fix your face and help you buy some new clothes," Margie grumbled at the breakfast table. She glared at Nell's usual attire. "And you might as well wear a gunnysack as that old outfit. You'd get just as much notice from the men, anyway."

"I don't want the men to notice me," Nell replied tersely.

"Well, you should," she said stubbornly. "That incident was a long time ago, Nell," she added with a fixed stare, "and not really as traumatic as you've made it out to be. And don't argue," she added when Nell bristled. "You were just a child, at a very impressionable age, and you'd had a crush on Darren. I'm not saying that you invited it, because we both know you didn't. But it's time you faced what a relationship really is between a man and a woman. You can't be a little girl forever."

"I'm not a little girl," Nell said through her teeth. She knew her cheeks were scarlet. "And I know what relationships are. I don't happen to want one."

"You should. You're going to wind up an old maid, and it's a pitiful waste." Margie folded her arms over the low bodice of her white peasant dress with its graceful flounces and ruffles. "Look, honey," she began, her voice softening, "I know it was mostly my fault. I'm sorry. But you can't let it ruin your whole life. You've never talked to me or to Bella. I wish you had, because we could have helped you."

"I don't need help," Nell said icily.

"Yes, you do," Margie persisted. "You've got to stop hiding from life—"

"There you are," Tyler said, interrupting Margie's tirade. "Your offspring have cornered a bull snake out in the yard. Curt says you won't mind if he keeps it for a pet."

Margie looked up, horrified.

Tyler chuckled at the expression on her face. "Okay. I'll make him turn it loose." He glanced at Nell, noticing the way she averted her eyes and toyed nervously with her coffee cup. "Some of the guests are going to services. I thought I'd drive them. I'm partial to a good sermon."

"Okay. Thanks," Nell said, ignoring Margie's obvious surprise.

"Did you think I was the walking image of sin?"

Tyler asked the prettier woman. "Sorry to put a stick in your spokes, but I'm still just a country boy from Texas, despite the lifestyle I used to boast."

"My, my." Margie shook her head amusedly. "The mind boggles." She darted a glance at Nell, sitting like a rock. "You ought to take Nell along. She and her hair shirt would probably enjoy it."

"I don't wear a hair shirt, and I can drive myself to church later." Nell got up and left the room, her stiff back saying more than words.

She did go to church, to the late morning service, in a plain gray dress that did nothing for her, with no makeup on and her honey-brown hair in a neat bun. She looked as she lived—plainly. Bella had driven her to town and was going to pick her up when the service was over. It would have been the last straw to go earlier with Tyler's group, especially after Margie's infuriating invitation at Tyler's expense.

So the last person she expected to find waiting for her was Tyler, in a neat gray suit, lounging against the ranch station wagon at the front of the church when services were over.

"Where's Bella?" Nell asked bluntly.

Tyler raised a dark eyebrow. "Now, now," he chided gently. "It's Sunday. And I'd hate to let you walk back to the ranch."

"Bella was supposed to pick me up," she said, refusing to move.

"No sense in letting her come all this way when I had to come back to town anyway, was there?" he asked reasonably.

She eyed him warily. "Why did you have to make two trips to town on Sunday?"

"To pick you up, of course. Get in."

It wasn't as if she had a choice. He escorted her to the passenger side and put her in like so much laundry, closing the door gently behind her.

"You're killing my ego," he remarked as he pulled out onto the road.

Her nervous hands twisted her soft gray leather purse. "You don't have an ego," she replied, glancing out at the expanse of open country and jagged mountains.

"Thank you," he replied, smiling faintly. "That's the first nice thing you've said to me in weeks."

She let out a quiet breath and stared at the purse in her hands. "I don't mean to be like this," she confessed. "It's just—" her shoulders lifted and fell "—I don't want you to think that I'm running after you." She grimaced. "After all, I guess I was pretty obnoxious those first days you were here."

He pulled the station wagon onto a pasture trail that led beyond a locked gate, and cut off the engine. His green eyes lanced over her while he lit a cigarette with slow, steady hands.

"Okay, let's put our cards on the table," he said quietly. "I'm flat busted. I work for your uncle because what I have left in the bank wouldn't support me for a week, and I can't save a lot. I've got debts that I'm trying to pay off. That makes me a bad prospect for a woman. I'm not looking for involvement…."

She groaned, torn by embarrassment, and fumbled her way out of the car, scarlet with humiliated pride.

He was one step behind, and before she could get

away he was in front of her, the threat of his tall, fit body holding her back against the station wagon.

"Please, you don't have to explain anything to me," she said brokenly. "I'm sorry, I never meant to—"

"Nell."

The sound of her name in that deep, slow drawl brought her hurt eyes up to his. Through a mist of gathering tears she saw his face harden, then his eyes begin to glitter again, as they had once before when he'd come close to her.

"You're all too vulnerable," he said, and there was something solemn and very adult in his look. "I'm trying to tell you that I never thought you were chasing me. You aren't the type."

She could have laughed at that statement. He didn't know that years ago she'd run shamelessly after Darren McAnders and almost begged for his love. But she didn't speak. Her eyes fell to the quick rise and fall of his broad chest under the well-fitting suit, and she wondered why he seemed so breathless. Her own breathing was much too quick, because he was close enough that she could feel his warmth, smell the expensive cologne that clung to him.

"I'm nervous around men," she said without looking up. "You were the first one who ever paid me any real attention. I guess I was so flattered that I went overboard, trying to make you happy here." She smiled faintly, glancing up and then down again. "But I never really thought it was anything except friendship on your part, you know. I'm not at all like Margie."

"What do you mean by that crack?" he asked sharply.

She shivered at his tone. "She's like the people in

your world, that's all. She's poised and sophisticated and beautiful…"

"There are many different kinds of beauty, Nell," he said, his voice softer than she'd ever heard it. With surprised pleasure she felt the touch of his lean fingers on her chin as he lifted her face up to his eyes. "It goes a lot deeper than makeup."

Her lips parted and she found that she couldn't quite drag her eyes away from his. He was watching her in a way that made her knees weak.

"We'd better go…hadn't we?" she asked in a husky whisper.

The timbre of her soft voice sent ripples down his spine. He searched her dark eyes slowly, finding secrets there, unvoiced longings. He could almost feel the loneliness in her, the hidden need.

And all at once, he felt a need spark within him to erase that pain from her soft eyes.

He dropped his cigarette absently to the ground and put it out with a sharp movement of his boot. His lean hands slid against her high cheekbones and past her ears.

"Tyler…!" she gasped.

"Shh." He eased her back until she was resting against the station wagon, with his chest touching her taut breasts, and all the time his eyes searched hers, locked with them, binding her to him.

Her nervous hands, purse and all, pressed against him, but not with any real protest, and he knew it. This close, she couldn't hide her hunger from him.

"But…" she began.

"Nell." He whispered her name just as his lips

brushed against hers. It wasn't a kiss at all. It was a breath of shivery sensation against her mouth, a tentative touch that made her stand very still, because she was afraid that he might stop if she moved.

His fingers toyed at her nape as they removed the hairpins and loosened her hair, and all the while his mouth was teasing hers, keeping her in thrall to him. He closed one of her hands around her hairpins and ran his fingers slowly through the mass of honey-streaked hair he'd loosened, enjoying its silky coolness.

"Open your mouth a little," he whispered as his teeth closed gently on her lower lip.

She blushed, but she obeyed him without pause.

His own mouth parted, and she watched it fit itself exactly to the contours of her lips. Her eyes glanced off his fiery ones, and then the sensation began to penetrate her shocked nerves, and she gasped as her eyes closed in aching pleasure.

He murmured something deep and rough, and then she felt the length of his hard body easing down against hers while birds called in the meadow and an airplane flew overhead and the sun beat down on her. She moaned in sweet oblivion.

He felt her tremble, heard the first cry from her lips. His mouth lifted just enough for him to see her face, and he was startled by the pleasure he found there. Her eyes opened, black pools of velvet. His hands slid gently down her back to her waist, and he realized that breathing had become an Olympic event.

"My God," he whispered, but with reverence, because not once in his life had he felt this overwhelming tenderness for a woman.

"You…you shouldn't hold me…like this," she whispered back, her voice shattering with mingled fear and need.

"Why not?" He brushed his nose against hers while he spoke and managed a faint smile for her.

She colored. "You know why not."

"No, I don't." His mouth covered hers slowly, and he felt her yield, felt her submission like a drug as he drowned in the softness of her body and the sweetness of her mouth. He relaxed, giving in to his own need. His hips slowly pressed against hers, letting her feel what she probably already knew…that he was feverishly aroused by her.

She stiffened and gasped, and without warning he felt her ardor turn to fear as she pushed at his chest in flaming embarrassment.

He drew away gently, releasing her from the soft crush of his body. His eyes searched her scarlet face, noting the way she kept her own eyes hidden.

"You haven't done this before," he said with sudden conviction.

"Not…not voluntarily, no," she replied with forced lightness. She gnawed on her lip. "I'm sorry. It's…it's a little scary." And she blushed again, even more.

He laughed softly, delighted. His mouth pressed gently against her forehead. He nuzzled her face with his. "I suppose it would be, to a quiet little virgin who doesn't chase men."

"Please don't make fun of me," she whispered.

"Was that how it sounded?" He lifted his head, touching her mouth with a slow, tender forefinger as he watched her. "I didn't mean it to. I'm not used to innocents, Nell. The world I came from didn't accept them very readily."

"Oh. I see."

"No, you don't, honey. And that's a good thing. It isn't my world any longer. I'm not sure I even miss it." He toyed with a long, silky strand of her hair. "You're trembling," he whispered.

"I'm…this is…it's new."

"It's new for me, too, although I imagine you don't believe it." He brushed the hair back from her face, and his green eyes searched her dark ones. "How long is it since a man kissed you…really kissed you?"

"I don't think anyone ever did, and meant it," she confessed.

"Why?"

"I don't attract men," she faltered.

"Really?" He smiled but without mirth as he caught her by the waist and pulled her to him. She flushed and tried to pull away, but this time he held her firmly.

"Tyler!" she protested, flustered.

"Just stand still," he said quietly, but he let her hips pull away without an argument. "You're twenty-four years old and damned ignorant about men. It's time you had a little instruction. I won't hurt you, but I can't kiss you from a safe distance."

"You shouldn't," she pleaded, looking up. "It isn't fair to…to play with me."

His dark eyes didn't blink. "Is that what I'm doing, Nell?" he asked softly. "Am I playing?"

"What else could you be doing?"

"What else, indeed," he breathed as his head bent. He pulled her up to meet the hard descent of his mouth, and he kissed her with passion and a little anger, because she was arousing him in ways she couldn't have dreamed. He couldn't stop what was happening, and that irritated him even more. Nell was the last woman in the world he should be kissing this way. He had no right to get involved with her when he had nothing to offer. But her mouth was sweet and gentle under his, softly parting; her body, after its first resistance, melting into his. He lifted her against his chest, drowning in the long, sweet, aching pleasure of the most chaste kiss he'd ever shared with a woman. His body fairly throbbed against her, but he kept himself in full control. This was an interlude that couldn't end in a bedroom; he had to remember that.

He groaned finally and listened to reason. He put her back on her feet, his hands gripping her soft arms hard as he held her in front of him and struggled for both breath and sanity.

Nell was dazed. Her eyes searched his glittery ones, and she could feel the fine tremor in his hands as he held her. He was breathing as roughly as she was. He wanted her. She knew it suddenly and without a doubt. With a sense of shock, she realized how much a man he really was.

"I need to sit down," she said shakily.

"I'm just that unsteady myself, if you want the truth," he said on a rough sigh. He opened the door and let her into the station wagon before he slid his long legs inside and got in under the wheel.

He lit a cigarette and sat quietly, not speaking, while Nell fumbled her hairpins into her purse and dug out a small brush to run through her long, disheveled hair.

She would have liked to check her appearance in a mirror, but that would look suspicious. She didn't want him to know how desperately sweet that interlude had been for her.

She put the brush back into her purse and closed it and stared down into her lap. Now that it was all over, she wondered how he felt. Would he think she was that starved for affection that she'd have reacted the same way to any man? She glanced at him nervously, but he seemed oblivious to her presence. He was staring out the windshield, apparently deep in thought.

In fact, he was trying to breathe normally. It was unusual for him to feel so shaken by such an innocent kiss. He couldn't remember the last time a woman had thrown him off balance. But Nell seemed to do it effortlessly, and that bothered him. Loss of control was the last thing he could afford with a virgin. He had to put on the brakes, and fast. The question was, how was he going to do that without making Nell think that he was little more than a playboy having fun?

He turned his head and found her watching the landscape without any particular expression on her soft face.

"We'll be late for lunch," Nell remarked without looking at him. She couldn't. She was too embarrassed by her reaction to his kiss.

He searched for the right words to explain what had happened, but Nell was far too unsophisticated for that kind of discussion. She seemed remarkably naive in a number of ways. He imagined her own abandon had been as embarrassing to her as his lack of control had been disturbing to him.

Better to let things lie, he supposed, for the time

being. He started the station wagon without another word and headed for the ranch.

MARGIE GOT THE boys ready to go early in the afternoon, and Tyler volunteered to take them back to Tucson. That seemed to thrill Margie, and it was a relief to Nell, who'd dreaded being alone with her sister-in-law. Margie had a way of dragging information out of her, and Nell didn't want to share what had happened with Tyler. It was a secret. A sweet, very private secret, which she was going to live on for a long time.

"You're not brooding again, are you?" Bella asked that evening as they washed supper dishes.

Nell shook her head. "No. I'm just grateful for a little peace. Margie was on her soapbox again about gussying me up." She sighed. "I don't think I'd like being a fashion plate, even if I had the raw material. I like me the way I am."

"Frumpy," Bella agreed.

She glared at the housekeeper. Nell's soapy hands lifted out of the water. "Look who's talking about frumpy!"

Bella glared back. "I ain't frumpy." She shifted her stance and shook back her wild silvery-black hair. "I'm unique."

Nell couldn't argue with that. "Okay, I give up. I'm frumpy."

"You could do with a little improvement. Maybe Margie isn't the terror we think she is. You know, she does care about you, in her way. She's only trying to help."

"She's trying to help herself into a relationship with Tyler," Nell corrected.

"She's lonely," Bella said. Her knowing eyes sought Nell's suddenly vulnerable face. "Aren't you?"

Nell stared at the soapsuds. "I think most people are," she said slowly. "And I guess Tyler could do worse. At least Margie makes him smile."

"You could, if you'd get that chip off your shoulder."

"I got hurt," Nell muttered.

"That's no reason to bury yourself. You're just twenty-four. You've got a lot of years left to be alone if you don't turn around pretty soon. You don't gain anything if you're afraid to take a chance. That isn't any way for a young woman to live."

Nell's mind had already gone back to the morning, to Tyler's warm mouth so hungry against her own, to the feel of his lean, strong body against hers. She colored at the sweet memory, and at that moment, she knew she was going to die if she could never have it again.

But Tyler didn't want her. He'd said that he didn't have room in his life for a woman—more than once. She had to keep her head. She couldn't run after him. Not when she was certain to be rejected.

"Bella, maybe I'm meant to be an old maid," she murmured thoughtfully. "Some women are, you know. It just works out that way. It's the beautiful women who marry—"

"I ain't beautiful and I married," Bella reminded her with an arrogant sniff. "Besides, looks fade. Character lasts. And you got plenty of that, child."

Nell smiled. "You're a nice lady."

"I'm glad you like me. I like me, too, just occasionally. Now wash off that spot, Nell, so we don't get food poisoning. When you have your own house and kitchen, you'll have to do all this without me to remind you."

Nell had to stifle a giggle. Bella could be imposing, but she was an angel.

TYLER THREW HIMSELF into his work for the next couple of days, and Nell hardly saw him. He came to meals, but he was looking more and more haggard, and he was coughing. Since the Sunday he'd picked her up at church, they'd hardly spoken. He'd been polite but remote, and Nell began to think he was avoiding her. She understood the reason for it—he didn't want to get involved. He was probably afraid she'd read too much into those warm kisses. Well, she told herself, there was no need for him to worry. She wasn't going to throw herself at him. She just wished she could tell him so, again. But it was too embarrassing to contemplate.

All the same, she couldn't stop being concerned about him. He did look bad. Inevitably, there came a day later in the week when he didn't show up for supper.

Bella went down to the foreman's cabin to find out why. She'd asked Nell to go, but Nell had refused instantly. Another confrontation with Tyler was the last thing she needed now.

Bella came back a half hour later looking thoughtful. "He don't look too good," she remarked. "He's pale and he says he's not hungry. I hope he's not coming down with that virus that went through the bunkhouse last week."

"Is he all right?" Nell asked too quickly.

"He says a night's sleep will do him good. We'll see."

Nell watched her amble off to the kitchen and had to force herself not to go rushing down to the cabin to see Tyler. He was the epitome of good health. She knew because he'd told them that he was never sick. But there was always a first time, and he'd worked like a horse since his arrival.

Sometimes it seemed that he was working off more than the loss of his ranch back in Texas. Perhaps there'd been a girl he'd wanted who hadn't wanted him when he lost everything. That put a new perspective on things and Nell started worrying even more. She hadn't thought of him having a girlfriend. But he was a handsome man, and he was experienced. Very experienced, even to her innocent mind. There had to have been women in his past. He might even have been engaged. She groaned. She didn't like to consider the possibility that he might have kissed her because he was missing some woman he'd left behind in Texas. But it might be true. Oh, if only there was some way to find out!

She paced the living room floor until Bella complained that she was wearing out the rug. She went up to bed, where she could pace uninterrupted.

But the more she paced, the more confused things got. In the end, she undressed, put on her soft long gown and climbed into bed. Minutes later she was blessedly asleep, beyond the reach of all her problems.

THE NEXT MORNING, Nell's first thought was of Tyler. She dressed in jeans and a yellow knit top, looped her long hair into a ponytail, and ran downstairs with her boots barely on.

"Have you been to see Tyler?" she asked Bella.

The older woman scowled at her from a pan of biscuits she was just making up. "I will as soon as I get these biscuits in the oven...."

"I'll go."

Bella didn't say a word. But she grinned to herself as Nell went tearing out the back door.

The foreman's cabin was nice. It was big enough for a small family, but nothing fancy. Nell knocked on the door. Nobody answered. She knocked again. Still nothing.

She paused, wondering what to do. But there was really no choice. If he didn't answer, he was either asleep, which was unlikely, or gone, which was equally unlikely, or too sick to get up.

She opened the door, glad to find it unlocked, and peeked in. It was in good order for a bachelor's establishment. The Indian rugs on the floor were straight, and there were no clothes thrown over the old leather couch and chair.

Her heart beat wildly as she eased farther into the living room. "Tyler?" she called.

There was a soft groan from the bedroom. She followed it, half-afraid that she might find him totally unclothed. She looked around the door hesitantly. "Tyler?"

He was under the covers, but his hair-matted chest was bare, like his tanned, muscular arms. He opened his eyes briefly. "Nell. God, I feel rough. Can you get Bella, honey?"

"What for?" she asked gently, moving closer.

"To call a doctor," he said wearily. "I haven't slept and my chest hurts. I think I've got bronchitis." He coughed.

"I can call a doctor," she said gently. She felt his forehead. It was burning hot. "Just lie there and don't move. I'll bring you something cold to drink, and then I'll get the doctor. I'll take care of you."

He caught her eyes, searching them strangely. It felt odd, the sensation her words had sent through his body. He'd never had to be taken care of, but it occurred to him that there was nobody he'd rather have nursing him than Nell.

"Be right back," she said, hiding her concern under a faint smile. She rushed out, all the antagonism gone in the rush of concern she felt for him. He had to be all right, he just had to!

CHAPTER FOUR

NELL GOT TYLER a cold soft drink from his small refrigerator and helped him get a few swallows of it down before she rushed back to the main house to phone the doctor.

Bella stood listening in the doorway while Nell described the symptoms to Dr. Morrison and was told to bring Tyler in to his clinic as soon as she could get him there.

She felt insecure when she hung up. "I'll bet he thinks it could be pneumonia," Nell told the older woman worriedly. "And I guess it could be. He's coughing something terrible and burning up with fever."

"I'll go get Chappy to help you get him into the station wagon," Bella said. "Or I'll go…"

"No, that's all right," Nell replied. "Chappy can come with us. We'll have to postpone the daily shopping trip with the guests, but Chappy can drive the Simses and the others to the mall as soon as we get back."

"He'll hate that." Bella chuckled.

"I know, but somebody's got to look after Tyler."

Bella almost strangled herself trying to keep quiet. She could have looked after Tyler, but it was pretty obvious that Nell had already assigned that chore to herself. And Bella wasn't about to interfere. "That's right," she said, grinning. "I'll get Chappy."

But as they went out the door together, they noticed immediately that the station wagon was missing. So was the pickup truck.

"Where's he gone?" Bella yelled to Marlowe, who was leading a saddled horse out of the stable.

"Chappy had to run into town to pick up that stomach medicine for the sick calves. He's been gone a half hour, so he should be back anytime."

"Where's the pickup?" Nell called.

Marlowe shrugged. "Sorry, ma'am, I don't know."

"Great," Nell muttered. She glanced at Bella. "Well, send Chappy down to the cabin the minute he comes back. I just hope he's not inclined to linger at the vet's office."

"I'll phone the vet and make sure," Bella replied. "Don't worry. Tyler's tough."

"I guess he is." Nell sighed. She forced a smile and quickly went down the path to the cabin.

Tyler was sprawled against the pillows asleep when Nell got back to him. She sighed, wondering how on earth he was going to dress himself.

"Tyler?" she called gently, touching his bare shoulder lightly. "Tyler, wake up."

His eyes opened instantly, a little glazed from sleep and fever. "Nell?" he murmured, shifting under the covers.

"Dr. Morrison wants me to bring you to his office," she said. "We have to get you dressed."

He laughed weakly. "That's going to be harder than you think. I'm as weak as a kitten." A sudden bout of coughing doubled him up and he grimaced at the pain it caused him. "Damn! It feels like I've got a broken rib."

Nell's heart sank. It was almost surely pneumonia. Her mother had died of it, and it held hidden terrors for her because of the memory.

"Can you dress yourself?" she asked hesitantly.

He sighed jerkily. "I don't think so, Nell."

"Chappy isn't here," she said thoughtfully. "But there's Marlowe, or Bella—"

"No," he said shortly. He glared up at her with fever-bright eyes. "As strange as it may seem to you, I don't like the thought of having myself dressed by ya-hoos and grinning old women. No way. If you want me dressed, honey, I'll let you help. But nobody else. Not even Chappy."

That was surprising. She hadn't thought men minded people looking at them. But then, Tyler wasn't like other men.

She hesitated. "Okay. If you can get the—" she cleared her throat "—the first things on, I guess I can help with the rest."

"Haven't you seen a man without clothes?" he asked with faint humor.

"No. And I don't really want to," she said nervously.

"You may not have a choice." He started coughing again and had to catch his breath before he could speak. "Underwear and socks are in the top drawer of the dresser," he said. "Shirts and jeans in the closet."

She paused, but only for a minute. The important thing was to get him to the doctor. She had to remember that and put his health before her outraged modesty. Since he wouldn't let anybody else help, she didn't have a choice.

As quickly as possible, she laid out everything he was going to need. But when he started trying to sit up, he held his chest and lay right back down again.

"God, that hurts, Nell," he said huskily. "It must have been the dust. We got into a cloud of it a few days ago bringing back some straying cattle, and I inhaled about half an acre, I think. I've had a lot of congestion, but I thought it was just an allergy. Until this morning, anyway."

"Oh, Tyler," she moaned.

"Should have worn my bandanna," he murmured. "That's why the old-timers wore them, you know, to pull up over their faces in dust storms and such."

"How are you going to dress?" she wailed.

He gave her a knowing look. "You mean, how are you going to dress me," he replied. "If it helps, it isn't something I'd choose to saddle you with. I don't even like stripping in front of men."

She colored. "I don't think I can," she whispered.

"It won't be that bad, I promise," he said softly. "Pull the sheet up over my hips and slide my briefs up as far as you feel comfortable. I think I can manage it from there."

The blush got worse as she picked them up. "I'm sorry," she muttered, fumbling the briefs over his feet and ankles. "Old maids aren't very good at this sort of thing."

"Neither are old bachelors." He coughed, groaning. "Come on, Nell, you can do it. Just close your eyes and push."

She laughed involuntarily. "That might be the only way." She eased them up, her hands cold against the warm, hard muscles of his thighs. She couldn't help but feel how well made he was, how powerful. She got them just under the sheet and her nerve gave way. "Is that...far enough?" she asked huskily.

"I'll manage." He eased his hands under the sheet and tugged and then lay back with a rough sigh. "Okay. The rest is up to you, honey."

She slid his socks on his feet. He had nice feet, very well proportioned if a little big, and even nice ankles. His legs were as tanned as his face and arms, and it almost had to be natural, because he certainly hadn't been sunbathing the past few weeks.

"This is the first time in my adult life that I've ever been dressed by a woman," he remarked weakly as she eased his undershirt over his head and pulled it down over his broad, hair-matted chest.

"They tell me there's a first time for everything," she returned, but her eyes were on the rippling muscles of his chest. She could feel the warmth of his skin, feel the thick abrasiveness of the hair that covered the broad expanse until it wedged down to his undershorts. When she reached under his arms to pull the undershirt down over his back, her face was almost pressed to his skin, and she had to grit her teeth not to kiss him there. The most unwanted sensations were washing over her body like fire. This wasn't the time or the place, she had to remind herself. He was a sick man, and she had to get him to a doctor. Besides all that, it was suicidal to feel that way about a man who'd already warned her off.

"You look like boiled lobster," he remarked. "It wasn't as bad as you thought, was it?"

"No, not really," she agreed with a thin smile. She helped him into his chambray shirt and snapped the cuffs and then the snaps down the front of it. "It's just new."

"Didn't you ever have to dress your brother?" he grinned weakly.

"No. Ted was much older than I was," she said. "And he went away to school, so we didn't spend a lot of time together. Dad and Mom worshipped him. He was their world. I guess I was more or less an accident. But they tried not to let me feel left out."

"My father never wanted kids at all," Tyler remarked. "He did his damnedest to break my spirit, and he almost did break my sister Shelby's. But we survived. It's ironic that the ranch had to be sold. He'd have sacrificed both of us to hold on to it."

She unfolded his jeans. "You'll have your own ranch one day," she said gently. "And you won't break your children's spirits to keep it, either."

"If I have children," he replied. "Some men never marry. I may be one of them."

"Yes. I guess you might." She eased his jeans onto his long legs and pulled them up as far as she was able. They were tight and the material was thick, and it took most of her strength just to get them to his upper thighs. She knew that he'd never be able to pull them the rest of the way, not with his chest hurting so badly.

"If you can lift up, I think I can get them over your hips," she said through her teeth, and she didn't look at him as she eased the sheet away and tried not to blush at the sight of his undershorts.

"Sorry, little one," he said huskily. "But I do hurt like hell."

"I know," she said gently. "I'm not a child, after all," she said for her own benefit, as well as his. "Here goes."

She closed her eyes and pulled and tugged until she got the jeans over his hips. But she balked at the zipper, going hot all over.

"Fetch my boots, will you, honey?" he asked. He saw her hesitation and understood it. "I can manage this."

She almost wept with relief as she went to the closet to get his dress boots. She'd seen them there when she'd found his shirts and jeans. They were Tony Lama boots, exquisite and expensive, black and gleaming like wet coal.

"These are going to be hard to get on you," she said worriedly.

"You push and I'll push," he said. "They're not all that tight."

"Okay."

Between them, they worked the boots onto his feet. Then Nell got a comb and fixed his disheveled hair. And all the while he lay there against his pillow, his feverish eyes watching her, studying her in a silence that was unnerving.

The roar of a car arriving interrupted the tension. "That must be Chappy," Nell said. She caught her breath. "Tyler, you won't tell him that I…"

"That you helped me dress?" He smiled gently. "I won't tell anyone. It's between you and me, and no one else," he said, and the smile faded into an exchanged look that was slow and intensely disturbing. Nell's heart ran wild until she dragged her eyes away and got up to let Chappy in.

Between them, they got Tyler into the backseat of the station wagon, where he could lie down, and to Dr. Morrison's office.

The nurse helped Tyler to the examination room, while Chappy paced and Nell chewed on a fingernail. It took a long time, and she was expecting Tyler to come out with the nurse, but Dr. Morrison came to the doorway and motioned for Nell to follow him.

He beckoned her into his office, but Tyler was nowhere in sight.

"He'll be fine," he told her, perching himself on the corner of his desk, "but he's got acute bronchitis."

"I was so afraid that it was pneumonia," Nell said, slumping into a chair with relief. "That pain in his chest—"

"That pain in his chest is from a pulled muscle, because he's coughed so much," he said with a tolerant smile. He folded his arms across his chest. "I want him in bed until the fever goes. He can get up then, but he can't work for a full week. And then I want to see him again. I've written him two prescriptions. One's an antibiotic, the other's an expectorant for the cough. Give him aspirin for fever and keep him in bed. If he gets worse, call me."

"Did you tell him all this?" she asked.

"Sure. He said like hell he'd lay around for a week. That's why I wanted to talk to you."

She smiled. "Thanks. He's working wonders out at the ranch. I'd hate to bury him on it."

"He seems pretty capable to me," he agreed. "Mind that he doesn't sneak out and start back to work before you realize it."

"I'll tie him in his bed," she promised.

"Bombard him with fluids while you're at it," the doctor added as he got up and opened the door. "He'll be as docile as a kitten until that antibiotic takes hold, then look out."

"I'll post guards at his door," she said with a grin. She felt lighter than air. Tyler was going to be all right. The relief was delicious. "Thank you!"

"My pleasure. He's all yours."

She smiled as she went out. If only that were true.

She called Chappy to help her get Tyler out to the station wagon, but only after she'd whispered to the receptionist to send the bill out to the ranch. She had a feeling that Tyler wouldn't appreciate having her pay his medical bill, but that was something they could argue about when he was back on his feet.

All the way home, she wondered how she was going to manage getting him undressed again. But he solved that problem himself. When they got into the cabin, he sighed and murmured, "Don't worry, Nell. I think I can manage getting out of this rig by myself."

"I'll go up to the house and get Bella to make some chicken soup for you," Nell said quickly, and darted out the door. It was easier than she'd imagined.

She sent Chappy back to town to get the prescriptions filled, because it had seemed more sensible to bring Tyler home first. She gathered the few things she might need and told Bella where she was going.

"He's not much of a threat in his present condition, I

guess," Bella said, and nodded, ignoring Nell's outraged glare. "You can sleep on his sofa. But if you need me, I'm here. I can sit with him while you sleep if he gets worse in the night."

"You're a doll," Nell said.

"I have a secret Florence Nightingale streak," she corrected. "Wanted to be a nurse, once, but I faint at the sight of blood."

"They say some doctors do the first time they see an operation," Nell replied. "But I'm glad you wanted to cook, instead. You're kind of special to me."

Bella beamed, unaccustomed to the praise. "I'll have that carved on my tombstone one day. Meanwhile, you fill Tyler full of that juice I gave you and don't let him rope cattle out the window."

"I won't. Thanks, Bella."

The older woman shrugged. "I'll bring the chicken soup when it's made. I'll put some in a thermos for you."

"It'll be welcome by then. And some coffee, too, please. I don't know if Tyler has a coffeepot, but I kind of doubt it."

"He carries his around in a thermos," Bella said surprisingly. "I fill one up for him every morning and every afternoon."

"Okay. I'll get going before he escapes. See you later."

She found Tyler asleep again, apparently back in the altogether under the single sheet that covered him. Nell watched his face for a long moment, seeing the lines erased in sleep, the masculine beauty of his mouth. Just the sight of him was like a banquet to her eyes. She had to tear herself away. While he slept, she might as well make herself useful by tidying up his kitchen.

She put the juice Bella had sent in the small refrigerator, and then she washed the few dishes and cleared the counter. With that done, she checked to make sure he was still asleep before she went to the bookcase in the living room to find something to read.

Apparently he was a mystery fan, because he had plenty of books by Sir Arthur Conan Doyle and Agatha Christie on the shelves. There were some biographies and some history books about the old West, and even a book about ancient Rome. She chose a work on the Apache tribe and sat down to read it, glancing curiously at the photograph atop the bookcase. It was of a young woman with long dark hair and green eyes and a rather sad expression on her beautiful face. Beside it was a smaller photo of the same woman in white, standing beside a tall, fierce-looking man in a suit. That, she decided, had to be Tyler's sister, Shelby. Nell knew Shelby had gotten married recently, because Tyler had gone to Texas for the wedding. That man was probably her new husband. He wasn't much to look at, but perhaps he had saving graces, Nell decided.

She didn't see any other photos. That had to be a good sign. If there had been a special woman in his life, surely he'd have a picture of her. Or maybe not. If he'd lost her to someone else, he might be too bitter to keep a picture of her in a prominent place.

Feeling gloomy, she went back to the book and started reading.

Bella brought chicken soup, and Chappy brought medicine. Tyler was still asleep, but when the visitors left, Nell took his medicine, a glass of juice and a bowl of soup into the bedroom on a tray. The medicine was important, and he needed nourishment. He hadn't eaten anything all day.

She sat down gently on the bed beside him, her eyes going helplessly over his broad, bare chest and his face. "Tyler?" she said softly. He didn't stir. She reached out and hesitatingly laid one slender hand on his chest, thrilling to its hard warmth. It was the first time she'd touched a man this way, and despite the circumstances, it was blatantly pleasurable.

"Tyler, I've got your medicine," she said.

He sighed and opened his eyes slowly. "I hate medicine," he said weakly. "How about a steak?"

"Dream on. Right now, it's going to be chicken soup and encouragement. I brought you a tray."

"What time is it?"

"Almost dark," she replied. "Chappy took the guests to town to shop, and now he's holding court at the supper table. I can hear him telling tall tales through the kitchen window, and everybody's laughing."

"He tells a mean story," Tyler agreed. He breathed heavily and touched his side, encountering Nell's warm hand as his own worked its way up his chest. "You're cool," he murmured.

"Only because you have a fever," she said, thrilling to the touch of his fingers on her soft skin. "Here. Let's get some medicine into you, and then you can have soup and juice. Are you hungry?"

"Half-starved," he said. "But I don't have much appetite."

She gave him the antibiotic with a swallow of juice, and then ladled the cough syrup into his mouth.

"That tastes terrible," he muttered.

"Most medicine does," she agreed. "Can you manage to sit up while you eat?"

"Under protest." He let her prop him up with pillows and dragged himself into a sitting position. The sheet lay loosely over his hips, but she caught a glimpse of underwear, not bare skin, as he moved. "That's for your benefit," he said dryly, smiling at her color. "I drew the line at pajamas, but I wouldn't outrage your modesty too much this way."

"Thank you," she said shyly.

"Thank you," he replied. "You're stuck with me, I gather. Didn't Bella rush to play nurse?"

"She did, but I headed her off. Crowbait would have to do the cooking if she came down here, and the whole outfit would quit on the spot."

"He's not that bad," he said. "The military would love to get their hands on him. Imagine, a cook who can make a lethal weapon of an innocent biscuit."

"Shame on you," she said.

He sighed and grimaced. "I guess my biscuits aren't much better, so I don't have a lot of room to talk. Nell, I'm sorry to cave in on you like this...."

"Anybody can get sick," she said easily, and began to feed him the soup without thinking about how much feeling that simple act betrayed. "It's amazing how many people come out here from the East, thinking that their allergies will go away overnight. What they don't realize is that the dust can be as bad as pollen, and that the soil itself harbors plenty of allergens. Just listen to Mr. Davis sneeze and wheeze on trail rides, if you don't believe me."

"Well, it's the first time in my life I've had bronchitis, but I'll buck it," he said quietly. "And I'll be back at work day after tomorrow."

"No, you won't," she replied. "Dr. Morrison said you couldn't get out of bed until the fever's gone, and you can't work for a week."

He eyed her warily. "Did he tell you that?"

"He sure did," she said with a mischievous grin. "So don't try to get around me. If you do, I'll call my uncle, and then where will you be?"

"Out of work and sick, I guess," he said wearily. "Okay. I'll stay put. Under protest, you understand."

"I understand. You'll get through it. Have some more soup."

He might get through it, she thought, but would she? He slept through the night without waking, although she checked on him every hour or so until she was forced to curl up on the couch and sleep.

The next day was pretty much the same. She fed him and gave him his medicine, and he slept most of the day and all night through. But the following day he felt much better and nothing suited him. The breakfast Bella had sent over was too everything. Too hot, too much, too salty, too filling and too starchy. He didn't want to stay in bed, he had to start planning for winter, and he had to get the cattle operation in hand. That meant more work than ever, in between getting the calves ready for the fall sale. He didn't like the medicine, he hated the confinement and Nell was beginning to wear on him, too, come to think of it.

She glared at him from red-rimmed dark eyes framed by long disheveled honey-brown hair, in the rumpled yellow knit shirt and faded jeans she'd slept in. She hadn't even bothered to put on her boots, having met Chappy at the door for the breakfast tray.

"If I wear on you, that's just too bad, Mr. Jacobs," she said shortly. "Somebody's got to keep you penned up, and everybody else is too busy. It's just the second day. The antibiotic's taking hold, and you want to fight tigers. Great. But fight them while you're asleep, please. I don't like people committing suicide on my ranch."

"It isn't your ranch yet, according to your uncle," he reminded her curtly.

"It will be," she said with cool determination. "Now you just lie down and get well."

"I don't want to lie down. I want to go to work. Hand me my clothes," he said firmly, nodding to where Chappy had draped them over his straight chair.

"Oh, no, I'm not going through that again," she said, reddening. "And you're not able to dress yourself yet—"

"Like hell I'm not able!" He pulled himself painfully into a sitting position, drew in a deep breath and tried to get his feet on the floor. He grimaced and groaned and lay back down, turning the air blue on the way down.

"Damn it, damn this disease and damn you, too!" he swore furiously.

"Thank you. What a kind thing to say to someone who's given up regular meals and sleeping to wait on you for two days," she said icily.

"I didn't ask you to!"

"Somebody had to!" she shot back. She stuck her hands on her slender hips and glared at him. He looked all too good that way, lying back against pillows with crisp white cotton pillowcases. His chest was still bare, and his black hair hung down over his forehead, straight and thick. He looked exquisitely masculine, and the sight of his half-clothed body wasn't doing Nell's nerves any good.

"All right, thank you," he said. "You're an angel in disguise and I'll remember you in my will. Now will you get out of here and let me go back to work?"

"You can't work for a week—Dr. Morrison said so," she replied for the tenth time in as many minutes. "And he wants to see you again to make sure you're on the road to recovery. He told me not to let you on a horse."

"I don't take orders from women," he said shortly. "I work for your uncle, and I answer only to him. You don't and never have told me what to do."

"Will you listen to reason?" she demanded, passing over that bit of insolence.

"Sure. If you'll get me my pants."

"Well, I won't."

"Then I'll get them myself," he said shortly.

She folded her arms across her chest with a smile. She knew he had on his underwear, so he wasn't going to frighten her off. "Okay. Go ahead," she invited.

She didn't realize her mistake until he gave her a hard glare and abruptly threw off the sheet. Her face went from pale pink to scarlet red in seconds as he gingerly slid his long, powerful bare legs over the bed and stood up. Without a stitch of clothing on.

CHAPTER FIVE

NELL WAS GRATEFUL that she didn't faint. What she did do was flush from the neck up and, after one long, shocked glance, turn and run out of the room.

Tyler immediately felt like a heel. He sat back down, his bad temper forgotten, and pulled the sheet over his hips. "Nell," he called gently.

She didn't answer him. She was staring out the living room window, with her arms folded tightly across her yellow shirt, trying to decide whether to stay or go. If he was going to be that difficult, she didn't know how she was going to cope. The sight of him had set her back a bit. Due to her experience with Darren McAnders when she was young, she'd led a pretty sheltered life. But she lived on a ranch, and because of that, she knew all about the technicalities of reproduction. But a nude man was a new experience. And a nude Tyler was...extraordinary. She was still shaking when she heard him calling her, more insistently.

With a deep breath, she turned and gritted her teeth and walked back to the doorway, pale and subdued.

"I'm sorry," he said tersely when he saw her face. "I won't do that again."

She shifted a little. "If you're that determined to kill

yourself, I can't stop you. But for your own sake, I wish you'd do what the doctor wants."

His green eyes searched her frozen features. "I'll do damned near anything to get that look off your face. Including," he added wearily as he lay back down, "staying in the bed."

He looked tired. Probably he was, and she wished she'd been older and more sophisticated so that she wouldn't have made such a fool of herself. He made her feel about thirteen.

"Can I get you anything?" she asked.

"I could do with some more juice," he said. "And if you'll dig me out some fresh underwear, I'll put it back on again."

She felt hot all over and tried to hide her reaction to him as she got him a glass of juice and then took a pair of briefs from the dresser. As she put them beside him, he caught her wrist and pulled her down onto the bed, holding her there firmly while he looked at her.

"How can you be twenty-four years old and so damned innocent?" he asked quietly. "Especially with all the people who pass through here in a year's time?"

"I don't mix with people very much," she said. Her eyes slid helplessly over his broad, bare chest. "I socialize only to the extent that I have to, and since most people who come here keep to themselves except for organized activities, I don't have many problems. If I had my own way, this would be just a cattle ranch and I wouldn't take in paying guests. But the dude ranch part is paying for the cattle operation, so I don't have much choice."

"Do you date?"

She kept her eyes down. "No, I don't have time."

"So many secrets between us, Nell," he said, caressing her hand lightly. "Too many."

"You told me you weren't interested in involvement. Well, I'm not, either," she lied.

"Really? Or is it that you don't think you attract men?"

She remembered when she'd said that and what he'd done about it on the way home from church. Her lips parted as she remembered the hungry kiss they'd shared, and she had to fight not to throw herself down against him and beg him to do it again.

"I can't attract men," she replied tersely.

"You're a pretty woman," he said. "You downplay your attractions, but they're there. Why don't you buy a new dress, have your hair done and put on some makeup for the next Saturday square dance?" he murmured, reaching up to tug on a long lock of her hair. "And I'll teach you to dance."

Breathing grew harder by the minute. She felt nervous and insecure, and the slow tracing of his long fingers on her hand and wrist was beginning to stir her blood.

"It's not practical," she said inanely, because she could hardly think at all.

"Why not?"

"Because…because you're…" She bit her lip. "You're just bored, Tyler, and when you're back on your feet again, when you're working for yourself again… Oh, I'm just muddling it."

"You think I'm playing."

She sighed. "Yes."

He took her hand and pulled it to his chest, pressing it
hard over the hair-covered expanse where his heart was
beating like a bass drum. "Nell, am I callous enough to
play with a virgin?" he asked softly.

Of course he wasn't, but she couldn't keep her
thoughts clear. The effect he had on her was incredible, and she was hungry for an affection she'd never
had from a man.

"It doesn't matter," he said huskily, pulling on her
hand. "Come here."

"Tyler, you're sick—"

"I don't have any fever, and I feel like a new man."
He eased her across him until she was on her back in
the bed with his lean bare torso above her, his green
eyes glittering down at her. "I've never seen a woman
with less self-confidence than you have, Nell," he said.
"There's nothing wrong with the way you look or the
way you are."

"Tyler, you're scaring me," she whispered. Her hands
went to his chest, and part of her tried to protest. This
was bringing back terrible memories of another man
she'd loved, or thought she loved, and his harsh, hurt-
ful treatment of her. But Tyler wasn't McAnders, and
the look on his face was intoxicating. He wanted her.
Not as a substitute for another woman, but for herself.

"No, that won't work," he said gently. His lean hands
cupped her chin and held her face tilted up to his. "I'm
not going to be rough with you, not ever. And anything
we do together will be because you want it."

That was as new as her proximity to him, and she
began to relax. There was nothing threatening about
him. He seemed fully in control and lazily indulgent.

"Yes, that's it," he said as he felt the tension draining out of her body. "I'm not going to hurt you."

As he spoke, his dark head bent. She felt his mouth whispering over her eyelids, closing them, brushing her nose, her chin, and then settling softly over her mouth. Her breath seemed suspended while he found just the right pressure, the right mingling of tenderness and expertise to make her lips part for him. And while he kissed her, his lean hands slid under her blouse at the back, and she thrilled to the faint roughness of their touch on her bare skin.

He was addictive, she thought dizzily, enraptured by the warmth of his caresses. She didn't think she could have pulled away to save her life. Every touch was more exciting than the one before. His mouth became a necessity. Without its warm crush she was sure to die.

Shyly, she flattened her hands against his chest and let them experience the thickness of hair, the strong padding of muscle beneath it. His breath caught against her mouth, and her eyes opened, questioning.

"I'm sorry, I didn't mean to…" she began quickly.

"It feels good," he said, smiling down into her shocked face. "I can drag that sound out of you the same way."

Her body coiled inside, like a kitten anticipating being stroked. She felt herself tremble and wondered at the mental pictures that were flashing sensually through her mind. His hands on her, touching her…there. Her lips parted. "You…you can?" she whispered, which wasn't what she wanted to say at all, but she was too shy and inexperienced to put it into words.

Tyler, with his greater experience, knew immediately

that she was going to welcome whatever he wanted to do. It went to his head, making his thoughts spin with new possibilities. His hands had already told him that Nell had been hiding her light, physically at least, under a barrel. He needed the intimacy with her as he'd needed nothing else in his life, although he still didn't quite understand the way she affected his senses.

"Yes," he breathed, bending again to her mouth. "I can."

As his lips toyed with hers, his hand went to the fastening of her bra. Subtly, almost without her knowing it, he released the catch and slid his fingers slowly, exploringly, under her arm to the soft edge of her breast.

She trembled, but she didn't pull away or protest, and his blood ran hot and fast through his veins. He wanted to look at her. He wanted to see her eyes when he touched her.

He lifted his head. The glitter of his eyes unnerved her at first, until she felt again the light tracing of his fingers against her skin. The sensations piled on each other until she went hot all over with the need to make him put his hand on her, to touch her. Her body was more demanding than her mind, because it tried to twist toward him, to force a contact he was deliberately denying her.

"Ty...ler?" she whispered brokenly.

His free hand was under her nape. It moved caressingly in her thick hair while his gaze searched her huge, hungry eyes. "Shh," he whispered gently. The hand under her arm moved again, tracing, and she arched, shuddering, while her big eyes pleaded with him. "It's all right," he whispered. "It's all right, honey."

And all the while, his fingers were driving her mad. She felt as if every single cell in her body was drawn as tight as a rope, as if the tension was going to break her in half. Her nails contracted on his muscular upper arms and dug in, and when she realized it, she was shocked at her own action.

"I'm...sorry," she whispered jerkily, caressing the red crescents she'd made in his skin. "I'm sorry, I...couldn't...help it."

"You haven't hurt me," he said gently. "You know that I'm doing this deliberately. Do you know why?"

"No," she whimpered, jerking as his fingertips edged a little farther onto her breast.

"It's very much like a symphony, little one," he whispered softly, and he managed a smile. "It starts slowly, softly, and builds and builds and builds to a crescendo. When I finally give you what you're pleading for, Nell, you're going to feel a kind of pleasure that I can't even describe to you."

Her teeth ground together, because the tension was growing unbearable. "But...when...?"

"Now." His mouth covered hers and his hand moved, at last, at last, at...last! It covered her breast, swallowing up the hard tip, giving her the tiny consummation her body had begged for.

And it was like fireworks. She cried out into his mouth, shuddered, arched with the anguished fulfillment. Her hand found his through the cloth of her shirt and pressed against it, holding it prisoner. She sobbed, and the hand at her neck contracted as his mouth grew feverishly hungry. For long, fiery seconds, the sounds of their breathing were audible in the quiet room.

"It isn't enough," he bit off against her mouth. While he held her, his hand began to unbutton her shirt. He lifted his head and looked into her eyes. "I won't go further than this, I promise you," he said huskily. "But I...need...to look at you."

Her eyelids felt heavy. She couldn't work up the effort to protest. What he'd just given her was like honey, and she was helpless with pleasure. She wanted more. She wanted his eyes on her.

It was extraordinary, she thought, watching him divest her of her shirt and bra. Extraordinary, that look in his eyes, on his face, as he eased her down against the pillows and sat gazing at her taut, swollen breasts.

"Ty," she whispered. "There was a movie I watched once, and it was just a little racy. But the man...he did more than touch her. He put his mouth..."

"Here?" he whispered back, brushing her taut breast with the backs of his fingers, his eyes intent on hers.

She jerked involuntarily with pleasure. "Yes."

"Do you want that, with me?"

She colored, but she was beyond pretending. "Oh, yes...!"

His mouth eased down over the soft flesh, smoothing her skin, sensitizing it. The sensation was beyond anything she'd ever imagined. She made little whimpers that sent his mind whirling out of control. He groaned against her breast and gathered her up close, giving in to the need to taste her, to pleasure her.

She didn't hear the knock the first time it came. But the second time it was louder. She lay still, listening, and felt Tyler stiffen above her.

He caught his breath slowly, glancing through the

open bedroom door toward the living room with glazed eyes and a mind that was still in limbo.

"Mr. Jacobs, I brought your mail. I'll slide it under the door."

It was Chappy's voice, and thank God he went away quickly. Nell colored furiously as she imagined what would have happened if Chappy had just walked in.

Tyler looked down at her quietly, letting his bold gaze go from her eyes to her swollen mouth to the alabaster skin of her breast.

"Are you all right?" he whispered softly. "I didn't frighten you?"

"No." She was looking at him as intently as he was studying her, measuring memory and imagination against the sweet reality of what they'd done together. "Not at all."

He touched her breast tenderly and smiled at her. "It was good," he whispered.

"Yes."

He eased down on his elbows and slowly drew his chest over her sensitized breasts, watching her shiver and gasp with the delicious sensation of it. "This is good, too," he breathed, bending again to her mouth. "I want you, Nell."

She tensed as his mouth brushed hers, and he smiled against her trembling lips.

"I'm not going to do anything about it," he reassured her. "Kiss me, and then you'd better get out of here."

She slid her arms up around his neck and gave him her mouth in a kiss as sweet and wild as the ones before. But seconds later he drew away and rolled over, taking her with him. He lay on his back, shuddering a little with a need he couldn't fulfill.

"You might as well get rid of the baggy britches and loose blouses," he murmured, holding her bare breasts against his broad chest. "I'll never fall for the camouflage again, after this."

"Am I too big?" she whispered, because it mattered if she was.

He brushed the hair away from her mouth. "No. You're just right. All of you." He brushed a warm kiss against her lips and loosened his arms. "You'd better get your things back on. I'm weak, but I'm still capable. I don't want this to get out of hand."

She touched his face, her fingers cold and nervous, tracing its hard contours, fascinated with him. "You can't imagine what it was like for me," she whispered. "I…well, it wasn't what I thought it would be."

He smiled. "Not even after you saw that racy movie?" he murmured dryly.

She swallowed, remembering when she'd told him about it and what had followed. "Well, no. Seeing and experiencing are different."

"Indeed they are." He helped her to sit up and spent a long minute looking at her before he gathered up her bra and blouse and proceeded to help her back into them. "No," he said when she tried to stop him. "You dressed me. Now it's my turn."

So she sat still and let him dress her, delighting in his gentle touch, in his obvious pleasure in her.

"You can't stay here tonight," he said. "I hope you realize why."

"Yes. I know why."

He buttoned her up to the throat and smoothed back her long disheveled hair. "I would like very much to take your clothes off and pull you under this sheet with me and love you up to the ceiling," he said seriously. "I could do that, despite your innocence. But I'd hate myself for abusing your trust, and you might hate me for backing you into a corner. I don't want anything to spoil what's building between us. I don't think you want that, either."

She linked her fingers into his as he toyed with her hair. "No. I don't want anything to spoil it, either," she whispered.

He drew her hand to his mouth and kissed it gently. "I won't sleep. I'll remember how it was while we were loving each other in this bed, and I'll ache to have you here with me."

She trembled at his description of what they'd done. It had felt like loving, even if he only meant that in a physical sense. Her warm eyes searched his, and her face was radiant with shared pleasure, with hope, with new dreams that seemed to be turning into reality.

"I never dreamed it would be this way," she said absently.

"How did you think it would be?"

"Frightening," she confessed without telling him why. McAnders had made it into a terrifying thing, a violent act that would have hurt if he'd succeeded. But what she'd experienced with Tyler wasn't terrifying. It had been beautiful.

"And it wasn't?" he persisted gently.

"Not frightening, no," she said with a demure smile. "A little scary, but in a nice way. So many sensations…"

"For me, too, Nell," he said somberly. His eyes held hers. "That was no casual diversion, and don't you forget it. I'm not a playboy."

"You're not a monk, either," she said. She smiled shakily. "I may be innocent, but I'm not stupid."

He sighed, smoothing her closed fingers with his thumb. "If you want the truth, yes, I've had women. But always women who couldn't or wouldn't consider marriage or anything permanent. And never for money. Lovemaking is too beautiful to reduce to a quick coupling that only satisfies a casual hunger."

She couldn't speak. She hadn't expected him to say anything like that, and it occurred to her that she didn't really know him very well. "I'm glad you think of it that way," she said.

"Don't you, honestly?" he asked.

"With you I do," she said after a minute. McAnders's angry handling was fading away like a bad dream. Now when she thought about physical expressions of affection, she was always going to feel Tyler's hands on her body.

He touched her lips with a long forefinger. "Go away," he said softly. "I want you terribly, Miss Regan."

She smiled tenderly. "I'm very glad of that. But I'll go."

She got up from the bed, her eyes possessive as they ran over his taut body.

"Would you like an anatomy lesson?" he asked with a dry smile. "I could pull this sheet away and teach you volumes about men."

She averted her eyes, her cheeks scarlet. "I'll just bet you could," she muttered, because she remembered how his body had changed when hers came into contact with it. "And stop making fun of me because I'm not clued in."

"I happen to like you that way, believe it or not," he mused. "Come back in the morning. We can have another argument."

"I don't really want to argue with you."

"The alternative could get us into real trouble."

She laughed because he sounded so morose and dryly amused all at once. Her face changed with the sound, brightened, went soft and radiant.

"You are lovely when you laugh," he said huskily. "And if you don't get out of here right now, I'm going to throw off this damned sheet and come after you."

She let out a low whistle and headed for the door. "The mind boggles," she murmured as she glanced over her shoulder and smiled at him. "Sleep tight."

"Oh, that's funny," he agreed. "A real screamer. I'll have to remember to put it in my memoirs."

"I won't sleep, either," she said softly, and left him reluctantly.

She went out the door smiling, her heart so light that it could have floated before her. She'd never been so happy in all her life. The most unexpected things happened sometimes. They'd argued and she'd been sure that there was no hope, and now he'd kissed her so hungrily, handled her so gently that she was building daydreams again. This had to be the real thing, she told herself doggedly. He'd told her he wasn't playing, so it had to be for real. It had to be!

And all of a sudden, she started thinking about the past, about a man who'd teased her and kissed her lazily once or twice, a man she'd thought she loved. And that man had betrayed her trust and tried to force her into bed, all because he'd wanted her bright, beautiful sister-in-law. It didn't bear thinking about. Surely history wasn't going to repeat itself with Tyler. Nell closed her eyes in faint fear. She couldn't bear the thought of that.

If Bella noticed that Nell's lips were swollen and her hair wildly disheveled and her face full of a new radiance mingled with fear, she kept it to herself. But she was less abrasive than usual as Nell helped with the dishes, and she was smiling when the younger woman went up to bed.

Nell awoke the next morning after a sleepless night to hear a furious commotion going on down in the kitchen.

She hurriedly dressed in jeans and a neat checked shirt, left her hair down around her shoulders and went to the kitchen for breakfast. She caught the tail end of a conversation that sounded curious at best.

Bella was still raging at someone. "…can't imagine what possessed him! Of course he didn't know—he isn't a mean kind of man. But we've got to get him out of here!"

"Can't be done." That was Chappy's voice, slow and measured. "Old Man Regan gave him the power to hire and fire. Even Nell can't override him in something like this. It's just a damned shame that one of you women didn't think to tell him!"

"Well, it ain't the kind of thing you talk about to outsiders," Bella grumbled.

"He was up and moving about last I looked. Should I go talk to him?"

"Hold off a few minutes. Give me time to think."

"Okay. Tell me when."

A door slammed. Nell hesitated before she went on into the room. When Bella saw her, she turned beet red.

"Nell! I wasn't expecting you this early," she said with a toothy grin that was as false as fool's gold.

"I heard you," Nell said. "What's going on? Is it something to do with the new men? They're supposed to show up today." She gnawed her lower lip. "I guess we can send them on over to Tyler. He was much better yesterday. He can't work, but he can still delegate—"

"You'd better sit down," Bella began.

"Why? Has he hired Jack the Ripper?" Nell grinned. She felt great. It was a beautiful day, and she wanted to get this over with so that she could see Tyler. Her whole life had changed overnight. Everything was beautiful.

"Worse." Bella took a deep breath. "Oh, there's just no use in pussyfooting around. He's hired Darren Mc-Anders."

There was a hush like death in the room. Of all the things Nell might have expected to hear, that was the last. She did sit down, heavily, with her heart in her throat. Nightmares were rushing in on her, old wounds were opening.

"How could he?" she asked huskily. "How could he give that man a job here? I thought Darren was working on a ranch in Wyoming."

"Obviously he came home, and it seems he thought nine years had healed old wounds."

"Not mine," Nell said, her dark eyes flashing. "Not ever. He used me. He hurt me, scared me out of my mind… Well, he isn't going to work here. Tell Chappy to fire him."

"You know Chappy can't do that. Neither can you," Bella said. "You'll have to go and tell Tyler what happened."

She went white. After what she and Tyler had shared the day before, the thought of telling him about what McAnders had done to her was sickening. Not only that, she'd have to tell him all of it. That McAnders had flirted with her and teased her, just as Tyler had done. That he'd made a little light love to her, and she'd gone off the deep end and thrown herself at him. It had never been all Darren's fault—even in the beginning. Nell hadn't been able to talk to Bella or Margie, to tell them how much at fault *she'd* been. But she'd loved Darren, or thought she had, and she'd assumed from his affectionate advances that he felt the same way. She'd had the shock of her young life when he'd come into her room, expecting her cooperation to help get Margie out of his blood, and found her unwilling and apparently scared to death. He'd had some harsh things to say, and he'd been drinking. She still didn't know if he'd have gone far enough to force her, because her screams had brought Bella and Margie running. Surely Darren didn't think Nell was still carrying a torch for him and would welcome him back? He had to know how she hated him.

"Tell Tyler what happened," Bella said. "He'll understand."

Nell wasn't at all sure that he would. She thought of approaching Darren, but she couldn't bear to talk to him. Nine years hadn't erased her shame and fear of him, or her embarrassment for her own behavior that had led to such a tragic confrontation.

"I'll try," Nell promised as she went out the back

door. She wasn't going to confess, she knew that. But maybe there was another way.

She knocked on Tyler's door, shaking in her boots. He called for her to come in, and she found him in the kitchen frying eggs.

He glanced at her with a strange reserve, as if he'd forgotten the day before or didn't want to remember it. "Good morning," he said quietly. His eyes slid over her and quickly away, back to what he was doing. "Do you want some breakfast?"

His coolness robbed her of courage. He didn't seem like the same man who'd kissed her half to death. Perhaps he was ashamed. Perhaps he regretted every kiss. Or perhaps he was just afraid she might throw herself at him. Shades of the past fell ominously over her head.

"I'm not hungry." She took a deep breath. "One of the new men you hired is Darren McAnders. I want you to let him go. Right now."

His black eyebrows arched. He moved the pan from the burner and shut off the stove before he turned slowly to face her. "I don't think I heard you right."

"I said I want you to fire McAnders right now," she returned stiffly. "I won't have him on this ranch."

"How many available cowboys do you think I can find at roundup time?" he asked shortly. "I'm already a man short, even with McAnders, and he comes highly recommended by the Wyoming outfit he was working for. He's steady, he doesn't drink and he knows what to do with a rope. And you want me to fire him before he's even started? You little fool, he could sue us to hell for that and bring down half the government on our heads!"

"You won't do it?" she asked coldly.

"No." He glowered at her. "Not without cause. If you want him fired, tell me why," he said, and his eyes were oddly intent.

She tried. She started to speak. Her sweet memories were turning black in her mind, and she was already mourning for what might have been. Tyler looked formidable. He also looked fighting mad. She'd gone about it all wrong. She should have tried honey instead of vinegar, but it was too late now. He'd see right through that tactic, anyway.

"We're old enemies," she said finally. "That's the best I can do by way of an explanation."

He smiled mockingly and there was a new coldness in his tone. "Now that's interesting," he said. "Because McAnders told me this morning that you were old friends. Very close friends, in fact."

CHAPTER SIX

NELL JUST STOOD, staring blankly at Tyler while she tried to decide what to say. His tone was enough to convince her that he was well on the way to believing that she'd lied to him. God knew what Darren had said about the past, but it had made a terrible difference in Tyler's attitude toward her. She could feel the distrust in him, and it chilled her.

"You don't have to agonize over an explanation," Tyler said when he saw her hesitation. It was obvious that McAnders had meant something to her. "But don't expect me to fire a man because he's one of your old flames," he added mockingly. "That isn't reason enough."

She didn't say another word. He was looking at her as if he was prepared to disbelieve anything she said. He didn't know her well enough to see that she'd never have asked him to fire a man out of some personal grudge. It went much deeper than that. McAnders was an unpleasant part of her past, a constant reminder of her own lack of self-control, her vulnerability. Tyler had shown her that physical desire wasn't the terrible thing she'd remembered. But that was over before it began, all because she couldn't bring herself to tell him the truth.

"Nothing else to say?" he asked.

She shook her head. "No, thank you. I'm sorry I disturbed you."

Tyler scowled as she left. She was subdued now when she'd been fiery-tempered before. What was McAnders to her? Was she still in love with him and afraid of succumbing? Or was it something more? He wished he'd made her tell him. Now, he had a terrible feeling that he might have left it too late.

Nell was keyed up and frightened of her first confrontation with Darren. It came unexpectedly that same day, at dusk, when he was passing the back porch as she went out the door.

She looked up and there he was. Her first love. Her first crush. Until Tyler had come along, her only crush. Darren McAnders had been in his early twenties nine years ago. Now he was in his early thirties, but he hadn't changed. He had dark auburn hair, threaded with gray at the temples now, and blue eyes. He was a little heavier than he had been. But it was his face that drew Nell's attention the most. He'd aged twenty years. He had lines where he shouldn't have had them, and the easygoing smile she remembered was gone completely.

"Hello, Nell," he said quietly.

She didn't flinch, although she felt like it. He brought back memories of her own stupidity and its near-disastrous consequences. He was walking proof that her self-control was a myth, and she didn't like it.

"Hello, Darren," she replied.

"I suppose you've given the word to have me thrown off the place by now," he said surprisingly. "Once I knew you still lived here, I was sure I'd made a mistake in hiring on without telling your new ramrod the truth."

He frowned slightly, pushing his battered hat back on his head. "You don't mind that I'm here?"

"Of course I mind," she said coldly, and her dark eyes flashed. "I mind that I made a fool of myself over you, and that you used me because of Margie. But if you don't mind the memories, then neither do I. Keep your job. I don't care one way or the other."

He searched her face for a long moment, and then what he could see of her body in her usual clothing, and a kind of sadness claimed his expression. "You might not believe it, but I had a lot of regrets about what happened. It's been heavy on my conscience all these years."

He looked as if it had, too, and that was the most surprising thing of all to Nell. She didn't speak because she couldn't think of anything to say.

He took a slow breath. "How is Marguerite?" he asked finally.

She'd suspected that Marguerite's widowhood had some place in McAnders's decision to take a job at the ranch. Even nine years hadn't dimmed his passion for Margie. Nell wondered how Margie would react.

"She's doing very well," Nell replied. "She and her sons live in Tucson. They come out here for an occasional weekend."

"I heard about your brother," he remarked. "I'm sorry. I always liked Ted. I hated betraying his trust that way."

"He never knew how you felt about her," she said. "Now if you'll excuse me…"

"You've changed," he said suddenly. "I wouldn't have known you in that getup."

She flushed with mingled temper and embarrassment as she remembered the close-fitting outfits she used to wear to try to catch his eye. "I guess not," she said tightly. "We all change with age."

"Not as much as you have." He grimaced. "Oh, Nell," he said softly. "Ted should have shot me for what I did to you. He should have shot me dead."

And he turned on his heels and walked away before she could reply. That wasn't the Darren McAnders she remembered. He was no longer the cocky, arrogant young man who'd alternately teased and toyed with her. He was older and far more mature, and the teasing streak seemed to have been buried. All the same, it was too soon to start trusting him, and Margie was going to have a fit when she heard that he was back on the ranch.

Bella had the same feeling, because after supper was cleared away she mentioned that it might be a good idea for Nell to call and tell Margie about their new hand.

"I won't," Nell said firmly. "She'll find out soon enough. She and the boys are coming this weekend."

Bella sighed. "Going to be fireworks," she said.

"Then she can complain to Tyler. I didn't hire him."

"Nell!"

She jumped. Tyler's deep voice carried even when he didn't raise it, but it was clearly raised now, and irritated as he came down the hall toward the kitchen.

"Is that you, or did somebody stick a pin in a mountain lion?" Nell asked with more courage than she felt.

He didn't smile. He was bareheaded and grim, and there were several bills held in one lean hand. "We've got to talk," he said.

Nell glanced apprehensively at Bella, but the older

woman began to whistle as if she hadn't heard a word. Nell put down the dishcloth and followed Tyler back down the hall to the front room that served as an office.

The desk was cluttered, and it looked as if Tyler had been at the books for at least a couple of hours. He'd been going over the ranch's finances for several weeks now, in his spare time, trying to make sense of Nell's hit-or-miss bookkeeping system. Apparently he'd just figured it out, and he didn't like what he saw.

"These—" he indicated a new set of books "—are the new books. I've boiled everything down to credits and debits. From now on, every purchase comes through me. If you want a needle and thread, you'll have to have a purchase order. This—" he held up a book of purchase orders "—is a book of them. It's going to be locked in the desk, and I have the only key."

"Why?" she asked.

He motioned her into a chair and perched himself on the corner of the desk to light a cigarette. "The way things have been run here, any cowboy could go to the hardware store and charge butane or vaccination supplies or go to the feed store for feed or salt and charge it without any authorization." He handed her the bills he'd been carrying. "Read a couple of those."

She frowned curiously, but she did as she was told. "A pair of spurs," she murmured, reading aloud, "a new saddle…" She looked up. "I never authorized those."

"I know you didn't." He smiled faintly. "That's the problem with giving carte blanche to the cowboys."

"Who had the saddle and spurs on here?" she demanded.

"Marlowe."

"You ought to fire him."

"I already have," he said. "Good thing I hired on two new men instead of one." He eyed the tip of his cigarette. "I saw you talking to McAnders. Is there still a problem?"

She didn't feel comfortable discussing it with him. "There won't be one. Darren and I will work things out."

That sounded ominous to him. As if she had ideas about recapturing the past. He scowled at her, his green eyes almost sparking with bad temper. "As long as you keep your dalliance after working hours, I don't care what you do."

She felt something inside her dying. He couldn't know how badly he was hurting her with his indifference. She supposed he wouldn't care if he did. She lowered her eyes to her jeans. "Have you told the men about the purchase orders?"

"I told the crew in the bunkhouse at supper. I'll tell the married hands in the morning. There are going to have to be other changes, as well." He picked up the ledger and went through it. "For one thing, we're going to have to cut back on the activities that require cowboy participation. It's getting time for roundup, and I'll need every man I've got. This open range may be fine for a big outfit, but it's hell on one this size. We'll spend the better part of a week just getting the saler calves into holding pens."

"We can borrow Bob Wyler's helicopter, if you want to," Nell said. "He always helps out that way, and he supplies the pilot, too."

"For what kind of payment?" Tyler asked narrowly.

Nell grinned involuntarily. "For a case of Bella's strawberry-rhubarb preserves," she said.

He chuckled, too, in spite of himself. "Okay. That's a deal. But can you manage the trail rides without Chappy?"

"I managed well enough before Ted died," she said. "I can do it again. What else?"

"This is the worst of it. We're spending a fortune on having a golf pro on the payroll for visitors who want to tee off on the Western Terrace greens. That's fine for the big dude ranches, but we're operating on a shoe-string here. I can show you on paper that only one out of every ten guests avails himself of this service, but the pro collects his fee just the same."

"That was Ted's idea," she said. "I've just let it drag on. You may have noticed that most of the people who come here aren't really very athletic." She blushed and he laughed.

"Yes, I've noticed." He searched her dark eyes slowly, and little sparks of attraction seemed to leap between them before he drew his gaze down to his cigarette. "Then I'll take care of the pro. As for this daily shopping trip into Tucson, is that mandatory?"

"We could cut back to every other day," she compromised. "I realize that it's pretty hard on the gas budget, what with the van being used for transportation. I guess the city tour is hard on the budget, too."

He nodded his dark head. "That was going to be my next question. Can we subcontract the tours out to an existing agency in town?"

"Sure! I know a terrific lady who'd love the business, and her fees are very reasonable."

"Okay. Give her a call and work something out."

"You've been working," Nell remarked, nodding toward all the ledgers and paperwork.

"It's been a long job. But I didn't want to make specific recommendations until I had a handle on how the ranch was run. You haven't done a bad job, Nell," he said surprisingly. "Except for a few places, you've budgeted to the bone. You've only continued old policies. But we're going to change some of those and get this place operating in the black again."

"You sound encouraging."

"It's a good little operation," he replied. "It shouldn't be hard to make it a paying one. Anyplace you think you may need more help?"

She thought for a minute, trying not to notice the way his jeans clung to his long, powerful legs, or the fact that the top three buttons of his red-checked shirt were unbuttoned over that tanned expanse of hair-covered chest. She remembered all too well how it had felt to touch him in passion.

"I'd like to have someone come with me on the trail ride while that man from back East is here," she confessed with a faint smile. "His wife is rather cold-eyed, and she seems to have some insane idea that I'm chasing him."

Tyler's eyes went narrow. "Yes, I saw how he tried to come on to you at the square dance. They leave Thursday, don't they?" He saw her nod. "I'll go on the next two trail rides with you. Chappy can keep things in order for Bella while we're out."

"Thanks."

"Unless you'd rather I let McAnders go with you?" he added with a mocking smile.

She wanted to protest, but that would be a little too revealing. She swallowed. "Whatever suits you," she said. "It doesn't matter to me."

Which wasn't the answer he wanted. He put out his cigarette with faint violence. "McAnders can go with you, then," he said. "I've got enough work to do without playing nursemaid."

The words were meant to sting, and they did. She got up, avoiding his eyes as she went to the door. "Thanks for all you're doing," she said over her shoulder.

"My pleasure. Good night."

"Good night."

She didn't see him alone after that. There was always some reason to have other people present or to put off discussions until she could arrange for reinforcements. But that didn't stop Tyler from cutting at her verbally at every opportunity.

What hurt the most was that Darren McAnders didn't mind accompanying her on trail rides, and seemed even to enjoy her taciturn company. He began to smile again, as if being with her brightened his life. She didn't understand why, and she understood even less Tyler's new antagonism.

But the fire hit the fan on the weekend, when Margie and the boys arrived by taxi.

Nell had just come back from the trail ride, with Darren McAnders at her side. Marguerite, immaculate in a white linen suit, stepped out of the cab she'd recklessly hired in Tucson, with her long reddish-gold hair wafting in the breeze, and looked straight up into Darren McAnders's stunned face.

"Darren!" she exclaimed, missing her step.

She went down on her knees in the dust, and Darren vaulted out of the saddle to pick her up, his hands strong and sure on her upper arms, his eyes intent on her flushed face.

"Margie," he said softly. "You haven't aged. You're as beautiful as ever."

"What are you doing here?" Margie gasped. She glanced at Nell, even more shocked to find Nell apparently voluntarily in Darren's company.

"He's our newest hand," Nell told her. "Tyler hired him."

"Doesn't he know?" Margie asked, and then flushed when she saw Darren's rueful smile. "Oh, I'm sorry. It's just that…"

"The past is only a problem if we let it be," Nell said stubbornly. "Darren and I are getting along very well. Aren't we, Darren?" she asked.

He smiled ruefully. "As well as could be expected. Nell's been very generous. It was this job or welfare, and I couldn't have blamed her if she'd thrown me off the place. It's as much as I deserved."

Margie searched his face slowly and then glanced up at Nell, sitting still on her horse. "It took a lot of courage for you to come back here, Darren," she remarked, even though she was looking at Nell, waiting, questioning.

"I found out that running away doesn't solve much," he said enigmatically. He glanced past Margie. "Are these your boys?" He asked the question softly, and his eyes echoed that softness as he looked at them. "Curt and Jess, aren't you? Your Aunt Nell's said a lot about you."

They piled out of the car like marauding pirates and stared at him enthusiastically. "Did she, really?" Curt asked. "Did she say nice stuff? Me and Jess are lots of help around the ranch—Tyler says so. We help him find snakes and lizards and stuff and keep them from eating up Aunt Nell's cattle!"

Aunt Nell's eyes widened with amusement. "Did Tyler tell you that?"

"Well, not really," Jess murmured. "But it sounds good, don't it?"

"Doesn't it," Margie corrected absently. She was just beginning to get her self-confidence back after the shock of seeing Darren. "Boys, we'd better get inside." She paid the driver, and Nell got off her horse to help with the luggage, but Darren was one step ahead of her.

"I'll take care of this if you can manage the horses, Nell," he said with a hopeful glance in her direction.

She knew he'd never gotten over Margie. It didn't surprise her that he was anxious to renew that acquaintance. What Margie felt was less easy to perceive. But it certainly wasn't like the older woman to lose her step and pitch headfirst into desert sand.

"Sure," Nell agreed easily. "I'll take them to the barn. Margie, I'll see you and the boys in a few minutes."

"That's fine," Margie said absently, but she was looking at Darren as if she'd been poleaxed.

Nell was faintly relieved. With Darren around, maybe Margie wouldn't bat her eyelashes so luxuriously at Tyler. Not that it mattered anymore. Tyler had certainly made it clear that he wasn't interested in Nell. He avoided her like the very plague.

She led the horses to the barn, where Chappy took the reins with a curious glance at her rigid features.

"You okay?" he asked.

She smiled. "I'm fine." She glanced around. "Where's Caleb?"

Caleb was the big black gelding that Tyler always rode. Asking for the horse's whereabouts was a little less obvious than inquiring about Tyler's.

Chappy saw right through her. "He's out riding the boundary fence we put up around the holding pens."

She blinked. "He hates riding fence."

"He overheard two of the boys talking about the way McAnders hangs around you since he's been here," the wrinkled cowboy said with a twinkle in his pale blue eyes. "He set them to cleaning out the stables, and he went off to ride fence. I don't reckon anybody will mention such things around him again, once word gets through the outfit."

She bit her lower lip. "Why should he care?"

Chappy started to lead the horses toward the stable, where two sweating, swearing cowboys were mucking out the stalls and pitching fresh hay. "You need glasses," he said dryly.

Nell drifted back to the house slowly, her eyes everywhere on the horizon, looking for a glimpse of Tyler. Things had been strained between them. That, and McAnders's presence, were making her life miserable. Not that she minded Darren being around. He'd changed so much from the shallow, careless man she'd known. She felt no remnant of the old crush she'd had on

him, nor any sense of bitterness. He was like a friendly
stranger whom she began to like, but nothing more.

If only she could go to Tyler and tell him that. But
despite his odd behavior this afternoon, he hadn't said
anything that would lead Nell to believe he had any
lasting affection for her. In fact, he'd said more than
once that there wasn't any place for a woman in his life
right now. And the thought of throwing herself at another man, after the misery her encounter with Darren
had brought her, was unwelcome. Tyler might be kind
about it, but she knew he wouldn't appreciate having
her "hang on his boots," as he'd mentioned to Bella.

She sighed. She knew so little about men. If only she
could talk to Margie, perhaps she could find a way out
of the corner she'd painted herself into.

She went into the house to help Bella get supper on
the table before the guests were called onto the elegant
patio to eat. The wooden tables each had umbrellas and
sat beside an Olympic-size swimming pool, which did
a lot of business during the day. All meals were taken
here, with Bella and Nell setting a buffet table from
which guests could choose their portions. All around
were palo verde trees, along with every conceivable
form of cactus known to the desert Southwest. It was
amusing to watch the guests from back East ask about
the flower garden mentioned in the brochure and then
see it for real. The native plants were surrounded by
rock borders, and their arrangement was both mysterious and compelling. In bloom, the cacti were beautiful, like the feathery palo verde with its fragrant yellow
blossoms.

"You aren't eating?" Nell asked when Margie sat

down a good distance away from the guests while, as a special treat, the boys had their meal in the bunkhouse with the cowboys.

Margie shook her head. She'd changed into designer jeans and a red tank top, and she looked elegant and moody. "I'm not hungry. How long has he been here?"

"A few days," Nell said. "Tyler hired him."

"And you let him stay?"

"Not voluntarily," Nell said after a minute. "I tried to bulldoze Tyler into letting him go, but he wouldn't. He wanted to know why." She lowered her eyes. "I couldn't tell him."

"Yes. I understand." She sat up suddenly, leaning her forearms on the table. "Nell, it isn't terribly bad, is it? Having him around?"

The intensity of the question was interesting. Nell smiled faintly. "No, it isn't terribly bad," she said gently. She studied the pale, beautiful features. "You still care about him, don't you?"

Margie stiffened. She actually flustered. "I…well, no, of course not. I didn't really care about him!"

"Ted has been dead for a long time," Nell said quietly. "And I'm sure he never meant for you to live without love forever. If you're asking me how I feel about Darren, he's very much like a nice stranger." She smiled gently. "I guess you and Bella were right about what happened. I blew it all out of proportion because I didn't have any experience to measure it against. I didn't exactly invite what happened, but I'd led him to believe that I wanted him without realizing it."

"It was my fault, too," Margie admitted. "But I never meant you to be hurt." She looked at the table instead

of at Nell. "I cared about him. Not in the way I loved
Ted, but in a different way. But I was married, and despite the way I teased him, I never would have had an
affair with him."

"I know that," Nell said.

Margie smiled at her sadly. "I've spent a lot of years
trying to make you over in my image, haven't I? Being
bossy, taking you for granted. But I meant it in the nicest way. I wanted to help. I just didn't know how."

"I don't need help," Nell told her dryly. "And I'm
not going to try to recapture the past with Darren Mc-
Anders."

"And Tyler?" Margie fished. "Where does he fit in?"

That question threw her again. Was Margie infatu-
ated with Tyler? Was her interest in Darren only pretended so that she could find out how Nell felt about
Tyler? Nell started drawing into herself again, defensively. "Tyler is my foreman, nothing more. He doesn't
give a hang about me in any way," Nell said tautly. She
got up from the table. "I'm not hungry, Margie. I think
I'll go watch TV."

"Okay. I've got to go get the boys."

"They're already on the way," Nell remarked with a
bitter smile, and gestured to where Tyler was coming
with both boys by the hand. They were laughing and
so was he. Margie was gazing at the group with such
naked hunger that Nell turned away. "See you later,"
she said, but Margie wasn't really listening. Her whole
attention was focused on Tyler. Actually, it was focused
on Darren, who was right behind Tyler, but Nell didn't
see the second man. She was sure now that Margie was
using Darren as an excuse to mask her feelings for Tyler.

Nell went inside and threw herself into housecleaning until she was nearly exhausted, getting rooms ready for the boys and Margie. When she came back downstairs, she was surprised to find Tyler in the living room, already watching the news.

He looked tired. Dead tired. He'd showered and changed, but he had an oblivious kind of expression on his face that brightened a little when he saw Nell come into the room.

"Can I get you a lemonade?" he asked, hoisting his.

"Not a brandy?" she mused.

"I don't drink. I never have."

She sat down in the armchair across from him, feeling her way. "Why?"

He shrugged. "I don't know. I don't like either the taste or the effect, I guess." His green eyes went over her like hands, and she flushed, because memories were glittering there. It was shocking to remember exactly how intimate he'd been with her, for all the distance that had been between them since then.

"I don't drink, either," she said absently. "I'm frightfully old-fashioned."

"Yes, I know," he said softly, and the memories were there again, warm and overwhelming. His eyes caught hers and held them relentlessly. "How do you feel about McAnders?"

She sat up straight. She had to hide her real feelings from him, so she said, "I'm not sure."

"Aren't you? You seem to spend enough time with him lately," he accused quietly.

"You spend plenty around Margie," she shot back.

He smiled mockingly. "Yes, I do, don't I? But you don't seem to spend much time considering why."

"It's obviously because she attracts you," she said haughtily. "I'm not blind."

"Oh, but you are," he said quietly. "More blind than you know."

"I can spend time with anyone I please," she continued coldly.

"Have you been intimate with McAnders?" he asked suddenly.

She gasped. Her face went bloodred as she remembered what had happened that night, what Darren had tried to do to her.

Tyler saw the expression, but he took it for guilt, and something inside him exploded. No wonder Nell had eyes for McAnders. He'd been her first love, and now he was back and he wanted her, and she'd let him touch her in all the ways Tyler had. Maybe even more. His eyes glittered at her furiously.

"How could you do that?" he asked bitterly.

She blinked. "Do what?"

He threw up his hands and paced angrily. "And all the time I thought—" He stopped short, turning. "Well, if it's McAnders you want, consider him yours. I'll run the business end of the ranch and take care of the livestock. But don't make the mistake of running after me if McAnders dumps you," he added venomously. "I don't want another man's castoff."

Nell gasped with outrage. "You lily-white purist!" she threw at him. "How many women have you cast off, if we're going to get personal?"

"That's none of your business," he said shortly.

"Well, Darren is none of yours." She clenched her hands, hating his arrogance.

He wanted to throw things. He hadn't realized until then just how deeply Nell was under his skin. He had to face the possibility that a man from her past was about to carry her off, and he didn't know what to do to stop it. She'd got the wrong end of the stick about Margie. He liked Margie, yet he saw right through her antics. But Nell was so insecure that she couldn't see the forest for the trees. Considering that insecurity it was a miracle that she could even contemplate a relationship with Darren McAnders. But she might love him...

He sighed heavily. "Fair enough," he said finally and with a long, quiet stare. "Do what you please, Nell. I won't interfere. As you say, your life is your own."

He turned to go and she felt sick all over at the way things were working out. She didn't care about Darren. She wanted to call him back and tell him the truth, but something stopped her. She couldn't tell him, she couldn't face his contempt when he knew that she'd invited Darren's advances, that she'd chased him all those years ago and brought it on herself. So she let him go, watching with sad eyes as he left the room only to run into Margie in the hall.

Nell heard him laughing and caught a glimpse of Margie's rapt expression. She couldn't bear it. She was going to lose him to Margie, and she couldn't bear it. She went back into the living room, forcing herself not to cry.

She'd let Tyler think she'd been deliberately intimate with Darren, and that was a lie. She sat down on the sofa, remembering what had happened all those years ago. She'd been mistaken about McAnders's feelings back then, and she'd become obsessed with him after he'd paid her a little attention. She recalled how she'd teased him until one night she went a little too far. Margie had given a party and that evening Nell had flirted with McAnders, who'd been rejected by Margie and had had too much to drink. McAnders had come to Nell's room and found her asleep in her scanty gown, and since she hadn't locked her door, he'd thought she was waiting for him. He'd climbed into bed with her and, despite her protests, he'd been about to seduce her when Bella had come to her rescue.

But that had been years ago, long before she knew Tyler. He hadn't been talking about the past, though. He'd asked her if she'd been intimate with Darren, and he was talking about the present.

The impact of the realization hit her between the eyes like a hammer. Now she'd done it! She'd inadvertantly let him think that what she'd shared with him she'd also shared with Darren. She'd stung his pride by letting him think that she could go straight from his arms into Darren's and without a twinge of conscience.

She got up, shaking with reaction, and wondered if she could go after him, explain.

But before she got to the door, Curt and Jess came careering down the hall, and she looked past them to where Tyler was holding Margie's arm, escorting her laughingly out the front door.

It was too late now to smooth things over, she knew. She'd left it just a few seconds too long. She'd lost him.

CHAPTER SEVEN

"HI, AUNT NELL," they chorused. "Can we watch that new science fiction movie on the DVD player?"

"Sure. Go ahead," she said with forced tolerance, but her heart was breaking. "Where'd your mother go?"

"Uncle Tyler's taking her into town," Curt volunteered disinterestedly as he searched for the right DVD. "I sure like Uncle Tyler."

"Yeah, me, too," Jess agreed.

So it was "uncle" already, Nell thought, groaning inwardly. She made some brief excuse and left the room before the boys could see the tears forming in her eyes.

After that day Nell started avoiding him again. Not that it was necessary. Tyler cut her dead every time he saw her, his eyes hard and accusing, as if she'd betrayed him somehow. Nell began to wilt emotionally.

Margie and the boys left, but she and Tyler had seemed to spend a lot of time together during that visit, and Margie had been very nervous and standoffish around Darren. So any hope Nell had that her sister-in-law might be interested in her old flame was washed away almost immediately. It was Tyler Margie wanted, and Nell didn't have a chance anymore. Not with Tyler nearly hating her for what he thought she'd done. As if she could have borne the touch of any man's hands but his; it seemed impossible that he didn't know that.

After Margie left, a morose Darren McAnders began to seek Nell out to talk about the way Margie had avoided him. He was hurt, just as she was, and their common pain brought them together as friends. She even found an odd kind of comfort in his presence.

It was an odd turn of events all around, she thought as she walked with Darren to the corral fence to see two new mares Tyler had bought. Darren was turning out to be a friend.

"You're looking moody lately," Darren remarked as they watched Chappy work one of the unbroken mares on a lunging rein. He glanced at her and smiled mischievously. "And the boss is explosive. The men are betting on how long it's going to be before he throws a punch at somebody just to let the pressure off."

She flushed. "It's complicated," she said.

He propped a boot on the lowest rail of the corral fence. "It's pretty funny for me to be offering you a shoulder to cry on, when I was your worst enemy at one time. But times have changed and so have I. And if you need somebody to listen, here I am, honey."

She looked up at him tearfully. He was different, all right. A new man altogether. She managed a smile.

He smiled back and pulled her against him to give her a friendly, totally platonic hug.

But Tyler happened to be looking out the window in the bunkhouse and he saw them. And what was a platonic hug didn't look that way to a man already trying to cope with emotions he was feeling for the first time in his life, and eaten up with unfamiliar jealousy,

to boot. Tyler let out a string of range language, turned
and stormed off to where he'd tied his horse. He swung
up into the saddle and rode away without the slightest
idea of where in hell he was going.

The square dance was the following Saturday night,
and most of the present guests were leaving on Sunday to make room for a new group of people. A one-
week stay was about standard for most of them. By that
time they were sore enough and rested enough to go
home and cope with their routines. Margie and the boys
showed up Saturday afternoon, and the older woman
thrust a huge box at Nell, with a mischievous smile.

"For you," she said with dancing eyes. "Open it."

Nell eyed her curiously, but she put the box on the
dining room table and opened it, aware of Bella's frank
interest as she did.

It was a square-dancing outfit. A red-checked full
skirt with oceans of petticoats and a pretty white Mexi-
can peasant blouse in cotton, both of which had probably cost the earth. Nell just stared at it without speaking.
It was the prettiest set she'd ever seen.

"For me?" she asked Margie blankly.

"For you," came the smiling reply. "And don't put
your hair up in a ponytail, will you?"

"But, Margie, I can't dance," she began.

"Wear that and someone will be sure to teach you,"
Margie promised.

So Nell wore the new outfit and brushed her long
honey-colored hair until it shone thick and gleaming
around her shoulders. Margie taught her how to put on
a thin coat of makeup, and they were both surprised
at the results. Nell didn't look like Nell anymore. She

wasn't beautiful, but she was certainly attractive enough to make a man notice her.

Margie was wearing a similar outfit, the difference being that Margie could do anything from a square dance to a samba. Nell was too aware that she herself had at least two left feet.

Once she tried to ask Margie about Tyler, but she lost her nerve. Margie was so beautiful, and she had a way of making every man she met want her. If Tyler fell victim to her charm, who could blame him?

Nell couldn't help but wonder, though, why Margie had bought her a dress. Did she possibly sense that Nell cared about Tyler, and was trying to help her get over him by attracting Darren? But surely Margie didn't think she was interested that way in Darren, because she'd already denied it.

Downstairs, Bella made a big fuss over Nell's new image, and Nell had a feeling it was to make up for the last time she'd dressed up and Bella had been worried about Tyler getting the wrong idea. But this time praise was certainly forthcoming.

The band could be heard tuning up in the barn, which had been cleared out for the dance. Bella grinned.

"Well, at least Tyler hasn't complained about that forty dollars we have to pay the band twice a month," she said dryly.

"Give him time." Nell sighed. "Lately he complains about most everything. I hear he even made Chappy take back a rope he bought without permission."

"In case you haven't heard," Bella told Margie, "Tyler is in a snit lately. He walks around glowering at people and talking to himself."

Margie lifted an eyebrow at Nell, who flushed angrily.

"I don't have anything to do with it," Nell said shortly. "Maybe he's missing your company."

Margie exchanged glances with Bella and smiled mischievously. "Well, that's possible, of course." She eyed Nell's averted face. "Shall we go find out? Bella, you're sure you can manage the boys? They're in their pajamas, waiting for that story you promised to read them."

"Sure, me and the boys will do fine." Bella picked up a book and started toward the staircase. "Don't you worry about us."

"What are you going to read them?" Margie asked.

Bella turned and grinned wickedly. "All about the pirate raids in the Caribbean, in gory detail."

Nell gasped, but Margie laughed. "Good for you."

"Won't they have nightmares?" Nell asked.

Margie shook her head. "They love that sort of thing. I'm told that most boys do—it's normal. Their young worlds are made up of monsters and battles."

"Isn't everybody's?" Bella chuckled. "Have fun."

Nell didn't have a wrap, and it was a chilly night, but she tried not to notice the goose bumps as she and Margie walked down to the barn. Things were already in full swing, and Nell noticed that Margie's eyes were restless, as if she were looking for someone. She sighed, thinking that Margie was apparently going to single out Tyler for the evening. Nell had once been certain that Darren was the recipient of Margie's affections, but she must have been wrong.

The guests were already dancing, with Chappy call-

ing the square dance with gleeful abandon and clapping
his hands as he stood at the microphone in front of the
band. Tyler was standing to one side, near the refreshment table, braiding three strands of rawhide carelessly
while he glared at the dancing. He had on jeans and a
blue-plaid Western shirt, and with his black hair neatly
combed and his face freshly shaven, he made Nell's
heart race. He was the handsomest man she'd ever seen.

"There you are!" Margie grinned, taking possession
of his arm. "How are you?"

"Fine." Tyler looked past her at Nell, glared even
more at Nell, then turned his attention back to Margie.
"You look like a dream, honey," he said in a tone that
would have attracted bees.

"Thank you," Margie purred. She glanced at Nell.
"Doesn't Nell look nice?" she added.

Nell colored and Tyler didn't say a word. He caught
Margie's hand in his. "Let's get in the circle," he told
her, and dragged her off without noticing the surprise
in her face.

Nell moved back out of the circle of dancers and sat
down in one of the chairs, feeling alone and rejected
and uncomfortable. It was there that Darren found her.
He was wearing a black shirt and red bandanna with
his jeans, and he looked almost as handsome as Tyler
but in a totally different way.

"Hi, pal," he said, smiling at Nell. "Hiding out?"

She shrugged. "I don't dance," she said with a rueful grin. "I never learned."

He cocked an eyebrow. "No time like the present," he
remarked. The band had just changed to a slow, dreamy
tune, and he held out his hand.

But she shook her head. "I'm not really in the mood."

He turned to look at the throng of dancers, and his face hardened when he saw Margie dancing with Tyler. He moved beside Nell to lean against one of the posts with folded arms, glaring at what he saw.

"He doesn't waste much time, does he?" he asked under his breath.

"They come from the same kind of world," Nell said quietly. "They've spent a lot of time together since he came here, and the boys love him."

"The boys don't exactly treat me like a plague victim," Darren said coldly. "Well, faint heart never won fair lady, Nell."

She smiled up at him. "In that case, good luck."

He smiled back. "Don't let him see you looking like that," he advised. "You'll blow your cover."

She sat up straighter. "God forbid."

He winked at her and moved into the dancers to tap Tyler curtly on the shoulder, nod and sweep Margie into his arms.

Tyler moved off the floor. He gave Nell a cursory glance before he picked up the rawhide strands he'd left on the corner of the refreshment table and began to braid them again.

"Lost your escort, I gather," he said coolly without looking down at her.

"What's the matter? Is the competition too much for you?" she shot back with uncharacteristic venom.

He blinked at the unfamiliar heat in her tone. His green eyes glanced over her composed features. "I thought that was your big problem, honey," he said. "Although you're dressed for it tonight."

"This old rag?" she said with a vacant smile. "Until just recently, it was the kitchen tablecloth."

He didn't smile. His eyes went to Margie and Darren, dancing like shadows, oblivious to the world.

"It's a nice crowd," Nell remarked when the silence between them lengthened.

"So it is." He finished the braid and tied it off.

"How are roundup plans coming?"

"Fine."

She took a deep breath. "My goodness, you'll talk my ear off."

"Will I?"

"You might offer to teach me to dance," she said shyly and not without reservations. Inside she was shaking as she tossed off the light remark. "You said once that you'd like it if I wore a dress, and you'd show me how."

His green eyes met hers like bullets. "Most men get poetic when they've been without a woman for a few months," he said with blunt insolence. "But you take things to heart, don't you, Nell?"

She felt the color run up her neck like fire. "I...I didn't mean..."

"Sorry, honey, but my taste doesn't run to tomboys," he said mockingly. "You might as well stick with your current favorite, if you can hold on to him. He seems to have a wandering eye."

She stood up. "That was unfair."

"Was it?" His eyes narrowed. "As for your offer, I don't want to dance with you, now or ever. And you might as well throw that—" he indicated her dress

"—in the trash if you bought it to catch my eye. I'm not interested in you."

She felt the world caving in around her. She looked up at him like a small, wounded animal, tears glistening in her eyes.

She couldn't even fight back for the pain his careless words had caused. She'd had such hopes. But then, he'd made no secret of his interest in Margie. She'd been crazy to pit her charms against her sister-in-law's!

"I'm sorry!" she whispered, but her voice broke. Without another word, she turned and ran out of the barn, her skirts flying against her legs as she darted onto the porch, into the house and up the stairs. She didn't stop until she was locked in her room, and the tears came like rain.

Tyler had watched her go with anguish. He hadn't expected that reaction, especially since she'd been sitting with McAnders. Well, maybe it was the sight of Margie dancing with her lost love that had set her off that way, and not what he'd said to her at all. He had to hold on to that thought. If he started believing that what he'd said to Nell had put those tears in her eyes, he wasn't sure he could stand it.

Nell had cried herself to sleep. She woke up dry-eyed and miserable, wondering how she was going to bear it if she had to see Tyler again. Margie had come by her room last night as if she wanted to talk, but Nell had feigned sleep. She didn't know what Margie had to say, but it was probably a lot of sighing memories of Tyler and the dance, and Nell didn't want to have to listen to her.

She was only sorry that she'd shown Tyler how he'd

hurt her. She never should have lost control that way. She should have thrown herself into the spirit of the dance, laughed and danced with Darren and given Tyler the cold shoulder. But she wasn't the kind of woman who could carry off that kind of charade. She wore her poor heart on her sleeve, and Tyler had crushed it.

She was surprised to find Tyler in the dining room when she went downstairs to breakfast, especially after the way they'd parted the night before.

"I want to talk to you," he began slowly.

"I can't imagine about what," she replied. She did look up then, and her dark eyes were almost black with cold rage.

"About last night," he said shortly. "I didn't mean what I said about your outfit. You looked lovely."

"Thank you," she said, but without warmth. "Last night that would have meant a lot."

"I got tired of watching you with McAnders," he admitted shortly.

She wasn't sure she'd heard him right. "Watching me with him?" she probed.

"Watching you throw yourself at him," he said with a mocking smile. "That's what it was, wasn't it? Dressing up in that fancy rig, putting on makeup. I hope he appreciated all your efforts."

She took a deep breath and felt her entire body bristling as she glared at him with her dark eyes flashing. "To be perfectly honest, I hadn't aimed my charms at Darren specifically. But thanks for the idea. Maybe I will 'throw myself' at Darren again! At least he told me I looked nice and offered to teach me to dance!"

"He felt sorry for you!" Tyler burst out without choosing his words.

"Doesn't everybody?" she shouted. "I know I'm not pretty! I'm just a stupid little tomboy who can't tell the right man from a hole in the south forty! And I'm glad he felt sorry for me—at least he didn't make fun of me!"

"Neither did I!"

"What would you call it?"

Bella came ambling into the room, her eyes like saucers, but neither of them noticed her.

"I got the wrong end of the stick!" he tried to explain.

"Well, why don't you get hold of the right end?" she invited. "And I'll tell you exactly where you can put it and how far!"

"Nell!" Bella burst out, shocked.

"If that's how you feel, we'll drop the whole subject," Tyler said through his teeth. One lean hand was almost crushing the brim of his hat, but he seemed to be beyond noticing it.

"Good! Why don't you go out and ride a horse or something?"

"You won't even listen…!"

"I did listen!" Nell raged, red-faced. "You said I might as well throw my clothes in the trash as wear them to impress you, that you weren't interested and that I took things to heart…!"

"Oh, God!" he groaned.

"And that it was just abstinence that was responsible for everything!" she concluded fiercely. "Well, that works both ways, cowboy! And you can get out of my dining room. You're curdling my eggs!"

His face was like rock, and his eyes blazed up like green fires. "Damn your eggs! Will you listen?"

"I will not, and I'm not eating the damned eggs. Here, you can have them, and welcome!" And she flung the plate at him, eggs and all, and stalked out of the room.

Tyler stood there, quite still, with egg literally on his face, his shirt, his jeans. A piece of egg had even landed in his hat.

Bella cocked her head warily as she waited for the explosion. He glared at her for a minute and deliberately stuck the hat on his head.

"Would you, uh, like some bacon to go with your eggs?" she asked.

"No, thanks," he said calmly. "I don't really have anyplace left to put it."

He turned and walked out, and Bella was hard put not to collapse with hysteria. Imagine, Nell actually shouting at anybody! That young lady was definitely getting herself together, and Tyler was going to be in for some hard times if Bella didn't miss her guess.

The cold war had truly begun. Nell sent messages to Tyler by Chappy during roundup and she never went near the holding pens. The most she did was to call Bob Wyler about the helicopter and make arrangements with the transport people to get the calves to the auction barn. Otherwise, she busied herself with the guests, who were enjoying the warm autumn climate and especially the cookouts and trail drives that Nell led herself.

Her confidence was beginning to grow, except where Tyler Jacobs was concerned. She felt like a new woman. She discarded her old wardrobe and bought a new one.

This time, she bought jeans that fit and tops that clung. She had her hair trimmed and shaped. She began to wear makeup. And she learned from Margie how to gracefully get out of potentially disturbing situations with male guests without hard feelings. She was beginning to bloom, like a delayed spring flower blossoming before winter.

Margie began spending more and more time at the ranch, and every time Nell looked out, she saw her sister-in-law with Tyler. Darren grew moody and frankly angry, and began cutting at Margie every time he saw her. She cut back. It got to the point that they were avoiding each other like the plague, but Tyler seemed to benefit from that, because Margie spent most all her time with him. He enjoyed it, too, if the expression on his face and in his eyes was anything to go by. The boys had even started teasing them about their preoccupation with each other. But it was a loving kind of teasing, because the boys were crazy about Tyler. Darren had captured at least some of their attention during the frequent visits, though, because they began to seek him out to show them about horses and cattle and tell them stories he'd heard from his grandfather about the old days in the West. That irritated Margie, but she couldn't make them stop following Darren around. And Tyler wouldn't. That, too, was puzzling to Nell.

Meanwhile, Tyler was becoming more and more unapproachable. He glared daggers through Nell when she was looking, and watched her hungrily when she wasn't. Bella knew, but she kept her mouth shut. It wouldn't do to interfere, she reckoned. Things had a way of working out better without meddling from interested bystanders. She'd learned her lesson.

Roundup ended and the calves brought a better than expected price at auction, which pleased Uncle Ted to no end. He praised Nell for the way things were going at the ranch and then asked with elaborate carelessness what she thought of his foreman.

Nell made an excuse to get off the phone without answering the question. It was too hard thinking up nice ways to tell her uncle that she thought his foreman would be best barbecued.

She'd no sooner hung up than the phone rang again. She picked it up. The voice on the line was a woman's and unfamiliar.

"Is this Nell Regan?" she was asked hesitantly.

"Yes."

"I'm Shelby Jacobs Ballenger," came the quiet reply. "I was hoping that I might be able to speak to my brother."

Nell sat down. "He's gone into town to pick up some supplies," she said, remembering the fondness Tyler's voice had betrayed when he mentioned his only relative, his sister, Shelby. "But he'll be back within the hour. Can I have him call you?"

"Oh, dear." Shelby sighed. "Justin and I are leaving for Jacobsville in just a few hours. We're just in Tucson on a quick business trip, and I was hoping that we could see him." She laughed self-consciously. "You see, he's been worried about me. Justin and I got off to a rocky start, but things are wonderful now and I wanted him to see us together, so that he'd be sure I was telling him the truth."

"Why don't you come down here," Nell offered impulsively. "We're only about thirty minutes out of Tucson. Have you a car?"

"Yes, Justin rented one for his meeting. It would be all right? You wouldn't mind having two strangers barge in on you?"

"You're not a stranger," Nell said with a smile. "Tyler's talked about you so much that we all feel as if we know you. We'd love for you to come. Bella can make a cake—"

"Oh, please, don't go to any trouble."

"It's no trouble, really. You just come on down." And she proceeded to give Shelby directions. Although God only knew why she should go to so much effort to give Tyler a nice surprise when he'd been simply horrible to her. It must have been a touch too much sun, she decided after she'd hung up.

"Tyler's sister, coming here?" Bella grinned from ear to ear. "I'll go bake a nice chocolate cake. You tidy up the living room."

Nell glowered. "It's already tidy."

"Good. Then lay a tray and make sure the silver's nice and polished."

Nell threw up her hands. "Botheration!"

"It was your idea to have them come down," she was reminded. Bella smiled with sickening superiority. "What a sweet surprise for Tyler. And here I thought you hated him. Slinging scrambled eggs all over him, yelling at him…"

"I'll just see about that silver," Nell murmured, and got out of Bella's sight.

A little more than half an hour later, a rented limousine pulled up at the sidewalk and two people got out. Nell recognized Shelby Jacobs Ballenger almost at once, because she looked so much like her brother. She was lovely, very slender and tall and elegant with her dark hair in a French twist and wearing a green silk dress. She was no surprise, but the tall man with her was. He was very masculine, that was apparent, but he wasn't handsome at all, and he looked as if he didn't smile much. Nell felt immediately intimidated and tried not to show it when she went to the door to greet them.

"You have to be Nell." Shelby smiled. She reached forward and hugged the younger woman warmly. "It's so nice to meet you. I'm Shelby, and this is Justin." She looked up at the tall man, her expression full of love.

He smiled back at her for an instant and then diverted his lancing dark gaze to Nell. "Nice to meet you."

Nell nodded, tongue-tied, she was glad that she'd put on clean jeans and a nice blue-checked blouse and brushed her hair. At least she didn't look scruffy.

She led them into the living room and Bella came in to be introduced, carrying a coffee tray laden with the necessities and a platter of fresh chocolate cake.

"My favorite," Justin murmured, grinning at Bella. "Thank you, but what are they going to eat?" he asked with an innocent glance at the women.

The ice was immediately broken. Nell relaxed visibly and sat down to pour coffee.

"When Tyler comes, waylay him and send him in, but don't tell him why," Nell called to Bella.

"I'll tell him you want to give him some more eggs," Bella said smugly and left the room.

Nell's color intrigued Shelby, who stirred cream into

her coffee absently and began to smile. "Eggs?" she probed.

Nell cleared her throat. "We had an, er, slight misunderstanding."

"Eggs?" Justin asked, looking dryly interested.

It was getting more uncomfortable by the second. "I sort of lost my temper and threw my breakfast at him," Nell confessed. She looked at Shelby pleadingly. "Well, he insulted me first."

"Oh, I can believe that." Shelby nodded, smiling. "I'm not going to put all the blame on you."

"How's he fitting in here?" Justin asked as he leaned back against the sofa with his coffee cup in one hand.

"He fits in fine with the men," Nell said restlessly. Justin's dark eyes were piercing, and they didn't seem to miss much.

Shelby was watching her just as closely, and with a faintly amused smile. "You know," she said, "you don't seem anything like Tyler's description of you at my wedding."

Nell cleared her throat. "Am I better or worse?" she asked.

"If you answer that, I'll disown you," came Tyler's deep voice from the doorway.

"Ty!" Shelby got up and ran into his arms, to be swung high and kissed while he smiled in a way Nell had never seen him smile. It made her see what she'd missed, and it made her sad.

"Good to see you again," Justin said, rising to shake hands with Tyler before he drew Shelby close to his side.

That simple gesture told Tyler how things were between the recently married couple. Justin looked at her with open possessiveness, and Shelby stayed as close to him as she could get. Apparently they'd solved their difficulties, because no couple could pretend the kind of explosive emotion that crackled between them like electricity. Tyler relaxed, sure of Shelby's future. That was one load off his mind. He'd been worried about the marriage's rocky start.

"We thought we'd call you before we left Tucson," Shelby explained while they drank coffee and ate chocolate cake. "But Nell invited us down to see you before we fly home to Texas."

"Nice of her, wasn't it?" Justin asked with that smug, lazy smile that made Tyler's neck hair bristle.

"Nice," Tyler said shortly. He didn't look at Nell, who was sitting in an armchair while he shared the sofa with Shelby and Justin.

"Don't strain yourself thanking me," Nell said with venomous politeness. "I'd have done the same thing for anyone."

Tyler's green eyes glittered at her across the coffee table. "I'm sure you would, you tenderhearted little thing."

He said it with deep sarcasm and Nell stiffened. "I used to have a tender heart all right," she told him flatly, "but I wore it out on men."

"That's right," he invited, "put all the blame on us. Men can't put a foot right where you're concerned, can they?"

"They can if they have a woman to lead them," Nell said, and smiled icily.

"Let me tell you, I won't live long enough to let a woman lead me anywhere! Furthermore..." He stopped, clearing his throat gruffly when he noticed the attention he was getting from the visitors. He smiled. "How are things back in Jacobsville?" he asked with pleasant interest.

It was to Justin's credit that he didn't fall on the floor laughing when he tried to answer that. Meanwhile, Shelby smiled into her coffee and exchanged a highly amused glance with her husband. They didn't need a program to see what was going on. It looked very much to Shelby as if Tyler had met his match, and not a minute too soon.

CHAPTER EIGHT

SHELBY AND JUSTIN stayed for another half hour, giving Tyler some interesting news from back home. Justin's brother, Calhoun, and sister-in-law, Abby, had flown to Europe for a belated honeymoon, and a neighbor had bought Geronimo, Tyler's prize stud stallion.

"I'm glad Harrison got him," Tyler murmured, his face faintly bitter because the remark reminded him of all he and Shelby had lost. "He was a good horse."

"He'll be well taken care of," Shelby added. "I'll make sure of it." She smiled at her brother. "Don't brood over it, will you? We can't do anything about the past."

Justin saw storm clouds coming and quickly headed them off. "I hate to cut this short," he said with a glance at his thin gold watch, "but we've got to go, honey."

Shelby clung to Justin's hand as they stood up, releasing it for just a minute while she hugged Tyler and then Nell. "Thanks for letting us come, Nell. Ty, try to write once in a while, or at least call and let us know you're alive."

He smiled at his sister. "I'll do my best. Take good care of her, Justin."

"Oh, that's the easy part," Justin said, and his expression as he smiled at his wife was loving and possessive and very sexy. Justin might look formidable, but Nell had a feeling he shared with Shelby a side of himself that no one else would ever see. That was what marriage should be, Nell thought. Not that she was ever going to have a chance at it.

She walked to the door with Tyler to see Justin and Shelby off. It was already dusk and getting darker by the minute. In the distance, the guest houses were all alight and there was the sound of a guitar and a harmonica playing down at the bunkhouse. Nell wrapped her arms around herself, reluctant to leave Tyler, but too nervous of him to stay.

She turned, only to find his hand sliding down to grasp hers.

"Not yet," he said, and there was a familiar deep note in his voice.

She should have had more willpower, but things had been strained between them for too long already, and the touch of his hand on hers made her weak.

"Come for a walk with me, Nell," he said quietly, and drew her along with him down the path that led to his cabin.

Even as she went along, she knew that she shouldn't go. He was leading up to a confrontation. But the night was perfumed with flowers, and the stars were above them, and silence drew around them like a dark blanket. His hand in hers was warm against the chill of the desert night, and she moved closer, feeling the strength of his body like a shield at her side. She sensed his sadness and bitterness, and all the hostility fell away from her. He needed someone to talk to; that was probably all he wanted. She understood that. She'd never had anyone who she could really talk to, until Darren McAnders had come back and become her friend. But she'd much rather have talked to Tyler. She couldn't do anything to change his past, but she could certainly listen.

He stopped at the corral fence and let go of her hand to light a cigarette while they listened to the night sounds and the silences.

"I like your sister," she said softly.

"So do I. She and I have been close all our lives. All we ever really had was each other when we were growing up. After our mother died, our father became greedy and grasping. He was hell to live with most of the time, and he wasn't above blackmail."

"Have she and Justin known each other a long time?" she asked curiously.

"Years." He took a draw of the cigarette, and his smile was reflected by the orange glow from its tip. "Six years ago they got engaged, but Shelby ended it. I never knew why, although I'm sure my father had a hand in it. Justin wasn't wealthy and Dad had just the right rich man picked out for Shelby. She didn't marry anyone as it turned out. Then when we lost everything, Justin went to see her because she had no one—I'd just come out here to work. And the next thing we knew, they were married. I thought he'd done that for revenge, that he was going to make her life miserable. She didn't seem very happy on their wedding day." He glanced down at her. "But I think they've worked things out. Did you notice the way they look at each other?"

Nell leaned against the fence and kept her face down. "Yes. They seem to be very happy."

"And very lucky. Most people don't get a second chance."

She lifted her eyes. "If that's a dig at me because I've avoided you since the square dance…"

"I was jealous, Nell," he said unexpectedly. He smiled faintly at the stunned expression on her face that was barely visible in the dim light from the house. "Jealous as hell. I'd seen you and McAnders in a clinch, and then you dressed up for him, I thought, when you'd never dressed up for me. I just blew up. I didn't really mean the things I said to you, but you wouldn't listen when I tried to explain."

"Jealous of me?" She laughed bitterly. "That'll be the day. I'm a tomboy, I'm plain, I'm shy—"

"And sadly lacking in self-confidence," he finished for her. "Don't you think that a man could want you for yourself? For the things you are instead of how you look?"

"Nobody ever has," she said shortly. "I'm twenty-four and I'll die an old maid."

"Not you, honey," he said softly. "You're too passionate to live and die alone."

Her face went hot. "Don't throw that up to me," she snapped, her eyes flashing. "I was…I was off balance and you're too experienced for me, that's all."

"Experienced, hell," he said shortly. "There haven't even been that many women, and you weren't off balance—you were starved for a little love."

"Thanks a lot!"

"Will you just shut up and listen?" he demanded. "You never would give me a chance to say anything about what happened, you just slung scrambled eggs at me and stomped off in a fury."

"I was entitled to be angry after what you said to me," she reminded him curtly.

"Oh, hell, maybe you were," he conceded tautly. "But you could have let me explain."

"The explanation was obvious," she replied. "Darren was poaching on what you considered your territory."

He smiled in spite of himself. "You might say that."

"Well, you don't have to worry about Margie," she said after a minute. "I mean, it's obvious that she's crazy about you. And the boys like you…"

"What are you talking about?" he asked pleasantly.

"Nobody could blame you for being attracted to her," she went on. "And I'm sorry if I've made things difficult for you—I didn't mean to. You've lost so much. You should have somebody to care about. Somebody who'll care about you."

"Coals of fire," he murmured, watching her as he smoked his cigarette. "Do you want me to be happy, Nell?"

"I want that very much," she said, her voice soft in the darkness. "I haven't meant to be difficult. It's just…"

"You don't have a scrap of self-confidence, that's just what it is," he said for her. "That's a shame, Nell, because you've got a lot going for you. I wish I knew why you had this hang-up about men."

"I got hurt once," she muttered.

"Most people get hurt once."

"Not like I did." She folded her arms across her breasts. "When I was in my middle teens, I had a terrible crush on one of the cowboys. I plagued him and followed him around and chased him mercilessly. To make a long story short, he was in love with a woman he couldn't have, and in a drunken stupor he decided to take me up on my offer." She laughed bitterly. "Until then, I had no idea that romance was anything except smiling at each other and maybe holding hands. It never actually occurred to me that people in love went to bed together. And what made it so bad was that physically I didn't feel anything for him. I guess that's why I panicked and screamed. Bella came and rescued me and the cowboy left in disgrace."

Tyler had listened intently. The cigarette burned away between his fingers without his noticing. "It was McAnders," he guessed with cold certainty.

"Yes. He was in love with Marguerite, but I didn't know it until he tried to make love to me. I realized that night what a terrible mistake I'd made." She smiled halfheartedly. "So then I knew that I couldn't trust my instincts or my judgment anymore. I stopped wearing sexy clothes and I stopped running after anybody."

"One bad egg doesn't make the whole carton spoil," he said.

"That's true, but how do you find the bad egg in time?" She shook her head. "I've never had the inclination to try again."

"Until I came along?"

She flushed. "I told you, I was only trying to make you feel welcome. You paid me a little attention and it flattered me."

"Where does McAnders fit into this now?" he asked. "I gather that you were fairly intimate with him before Bella came to the rescue, but how about today? Did you go from me to him?"

She shifted restlessly. "No," she said under her breath.

He brightened a little. "Why not?"

She had to remember that he was interested in Margie, not her. He might feel a little sorry for her, but he didn't want her for keeps. She straightened. "He still doesn't appeal to me physically."

He wondered if she realized what she was giving away with that remark. If she didn't want McAnders she probably didn't really love him. But he was going to have to make her see that, and it wouldn't be easy.

"I appealed to you physically, once," he said gently, his voice deep and drugging in the still night. He moved closer, his fingers lightly touching her face, her loosened hair. His warmth enveloped her, his breath was like a faint breeze, moving the hair at her temples, making her heart race. "If McAnders hadn't shown up, I might have appealed to you in other ways. We didn't have enough time to get to know each other."

She put her hands slowly, flatly against his shirtfront, hesitating as if she thought he might throw them away. But he caught them gently and pressed them to the soft cotton of his shirt.

"You wouldn't want to, now," she said, and her voice shook. "Margie's here half the time."

"And, of course, you think I'm madly in love with her."

"Aren't you?" she asked stubbornly.

"I'm not going to tell you that," he said. He lifted her chin. "You're going to have to come out of your shell, little one, and start looking around you. You can't learn to swim if you keep balking at the water."

"I don't understand."

"Very simply, Nell, if you want me, you're going to have to believe that I can want you back. You're going to have to believe in yourself a little and start trusting me not to hurt you."

"Trust comes hard," she said, although what he was saying was more tempting than he realized. She did want him, terribly, but she was playing for keeps. Was he?

"It comes hard to most people." He smoothed the hair away from her face. "It depends on whether or not you think it's worth the chance. Love doesn't come with a money-back guarantee. There comes a time when you have to trust your instincts and take a chance."

She shifted restlessly, but he wouldn't let go of her hands. "Why?" she asked abruptly. "You said you wanted me, but at the same time you said you weren't interested in any relationships with women."

"I said a lot, didn't I, honey?" he murmured dryly.

She searched what she could see of his dark face. "I'm not the kind of woman you could care about," she said miserably.

"My whole life has turned upside down, Nell," he told her. "I'm not the same man I used to be. I don't have wealth or position, and about all that's left is my good name and a lot of credit. That makes me pretty vulnerable, in case you've missed it."

"Vulnerable, how?" she asked.

"You might think I was interested in you because you're a woman of property."

"That'll be the day," she murmured dryly. "There's no way I can see you chasing a woman for her money."

His quiet eyes pierced the darkness, looking for her face. "At least you know me that well," he said. "But part of you is afraid of me."

"You want Marguerite," she moaned. "Why bother with me?"

"Margie sends out signals. You could learn to do that, too," he said conversationally. "You could waylay me in the office and kiss me stupid, or buy a new wardrobe to dazzle me with."

She blushed and her heart jumped into her throat. "Fat chance when you made Chappy take back a rope he bought," she reminded him to lighten the tension that was growing between them.

He grinned. "Buy a new dress. I promise not to fuss."

"Margie bought me a new dress and you made me feel dowdy when I wore it," she said.

"Yes, I know." He sighed. "I keep trying to apologize, but you don't hear me."

Her heart was running wild; while he spoke his hands had gone to her hips and pulled them slowly to his. She tried to step back, but he held her there very gently.

"No," he said softly. "You can't run away this time. I won't let you."

"I have to go inside," she said. Panic was rising in her at the intimacy of his hold. It was bringing back dangerously sweet memories.

"Frightened, Nell?" he asked quietly.

"I won't be just another conquest!" she groaned, struggling.

"Stand still, for God's sake." He gasped suddenly, and his powerful body stiffened. "God, Nell, that hurts!"

She stopped instantly. Her color was rising when she felt what he was talking about and realized that she was only complicating things.

"Then you shouldn't hold me like this," she whispered shakily.

He took a steadying breath and his hands contracted on her waist. "We've been a lot closer, though, haven't we?" he asked at her forehead, brushing his lips against her skin. "We've been together without a scrap of fabric between your breasts and my chest, and you pulled my head down and arched up to meet my mouth."

She buried her embarrassed face in his shirt, shaking with remembered pleasure. "I shouldn't have let you," she whispered.

"Then Chappy came to the door and broke the spell," he murmured at her cheek. "I didn't want to answer it. I wanted to go on loving you. But I guess it was a good thing he came along, because things were getting out of hand, weren't they? We wanted each other so much, Nell. I don't really know that we could have stopped in time."

He was right. That didn't make her guilt any easier to bear. "And that would have been a disaster, wouldn't it?" she asked, waiting stiffly for his answer.

"I'm an old-fashioned man, honey," he said finally. His hands smoothed down her back, holding her against him. "I wouldn't ask you to sleep with me, knowing that you're a virgin. You aren't that kind of woman."

She bit her lower lip hard. "I've got all these hang-ups..."

"Most of which we removed that day in my bed," he reminded her. "But your biggest hang-up, little Nell, is your mental block about your attractions. You're the only person around here who doesn't see what a dish you are."

"Me?" she asked breathlessly.

"You." He bent to her mouth and brushed it with his. "You've got a warm heart," he whispered, bending again. The kiss lingered this time, just a second longer. "You're caring." He kissed her again, and this time he parted her lips briefly before he raised his head. "You're intelligent." His mouth teased, brushing hers open breath by breath. "And you're the sexiest woman I've ever made love to…"

He whispered the words into her trembling lips before he took them, and this time he didn't draw back. His tongue began to penetrate her mouth in slow, exquisite thrusts. This was a kind of kiss Nell hadn't experienced before, not even that day in Tyler's cabin, and she was afraid of it.

She tried to draw back, but his lean hand at her nape held her mouth under his.

"Don't fight it," he whispered coaxingly. "I won't hurt you. Relax, Nell. Let me have your mouth. I'll treat it just as tenderly as I'd treat your body if you gave yourself to me, little one," he breathed, and his mouth whispered down onto hers.

The words in addition to the expert teasing of his tongue shook away every last bit of her reserve. She melted into the length of him, trembling with the fierce hunger he was arousing in her body. She moaned helplessly and felt his mouth smile against hers. Then he deepened the pressure and the slow thrust of his tongue into the sweet, soft darkness of her mouth.

But what about Margie? she wanted to ask. How can you hold me like this when you want her? She couldn't have asked him that to save her life, because he was working magic on her body. She wanted him. Tomorrow she could hate herself and him for leading her on, for toying with her. But tonight she wanted nothing except the sweet pleasure of his mouth and his hands and a few memories to carry through the long years ahead.

She felt his hands at the back of her thighs, pulling her shaking legs closer so that her hips were grinding into his, so that she knew how aroused he was. She didn't protest. Her hands found their way around him, to his back and down, returning the pressure shyly even as the first shudder of desire ripped through her and dragged a cry from her lips.

He lifted his head abruptly. His eyes glittered and he was trembling a little; his heartbeat was rough against her breasts. "Come home with me. I'll sit with you in that big leather armchair by the fireplace, and we'll love each other for a few minutes."

She was crying with reaction. "It's so dangerous," she pleaded, but it was no protest at all, and he had to know it.

"I've got to, Nell," he whispered, bending to lift her so gently into his arms. He turned, carrying her the rest of the way to his porch in the darkness. "I've got to, sweetheart."

Her arms went around his neck, and she buried her face in his warm, pulsating throat. "I can't...I can't sleep with you," she whispered.

"I'd never ask that of you," he breathed ardently. He caught her mouth hungrily with his while he fumbled the door open with one hand and carried her into the dark stillness of his cabin.

He kicked the door shut and moved to the big arm-chair, dropping into it with his mouth still hard and sure on her lips.

There was no more pretense left. He was hungry and he wasn't trying to hide it. He fought the buttons of her blouse out of his way and deftly removed it and the lacy covering beneath. His mouth found her warm breasts, and he nuzzled them hungrily, nibbling, kissing, tasting while she shuddered and arched her back to help him.

"So sweet, Nell," he groaned as his lips moved on her. "Oh, God, you taste like honey in my mouth."

Her hands touched his cool dark hair, savoring its clean thickness while she fed on the aching sweetness of his mouth. "Oh, please!" she moaned brokenly when he lifted his head to breathe. "Tyler, please…!"

He held her quietly while he tore open the snaps of his own shirt and dragged her inside it, pressing her breasts against the hair-covered warmth of his chest, moving her sensually from side to side so that her breathing became as rough and torturous as his own.

His mouth ground into hers then, rough with need, his restraint gone, his control broken by the sounds she was making against his lips, by the helpless movement of her body against him, silky and bare and terribly arousing.

His lean hands caressed her soft, bare back, holding her to him so that he could feel the hard tips of her breasts like tiny brands on his skin.

"Nell," he groaned. His mouth slid away from hers and into her throat, pressing hard against the wildly throbbing artery as he drew her up close and held her, rocked her, until the trembling need began to drain out of her.

"I ache all over," she whispered with tears in her voice. She clung closer. "Tyler, this is scary!"

"This is desire," he breathed at her ear, and his arms contracted. "This is the raw need to mate. Don't be afraid of it. I'm not going to take advantage of something you can't help. I want you just as much as you want me."

She shuddered helplessly. "It must be…so much worse for you," she whispered.

"A sweet ache," he confessed huskily, and his mouth brushed her cheek, her throat. "I don't have a single regret. Do you?"

"I shouldn't admit it."

He chuckled, delighted with her headlong response to him, with her helpless hunger. "Neither should I. But wasn't it good, Nell? Wasn't it delicious?"

"Oh, yes." She sighed, nestling closer with a tiny sound deep in her throat. "I want to stay with you all night."

"I want that, too, but we can't."

"I could just sleep with you," she murmured drowsily.

"Sure you could. Platonically. And nothing would happen." He turned up her face and kissed her mouth hard. "You know as well as I do that we'd devour each other if we got into a bed together. We're half-crazy to be together already, and I've barely touched you."

She pulled back a little. "You call that barely touching?" she asked, awed.

"Compared to what I'd do to you in bed, yes."

She hesitated, but he read the thought in her mind and chuckled helplessly.

"Shall I tell you?" he whispered softly.

"You wouldn't dare."

But he would. And he did, sensuously, whispering it into her ear while he touched her, lightly caressed her, brought every nerve in her body to singing, agonizing pleasure.

"I never dreamed…!" she gasped, hiding her face in his chest when he finished.

"You needed to know," he said gently. "You're still very innocent, despite what happened in your teens. I want you to understand that what you and I would share wouldn't be painful or frightening. Physical love is an expression of what two people feel for each other so strongly that words aren't enough to contain it. It isn't anything to dread."

"Certainly not with you it wouldn't be," she said tenderly. She touched his hard face, loving its strength, its masculine beauty. "Tyler…I could love you," she whispered hesitantly.

"Could you, honey?" He bent, brushing his mouth with exquisite softness against her lips. "If you want me, Nell, come after me."

"That isn't fair," she began.

"It's fair," he said. "For your own peace of mind, you need to regain the confidence you lost because of what happened with McAnders. Oh, I could back you into a corner and force you into a decision, but that would rob you of your right to choose. I won't do it for you. You have to do it, alone."

Her worried eyes studied his profile. "You said you didn't want a lasting relationship...." she said again.

He turned his head and looked down at her in the dimness of the unlit room. "Make me want one," he challenged. "Vamp me. Buy some sexy dresses and drive me crazy. Be the woman you can be. The woman you should have been."

"I'm not attractive," she argued faintly.

His hand swept slowly, lovingly, over her breasts. "You're beautiful, Nell," he said huskily. "Firm and soft and silky to touch."

"Tyler..."

"Come here," he groaned. He stood up with her in his arms and let her slide down his body, bent to kiss her hungrily before his hand shot out and fumbled with a light switch.

"No!" she protested, but it was too late. The soft light flooded the living room, and Tyler caught her hands before she could cover herself. He gazed down at her with an intent masculine appreciation of her attributes, which brought a wave of color up her neck and into her face. His chest rose and fell heavily, and his expression showed that he was having a monumental battle with his conscience to do nothing more than look.

"I'll live on this for a while," he breathed, lifting his eyes to hers.

Her lips parted as she stared back at him, all too aware of the tense swelling of her breasts, of their hard arousal, which he could see as well as feel.

"It embarrasses you, doesn't it?" he asked softly, searching her eyes. "I can see how lovely you are, how aroused I've made you. It's like letting me see you totally nude, isn't it? But you've seen me that way already, Nell. Remember?"

She lowered her eyes to his bare chest. "I couldn't forget if I tried. I thought you were perfect," she whispered shyly.

"I feel just that way about you. I love the way you look without your blouse. I'd give everything I have to carry you into my bedroom and love you in my bed. But as things stand, that's a decision I can't make." He let go of her hands and gazed at her one last time before he forced himself to turn his back and light a cigarette. "You'd better dress, sweetheart. I want you desperately right now, and I'm not quite as controlled as I thought I was."

She stared at his back for an instant, thinking of pressing herself against him. But she knew what would happen, and it would be her fault. She sighed softly and went to find her blouse and bra.

He got into his shirt and buttoned it and smoked half his cigarette before he turned around again. His eyes were dark with frustrated hunger as he looked at her. "We can't do much of that," he said with a tender smile. "It gets worse every time."

"Yes." She smiled back. "Oh, I want you so," she whispered helplessly.

"I want you, too." He held out his hand, and she put hers into it without hesitation. "I'd better walk you home."

"All right."

He went with her up the path in the darkness. He didn't speak and neither did she, but she clung to his hand and felt as if they'd become lovers in every sense of the word. There would never be, could never be, anyone after him. She felt that with a sense of faint despair, because she still didn't know where she stood with him.

He stopped at the front steps and turned her. His face was clearly visible in the light pouring out the window from the front room.

"No more pretense, Nell," he said softly. "If you want me, show me."

"But men don't like being chased," she whispered.

"Try it and see," he challenged with narrowed eyes. "You've got to believe in yourself before other people will."

"You won't mind?" she asked. "You're sure?"

He bent and put his mouth warmly against hers in a brief kiss. "I won't mind."

"But what about Margie?" she groaned.

"You'll find out about that all by yourself when you start putting your life back in order," he said simply. "It's right under your nose, but you just can't see it."

"Tell me," she whispered.

"No. You work it out. Good night, Nell."

Impulsively she moved closer and lifted her mouth. "Would you…kiss me again?" she whispered.

He did, half lifting her against him, and so thoroughly and hungrily that when he let her down again, she gasped.

"I like that," he said roughly. "You might try it again from time to time. Sleep well."

"You, too." She watched him turn and walk back the way they'd come, lighting a cigarette on the way. His stride was moody and thoughtful, but as she turned to go in, she heard him whistling a light, cheerful tune in the darkness. She smiled, because it was a popular love song. She knew that she might be reading too much into what they'd done, but her heart was on fire for him. Maybe he didn't really care that much about Margie. Maybe she could worm her way into his affection if she tried. But it was going to take some hard thinking before she risked her heart again. She needed time.

CHAPTER NINE

NELL WORRIED ALL night about Margie and Tyler and what she was going to do. Her own insecurities haunted her.

She went downstairs, her thoughts murky and still without concrete answers. She half expected Tyler to be there again, waiting for her, but he wasn't.

Bella bustled in with breakfast and sat down beside Nell. "Too early for the new arrivals to be up and hungry, so you and I can have ours in peace," she said, pouring two cups of coffee. "Tyler's having his in the bunkhouse."

"That's nothing unusual, is it?" Nell sighed. "He always seems to be eating down there lately."

"I don't think he's felt very welcome here in recent days," Bella told her bluntly. "Pity, because he sure is a nice fella and you could do worse."

"It isn't me he wants," Nell said curtly, glaring at the older woman as she helped herself to a fresh biscuit and buttered it. "It's Margie."

Bella sipped her coffee. "Did he tell you that?"

"No. But he didn't deny it, either."

The older woman spooned scrambled eggs onto her plate and reached for bacon. "Nell, I steered you wrong when Tyler came here. I should have encouraged you

to dress up and act like a young lady. I should have realized what kind of man he was. But I didn't, and I've
helped complicate things. I'm sorry."

"You didn't do anything," Nell said. She glowered at
her eggs. "I'm not the kind of woman a man like Tyler
needs. I'm just a country tomboy. I don't even know
how to dance."

"Stop running yourself down," Bella said gruffly.
"Listen, child, just because Darren McAnders couldn't
see past Margie to you is no reason for you to bury yourself in baggy britches forever. You're young and pretty,
and if you tried, you could be everything Tyler needs.
Don't forget, he isn't a rich man anymore. He doesn't
need a social butterfly, he needs a woman who can help
him build a new legacy for his children."

"Margie can work," Nell said halfheartedly.

"Oh, sure, like she does when she's here?" Bella
scoffed. "Fat chance. Tyler would be out of his mind
after the first week and you know it. She'd never cook
supper—she'd be too busy trying on dresses in town
or gossiping on the telephone."

"She's pretty and flamboyant."

"A sensible man doesn't want a wall decoration, he
wants a flesh-and-blood woman."

"I guess I'm flesh and blood," Nell agreed.

"And a hard worker, a good little cook and a companion who listens more than she talks. You're a jewel,"
Bella concluded. "You should think positively. At least
you've made a start. You're wearing clothes that really
fit, and you've put away that horrible slouchy hat and
let your hair down. You look like a different Nell."

"I decided that you and Margie were right about what

happened with Darren," she conceded. "I overreacted because I didn't know what a man was like when he was hungry for a woman. Well, not then, at least."

Bella's eyes widened. "And now you do?" she asked with a slow, wicked smile.

Nell felt the flush working its way up her neck. She reached blindly for her coffee and turned it over onto the tablecloth and herself.

"Oh, my, what little fumble fingers." Bella chuckled.

"I meant to do that," Nell protested as she got to her feet, brushing at a tiny spot on her blue-checked Western shirt and her new jeans. She glared at Bella. "I just hate coffee. And I don't fumble!" she added.

Then she turned around and tripped over the chair and fell flat on her face.

Bella doubled over laughing while Nell, bruised and furious, disentangled herself from the chair. She was turning the air blue when she saw a pair of boots come into view past her nose.

"She don't fumble," Bella explained to the boots, and walked off into the kitchen.

Nell scrambled to her feet, assisted by a familiar lean, strong hand.

"Having trouble?" Tyler asked pleasantly.

She did fumble then, nervous with him and still uncertain of her ground. She looked up into his dark face, wondering at the secret pleasure it gave her just to stare at him.

"I was looking for a contact lens," Nell said, flustered.

"You don't wear contact lenses," he pointed out.

She cleared her throat. "That doesn't mean that I can't look for one if I want to."

He smiled slowly. "Whatever turns you on," he said dryly.

She brushed back her unruly hair. "What can I do for you?" she asked abruptly.

"You can come on the campout trail ride with me this afternoon," he said. "Chappy's tied up with those new mares, so I told him we'd take the greenhorns out today."

She colored. "You and not Darren?"

He pursed his lips. "That's right. Is that a problem?" he added quietly.

She was still feeling her way, but telling the truth might be a good start, she decided. "No, it's not a problem," she said. "Darren has been a good friend. But I'd rather be with you."

He smiled slowly because her face flamed when she said it, and her shyness made her even more delectable to him. She was a pretty woman when she didn't dress like a baggy orphan.

"I'd rather be with you, too, sunshine," he said softly.

Her heart soared. Heaven must be this sweet, she thought dazedly. She smiled at him, her dark eyes like brown velvet.

Bella came through the door and broke the spell. Nell excused herself as the housekeeper giggled wickedly, and went out into the hall to get her hat. She did her usual chores, feeling as if she were walking on air, and the day was all too long until it was time to pack the bedrolls and the cooking utensils and the food that Bella had provided and head out for an overnight campout. The Double R Ranch was one of the few left that did it for real, complete with bedrolls and rough accommodations and no luxuries. Only a few hardy souls were willing to rough it the way the old-time cowboys had.

There were six people in the party, three couples. Four of that number were good riders already, and they weren't afraid of snakes or coyotes or rolling into the campfire in their sleep. It was a beautiful day, with the ragged mountains ringing around the flat grassy plain, and Nell felt on top of the world as she rode along at the head of the group with Tyler at her side. She kept looking back to make sure she wasn't losing any of their small parade.

"They're doing fine," Tyler told her as he lit a cigarette with steady hands. "Don't worry so much."

"Two of them have never even seen a real horse before," she reminded him.

"The Callaways?" He grinned, referring to a newly married, middle-aged couple who were, to put it politely, well fed. "No, but you've taught them how to stay on, at least, and they're getting the hang of it. Just relax."

She tried, but being a mother hen had become a habit, and she had a bad feeling about doing this campout without Chappy and the chuck wagon that usually came along with a bigger crowd.

And sure enough, things did begin to go wrong suddenly. They rode for an hour and then turned back toward the ranch house and stopped about a mile out to make camp just before dark.

Mrs. Callaway, a pleasant cheerful little blonde lady, came down off her horse too suddenly and caught her blouse on the pommel. There she hung, two inches above the desert floor, while the horse shook his head and pranced restlessly.

Tyler leaped forward to lift Mrs. Callaway while Nell soothed the horse and extricated the blouse.

"Are you all right, Mrs. Callaway?" Nell asked anxiously when the red-faced little woman had stopped shaking in her concerned husband's arms.

"Oh, I'm fine," she said with a grin. "What a story to tell the folks back home!"

Nell relaxed, but Mrs. Callaway's experience was only the beginning. Her husband went to help Tyler and the other men gather brush to make a fire and unearthed a long, fat, very unsocial rattlesnake.

He let out a war whoop, which startled Mrs. Donnegan, who backed into a cactus and let out a war whoop of her own. By the time the rattlesnake was disposed of by Tyler, and Mrs. Donnegan had her cactus spines removed by Nell, everybody was ready to eat. Tyler had a roaring fire going and had passed out wieners and buns and marshmallows and sticks for the guests while he brewed up a pot of black coffee.

"I really hate coffee," Mrs. Harris remarked. She was the only sour note in the bunch, a city woman who'd come to the desert only because her husband had coaxed her into it. She hated the desert, the cactus, the heat, the isolation—she hated everything, in fact. "I'd rather have a soft drink."

"No problem," her husband said. "We'll ride down to the ranch and get one."

"On that horse?" Mrs. Harris wailed, her black eyes

going even blacker. "I hurt in places I didn't even know I had!"

"Then you can drink coffee, can't you, sweetheart?" her husband continued.

She pouted, but she shut up. The Callaways sat close together, sharing condiments for the hot dogs while they munched on potato chips and carried on a casual conversation with the other guests on a variety of newsy subjects.

Nell enjoyed the quiet wonder of night on the desert as she never had, especially when Tyler started telling their guests about the surrounding territory and something of its history. She hadn't realized how much he knew about southeastern Arizona, and some of it she hadn't even known herself.

He talked about places like Cochise Stronghold, where the famous Apache chief was buried. There was a marker there, he added, telling that Indian Agent Tom Jeffords, a friend of Cochise, was the only white man privileged to know the exact spot of the chief's burial. The Apaches had run their horses over the ground and dragged it with brush behind them to conceal forever the place where Cochise rested.

There was also the famous Copper Queen Hotel in Bisbee, a landmark from old copper mining days in the Lavender Pit, where guests drank French champagne and were entertained by famous singers.

Farther south was Douglas, where Agua Prieta lay just over the border in Mexico. Pancho Villa had raided the border town, and a hotel in Douglas bore the marks of his horse on its marble staircase, which could still be seen today.

"You know a lot about this part of the state, Mr. Jacobs," Mr. Callaway remarked. "Do you come from around here?"

"No. I'm from south Texas." He smiled. "Near Victoria. My people founded a little place called Jacobsville, where I was raised."

"I love Texas," Mrs. Callaway said, sighing. "I guess you have cactus and mesquite and sagebrush..."

"Actually, it's more like magnolias, live oaks and dogwood trees," Tyler mused. "West Texas has those plants you're thinking about."

She blushed. "Sorry."

He laughed out loud. "Don't feel bad, a lot of people don't realize just how many different geographic sections there are in Texas. We've got everything from beach to desert to mountain country and plains. Texas had the option of becoming five separate states if it wanted to. But nobody ever did."

"I can see why," Mrs. Callaway said. "I've heard that you can drive from sunup to sunset and never leave Texas."

"That's very nearly true," he agreed.

"I suppose you'll go back there one day?" the small woman asked.

Tyler looked at Nell, his eyes narrow, thoughtful as they caressed hers until she caught her breath. "Maybe. Maybe not," he added softly, and smiled at Nell.

She felt lighter than air all over again, invincible. She laughed delightedly. "Anybody want more marshmallows?"

They roasted marshmallows until nobody could stuff another one into his mouth, and then they laid out the bedrolls and settled down for the night, while the orange flames of the campfire drifted lazily back and forth in the faint wind. It was cold on the desert at night. The guests had been told that and were prepared.

Nell moved her sleeping bag close to Tyler's, to his secret delight, and with a shy glance at him as he rested with his saddle for a pillow, she settled down beside him.

"Comfortable?" he asked, his voice deep and soft in the firelit darkness as he turned on his side to watch her.

"Yes." She gave in to the need to look at him, to memorize the lines and curves of his face, his body. She felt a kind of possessiveness toward him that she didn't really understand. "Do you miss Texas, Tyler?" she asked hesitantly.

"I got pretty homesick at first," he conceded. "But there's something about this desert that gets into your blood. It's full of history, but the cities are forward-looking, as well, and there are plenty of conservationists around who care about the land and water resources. Yes, I miss Texas. But I could live here, Nell," he said, smiling at her.

She wanted so badly to ask him if it was just because he liked the land, but she couldn't get the words to form properly. She blurted out, "With Margie?"

His eyebrows lifted. "Did I say with Margie?"

"No, but..."

He reached out a lean hand and touched her fingers where they lay cold and trembling on her stomach. His covered them, warmed them and made her tingle from head to toe. "I told you, Nell, you're going to have to

figure it out for yourself. I won't tell you how I feel
about Margie, or how I feel about you, for that matter."

"Why?" she asked more plaintively than she knew.

"Because I want you to understand a little more about
trust than you do, honey," he replied. "There's a part
of you that draws back and shies away from me. Until
you get it worked out, I'm not going to influence you
one way or the other."

She sighed. "I guess maybe I'll work it out, then."

"Want to come closer?" he coaxed with a warm
smile. "You're pretty safe, considering how we're surrounded by curious eyes."

She yielded to the temptation to be close. Inching
her way, she moved her sleeping bag right up against
his and turned on her side to rest beside him, with her
head pillowed on one of his hard arms.

"That's better," he said softly. He eased forward a
fraction of an inch and brushed her warm lips gently
with his, savoring their faint trembling, their helpless
response. "You might keep something in mind," he
whispered.

"Oh? What?" she breathed against his lips, and her
eyes opened straight into his.

"You aren't wearing makeup or a fancy dress," he
whispered quietly. "And I'm not drawing back because
you don't appeal to me the way you are."

Her fingers touched his face, loving its strength. "I'm
not pretty," she said.

"You are to me," he said. "That's all that matters in
the long run, if you'd open your eyes and see what's
right under your nose."

"I see you," she said, her voice achingly tender as she adored him with her eyes.

"That's what I mean," he replied. He drew her closer. The saddle protected their faces from prying eyes, and he bent slowly to press his mouth hard against hers. "I want you, Nell," he said into her parted lips as he bit at them.

She wanted him, too. Her body was already on fire, and all he was doing was kissing her. She nibbled helplessly at his teasing mouth, and her hand smoothed into his thick hair, trying to draw him down.

"No," he breathed. "You can't have my mouth that way, not tonight. I can't lose my head with you, honey. There are too many witnesses."

"What if we were alone?" she moaned under her breath. She slid her arms around his neck to press her breasts against his hard chest.

"Nell...damn it." He shuddered. He lifted his tormented eyes to the campfire. It was dying down and he needed to get up and put some fresh wood on it. The other campers were in their sleeping bags and turned toward the fire in a semicircle, which he and Nell were behind. No one could see them. He realized that now, and his powerful body trembled with the need to ease Nell onto her back and slide his leg between both of hers and show her how much he wanted her. He could feel her skin against his, the silken warmth of her breasts hardtipped under his broad chest, the cries that he could tease out of her throat while he seduced her body slowly and tenderly and penetrated its virginal purity....

He groaned. His fingers on her arms hurt, but she didn't mind. Something powerful and mysterious was working in him, and she was too hungry to be afraid of it. This was Tyler, and she loved him with all her heart. She wanted memories, all that she could get, to press to her mind in the years that would follow.

"What is it?" she asked.

He looked down at her. In the dim light he could see her soft eyes, he could feel her quickened breathing. His hand moved with quiet possession over her blouse and smoothed around her breast until he found the hard tip. He watched her bite her lip and jerk toward him, trying not to cry out lest someone heard her.

"This is not sane," he whispered as the arm under her nape contracted with desire. "Of all the stupid places to make love…."

"Touch me," she whispered brokenly.

His breath was audible as the words shattered his control and made him vulnerable. "Oh, Nell, you can't imagine what I'm thinking." He laughed huskily as his hand slid to the buttons of her blouse and began to lazily unfasten them. "You can't imagine what I want to do to you."

"Yes, I can," she whispered back, "because you told me, remember?" Her eyes met his searchingly. "You told me every single detail."

His powerful body trembled as he reached the last button. "Yes. And I dreamed it that night. Dreamed that I took you under me and felt your body like a field of flowers absorbing me so tenderly." He was whispering, but the tone of his voice drugged her. His fingers slid under the fabric and stopped with delighted surprise when he found nothing except soft warm skin.

Her lips parted. "I've never done this before," she

whispered unsteadily. "Gone without…without what I usually wear, I mean."

He could have jumped over the moon. His fingers delved farther under the soft fabric and found a hard tip that brought a pleasured gasp from her lips when he touched it. "Lie still, honey," he whispered, his voice as unsteady as her own as he peeled away the cotton. "And for God's sake, don't cry out when I put my mouth on you…."

She had to bite her lower lip almost until it bled to manage that, because his lips were hungry and demanding. When he took her inside the warm darkness of his mouth, she felt tears well up from her closed eyes because it was like a tiny fulfillment in itself. She writhed helplessly, her nails biting him, her mouth as hungry as his, while the stars boiled down around them in white-hot flame.

He drew back first, and suddenly fastened her blouse with trembling hands before he rolled away from her and got to his feet.

She lay there, on fire for him, her eyes watching him as he moved near the campfire. Her body trembled with a need she'd never felt before. She wanted him, she wanted him!

His back was arrow straight as he began to build up the fire. He stood there for a while, and by the time he came back to his bedroll, her heart was beating normally again and she could feel the tension easing out of her body. But when he climbed into his sleeping bag, the tension came back all over again.

"Tyler," she whispered achingly.

"It passes," he whispered back. "I'm sorry, little one.

I didn't mean to take you that far. It's impossible, in more ways than one."

She felt for his lean hand and curled her fingers into it trustingly. "I know. But it was sweet, all the same. I love it when you touch me like that. I'm not even embarrassed to tell you so."

His fingers contracted. "Then I don't mind telling you that I almost couldn't pull back." His head turned and his eyes searched hers in the blazing orange reflection of the fire beyond them. "One day I won't be able to stop. What then?"

Her lips parted. "I don't know."

"You'd better start thinking about it," he said bluntly. "Because things are getting totally out of hand. Either we part company or risk the consequences."

She lowered her worried eyes to the steady rise and fall of his chest. "I...don't want to lose you," she said, burying her pride.

He brought her hand to his mouth. "That would be harder than you realize. Do you still want me, or is it easing off?"

She flushed. "It's easing off," she whispered back.

"At least now you understand why I get short-tempered from time to time, don't you?" he mused.

"Yes." She nuzzled her face against his arm. "What are we going to do?"

"What are *you* going to do?" he said, rephrasing the question. "The ball's in your court, honey. Make your move."

"But what do you want?"

"You."

"Just my body?" she asked softly.

"All of you."

She took a slow breath. "For how long?" she asked bravely.

"I told you, Nell. Love doesn't come with a money-back guarantee—if you do love me. What you feel might be infatuation, or just your first sensual experience making you vulnerable to me."

She searched his face, trying to see if he really believed that. "Is that what you think?"

"Not really. Why don't you tell me what you feel?"

She hesitated, and despite what she did feel, she couldn't lower her pride enough to tell him. She moved her fingers closer into his, feeling his own part and accept them in a warm, strong clasp.

"That reserve is the biggest part of our problem," he murmured. "You won't give in because you don't think I want you."

"I know you want me," she corrected.

"But not how badly, or in what way," he returned. "You're still locked up in the past, afraid of being hurt again."

"I know you wouldn't hurt me," she said unexpectedly, and her eyes were eloquent. "I never knew that a man could be so gentle."

He brought her fingers to his mouth. "That seems to come naturally with you," he said softly. "I've never felt as tender with a woman until now."

She moved her head on his arm. "Tyler, is it just physical with you?"

"If it was," he replied with a dry smile, "would I give a damn about your old-fashioned ideas on chastity? Would I even try to pull back?"

She felt her cheeks burn, and then she laughed self-consciously. "No. Of course not."

"Take it from there and think about it. Now we'd better get some sleep. We've already talked and…other things…for more than an hour."

"It didn't seem that long," she said shyly.

"For me, either, Nell." He let their clasped hands relax between them and closed his eyes. "After tonight," he murmured drowsily, "you'll never be able to deny that we've slept together."

"No, I won't." She curled a little closer and closed her own eyes. Her last thought before she fell asleep was that she'd never felt more secure or happy in all of her life.

SHE WOKE AT dawn to the delicious smell of percolating coffee and bacon and eggs being fried. Tyler was already hard at work on breakfast, with a little good-intentioned help from a couple of the guests. Everyone ate quietly, enjoying the silence of the desert at dawn and the incredible colors of the sky on the horizon.

"I've never seen anything so beautiful," Mrs. Callaway said with a sigh, nestling close to her husband.

"A living art gallery," Tyler agreed, smiling at Nell. "With a new canvas every minute of the day. It certainly is beautiful." *Like you,* his eyes were telling Nell, wooing her.

She sighed, her heart in her eyes, in her smile, in her rapt attention. His gaze locked with hers while he smoked his cigarette, and the exchange lasted long enough to make her blood run wildly through her veins and her knees get weak.

They rode back to the ranch a few minutes later, and Nell helped Tyler get the horses unsaddled, unbridled and put back in their stalls.

"I've never enjoyed anything more," Nell told him honestly, and laughed uninhibitedly. "It was wonderful."

"I thought so myself," he murmured. He leaned against a closed stall, and his green eyes glittered over her. "Come here," he challenged from deep in his throat.

Her heart raced. She didn't hesitate. She went straight to him and deliberately let her hips melt into his, her legs rest against the powerful strength of his own.

She raised her face for his kiss, blatantly inviting, without fear or inhibitions or reservations.

"Now I want an answer," he said solemnly. "I want to know what you feel for me. I want to know where I stand. You're going to have to trust me enough to tell me."

"That isn't quite fair," she argued. "I have to lower my pride, and you won't lower yours."

"I'm not the one with all the hang-ups," he reminded her. "Any good relationship has to be built on absolute trust to be successful."

"Yes, I know. But…" She avoided his gaze.

He tilted her face up to his. "Take a chance, Nell."

She took a deep breath, gathered her courage and started to speak. And just as she opened her mouth, a familiar voice called, "Tyler, darling, there you are! The boys and I arrived yesterday evening, and we're going to spend the week—isn't that nice?"

Nell moved away from Tyler as Margie came laughing into the stable and threw her arms around him. "Oh, you darling man, how have I managed to live all these years without you? Nell, isn't he wonderful? I'm so happy! Tyler, have you told her our news?" she prompted, her face radiant.

"No, he hasn't," Nell said, turning away. "But he doesn't need to, now. I can guess. See you later. I need a bath and a change of clothing."

"Nell," Tyler called after her, but she wasn't listening. She kept going into the house, with her dreams around her ears. Only a blind fool wouldn't know what Margie had hinted at. She and Tyler had something going, it was just plain obvious. And how could he have touched Nell so hungrily only last night, knowing that Margie was going to be here, waiting for him? Nell could have thrown things. Once again she'd been taken in by her own stupid, trusting nature. Well, this was the last straw. She was going to call Uncle Ted and tell him he could keep the ranch forever—she was going to leave and find something else to do. And as far away from Arizona and Tyler Jacobs as she could get!

CHAPTER TEN

"WHAT DO YOU look so unhappy for?" Bella asked Nell. "Didn't you enjoy the campout?"

"It was all right," Nell said with deliberate carelessness. She didn't want to remember what she and Tyler had done together. Margie had spoiled everything. Whatever Tyler had been going to say would never be said, and it looked as though Margie had pulled out all the stops and was going after him headlong.

"Hand me that mixer." Bella nodded toward the appliance she was going to use on a cake mix. "That Mrs. Norman was back in here again complaining about the menu. She's another Mrs. Harris, but at least Mr. Harris is here. Mrs. Norman doesn't like the way I cook. And besides all that, she thinks the entertainment stinks and there's nothing to do but ride horses."

Nell's eyes bulged. "Did you tell her that this is a dude ranch? People come here to ride horses."

"I told her that and plenty more." Bella looked at the younger woman sheepishly. "She's packing to leave. She says she's going to tell the whole world what a miserable operation we've got here. Oh, and we don't even have a tennis pro," she added.

"Tyler fired him, along with the golf pro," Nell reminded her. "He said they weren't paying their way."

"You mad at me?" Bella asked.

Nell put her arms around the older woman. "I love you. If people say cruel things about your cooking, they deserve to be sent packing. I think you're terrific."

Bella smiled and hugged her back. "That goes double for me. But I'll apologize all the same, if you want me to."

"No. Mrs. Norman may leave, with my blessing. In fact," she said, moving toward the door, "I'll even refund her money."

"Tyler won't like that," Bella called after her.

"Tyler can eat worms and die," Nell muttered.

"So that's it," Bella said to herself, and giggled once Nell was out of earshot.

Mrs. Norman had finished packing. She had her full-length mink coat wrapped around her thin body and her black eyes were flashing. "I am leaving," she told Nell, who was waiting outside the apartment when the older woman came out with her nose haughtily in the air. "You may have someone bring my luggage and call me a cab."

"With pleasure," Nell said, and even smiled. "If you'll stop by the office, I'll gladly refund your money."

Mrs. Norman eyed her suspiciously. "Why?"

"You don't like it here," Nell said. "There's no reason you should pay to be made miserable. The cooking is terrible, there's nothing to do…"

Mrs. Norman actually squirmed and pulled the mink coat closer, despite the fact that it was ninety degrees outside and she was already sweating. "That won't be necessary," she said. "Money is the least of my problems." She averted her eyes, then suddenly blurted out,

"I'm allergic to horses and the dust is choking me. All my husband's friends go to dude ranches, and he sent me here because he didn't want to take me to Europe with him." She lifted her chin proudly, even though it trembled. "It's just that…that this room…is so empty," she finished, choking the words out. "I'm so alone."

She broke down into tears and Nell did what came naturally. She took the weeping woman in her arms and just stood holding her and rocking her and murmuring soft words of reassurance.

"There's nothing wrong with the food," Mrs. Norman said with a hiccup. Mascara ran like black tears from her huge, hurting eyes. "It's delicious. And the people are nice, too, but they're all couples. My husband only married me as a business proposition—he doesn't even like me. He never tried to make our marriage anything else."

"You might consider that men don't read minds," Nell told her gently, and even as she said it she smiled inwardly at the irony of telling this sophisticated woman anything about men, when her own love life was so confusing and unfamiliar. "Your husband might think you didn't want to go with him."

Mrs. Norman pulled away self-consciously and dried her eyes with a pure white linen handkerchief. Then she smiled a little shakily. "I'm sorry, I never go to pieces like this." She blew her nose. "Actually, he asked me if I wanted to go, and I laughed at him. He's not a handsome man, but I…I do love him." She glanced at Nell. "Can I make a long-distance call to Europe and have it charged to my account?"

"Of course you can!" Nell smiled. "He might even decide to come back home."

Mrs. Norman smiled back, suddenly looking ten years younger. "I'll do it right now." She took off the mink coat. "That's my security blanket," she added ruefully, draping it over one arm. "I hate the damned thing, it makes me sneeze, and it's too hot to wear it anywhere except during blizzards in Alaska. I'll just make that phone call." She went inside the apartment, and before she closed the door she turned to look at Nell. "Thank you," she said sincerely.

Nell couldn't get over what had just happened. She felt on top of the world; she'd just learned a valuable lesson about human nature, and she might have helped save a marriage.

It wasn't a good time for Tyler to come around the corner of the apartment block, glaring into space.

He stopped, looking at her. "Are you lost?" he asked.

"Not lately." She put her hands in her back pockets and studied him quietly. "You look peaked."

"Do I? Why did you go rushing out of the stable?" he demanded.

She lifted her eyebrows. "Three is still a crowd, isn't it?"

"You thought I might have been waiting breathlessly for you to leave so that I could seduce Margie in one of the stalls?" he said with a cold tone to his deep voice.

Put that way, it sounded ridiculous. "Well, I guess not. But she was waiting for you."

"She had some good news. You won't get to hear it, of course," he continued. He lit a cigarette and threw her a mocking smile. "Margie and I don't think you de-

serve to hear it. You jump to conclusions on the shab-
biest evidence, and you won't listen to explanations.
You're still running away from involvement."

"I've had some hard knocks in the past," she defended herself.

"I know all about that," he said. "I wormed the rest of
it out of Margie, and I'm sorry about what happened to
you. But I thought you and I were on the way to something more important than a few stolen kisses—yet I
still can't get close to you."

She flushed, remembering the trail ride. "I wouldn't
exactly say that," she faltered.

"I'm not talking about physical closeness," he said
curtly. "I can't get close to you emotionally. You back
away from me."

"I have good reason to!" she shot back.

"Not with me, you don't," he said, his voice deep and
quiet as he watched her. "I'm not asking you to move in
with me, or even to spend the night with me in a non-
platonic way. I want you to trust me, Nell."

"But I do trust you," she began.

"Not in the way that counts." He drew in a slow
breath. "Well, I've had all I can take. I won't run after
you, honey. If you want anything more to happen between us, you'll have to make the first move. I'm not
going to touch you again. You're going to have to decide."

He moved away without another word, leaving Nell
to stand there and watch him leave with her heart down
around her ankles.

Mrs. Norman left in a delighted flurry that afternoon. Her husband had been thrilled to hear from her,

and he'd decided to come home and meet her in Ver-
mont for a second honeymoon. Nell had driven the older
woman to the airport and had been fervently hugged
before Mrs. Norman ran like a teenage girl to catch
her plane.

At least someone was happy, Nell thought miserably.
But it sure wasn't her. She still didn't understand why
Tyler was trying to make her chase him. It didn't really
make sense. He was the man, and the man was supposed
to make all the moves, not the woman; at least, not in
Nell's old-fashioned world.

Of course, Tyler was old-fashioned, too. That was
the hard thing to reconcile. And with his attitude, it
didn't really make sense that he'd be hanging around
Nell when he wanted Margie. And he had to want Margie. Every man did. Margie was beautiful and cultured
and sophisticated, just the right kind of woman for a
man like Tyler.

During the next few days, Margie kept very much
to herself. She smiled at Nell as if nothing were wrong,
but she spent a lot of time where the men—especially
Tyler—were, and she kept the boys with her. She
seemed to understand that her presence irritated Nell,
and she did everything she could to make it bearable
for the younger woman, right down to sleeping late and
going to bed early.

Nell was actually looking for an excuse for a confrontation, because there was a lot she wanted to say to her
sister-in-law. But Margie made that impossible, and
even Tyler interfered if it looked as though Nell might
find an opportunity. So the days went by with Nell getting more frustrated by the minute. What she didn't

know was that Darren McAnders had been furious that Margie was spending time with Tyler, and had begun to make his presence felt and heard while Tyler and Nell were away on the campout. He and Margie had it out that very evening while the campout was in full swing. The argument shortly began to have results. When no one was looking, McAnders picked Margie up and carried her off to a quiet spot under the big palo verde tree near the apartments. And there he kissed her until she couldn't stand up or protest. Then he began to tell her how he felt and what he wanted. When he finished, she was smiling. And the next kiss was instigated by her. But they kept their secret, because Margie didn't want to spring anything on Nell until Tyler had a chance to patch things up with his lady. Margie was getting impatient, though. Tyler and Nell seemed to have reached an impasse.

Nell went on teaching the daily riding lessons and avoided going to the dinner table until she was sure it was too late for Tyler to be there, if he'd decided to eat at the big house, that was. He spent more and more time in the bunkhouse or his own cabin.

Nights got longer and Nell's temper got shorter. Until Tyler had come along, she'd never known that she even had a temper, but he seemed to bring out the beast in her.

It was like being half a person. She strained for glimpses of him; she spun beautiful daydreams about him. Her eyes followed him everywhere. But she kept to herself, and spoke to him only when he asked her something directly. Which was all she could do, because he was still spending time with Margie. Actually he was chaperoning her with McAnders so that Bella wouldn't figure out their secret and spill the beans too soon, but Nell didn't know that and she didn't trust him.

Tyler was brooding, too. He almost gave up. Nell seemed more unapproachable now than she ever had, and she was retreating by the day. He wondered if he was ever going to be able to reach her again.

Texas seemed so far away. He remembered how he'd taken Abby Clark out on a date and how sweet it had been to dance with her. But it was nothing compared to the feel of Nell's body in his arms, her soft, shy mouth under the crush of his, welcoming him. She had a big heart and he wanted it, but Nell didn't seem to want him back.

She thought he was stuck on Margie, and that was a real laugh. Margie reminded him too much of the world he'd had to give up, of all he'd lost. He was going to need a woman who wasn't interested in frills and fancies, a woman who'd be willing to work at his side and help him start over. Nell was just right, in every way, and he cared about her deeply. The problem was getting her to believe he loved her when she had such poor self-image. She couldn't or wouldn't believe that she was infinitely desirable to him. And until he could break her out of that self-ordained mold, he was never going to reach her.

His green eyes glittered as he saw her riding back in from the trail ride with Darren McAnders at her side. Damn McAnders. Why couldn't he stop interfering?

He watched them dismount. McAnders took Nell's mount by the bridle and led both horses into the stable, with a grin and a cheerful greeting to Tyler.

Tyler didn't acknowledge it. He stood glaring at Nell for a long moment, and then he strode toward her.

She watched the way he walked, so tall and easy, which was deceptive. He was all muscle, and she knew the power in that exquisitely male body, the sweetness of being held by him while he brought her every nerve alive. He had on a beige shirt that emphasized his dark coloring, made his green eyes even greener. He came close and she felt the tension grow between them almost instantly.

"Having fun?" he asked.

She didn't like his tone. It was insulting. "No, I'm not," she replied tersely. "I hate running a dude ranch. I'm scared to death that a rattlesnake is going to bite somebody or a horse is going to run away with a green-horn rider or that we're going to lose somebody out on that desert and find them several days later. I hate budgeting, I don't like the need to cut out half of our recreational facilities, and if I have to hear one more remark about how desolate and disgusting my desert is, I'm going to scream!"

"I just asked if you were having fun," he pointed out. "I didn't ask for a rundown on world economy."

"Don't mind me," she said mockingly. "Pat yourself on the back."

He did, and her face flamed with bad temper.

"Why don't you go back to Texas?" she muttered.

"Oh, I like it here," he told her. "Dust and rattle-snakes grow on a man."

Her eyes narrowed. "Don't you start," she dared.

His eyebrows lifted. "What a nasty temper you're in,

little Nell. Why don't you go and eat something bland and see if it'll take the pepper off your tongue?"

"I'm going to tell my uncle how you're ruining the place," she threatened.

"He won't listen," he said with a lazy grin. "He's too busy depositing the money we've been making lately."

She took a sharp breath. "That's it, go ahead, put all the blame on me!"

"Mind you don't split a blood vessel with all that temper, honey," he said.

"Don't call me honey!"

"How about vinegar?"

She aimed a kick at his shin, but he was faster. He caught her up in his arms and carried her toward the corral, where the horses' watering trough was sitting innocently.

Through her kicking and cursing, she noticed where he was headed and clung to his neck.

"You wouldn't dare," she snapped.

He chuckled. "Of course I would."

Her arms tightened. "I'll take you with me."

"Promises, promises," he breathed huskily, and his mouth lowered so that it almost touched hers. "Will you, indeed?"

The threat of his lips made her heart race. She felt her breasts pressed against his chest; she smelled the leather and tobacco scent of his body mingling with the cologne he wore. She felt the strength of the arms under her and a kind of feminine delight in his maleness grew within her.

"Will I what?" she breathed. Her nails scraped gently

against his nape as unfamiliar sensations trembled through her.

"Don't tease," he whispered. "If I start kissing you now, we're going to have the biggest audience this side of Denver."

Her lips parted. "I'm not teasing," she said softly.

His face hardened. "No? Then tell me how I feel about Margie."

She felt the spell shatter. "I don't know," she muttered. "Anyway, it's none of my business."

"The hell it isn't. You blind little bat!"

And with a suddenness that put her between shock and fear, his mouth went down on hers savagely for one long instant before he took advantage of her helpless reaction and threw her, bottom first, right into the horses' trough.

CHAPTER ELEVEN

TYLER HAD STRODE off in a black temper by the time Nell dragged herself, dripping and swearing, out of the horses' trough. A couple of the men were watching, and she gave them her best glare as she sloshed off toward the house. It didn't help her dignity that they were laughing behind her.

She stormed into the house and upstairs to shower and change her clothes before anybody got a good look at her and guffawed some more. Then she returned downstairs, cooler but still fuming, and dialed her Uncle Ted's number with fingers that trembled in her haste. And all the while she wanted to fling Tyler and Margie down a mine shaft.

"Hello?" A deep, masculine voice came over the other end.

"Hello, yourself. I don't want to run this ranch anymore," she said without preamble. "I don't care if it means I lose everything, I won't stay at the same place with that foreman of yours!"

Uncle Ted was getting a new lease on life. His man-hating niece was suddenly losing her temper, something she never did, and over a real live man! He could have jumped for joy. He knew it had been a good idea to send Tyler Jacobs out to the Double R.

"Now, now," Uncle Ted soothed, "I can't let you throw away your inheritance, Nell. No, you'll just have to stay there and work things out, I'm afraid."

"I can't!" she wailed. "Look, I'll sign everything over to you—"

"No." He hung up.

She stared at the dead receiver as if it had sprouted flowers. Talk about finality! He hadn't even said goodbye.

She slammed the receiver down with a bang and glared at it. "I hate you!" she raged. "I think you're an overbearing male chauvinist, and just because you're rich doesn't give you the right to try and run people's lives for them!"

She was screaming by now, and Curt and Jess, standing unnoticed in the doorway, were watching her with saucer-size eyes. They motioned to their mother, who joined the rapt audience.

"I don't want him here," she fumed at the telephone. "I never did! I don't understand why you wouldn't give me a chance to straighten things out by myself before you stuck your big nose into my business. It's my ranch, my father left it to me and Teddy, and he never meant for you to dangle it over my head like a guillotine!"

"What's a guillotine?" Jess whispered to his mother.

"It's stuff you put on your joints when you have rheumatism," Curt whispered.

"Hush!" said their mother.

"Well, you can just tell him to go back to Texas, or I'll go there and live myself and he can have the ranch! I hate him, and I hate you, and I hate Margie, too!"

"It must be the insecticides in the groundwater table affecting your brain," Margie said, shaking her head.

Nell whirled, aghast to find three pairs of eyes staring at her. She stared back, speechless.

"Aunty Nell, why are you talking to the telephone?" Curt wanted to know.

"I was talking to your Great-Uncle Ted," she said with mangled dignity.

"Wouldn't you communicate better by talking into the receiver?" Margie mused.

Nell glared at her. "I haven't congratulated you yet. I'll make sure I send you a suitable gift when the time comes."

"How sweet of you, Nell." Margie sighed. "He's soo handsome, and I can't believe he really loves me."

"We love him, too," the boys chorused, grinning. "And we can come and live here now—"

Nell screamed. She actually screamed. She did it and then stood stock-still, astonished that the sound had really come from her throat.

"I love you, too." Margie added fuel to the fire, making a kissing motion with her lips. "We'll be one big happy family."

"Like hell we will!" Nell burst out, and tears fell from her eyes. "I'm leaving, right now!"

"Leaving for where?" Margie asked.

"I don't know and I don't…care." She hiccuped from stuffy tears. "Oh, Margie, how could you!"

"Boys, go and find a new lizard to scare me with," Margie told her sons. She shooed them out and closed the door.

"I want to leave," Nell wailed.

"After you listen to me," Margie said. "Now dry up for a minute. How do you feel about Tyler?"

Nell tried to avoid the question, but Margie wouldn't budge. She drew in a shaky breath. "I...love him," she bit off.

Margie smiled. "Do you? A lot?"

"Yes."

"But you think that he's the kind of man who plays with one woman at the same time he's courting somebody else?"

Nell blinked. She turned her head slightly, and her great, dark eyes fixed on Margie's face. "Well, no, actually, he isn't," she admitted. "He's kind of old-fashioned about things."

Margie nodded. "That's right. You're doing very well, darling. Keep going."

"If he'd been going to marry you, he'd have told me himself," Nell ventured. "He wouldn't have let me find out by accident from someone else."

"Yes. And?"

Nell drew in a slow, exquisite breath. "He'd never play around with an innocent woman unless he was serious about her. Unless he was playing for keeps."

Margie smiled gently. "And you were going to cuss out Uncle Ted and run away."

Nell dried her tears. "I've been such a fool. I was scared, you know, Margie."

"We're all scared. Commitment isn't easy, even when people love each other." She went close to Nell, smiling. "I'm going to marry Darren. Will you be my maid of honor?"

Nell burst out laughing. "Oh, Margie, of course I

will!" She hugged the older woman fervently, laughing and crying all at once. "I'm so sorry for the things I said. I was so jealous, and my heart was broken! But now I think I'm going to be all right, after all."

"I know you are. Wouldn't you like to take a nice, refreshing walk?" she added. "You might walk down by the holding pens. The scenery there is really something."

"Nice, is it?" Nell probed.

"Dark and handsome, to coin a phrase." Margie grinned. "But it may not last long, so you'd better hurry."

"I'll do that. But first, can you lend me a dress? Something very feminine and lighter than air and suitable for a woman to chase a man in?"

Margie was delighted. "You bet I can. Come on!"

It was a dream of a dress in creamy spring green with a full, flowing skirt and a pretty rounded neckline and puffy sleeves. Nell felt like a young girl again, all heart and nerves as she brushed her long, clean hair and put on makeup and a little perfume.

Nell smiled, thinking how sweet it was going to be to make her first move toward Tyler, to flirt openly with him, sure of herself at last.

She slipped on a pair of soft shoes and tore down the staircase and out the door toward the holding pens. It seemed to take forever to get there, and she was breathless from her haste when she finally reached them.

The pens were empty now, with roundup over, but Tyler was leaning back lazily against the fence with a cigarette in his fingers, his long legs crossed and one arm propped on the second fence rail. His hat was pulled low over his eyes so that Nell couldn't quite see them through the shadows, but he looked approachable enough.

"Hello," she said nervously.

He nodded. His green eyes glittered over her possessively before he turned back to the horizon and took a draw from his cigarette. "Lose your way?"

"Not this time." She went closer and stood beside him to look over the pasture. "Do you make a habit of throwing women into water troughs? Because if you do, we're going to have a rocky life together."

He couldn't believe he'd heard that. He turned, his eyes hungry on her face, his pulse racing. She'd dressed up and fixed her face and hair, and she looked radiant. "No, I don't make a habit of it," he replied. "But at the time I'd had about all I could stand. Nell, I'm thinking of going back to Texas."

"Running out on me?" she asked with pure bravado. "I'll come after you."

He touched his forehead unobtrusively to see if he was dying of fever or having hallucinations. "I beg your pardon?"

She gathered up her shaken nerve. "I said, I'll follow you back to Texas."

He finished the cigarette and ground it out under his boot, taking so long to speak that Nell felt her knees getting ready to buckle in case she'd gotten it wrong and he didn't care.

"No doubts?" he asked suddenly, and his eyes met hers with a fiercely sensual impact.

It was hard to get enough breath to answer him, because he was even closer now, and she had to fight not to put her body right against his and hold on for dear

life. "No doubts, Ty," she whispered. She looked up at
him and went for broke. "I love you."

His eyes closed for an instant and then opened on a
heavy exhaled breath. "My God." He drew her into his
arms and held her there, rocking her hungrily from side
to side, with his lips on her cheek, her ear, her neck,
and finally, crushing into the warmth of her soft mouth.

She held on to him with all her strength, loving the
furious beating of her heart, the weakness he engen-
dered in her body, the warm wonder of knowing that
he cared about her, too. She sighed under his devour-
ing mouth and it lifted, fractionally, while he searched
her eyes with all the barriers gone.

"Did Margie tell you that it isn't me she's going to
marry?" he asked quietly.

"Not really," she hedged, because it was a dangerous time to go into all the details.

He frowned. "She didn't talk to you?"

"It was more a case of her making *me* talk. And I
worked it out by myself." She smiled tenderly at him.
"If you were going to marry Margie," she began quietly,
"you'd never have touched me, not even out of pity."

He didn't move for a minute. Then he began to stroke
her bare arms very gently with his warm, work-rough-
ened hands. "It took you a long time to realize that,"
he said deeply, and his heart sang because of the look
in her eyes.

"Yes," she said with a faint grin. "Of course, I didn't
work it out at first. After I got out of the horses' trough
and dried off," she said with a glare that didn't faze
him, "I called Uncle Ted and yelled at him and told him
what he could do with the ranch and that I was leaving

forever. He just hung up on me. I guess I'll have to call him back and apologize."

"I wouldn't just yet," Tyler advised. "He's probably laughing too hard. I get the idea that before I came along, you never yelled at anybody."

She nodded. "There was never any reason to." She sighed, looking hungrily at his dark face. "Oh, I want you," she whispered, letting down her pride. "I want to live with you and have children with you and grow old with you."

"And what do I want, do you think?" he asked, leading her on.

It didn't work. She just smiled. "You want me, of course."

He burst out laughing, the sound full with joy and delight. He lifted her up against his chest to kiss her with exquisite tenderness. "I'm sorry about the horses' trough. I'd waited and hoped, and we were almost there, and then Margie came along after the campout and set us back several weeks. She didn't mean to. Her news, of course, was that she and McAnders were engaged. But when you took off, she decided to keep the secret awhile longer."

"I'm sorry about that," she murmured. "I didn't think I could compete with her. I never dreamed that you could feel for me what I felt for you. It was like wishing for the moon."

"Not anymore, is it?" he mused, and brushed his mouth sensually across hers.

"Not anymore," she agreed huskily.

"When were you sure that I didn't want Margie?"

"When I remembered that you'd made the sweetest kind of love to me, without asking me to go all the way with you," she whispered, and for the first time, she kissed him, with shy hunger. "And a man like you wouldn't do that unless he had something permanent in mind. Because I'm still a virgin," she breathed into his mouth. "And you're an old-fashioned man. You even said so."

"It took you long enough to remember it," he murmured dryly. He nuzzled her cheek with his, floating, warm from the touch of her body against his, the clasp of her soft arms. "I love you, Nell," he whispered huskily. "And I do want you for keeps. You and a houseful of children and the best future we can make together."

"I love you, too," she whispered fervently.

"You grew on me," he mused, lifting his head to search her soft eyes. "But long before that time I was sick and you nursed me, I knew I'd lost my heart. I wasn't able to think about another woman after that."

"I'm very glad. I loved you from the beginning, although I was afraid to. You see, I thought you were just being nice to me because you felt sorry for me."

"I liked you," he said simply. "And when you started avoiding me, it was like a knife in my heart."

"I didn't think you could care about someone like me," she said quietly. "Then after you began to talk about my low self-image and my lack of confidence, I started thinking about things. I guess none of us is perfect, but that doesn't mean we can't be loved. It doesn't have much to do with beauty and sophistication and money, does it? Love is more than that."

"Much more." He framed her face and bent slowly

to her mouth. "I'll cherish you all my life. I don't have a lot to give you, but you can have my heart."

She smiled against his mouth. "I'd rather have that than anything else in the whole world. I'll give you mine for it."

He smiled back. "That," he whispered before he kissed her, "is a deal."

A long time later, they walked back to the house hand in hand, and Margie and the boys and Bella stood on the porch, anxious to find out what had happened.

"Well?" Bella demanded, out of patience. "Is it going to be a wedding or a farewell party?"

"A wedding." Nell laughed and ran forward to hug Bella and Margie and the boys. "And we're going to be so happy together."

"As if anybody could believe otherwise," Bella said, sniffing. "Well, I'll go cook supper. Something special." Her eyes narrowed in thought. "And a cake…"

"You snake in the grass, leading me on like that!" Nell accused Margie. "Making me so jealous that I couldn't stand it!"

"I knew it would either open your eyes or close them for good." Margie smiled. "You could have gone on forever the way you were, untrusting and alone. I thought you needed a chance."

"Well, thank you," Nell said. She glanced at Tyler's radiant expression and then back at Margie as the other woman started to speak.

"I love Darren so much, Nell. Are you going to mind having us both on the place? Because he insists that he's going to support me."

"I don't have any problem at all with that," Nell said at once.

"I called Uncle Ted back after you went out to meet Tyler," Margie said with a secretive smile. "He said if you and Tyler got married, he'd turn over control of the ranch early—as a wedding present."

Tyler didn't say anything, and Nell went close to him. "Look," she said, "it isn't much of a ranch right now. It's lost a lot of money and times are still pretty bad. You are getting nothing but a headache, so don't look on it as a handout."

That took the bitter look off his face. "Then I guess you and I are going to have the challenge of building it up again," he said finally, and his hard features relaxed. He had to start back somewhere, and he loved Nell. The two of them together, working to build a future and a family. Yes, that sounded good. He smiled down at her. "Okay, honey. We'll give it a try."

"And Darren and I can live in the cabin with the boys," Margie suggested. "Or we can build a house close by. I think I'd rather do that. I still have a nest egg, and so does Darren—he's been saving for years. We'll do that. Your foreman will have to have some-place to live."

Tyler glanced amusedly at Nell. "I thought we might offer it to Chappy. He's been here a long time, and he bosses everybody around anyway. What do you think?"

Nell laughed. "I think it's a great idea!"

"So do I," Margie agreed. "Well, shall we go inside and call Uncle Ted one more time?"

Nell slid her hand into Tyler's, and they followed the others back inside. Tyler looked down at her just before they went through the open door. The look on his face made Nell catch her breath. The awe and wonder of love blazed from it as surely as the Arizona sun warmed the desert. Nell's own face reflected a love for her long, tall Texan that would last forever.

* * * * *

SUTTON'S WAY

To Barry Call
of Charbons in Gainesville, GA
Many thanks

CHAPTER ONE

THE NOISE OUTSIDE the cabin was there again, and Amanda shifted restlessly with the novel in her lap, curled up in a big armchair by the open fireplace in an Indian rug. Until now, the cabin had been paradise. There was three feet of new snow outside, she had all the supplies she needed to get her through the next few wintery weeks of Wyoming weather, and there wasn't a telephone in the place. Best of all, there wasn't a neighbor.

Well, there was, actually. But nobody in their right mind would refer to that man on the mountain as a neighbor. Amanda had only seen him once and once was enough.

She'd met him, if their head-on encounter could be referred to as a meeting, on a snowy Saturday last week. Quinn Sutton's majestic ranch house overlooked this cabin nestled against the mountainside. He'd been out in the snow on a horse-drawn sled that contained huge square bales of hay, and he was heaving them like feather pillows to a small herd of red-and-white cattle. The sight had touched Amanda, because it indicated concern. The tall, wiry rancher out in a blizzard feeding his starving cattle. She'd even smiled at the tender picture it made.

And then she'd stopped her four-wheel-drive vehicle and stuck her blond head out the window to ask directions to the Blalock Durning place, which was the cabin one of her aunt's friends was loaning her. And the tender picture dissolved into stark hostility.

The tall rancher turned toward her with the coldest black eyes and the hardest face she'd ever seen in her life. He had a day's growth of stubble, but the stubble didn't begin to cover up the frank homeliness of his lean face. He had amazingly high cheekbones, a broad forehead and a jutting chin, and he looked as if someone had taken a straight razor to one side of his face, which had a wide scratch. None of that bothered Amanda because Hank Shoeman and the other three men who made music with her group were even uglier than Quinn Sutton. But at least Hank and the boys could smile. This man looked as if he invented the black scowl.

"I said," she'd repeated with growing nervousness, "can you tell me how to get to Blalock Durning's cabin?"

Above the sheepskin coat, under the battered gray ranch hat, Quinn Sutton's tanned face didn't move a muscle. "Follow the road, turn left at the lodgepoles," he'd said tersely, his voice as deep as a rumble of thunder.

"Lodgepoles?" she'd faltered. "You mean Indian lodgepoles? What do they look like?"

"Lady," he said with exaggerated patience, "a lodgepole is a pine tree. It's tall and piney, and there are a stand of them at the next fork in the road."

"You don't need to be rude, Mr...?"

"Sutton," he said tersely. "Quinn Sutton."

"Nice to meet you," she murmured politely. "I'm Amanda." She wondered if anyone might accidentally recognize her here in the back of beyond, and on the off chance, she gave her mother's maiden name instead of her own last name. "Amanda Corrie," she added untruthfully. "I'm going to stay in the cabin for a few weeks."

"This isn't the tourist season," he'd said without the slightest pretense at friendliness. His black eyes cut her like swords.

"Good, because I'm not a tourist," she said.

"Don't look to me for help if you run out of wood or start hearing things in the dark," he added coldly. "Somebody will tell you eventually that I have no use whatsoever for women."

While she was thinking up a reply to that, a young boy of about twelve had come running up behind the sled.

"Dad!" he called, amazingly enough to Quinn Sutton. "There's a cow in calf down in the next pasture. I think it's a breech!"

"Okay, son, hop on," he told the boy, and his voice had become fleetingly soft, almost tender. He looked back at Amanda, though, and the softness left him. "Keep your door locked at night," he'd said. "Unless you're expecting Durning to join you," he added with a mocking smile.

She'd stared at him from eyes as black as his own and started to tell him that she didn't even know Mr. Durning, who was her aunt's friend, not hers. But she bit her tongue. It wouldn't do to give this man an opening. "I'll do that little thing," she agreed. She glanced at the boy, who was eyeing her curiously from his perch on the sled. "And it seems that you do have at least one use for women," she added with a vacant smile. "My condolences to your wife, Mr. Sutton."

She'd rolled up the window before he could speak and she'd whipped the four-wheel-drive down the road with

little regard for safety, sliding all over the place on the
slick and rutted country road.

She glared into the flames, consigning Quinn Sutton
to them with all her angry heart. She hoped and prayed
that there wouldn't ever be an accident or a reason she'd
have to seek out his company. She'd rather have asked
help from a passing timber wolf. His son hadn't seemed
at all like him, she recalled. Sutton was as dangerous
looking as a timber wolf, with a face like the side of
a bombed mountain and eyes that were coal-black and
cruel. In the sheepskin coat he'd been wearing with that
raunchy Stetson that day, he'd looked like one of the old
mountain men might have back in Wyoming's early days.
He'd given Amanda some bad moments and she'd hated
him after that uncomfortable confrontation. But the boy
had been kind. He was redheaded and blue-eyed, nothing like his father, not a bit of resemblance.

She knew the rancher's name only because her aunt
had mentioned him, and cautioned Amanda about going
near the Sutton ranch. The ranch was called Ricochet, and
Amanda had immediately thought of a bullet going awry.
Probably one of Sutton's ancestors had thrown some lead
now and again. Mr. Sutton looked a lot more like a bandit
than he did a rancher, with his face unshaven, that wide,
awful scrape on his cheek and his crooked nose. It was
an unforgettable face all around, especially those eyes....

She pulled the Indian rug closer and gave the book
in her slender hand a careless glance. She wasn't really
in the mood to read. Memories kept tearing her heart.
She leaned her blond head back against the chair and
her dark eyes studied the flames with idle appreciation
of their beauty.

The nightmare of the past few weeks had finally caught up with her. She'd stood onstage, with the lights beating down on her long blond hair and outlining the beige leather dress that was her trademark, and her voice had simply refused to cooperate. The shock of being unable to produce a single note had caused her to faint, to the shock and horror of the audience.

She came to in a hospital, where she'd been given what seemed to be every test known to medical science. But nothing would produce her singing voice, even though she could talk. It was, the doctor told her, purely a psychological problem, caused by the trauma of what had happened. She needed rest.

So Hank, who was the leader of the group, had called her Aunt Bess and convinced her to arrange for Amanda to get away from it all. Her aunt's rich boyfriend had this holiday cabin in Wyoming's Grand Teton Mountains and was more than willing to let Amanda recuperate there. Amanda had protested, but Hank and the boys and her aunt had insisted. So here she was, in the middle of winter, in several feet of snow, with no television, no telephone and facilities that barely worked. Roughing it, the big, bearded bandleader had told her, would do her good.

She smiled when she remembered how caring and kind the guys had been. Her group was called Desperado, and her leather costume was its trademark. The four men who made up the rest of it were fine musicians, but they looked like the Hell's Angels on stage in denim and leather with thick black beards and mustaches and untrimmed hair. They were really pussycats under that rough exterior, but nobody had ever been game enough to try to find out if they were.

Hank and Deke and Jack and Johnson had been trying to get work at a Virginia night spot when they'd run
into Amanda Corrie Callaway, who was also trying to
get work there. The club needed a singer and a band, so
it was a match made in heaven, although Amanda with
her sheltered upbringing had been a little afraid of her
new backup band. They, on the other hand, had been nervous around her because she was such a far cry from the
usual singers they'd worked with. The shy, introverted
young blonde made them self-conscious about their appearance. But their first performance together had been a
phenomenal hit, and they'd been together four years now.

They were famous, now. Desperado had been on the
music videos for two years, they'd done television shows
and magazine interviews, and they were recognized everywhere they went. Especially Amanda, who went by
the stage name of Mandy Callaway. It wasn't a bad life,
and it was making them rich. But there wasn't much rest
or time for a personal life. None of the group was married except Hank, and he was already getting a divorce. It
was hard for a homebound spouse to accept the frequent
absences that road tours required.

She still shivered from the look Quinn Sutton had
given her, and now she was worried about her Aunt Bess,
though the woman was more liberal minded and should
know the score. But Sutton had convinced Amanda that
she wasn't the first woman to be at Blalock's cabin. She
should have told that arrogant rancher what her real relationship with Blalock Durning was, but he probably
wouldn't have believed her.

Of course, she could have put him in touch with Jerry
and proved it. Jerry Allen, their road manager, was one

of the best in the business. He'd kept them from starving during the beginning, and they had an expert crew of electricians and carpenters who made up the rest of the retinue. It took a huge bus to carry the people and equipment, appropriately called the "Outlaw Express."

Amanda had pleaded with Jerry to give them a few weeks rest after the tragedy that had cost her her nerve, but he'd refused. Get back on the horse, he'd advised. And she'd tried. But the memories were just too horrible.

So finally he'd agreed to Hank's suggestion and she was officially on hiatus, as were the other members of the group, for a month. Maybe in that length of time she could come to grips with it, face it.

It had been a week and she felt better already. Or she would, if those strange noises outside the cabin would just stop! She had horrible visions of wolves breaking in and eating her.

"Hello?"

The small voice startled her. It sounded like a boy's. She got up, clutching the fire poker in her hand and went to the front door. "Who's there?" she called out tersely.

"It's just me. Elliot," he said. "Elliot Sutton."

She let out a breath between her teeth. Oh, no, she thought miserably, what was he doing here? His father would come looking for him, and she couldn't bear to have that...that savage anywhere around!

"What do you want?" she groaned.

"I brought you something."

It would be discourteous to refuse the gift, she guessed, especially since he'd apparently come through several feet of snow to bring it. Which brought to mind a really interesting question: where was his father?

She opened the door. He grinned at her from under a thick cap that covered his red hair.

"Hi," he said. "I thought you might like to have some roasted peanuts. I did them myself. They're nice on a cold night."

Her eyes went past him to a sled hitched to a sturdy draft horse. "Did you come in that?" she asked, recognizing the sled he and his father had been riding the day she'd met them.

"Sure," he said. "That's how we get around in winter, what with the snow and all. We take hay out to the livestock on it. You remember, you saw us. Well, we usually take hay out on it, that is. When Dad's not laid up," he added pointedly, and his blue eyes said more than his voice did.

She knew she was going to regret asking the question before she opened her mouth. She didn't want to ask. But no young boy came to a stranger's house in the middle of a snowy night just to deliver a bag of roasted peanuts.

"What's wrong?" she asked with resigned perception.

He blinked. "What?"

"I said, what's wrong?" She made her tone gentler. He couldn't help it that his father was a savage, and he was worried under that false grin. "Come on, you might as well tell me."

He bit his lower lip and looked down at his snow-covered boots. "It's my dad," he said. "He's bad sick and he won't let me get the doctor."

So there it was. She knew she shouldn't have asked. "Can't your mother do something?" she asked hopefully.

"My mom ran off with Mr. Jackson from the livestock association when I was just a little feller," he replied, registering Amanda's shocked expression. "She and Dad got divorced and she died some years ago, but Dad doesn't talk about her. Will you come, miss?"

"I'm not a doctor," she said, hesitating.

"Oh, sure, I know that," he agreed eagerly, "but you're a girl. And girls know how to take care of sick folks, don't they?" The confidence slid away and he looked like what he was—a terrified little boy with nobody to turn to. "Please, lady," he added. "I'm scared. He's hot and shaking all over and—!"

"I'll get my boots on," she said. She gathered them from beside the fireplace and tugged them on, and then she went for a coat and stuffed her long blond hair under a stocking cap. "Do you have cough syrup, aspirins, throat lozenges—that sort of thing?"

"Yes, ma'am," he said eagerly, then sighed. "Dad won't take them, but we have them."

"Is he suicidal?" Amanda asked angrily as she went out the door behind him and locked the cabin before she climbed on the sled with the boy.

"Well sometimes things get to him," he ventured. "But he doesn't ever get sick, and he won't admit that he is. But he's out of his head and I'm scared. He's all I got."

"We'll take care of him," she promised, and hoped she could deliver on the promise. "Let's go."

"Do you know Mr. Durning well?" he asked as he called to the draft horse and started him back down the road and up the mountain toward the Sutton house.

"He's sort of a friend of a relative of mine," she said evasively. The sled ride was fun, and she was enjoying the cold wind and snow in her face, the delicious moun-

tain air. "I'm only staying at the cabin for a few weeks.
Just time to…get over something."

"Have you been sick, too?" he asked curiously.

"In a way," she said noncommittally.

The sled went jerkily up the road, around the steep
hill. She held on tight and hoped the big draft horse had
steady feet. It was a harrowing ride at the last, and then
they were up, and the huge redwood ranch house came
into sight, blazing with light from its long, wide front
porch to the gabled roof.

"It's a beautiful house," Amanda said.

"My dad added on to it for my mom, before they married," he told her. He shrugged. "I don't remember much
about her, except she was redheaded. Dad sure hates
women." He glanced at her apologetically. "He's not going
to like me bringing you…."

"I can take care of myself," she returned, and smiled
reassuringly. "Let's go see how bad it is."

"I'll get Harry to put up the horse and sled," he said,
yelling toward the lighted barn until a grizzled old man
appeared. After a brief introduction to Amanda, Harry
left and took the horse away.

"Harry's been here since Dad was a boy," Elliot told
her as he led her down a bare-wood hall and up a steep
staircase to the second storey of the house. "He does most
everything, even cooks for the men." He paused outside
a closed door, and gave Amanda a worried look. "He'll
yell for sure."

"Let's get it over with, then."

She let Elliot open the door and look in first, to make
sure his father had something on.

"He's still in his jeans," he told her, smiling as she blushed. "It's okay."

She cleared her throat. So much for pretended sophistication, she thought, and here she was twenty-four years old. She avoided Elliot's grin and walked into the room.

Quinn Sutton was sprawled on his stomach, his bare muscular arms stretched toward the headboard. His back gleamed with sweat, and his thick, black hair was damp with moisture. Since it wasn't hot in the room, Amanda decided that he must have a high fever. He was moaning and talking unintelligibly.

"Elliot, can you get me a basin and some hot water?" she asked. She took off her coat and rolled up the sleeves of her cotton blouse.

"Sure thing," Elliot told her, and rushed out of the room.

"Mr. Sutton, can you hear me?" Amanda asked softly. She sat down beside him on the bed, and lightly touched his bare shoulder. He was hot, all right—burning up. "Mr. Sutton," she called again.

"No," he moaned. "No, you can't do it…!"

"Mr. Sutton…"

He rolled over and his black eyes opened, glazed with fever, but Amanda barely noticed. Her eyes were on the rest of him, male perfection from shoulder to narrow hips. He was darkly tanned, too, and thick, black hair wedged from his chest down his flat stomach to the wide belt at his hips. Amanda, who was remarkably innocent not only for her age, but for her profession as well, stared like a star-struck girl. He was beautiful, she thought, amazed at the elegant lines of his body, at the ripple of muscle and the smooth, glistening skin.

"What the hell do you want?" he rasped.

So much for hero worship, she thought dryly. She lifted her eyes back to his. "Elliot was worried," she said quietly. "He came and got me. Please don't fuss at him. You're raging with fever."

"Damn the fever, get out," he said in a tone that might have stopped a charging wolf.

"I can't do that," she said. She turned her head toward the door where Elliot appeared with a basin full of hot water and a towel and washcloth over one arm.

"Here you are, lady," he said. "Hi, Dad," he added with a wan smile at his furious father. "You can beat me when you're able again."

"Don't think I won't," Quinn growled.

"There, there, you're just feverish and sick, Mr. Sutton," Amanda soothed.

"Get Harry and have him throw her off my land," Quinn told Elliot in a furious voice.

"How about some aspirin, Elliot, and something for him to drink? A small whiskey and something hot—"

"I don't drink whiskey," Quinn said harshly.

"He has a glass of wine now and then," Elliot ventured.

"Wine, then." She soaked the cloth in the basin. "And you might turn up the heat. We don't want him to catch a chill when I sponge him down."

"You damned well aren't sponging me down!" Quinn raged.

She ignored him. "Go and get those things, please, Elliot, and the cough syrup, too."

"You bet, lady!" he said grinning.

"My name is Amanda," she said absently.

"Amanda," the boy repeated, and went back downstairs.

"God help you when I get back on my feet," Quinn said with fury. He laid back on the pillow, shivering when she touched him with the cloth. "Don't...!"

"I could fry an egg on you. I have to get the fever down. Elliot said you were delirious."

"Elliot's delirious to let you in here," he shuddered. Her fingers accidentally brushed his flat stomach and he arched, shivering. "For God's sake, don't," he groaned.

"Does your stomach hurt?" she asked, concerned. "I'm sorry." She soaked the cloth again and rubbed it against his shoulders, his arms, his face.

His black eyes opened. He was breathing roughly, and his face was taut. The fever, she imagined. She brushed back her long hair, and wished she'd tied it up. It kept flowing down onto his damp chest.

"Damn you," he growled.

"Damn you, too, Mr. Sutton." She smiled sweetly. She finished bathing his face and put the cloth and basin aside. "Do you have a long-sleeved shirt?"

"Get out!"

Elliot came back with the medicine and a small glass of wine. "Harry's making hot chocolate," he said with a smile. "He'll bring it up. Here's the other stuff."

"Good," she said. "Does your father have a pajama jacket or something long-sleeved?"

"Sure!"

"Traitor," Quinn groaned at his son.

"Here you go." Elliot handed her a flannel top, which she proceeded to put on the protesting and very angry Mr. Sutton.

"I hate you," Quinn snapped at her with his last ounce of venom.

"I hate you, too," she agreed. She had to reach around him to get the jacket on, and it brought her into much too close proximity to him. She could feel the hair on his chest rubbing against her soft cheek, she could feel her own hair smoothing over his bare shoulder and chest. Odd, that shivery feeling she got from contact with him. She ignored it forcibly and got his other arm into the pajama jacket. She fastened it, trying to keep her fingers from touching his chest any more than necessary because the feel of that pelt of hair disturbed her. He shivered violently at the touch of her hands and her long, silky hair, and she assumed it was because of his fever.

"Are you finished?" Quinn asked harshly.

"Almost." She pulled the covers over him, found the electric-blanket control and turned it on. Then she ladled cough syrup into him, gave him aspirin and had him take a sip of wine, hoping that she wasn't overdosing him in the process. But the caffeine in the hot chocolate would probably counteract the wine and keep it from doing any damage in combination with the medicine. A sip of wine wasn't likely to be that dangerous anyway, and it might help the sore throat she was sure he had.

"Here's the cocoa," Harry said, joining them with a tray of mugs filled with hot chocolate and topped with whipped cream.

"That looks delicious. Thank you so much," Amanda said, and smiled shyly at the old man.

He grinned back. "Nice to be appreciated." He glared at Quinn. "Nobody else ever says so much as a thank-you!"

"It's hard to thank a man for food poisoning," Quinn rejoined weakly.

"He ain't going to die," Harry said as he left. "He's too damned mean."

"That's a fact," Quinn said and closed his eyes.

He was asleep almost instantly. Amanda drew up a chair and sat down beside him. He'd still need looking after, and presumably the boy went to school. It was past the Christmas holidays.

"You go to school, don't you?" she asked Elliot.

He nodded. "I ride the horse out to catch the bus and then turn him loose. He comes to the barn by himself. You're staying?"

"I'd better, I guess," she said. "I'll sit with him. He may get worse in the night. He's got to see a doctor tomorrow. Is there one around here?"

"There's Dr. James in town, in Holman that is," he said. "He'll come out if Dad's bad enough. He has a cancer patient down the road and he comes to check on her every few days. He could stop by then."

"We'll see how your father is feeling. You'd better get to bed," she said and smiled at him.

"Thank you for coming, Miss…Amanda," Elliot said. He sighed. "I don't think I've ever been so scared."

"It's okay," she said. "I didn't mind. Good night, Elliot."

He smiled at her. "Good night."

He went out and closed the door. Amanda sat back in her chair and looked at the sleeping face of the wild man. He seemed vulnerable like this, with his black eyes closed. He had the thickest lashes she'd ever seen, and his eyebrows were thick and well shaped above his deep-

set eyes. His mouth was rather thin, but it was perfectly
shaped, and the full lower lip was sensuous. She liked
that jutting chin, with its hint of stubbornness. His nose
was formidable and straight, and he wasn't that bad looking…asleep. Perhaps it was the coldness of his eyes that
made him seem so much rougher when he was awake.
Not that he looked that unintimidating even now. He had
so many coarse edges….

She waited a few minutes and touched his forehead.
It was a little cooler, thank God, so maybe he was going
to be better by morning. She went into the bathroom and
washed her face and went back to sit by him. Somewhere
in the night, she fell asleep with her blond head pillowed
on the big arm of the chair. Voices woke her.

"Has she been there all night, Harry?" Quinn was
asking.

"Looks like. Poor little critter, she's worn out."

"I'll shoot Elliot!"

"Now, boss, that's no way to treat the kid. He got
scared, and I didn't know what to do. Women know things
about illness. Why, my mama could doctor people and
she never had no medical training. She used herbs and
things."

Amanda blinked, feeling eyes on her. She found Quinn
Sutton gazing steadily at her from a sitting position on
the bed.

"How do you feel?" she asked without lifting her
sleepy head.

"Like hell," he replied. "But I'm a bit better."

"Would you like some breakfast, ma'am?" Harry asked
with a smile. "And some coffee?"

"Coffee. Heavenly. But no breakfast, thanks, I won't

impose," she said drowsily, yawning and stretching uninhibitedly as she sat up, her full breasts beautifully out-
lined against the cotton blouse in the process.

Quinn felt his body tautening again, as it had the night
before so unexpectedly and painfully when her hands had
touched him. He could still feel them, and the brush of
her long, silky soft hair against his skin. She smelled of
gardenias and the whole outdoors, and he hated her more
than ever because he'd been briefly vulnerable.

"Why did you come with Elliot?" Quinn asked her
when Harry had gone.

She pushed back her disheveled hair and tried not to
think how bad she must look without makeup and with
her hair uncombed. She usually kept it in a tight braid
on top of her head when she wasn't performing. It made
her feel vulnerable to have its unusual length on display
for a man like Quinn Sutton.

"Your son is only twelve," she answered him belatedly.
"That's too much responsibility for a kid," she added.
"I know. I had my dad to look after at that age, and no
mother. My dad drank," she added with a bitter smile.
"Excessively. When he drank he got into trouble. I can
remember knowing how to call a bail bondsman at the
age of thirteen. I never dated, I never took friends home
with me. When I was eighteen, I ran away from home. I
don't even know if he's still alive, and I don't care."

"That's one problem Elliot won't ever have," he replied
quietly. "Tough girl, aren't you?" he added, and his black
eyes were frankly curious.

She hadn't meant to tell him so much. It embarrassed
her, so she gave him her most belligerent glare. "Tough
enough, thanks," she said. She got out of the chair. "If

you're well enough to argue, you ought to be able to take care of yourself. But if that fever goes up again, you'll need to see the doctor."

"I'll decide that," he said tersely. "Go home."

"Thanks, I'll do that little thing." She got her coat and put it on without taking time to button it. She pushed her hair up under the stocking cap, aware of his eyes on her the whole time.

"You don't fit the image of a typical hanger-on," he said unexpectedly.

She glanced at him, blinking with surprise. "I beg your pardon?"

"A hanger-on," he repeated. He lifted his chin and studied her with mocking thoroughness. "You're Durning's latest lover, I gather. Well, if it's money you're after, he's the perfect choice. A pretty little tramp could go far with him... Damn!"

She stood over him with the remains of his cup of hot chocolate all over his chest, shivering with rage.

"I'm sorry," she said curtly. "That was a despicable thing to do to a sick man, but what you said to me was inexcusable."

She turned and went to the door, ignoring his muffled curses as he threw off the cover and sat up.

"I'd cuss, too," she said agreeably as she glanced back at him one last time, her eyes running helplessly over the broad expanse of hair-roughened skin. "All that sticky hot chocolate in that thicket on your chest," she mused. "It will probably take steam cleaning to remove it. Too bad you can't attract a 'hanger-on' to help you bathe it out. But, then, you aren't as rich as Mr. Durning, are you?"

And she walked out, her nose in the air. As she went toward the stairs, she imagined that she heard laughter. But of course, that couldn't have been possible.

CHAPTER TWO

AMANDA REGRETTED THE hot-chocolate incident once she was back in the cabin, even though Quinn Sutton had deserved every drop of it. How dare he call her such a name!

Amanda was old-fashioned in her ideas. A real country girl from Mississippi who'd had no example to follow except a liberated aunt and an alcoholic parent, and she was like neither of them. She hardly even dated these days. Her working gear wasn't the kind of clothing that told men how conventional her ideals were. They saw the glitter and sexy outfit and figured that Amanda, or just "Mandy" as she was known onstage, lived like her alter ego looked. There were times when she rued the day she'd ever signed on with Desperado, but she was too famous and making too much money to quit now.

She put her hair in its usual braid and kept it there for the rest of the week, wondering from time to time about Quinn Sutton and whether or not he'd survived his illness. Not that she cared, she kept telling herself. It didn't matter to her if he turned up his toes.

There was no phone in the cabin, and no piano. She couldn't play solitaire, she didn't have a television. There was only the radio and the cassette player for company, and Mr. Durning's taste in music was really extreme. He liked opera and nothing else. She'd have died for some soft rock, or just an instrument to practice on. She could play drums as well as the synthesizer and piano, and she wound up in the kitchen banging on the counter with two stainless-steel knives out of sheer boredom.

When the electricity went haywire in the wake of two inches of freezing rain on Sunday night, it was almost a relief. She sat in the darkness laughing. She was trapped in a house without heat, without light, and the only thing she knew about fireplaces was that they required wood. The logs that were cut outside were frozen solid under the sleet and there were none in the house. There wasn't even a pack of matches.

She wrapped up in her coat and shivered, hating the solitude and the weather and feeling the nightmares coming back in the icy night. She didn't want to think about the reason her voice had quit on her, but if she spent enough time alone, she was surely going to go crazy reliving that night onstage.

Lost in thought, in nightmarish memories of screams and her own loss of consciousness, she didn't hear the first knock on the door until it came again.

"Miss Corrie!" a familiar angry voice shouted above the wind.

She got up, feeling her way to the door. "Keep your shirt on," she muttered as she threw it open.

Quinn Sutton glared down at her. "Get whatever you'll need for a couple of days and come on. The power's out. If you stay here you'll freeze to death. It's going below zero tonight. My ranch has an extra generator, so we've still got the power going."

She glared back. "I'd rather freeze to death than go anywhere with you, thanks just the same."

He took a slow breath. "Look, your morals are your own business. I just thought—"

She slammed the door in his face and turned, just in time to have him kick in the door and come after her.

"I said you're coming with me, lady," he said shortly. He bent and picked her up bodily and started out the door. "And to hell with what you'll need for a couple of days."

"Mr....Sutton!" she gasped, stunned by the unexpected contact with his hard, fit body as he carried her easily out the door and closed it behind them.

"Hold on," he said tautly and without looking at her. "The snow's pretty heavy right through this drift."

In fact, it was almost waist deep. She hadn't been outside in two days, so she hadn't noticed how high it had gotten. Her hands clung to the old sheepskin coat he was wearing. It smelled of leather and tobacco and whatever soap he used, and the furry collar was warm against her cold cheek. He made her feel small and helpless, and she wasn't sure she liked it.

"I don't like your tactics," she said through her teeth as the wind howled around them and sleet bit into her face like tiny nails.

"They get results. Hop on." He put her up on the sled, climbed beside her, grasped the reins and turned the horse back toward the mountain.

She wanted to protest, to tell him to take his offer and go to hell. But it was bitterly cold and she was shivering too badly to argue. He was right, and that was the hell of it. She could freeze to death in that cabin easily enough, and nobody would have found her until spring came or until her aunt persuaded Mr. Durning to come and see about her.

"I don't want to impose," she said curtly.

"We're past that now," he replied. "It's either this or bury you."

"I'm sure I know which you'd prefer," she muttered, huddling in her heavy coat.

"Do you?" he asked, turning his head. In the daylight glare of snow and sleet, she saw an odd twinkle in his black eyes. "Try digging a hole out there."

She gave him a speaking glance and resigned herself to going with him.

He drove the sled right into the barn and left her to wander through the aisle, looking at the horses and the two new calves in the various stalls while he dealt with unhitching and stalling the horse.

"What's wrong with these little things?" she asked, her hands in her pockets and her ears freezing as she nodded toward the two calves.

"Their mamas starved out in the pasture," he said quietly. "I couldn't get to them in time."

He sounded as if that mattered to him. She looked up at his dark face, seeing new character in it. "I didn't think a cow or two would matter," she said absently.

"I lost everything I had a few months back," he said matter-of-factly. "I'm trying to pull out of bankruptcy, and right now it's a toss-up as to whether I'll even come close. Every cow counts." He looked down at her. "But it isn't just the money. It disturbs me to see anything die from lack of attention. Even a cow."

"Or a mere woman?" she said with a faint smile. "Don't worry, I know you don't want me here. I'm... grateful to you for coming to my rescue. Most of the firewood was frozen and Mr. Durning apparently doesn't smoke, because there weren't a lot of matches around."

He scowled faintly. "No, Durning doesn't smoke. Didn't you know?"

She shrugged. "I never had reason to ask," she said, without telling him that it was her aunt, not herself, who would know about Mr. Durning's habits. Let him enjoy his disgusting opinion of her.

"Elliot said you'd been sick."

She lifted a face carefully kept blank. "Sort of," she replied.

"Didn't Durning care enough to come with you?"

"Mr. Sutton, my personal life is none of your business," she said firmly. "You can think whatever you want to about me. I don't care. But for what it's worth, I hate men probably as much as you hate women, so you won't have to hold me off with a stick."

His face went hard at the remark, but he didn't say anything. He searched her eyes for one long moment and then turned toward the house, gesturing her to follow.

Elliot was overjoyed with their new house guest. Quinn Sutton had a television and all sorts of tapes, and there was, surprisingly enough, a brand-new keyboard on a living-room table.

She touched it lovingly, and Elliot grinned at her. "Like it?" he asked proudly. "Dad gave it to me for Christmas. It's not an expensive one, you know, but it's nice to practice on. Listen."

He turned it on and flipped switches, and gave a pretty decent rendition of a tune by Genesis.

Amanda, who was formally taught in piano, smiled at his efforts. "Very good," she praised. "But try a B-flat instead of a B at the end of that last measure and see if it doesn't give you a better sound."

Elliot cocked his head. "I play by ear," he faltered.

"Sorry." She reached over and touched the key she wanted. "That one." She fingered the whole chord. "You have a very good ear."

"But I can't read music," he sighed. His blue eyes searched her face. "You can, can't you?"

She nodded, smiling wistfully. "I used to long for piano lessons. I took them in spurts and then begged a...friend to let me use her piano to practice on. It took me a long time to learn just the basics, but I do all right."

"All right" meant that she and the boys had won a Grammy award for their last album and it had been one of her own songs that had headlined it. But she couldn't tell Elliot that. She was convinced that Quinn Sutton would have thrown her out the front door if he'd known what she did for a living. He didn't seem like a rock fan, and once he got a look at her stage costume and her group, he'd probably accuse her of a lot worse than being his neighbor's live-in lover. She shivered. Well, at least she didn't like Quinn Sutton, and that was a good thing. She might get out of here without having him find out who she really was, but just in case, it wouldn't do to let herself become interested in him.

"I don't suppose you'd consider teaching me how to read music?" Elliot asked. "For something to do, you know, since we're going to be snowed in for a while, the way it looks."

"Sure, I'll teach you," she murmured, smiling at him. "If you dad doesn't mind," she added with a quick glance at the doorway.

Quinn Sutton was standing there, in jeans and red-checked flannel shirt with a cup of black coffee in one hand, watching them.

"None of that rock stuff," he said shortly. "That's a bad influence on kids."

"Bad influence?" Amanda was almost shocked, despite the fact that she'd gauged his tastes very well.

"Those raucous lyrics and suggestive costumes, and satanism," he muttered. "I confiscated his tapes and put them away. It's indecent."

"Some of it is, yes," she agreed quietly. "But you can't lump it all into one category, Mr. Sutton. And these days, a lot of the groups are even encouraging chastity and going to war on drug use..."

"You don't really believe that bull, do you?" he asked coldly.

"It's true, Dad," Elliot piped up.

"You can shut up," he told his son. He turned. "I've got a lot of paperwork to get through. Don't turn that thing on high, will you? Harry will show you to your room when you're ready to bed down, Miss Corrie," he added, and looked as if he'd like to have shown her to a room underwater. "Or Elliot can."

"Thanks again," she said, but she didn't look up. He made her feel totally inadequate and guilty. In a small way, it was like going back to that night...

"Don't stay up past nine, Elliot," Quinn told his son.

"Okay, Dad."

Amanda looked after the tall man with her jaw hanging loose. "What did he say?" she asked.

"He said not to stay up past nine," Elliot replied. "We all go to bed at nine," he added with a grin at her expression. "There, there, you'll get used to it. Ranch life, you know. Here, now, what was that about a B-flat? What's a B-flat?"

She was obviously expected to go to bed with the chickens and probably get up with them, too. Absently she picked up the keyboard and began to explain the basics of music to Elliot.

"Did he really hide all your tapes?" she asked curiously.

"Yes, he did," Elliot chuckled, glancing toward the stairs. "But I know where he hid them." He studied her with pursed lips. "You know, you look awfully familiar somehow."

Amanda managed to keep a calm expression on her face, despite her twinge of fear. Her picture, along with that of the men in the group, was on all their albums and tapes. God forbid that Elliot should be a fan and have one of them, but they were popular with young people his age. "They say we all have a counterpart, don't they?" she asked and smiled. "Maybe you saw somebody who looked like me. Here, this is how you run a C scale...."

She successfully changed the subject and Elliot didn't bring it up again. They went upstairs a half hour later, and she breathed a sigh of relief. Since the autocratic Mr. Sutton hadn't given her time to pack, she wound up sleeping in her clothes under the spotless white sheets. She only hoped that she wasn't going to have the nightmares here. She couldn't bear the thought of having Quinn Sutton ask her about them. He'd probably say that she'd gotten just what she deserved.

But the nightmares didn't come. She slept with delicious abandon and didn't dream at all. She woke up the next morning oddly refreshed just as the sun was coming up, even before Elliot knocked on her door to tell her that Harry had breakfast ready downstairs.

She combed out her hair and rebraided it, wrapping it around the crown of her head and pinning it there as she'd had it last night. She tidied herself after she'd washed up, and went downstairs with a lively step.

Quinn Sutton and Elliot were already making great inroads into huge, fluffy pancakes smothered in syrup when she joined them.

Harry brought in a fresh pot of coffee and grinned at her. "How about some hotcakes and sausage?" he asked.

"Just a hotcake and a sausage, please," she said and grinned back. "I'm not much of a breakfast person."

"You'll learn if you stay in these mountains long," Quinn said, sparing her a speaking glance. "You need more meat on those bones. Fix her three, Harry."

"Now, listen…" she began.

"No, you listen," Quinn said imperturbably, sipping black coffee. "My house, my rules."

She sighed. It was just like old-times at the orphanage, during one of her father's binges when she'd had to live with Mrs. Brim's rules. "Yes, sir," she said absently.

He glared at her. "I'm thirty-four, and you aren't young enough to call me 'sir.'"

She lifted startled dark eyes to his. "I'm twenty-four," she said. "Are you really just thirty-four?" She flushed even as she said it. He did look so much older, but she hadn't meant to say anything. "I'm sorry. That sounded terrible."

"I look older than I am," he said easily. "I've got a friend down in Texas who thought I was in my late thirties, and he's known me for years. No need to apologize." He didn't add that he had a lot of mileage on him, thanks to his ex-wife. "You look younger than twenty-four," he did add.

He pushed away his empty plate and sipped coffee, staring at her through the steam rising from it. He was wearing a blue-checked flannel shirt this morning, buttoned up to his throat, with jeans that were well fitting but not overly tight. He didn't dress like the men in Amanda's world, but then, the men she knew weren't the same breed as this Teton man.

"Amanda taught me all about scales last night," Elliot said excitedly. "She really knows music."

"How did you manage to learn?" Quinn asked her, and she saw in his eyes that he was remembering what she'd told him about her alcoholic father.

She lifted her eyes from her plate. "During my dad's binges, I stayed at the local orphanage. There was a lady there who played for her church. She taught me."

"No sisters or brothers?" he asked quietly.

She shook her head. "Nobody in the world, except an aunt." She lifted her coffee cup. "She's an artist, and she's been living with her latest lover—"

"You'd better get to school, son," Quinn interrupted tersely, nodding at Elliot.

"I sure had, or I'll be late. See you!"

He grabbed his books and his coat and was gone in a flash, and Harry gathered the plates with a smile and vanished into the kitchen.

"Don't talk about things like that around Elliot," Quinn said shortly. "He understands more than you think. I don't want him corrupted."

"Don't you realize that most twelve-year-old boys know more about life than grown-ups these days?" she asked with a faint smile.

"In your world, maybe. Not in mine."

She could have told him that she was discussing the way things were, not the way she preferred them, but she knew it would be useless. He was so certain that she was wildly liberated. She sighed. "Maybe so," she murmured.

"I'm old-fashioned," he added. His dark eyes narrowed on her face. "I don't want Elliot exposed to the liberated outlook of the so-called modern world until he's old enough to understand that he has a choice. I don't like a society that ridicules honor and fidelity and innocence. So I fight back in the only way I can. I go to church on Sunday, Miss Corrie," he mused, smiling at her curious expression. "Elliot goes, too. You might not know it from watching television or going to movies, but there are still a few people in America who also go to church on Sunday, who work hard all week and find their relaxation in ways that don't involve drugs, booze or casual sex. How's that for a shocking revelation?"

"Nobody ever accused Hollywood of portraying real life," she replied with a smile. "But if you want my honest opinion, I'm pretty sick of gratuitous sex, filthy language and graphic violence in the newer movies. In fact, I'm so sick of it that I've gone back to watching the old-time movies from the 1940s." She laughed at his expression. "Let me tell you, these old movies had real handicaps—the actors all had to keep their clothes on and they couldn't swear. The writers were equally limited, so they created some of the most gripping dramas ever produced. I love them. And best of all, you can even watch them with kids."

He pursed his lips, his dark eyes holding hers. "I like George Brent, George Sanders, Humphrey Bogart, Bette Davis and Cary Grant best," he confessed. "Yes, I watch them, too."

"I'm not really all that modern myself," she confessed, toying with the tablecloth. "I live in the city, but not in the fast lane." She put down her coffee cup. "I can understand why you feel the way you do, about taking Elliot to church and all. Elliot told me a little about his mother…"

He closed up like a plant. "I don't talk to outsiders about my personal life," he said without apology and got up, towering over her. "If you'd like to watch television or listen to music, you're welcome. I've got work to do."

"Can I help?" she asked.

His heavy eyebrows lifted. "This isn't the city."

"I know how to cut open a bale of hay," she said. "The orphanage was on a big farm. I grew up doing chores. I can even milk a cow."

"You won't milk the kind of cows I keep," he returned. His dark eyes narrowed. "You can feed those calves in the barn, if you like. Harry can show you where the bottle is."

Which meant that he wasn't going to waste his time on her. She nodded, trying not to feel like an unwanted guest. Just for a few minutes she'd managed to get under that hard reserve. Maybe that was good enough for a start. "Okay."

His black eyes glanced over her hair. "You haven't worn it down since the night Elliot brought you here," he said absently.

"I don't ever wear it down at home, as a rule," she

said quietly. "It...gets in my way." It got recognized, too, she thought, which was why she didn't dare let it loose around Elliot too often.

His eyes narrowed for an instant before he turned and shouldered into his jacket.

"Don't leave the perimeter of the yard," he said as he stuck his weather-beaten Stetson on his dark, thick hair. "This is wild country. We have bears and wolves, and a neighbor who still sets traps."

"I know my limitations, thanks," she said. "Do you have help, besides yourself?"

He turned, thrusting his big, lean hands into work gloves. "Yes, I have four cowboys who work around the place. They're all married."

She blushed. "Thank you for your sterling assessment of my character."

"You may like old movies," he said with a penetrating stare. "But no woman with your kind of looks is a virgin at twenty-four," he said quietly, mindful of Harry's sharp ears. "And I'm a backcountry man, but I've been married and I'm not stupid about women. You won't play me for a fool."

She wondered what he'd say if he knew the whole truth about her. But it didn't make her smile to reflect on that. She lowered her eyes to the thick white mug. "Think what you like, Mr. Sutton. You will anyway."

"Damned straight."

He walked out without looking back, and Amanda felt a vicious chill even before he opened the door and went out into the cold white yard.

She waited for Harry to finish his chores and then went

with him to the barn, where the little calves were curled up in their stalls of hay.

"They're only days old," Harry said, smiling as he brought the enormous bottles they were fed from. In fact, the nipples were stretched across the top of buckets and filled with warm mash and milk. "But they'll grow. Sit down, now. You may get a bit dirty…"

"Clothes wash," Amanda said easily, smiling. But this outfit was all she had. She was going to have to get the elusive Mr. Sutton to take her back to the cabin to get more clothes, or she'd be washing out her things in the sink tonight.

She knelt down in a clean patch of hay and coaxed the calf to take the nipple into its mouth. Once it got a taste of the warm liquid, it wasn't difficult to get it to drink. Amanda loved the feel of its silky red-and-white coat under her fingers as she stroked it. The animal was a Hereford, and its big eyes were pink rimmed and soulful. The calf watched her while it nursed.

"Poor little thing," she murmured softly, rubbing between its eyes. "Poor little orphan."

"They're tough critters, for all that," Harry said as he fed the other calf. "Like the boss."

"How did he lose everything, if you don't mind me asking?"

He glanced at her and read the sincerity in her expression. "I don't guess he'd mind if I told you. He was accused of selling contaminated beef."

"Contaminated…how?"

"It's a long story. The herd came to us from down in the Southwest. They had measles. Not," he added when he saw her puzzled expression, "the kind humans get.

Cattle don't break out in spots, but they do develop cysts
in the muscle tissue and if it's bad enough, it means that
the carcasses have to be destroyed." He shrugged. "You
can't spot it, because there are no definite symptoms, and
you can't treat it because there isn't a drug that cures it.
These cattle had it and contaminated the rest of our herd.
It was like the end of the world. Quinn had sold the beef
cattle to the packing-plant operator. When the meat was
ordered destroyed, he came back on Quinn to recover his
money, but Quinn had already spent it to buy new cattle.
We went to court... Anyway, to make a long story short,
they cleared Quinn of any criminal charges and gave him
the opportunity to make restitution. In turn, he sued the
people who sold him the contaminated herd in the first
place." He smiled ruefully. "We just about broke even,
but it meant starting over from scratch. That was last
year. Things are still rough, but Quinn's a tough customer
and he's got a good business head. He'll get through it.
I'd bet on him."

Amanda pondered that, thinking that Quinn's recent
life had been as difficult as her own. At least he had Elliot. That must have been a comfort to him. She said as
much to Harry.

He gave her a strange look. "Well, yes, Elliot's special
to him," he said, as if there were things she didn't know.
Probably there were.

"Will these little guys make it?" she asked when the
calf had finished his bottle.

"I think so," Harry said. "Here, give me that bottle
and I'll take care of it for you."

She sighed, petting the calf gently. She liked farms
and ranches. They were so real, compared to the artificial

life she'd known since she was old enough to leave home. She loved her work and she'd always enjoyed performing, but it seemed sometimes as if she lived in another world. Values were nebulous, if they even existed, in the world where she worked. Old-fashioned ideas like morality, honor, chastity were laughed at or ignored. Amanda kept hers to herself, just as she kept her privacy intact. She didn't discuss her inner feelings with anyone. Probably her friends and associates would have died laughing if they'd known just how many hang-ups she had, and how distant her outlook on life was from theirs.

"Here's another one," Quinn said from the front of the barn.

Amanda turned her head, surprised to see him because he'd ridden out minutes ago. He was carrying another small calf, but this one looked worse than the younger ones did.

"He's very thin," she commented.

"He's got scours." He laid the calf down next to her. "Harry, fix another bottle."

"Coming up, boss."

Amanda touched the wiry little head with its rough hide. "He's not in good shape," she murmured quietly.

Quinn saw the concern on her face and was surprised by it. He shouldn't have been, he reasoned. Why would she have come with Elliot in the middle of the night to nurse a man she didn't even like, if she wasn't a kind woman?

"He probably won't make it," he agreed, his dark eyes searching hers. "He'd been out there by himself for a long time. It's a big property, and he's a very small calf," he defended when she gave him a meaningful look. "It wouldn't be the first time we missed one, I'm sorry to say."

"I know." She looked up as Harry produced a third bottle, and her hand reached for it just as Quinn's did. She released it, feeling odd little tingles at the brief contact with his lean, sure hand.

"Here goes," he murmured curtly. He reached under the calf's chin and pulled its mouth up to slide the nipple in. The calf could barely nurse, but after a minute it seemed to rally and then it fed hungrily.

"Thank goodness," Amanda murmured. She smiled at Quinn, and his eyes flashed as they met hers, searching, dark, full of secrets. They narrowed and then abruptly fell to her soft mouth, where they lingered with a kind of questioning irritation, as if he wanted very much to kiss her and hated himself for it. Her heart leaped at the knowledge. She seemed to have a new, built-in insight about this standoffish man, and she didn't understand either it or her attitude toward him. He was domineering and hardheaded and unpredictable and she should have disliked him. But she sensed a sensitivity in him that touched her heart. She wanted to get to know him.

"I can do this," he said curtly. "Why don't you go inside?"

She was getting to him, she thought with fascination. He was interested in her, but he didn't want to be. She watched the way he avoided looking directly at her again, the angry glance of his eyes.

Well, it certainly wouldn't do any good to make him furious at her, especially when she was going to be his unwanted houseguest for several more days, from the look of the weather.

"Okay," she said, giving in. She got to her feet slowly. "I'll see if I can find something to do."

"Harry might like some company while he works in the kitchen. Wouldn't you, Harry?" he added, giving the older man a look that said he'd damned sure better like some company.

"Of course I would, boss," Harry agreed instantly.

Amanda pushed her hands into her pockets with a last glance at the calves. She smiled down at them. "Can I help feed them while I'm here?" she asked gently.

"If you want to," Quinn said readily, but without looking up.

"Thanks." She hesitated, but he made her feel shy and tongue-tied. She turned away nervously and walked back to the house.

Since Harry had the kitchen well in hand, she volunteered to iron some of Quinn's cotton shirts. Harry had the ironing board set up, but not the iron, so she went into the closet and produced one. It looked old, but maybe it would do, except that it seemed to have a lot of something caked on it.

She'd just started to plug it in when Harry came into the room and gasped.

"Not that one!" he exclaimed, gently taking it away from her. "That's Quinn's!"

She opened her mouth to make a remark, when Harry started chuckling.

"It's for his skis," he explained patiently.

She nodded. "Right. He irons his skis. I can see that."

"He does. Don't you know anything about skiing?"

"Well, you get behind a speedboat with them on…"

"Not waterskiing. *Snow* skiing," he emphasized.

She shrugged. "I come from southern Mississippi." She grinned at him. "We don't do much business in snow, you see."

"Sorry. Well, Quinn was an Olympic contender in giant slalom when he was in his late teens and early twenties. He would have made the team, but he got married and Elliot was on the way, so he gave it up. He still gets in plenty of practice," he added, shuddering. "On old Ironside peak, too. Nobody, but nobody, skis it except Quinn and a couple of other experts from Larry's Lodge over in Jackson Hole."

"I haven't seen that one on a map..." she began, because she'd done plenty of map reading before she came here.

"Oh, that isn't its official name, it's what Quinn calls it." He grinned. "Anyway, Quinn uses this iron to put wax on the bottom of his skis. Don't feel bad, I didn't know any better, either, at first, and I waxed a couple of shirts. Here's the right iron."

He handed it to her, and she plugged it in and got started. The elusive Mr. Sutton had hidden qualities, it seemed. She'd watched the winter Olympics every four years on television, and downhill skiing fascinated her. But it seemed to Amanda that giant slalom called for a kind of reckless skill and speed that would require ruthlessness and single-minded determination. Considering that, it wasn't at all surprising to her that Quinn Sutton had been good at it.

CHAPTER THREE

AMANDA HELPED HARRY do dishes and start a load of clothes in the washer. But when she took them out of the dryer, she discovered that several of Quinn's shirts were missing buttons and had loose seams.

Harry produced a needle and some thread, and Amanda set to work mending them. It gave her something to do while she watched a years-old police drama on television.

Quinn came in with Elliot a few hours later.

"Boy, the snow's bad," Elliot remarked as he rubbed his hands in front of the fire Harry had lit in the big stone fireplace. "Dad had to bring the sled out to get me, because the bus couldn't get off the main highway."

"Speaking of the sled," Amanda said, glancing at Quinn, "I've got to have a few things from the cabin. I'm really sorry, but I'm limited to what I'm wearing…."

"I'll run you down right now, before I go out again."

She put the mending aside. "I'll get my coat."

"Elliot, you can come, too. Put your coat back on," Quinn said unexpectedly, ignoring his son's surprised glance.

Amanda didn't look at him, but she understood why he wanted Elliot along. She made Quinn nervous. He was attracted to her and he was going to fight it to the bitter end. She wondered why he considered her such a threat.

He paused to pick up the shirt she'd been working on, and his expression got even harder as he glared at her. "You don't need to do that kind of thing," he said curtly.

"I've got to earn my keep somehow." She sighed. "I can feed the calves and help with the housework, at least. I'm not used to sitting around doing nothing," she added. "It makes me nervous."

He hesitated. An odd look rippled over his face as he studied the neat stitches in his shirtsleeve where the rip had been. He held it for a minute before he laid it gently back on the sofa. He didn't look at Amanda as he led the way out the door.

It didn't take her long to get her things together. Elliot wandered around the cabin. "There are knives all over the counter," he remarked. "Want me to put them in the sink?"

"Go ahead. I was using them for drumsticks," she called as she closed her suitcase.

"They don't look like they'd taste very good." Elliot chuckled.

She came out of the bedroom and gave him an amused glance. "Not that kind of drumsticks, you turkey. Here." She put down the suitcase and took the blunt stainless-steel knives from him. She glanced around to make sure Quinn hadn't come into the house and then she broke into an impromptu drum routine that made Elliot grin even more.

"Say, you're pretty good," he said.

She bowed. "Just one of my minor talents," she said. "But I'm better with a keyboard. Ready to go?"

"Whenever you are."

She started to pick up her suitcase, but Elliot reached down and got it before she could, a big grin on his freckled face. She wondered again why he looked so little like his father. She knew that his mother had been a redhead, too, but it was odd that he didn't resemble Quinn in any way at all.

Quinn was waiting on the sled, his expression unreadable, impatiently smoking his cigarette. He let them get on and turned the draft horse back toward his own house. It was snowing lightly and the wind was blowing, not fiercely but with a nip in it. Amanda sighed, lifting her face to the snow, not caring that her hood had fallen back to reveal the coiled softness of her blond hair. She felt alive out here as she never had in the city, or even back East. There was something about the wilderness that made her feel at peace with herself for the first time since the tragedy that had sent her retreating here.

"Enjoying yourself?" Quinn asked unexpectedly.

"More than I can tell you," she replied. "It's like no other place on earth."

He nodded. His dark eyes slid over her face, her cheeks flushed with cold and excitement, and they lingered there for one long moment before he forced his gaze back to the trail. Amanda saw that look and it brought a sense of foreboding. He seemed almost angry.

In fact, he was. Before the day was out, it was pretty apparent that he'd withdrawn somewhere inside himself and had no intention of coming out again. He barely said two words to Amanda before bedtime.

"He's gone broody," Elliot mused before he and Amanda called it a night. "He doesn't do it often, and not for a long time, but when he's got something on his mind, it's best not to get on his nerves."

"Oh, I'll do my best," Amanda promised, and crossed her heart.

But that apparently didn't do much good, in her case, because he glared at her over breakfast the next morning and over lunch, and by the time she finished mending a window curtain in the kitchen and helped Harry bake a cake for dessert, she was feeling like a very unwelcome guest.

She went out to feed the calves, the nicest of her daily chores, just before Quinn was due home for supper. Elliot had lessons and he was holed up in his room trying to get them done in time for a science-fiction movie he wanted to watch after supper. Quinn insisted that homework came first.

She fed two of the three calves and Harry volunteered to feed the third, the little one that Quinn had brought home with scours, while she cut the cake and laid the table. She was just finishing the place settings when she heard the sled draw up outside the door.

Her heart quickened at the sound of Quinn's firm, measured stride on the porch. The door opened and he came in, along with a few snowflakes.

He stopped short at the sight of her in an old white apron with wisps of blond hair hanging around her flushed face, a bowl of whipped potatoes in her hands.

"Don't you look domestic?" he asked with sudden, bitter sarcasm.

The attack was unexpected, although it shouldn't have been. He'd been irritable ever since the day before, when he'd noticed her mending his shirt.

"I'm just helping Harry," she said. "He's feeding the calves while I do this."

"So I noticed."

She put down the potatoes, watching him hang up his hat and coat with eyes that approved his tall, fit physique, the way the red-checked flannel shirt clung to his muscular torso and long back. He was such a lonely man, she thought, watching him. So alone, even with Elliot and Harry here. He turned unexpectedly, catching her staring and his dark eyes glittered.

He went to the sink to wash his hands, almost vibrating with pent-up anger. She sensed it, but it only piqued her curiosity. He was reacting to her. She felt it, knew it, as she picked up a dish towel and went close to him to wrap it gently over his wet hands. Her big black eyes searched his, and she let her fingers linger on his while time seemed to end in the warm kitchen.

His dark eyes narrowed, and he seemed to have stopped breathing. He was aware of so many sensations. Hunger. Anger. Loneliness. Lust. His head spun with them, and the scent of her was pure, soft woman, drifting up into his nostrils, cocooning him in the smell of cologne and shampoo. His gaze fell helplessly to her soft bow of a mouth and he wondered how it would feel to bend those few inches and take it roughly under his own. It had been so long since he'd kissed a woman, held a woman. Amanda was particularly feminine, and she appealed to everything that was masculine in him. He almost vibrated with the need to reach out to her.

But that way lay disaster, he told himself firmly. She was just another treacherous woman, probably bored with confinement, just keeping her hand in with attracting men. He probably seemed like a push-over, and she was going to use her charms to make a fool of him. He took a deep, slow breath and the glitter in his eyes became even more pronounced as he jerked the towel out of her hands and moved away.

"Sorry," she mumbled. She felt her cheeks go hot, because there had been a cold kind of violence in the action that warned her his emotions weren't quite under control. She moved away from him. Violence was the one thing she did expect from men. She'd lived with it for most of her life until she'd run away from home.

She went back to the stove, stirring the sauce she'd made to go with the boiled dumpling.

"Don't get too comfortable in the kitchen," he warned her. "This is Harry's private domain and he doesn't like trespassers. You're just passing through."

"I haven't forgotten that, Mr. Sutton," she replied, and her eyes kindled with dark fire as she looked at him. There was no reason to make her feel so unwelcome. "Just as soon as the thaw comes, I'll be out of your way for good."

"I can hardly wait," he said, biting off the words.

Amanda sighed wearily. It wasn't her idea of the perfect rest spot. She'd come away from the concert stage needing healing, and all she'd found was another battle to fight.

"You make me feel so at home, Mr. Sutton," she said wistfully. "Like part of the family. Thanks so much for your gracious hospitality, and do you happen to have a jar of rat poison...?"

Quinn had to bite hard to keep from laughing. He

turned and went out of the kitchen as if he were being chased.

After supper, Amanda volunteered to wash dishes, but Harry shooed her off. Quinn apparently did book work every night, because he went into his study and closed the door, leaving Elliot with Amanda for company. They'd watched the science-fiction movie Elliot had been so eager to see and now they were working on the keyboard.

"I think I've got the hang of C major," Elliot announced, and ran the scale, complete with turned under thumb on the key of F.

"Very good," she enthused. "Okay, let's go on to G major."

She taught him the scale and watched him play it, her mind on Quinn Sutton's antagonism.

"Something bothering you?" Elliot asked suspiciously.

She shrugged. "Your dad doesn't want me here."

"He hates women," he said. "You knew that, didn't you?"

"Yes. But why?"

He shook his head. "It's because of my mother. She did something really terrible to him, and he never talks about her. He never has. I've got one picture of her, in my room."

"I guess you look like her," she said speculatively.

He handed her the keyboard. "I've got red hair and freckles like she had," he confessed. "I'm just sorry that I...well, that I don't look anything like Dad. I'm glad he cares about me, though, in spite of everything. Isn't it great that he likes me?"

What an odd way to talk about his father, Amanda

thought as she studied him. She wanted to say something else, to ask about that wording, but it was too soon. She hid her curiosity in humor.

"'There are more things in heaven and earth, Horatio, than are dreamt of in your philosophy,'" she intoned deeply.

He chuckled. "Hamlet," he said. "Shakespeare. We did that in English class last month."

"Culture in the high country." She applauded. "Very good, Elliot."

"I like rock culture best," he said in a stage whisper. "Play something."

She glanced toward Quinn's closed study door with a grimace. "Something soft."

"No!" he protested, and grinned. "Come on, give him hell."

"Elliot!" she chided.

"He needs shaking up, I tell you, he's going to die an old maid. He gets all funny and red when unmarried ladies talk to him at church, and just look at how grumpy he's been since you've been around. We've got to save him, Amanda," he said solemnly.

She sighed. "Okay. It's your funeral." She flicked switches, turning on the auto rhythm, the auto chords, and moved the volume to maximum. With a mischievous glance at Elliot, she swung into one of the newest rock songs, by a rival group, instantly recognizable by the reggae rhythm and sweet harmony.

"Good God!" came a muffled roar from the study.

Amanda cut off the keyboard and handed it to Elliot.

"No!" Elliot gasped.

But it was too late. His father came out of the study and saw Elliot holding the keyboard and started smoldering.

"It was her!" Elliot accused, pointing his finger at her.

She peered at Quinn over her drawn-up knees. "Would I play a keyboard that loud in your house, after you warned me not to?" she asked in her best meek voice.

Quinn's eyes narrowed. They went back to Elliot.

"She's lying," Elliot said. "Just like the guy in those truck commercials on TV…!"

"Keep it down," Quinn said without cracking a smile. "Or I'll give that thing the decent burial it really needs. And no more damned rock music in my house! That thing has earphones. Use them!"

"Yes, sir," Elliot groaned.

Amanda saluted him. "We hear and obey, excellency!" she said with a deplorable Spanish accent. "Your wish is our command. We live only to serve…!"

The slamming of the study door cut her off. She burst into laughter while Elliot hit her with a sofa cushion.

"You animal," he accused mirthfully. "Lying to Dad, accusing me of doing something I never did! How could you?"

"Temporary insanity," she gasped for breath. "I couldn't help myself."

"We're both going to die," he assured her. "He'll lie awake all night thinking of ways to get even and when we least expect it, pow!"

"He's welcome. Here. Run that G major scale again."

He let her turn the keyboard back on, but he was careful to move the volume switch down as far as it would go.

It was almost nine when Quinn came out of the study and turned out the light.

"Time for bed," he said.

Amanda had wanted to watch a movie that was coming on, but she knew better than to ask. Presumably they did occasionally watch television at night. She'd have to ask one of these days.

"Good night, Dad. Amanda," Elliot said, grinning as he went upstairs with a bound.

"Did you do your homework?" Quinn called up after him.

"Almost."

"What the hell does that mean?" he demanded.

"It means I'll do it first thing in the morning! 'Night, Dad!"

A door closed.

Quinn glared at Amanda. "That won't do," he said tersely. "His homework comes first. Music is a nice hobby, but it's not going to make a living for him."

Why not, she almost retorted, it makes a six-figure annual income for me, but she kept her mouth shut.

"I'll make sure he's done his homework before I offer to show him anything else on the keyboard. Okay?"

He sighed angrily. "All right. Come on. Let's go to bed."

She put her hands over her chest and gasped, her eyes wide and astonished. "Together? Mr. Sutton, really!"

His dark eyes narrowed in a veiled threat. "Hell will freeze over before I wind up in bed with you," he said icily. "I told you, I don't want used goods."

"Your loss," she sighed, ignoring the impulse to lay a lamp across his thick skull. "Experience is a valuable commodity in my world." She deliberately smoothed her hands down her waist and over her hips, her eyes faintly coquettish as she watched him watching her movements. "And I'm very experienced," she drawled. In music, she was.

His jaw tautened. "Yes, it does show," he said. "Kindly keep your attitudes to yourself. I don't want my son corrupted."

"If you really meant that, you'd let him watch movies and listen to rock music and trust him to make up his own mind about things."

"He's only twelve."

"You aren't preparing him to live in the real world," she protested.

"This," he said, "is the real world for him. Not some fancy apartment in a city where women like you lounge around in bars picking up men."

"Now you wait just a minute," she said. "I don't lounge around in bars to pick up men." She shifted her stance. "I hang out in zoos and flash elderly men in my trench coat."

He threw up his hands. "I give up."

"Good! Your room or mine?"

He whirled, his dark eyes flashing. Her smile was purely provocative and she was deliberately baiting him, he could sense it. His jaw tautened and he wanted to pick her up and shake her for the effect her teasing was having on him.

"Okay, I quit," Amanda said, because she could see that he'd reached the limits of his control and she wasn't quite brave enough to test the other side of it. "Good night. Sweet dreams."

He didn't answer her. He followed her up the stairs and watched her go into her room and close the door. After a minute, he went into his own room and locked the door.

He laughed mirthlessly at his own rash action, but he hoped she could hear the bolt being thrown.

She could. It shocked her, until she realized that he'd done it deliberately, probably trying to hurt her. She laid back on her bed with a long sigh. She didn't know what to do about Mr. Sutton. He was beginning to get to her in a very real way. She had to keep her perspective. This was only temporary. It would help to keep it in mind.

Quinn was thinking the same thing. But when he turned out the light and closed his eyes, he kept feeling Amanda's loosened hair brushing down his chest, over his flat stomach, his loins. He shuddered and woke up sweating in the middle of the night. It was the worst and longest night of his life.

The next morning, Quinn glared at Amanda across the breakfast table after Elliot had left for school.

"Leave my shirts alone," he said curtly. "If you find any more tears, Harry can mend them."

Her eyebrows lifted. "I don't have germs," she pointed out. "I couldn't contaminate them just by stitching them up."

"Leave them alone," he said harshly.

"Okay. Suit yourself." She sighed. "I'll just busy myself making lacy pillows for your bed."

He said something expressive and obscene; her lips fell open and she gaped at him. She'd never heard him use language like that.

It seemed to bother him that he had. He put down his fork, left his eggs and went out the door as if leopards were stalking him.

Amanda stirred her eggs around on the plate, feeling vaguely guilty that she'd given him such a hard time that he'd gone without half his breakfast. She didn't know why she needled him. It seemed to be a new habit, maybe to keep him at bay, to keep him from noticing how attracted she was to him.

"I'm going out to feed the calves, Harry," she said after a minute.

"Dress warm. It's snowing again," he called from upstairs.

"Okay."

She put on her coat and hat and wandered out to the barn through the path Quinn had made in the deep snow. She'd never again grumble at little two- and three-foot drifts in the city, she promised herself. Now that she knew what real snow was, she felt guilty for all her past complaints.

The barn was warmer than the great outdoors. She pushed snowflakes out of her eyes and face and went to fix the bottles as Harry had shown her, but Quinn was already there and had it done.

"No need to follow me around trying to get my attention," Amanda murmured with a wicked smile. "I've already noticed how sexy and handsome you are."

He drew in a furious breath, but just as he was about to speak she moved closer and put her fingers against his cold mouth.

"You'll break my heart if you use ungentlemanly language, Mr. Sutton," she told him firmly. "I'll just feed the calves and admire you from afar, if you don't mind. It seems safer than trying to throw myself at you."

He looked torn between shaking her and kissing her. She stood very still where he towered above her, even bigger than usual in that thick shepherd's coat and his tall, gray Stetson. He looked down at her quietly, his narrowed eyes lingering on her flushed cheeks and her soft, parted mouth.

Her hands were resting against the coat, and his were on her arms, pulling. She could hardly breathe as she realized that he'd actually touched her voluntarily. He jerked her face up under his, and she could see anger and something like bitterness in the dark eyes that held hers until she blushed.

"Just what are you after, city girl?" he asked coldly.

"A smile, a kind word and, dare I say it, a round of hearty laughter?" she essayed with wide eyes, trying not to let him see how powerfully he affected her.

His dark eyes fell to her mouth. "Is that right? And nothing more?"

Her breath came jerkily through her lips. "I…have to feed the calves."

His eyes narrowed. "Yes, you do." His fingers on her arms contracted, so that she could feel them even through the sleeves of her coat. "Be careful what you offer me," he said in a voice as light and cold as the snow outside the barn. "I've been without a woman for one hell of a long time, and I'm alone up here. If you're not what you're making yourself out to be, you could be letting yourself in for some trouble."

She stared up at him only half comprehending what he was saying. As his meaning began to filter into her consciousness, her cheeks heated and her breath caught in her throat.

"You…make it sound like a threat," she breathed.

"It is a threat, Amanda," he replied, using her name for the first time. "You could start something you might not want to finish with me, even with Elliot and Harry around."

She bit her lower lip nervously. She hadn't considered that. He looked more mature and formidable than he ever had before, and she could feel the banked-down fires in him kindling even as he held her.

"Okay," she said after a minute.

He let her go and moved away from her to get the bottles. He handed them to her with a long, speculative look.

"It's all right," she muttered, embarrassed. "I won't attack you while your back is turned. I almost never rape men."

He lifted an eyebrow, but he didn't smile. "You crazed female sex maniac," he murmured.

"Goody Two Shoes," she shot back.

A corner of his mouth actually turned up. "You've got that one right," he agreed. "Stay close to the house while it's snowing like this. We wouldn't want to lose you."

"I'll just bet we wouldn't," she muttered and stuck her tongue out at his retreating back.

She knelt down to feed the calves, still shaken by her confrontation with Quinn. He was an enigma. She was almost certain that he'd been joking with her at the end of the exchange, but it was hard to tell from his poker face. He didn't look like a man who'd laughed often or enough.

The littlest calf wasn't responding as well as he had earlier. She cuddled him and coaxed him to drink, but he did it without any spirit. She laid him back down with a sigh. He didn't look good at all. She worried about him for the rest of the evening, and she didn't argue when the television was cut off at nine o'clock. She went straight to bed, with Quinn and Elliot giving her odd looks.

CHAPTER FOUR

AMANDA WAS SUBDUED at the breakfast table, more so when Quinn started watching her with dark, accusing eyes. She knew she'd deliberately needled him for the past two days, and now she was sorry. He'd hinted that her behavior was about to start something, and she was anxious not to make things any worse than they already were.

The problem was that she was attracted to him. The more she saw of him, the more she liked him. He was different from the superficial, materialistic men in her own world. He was hardheaded and stubborn. He had values, and he spoke out for them. He lived by a rigid code of ethics, and *honor* was a word that had great meaning for him. Under all that, he was sensitive and caring. Amanda couldn't help the way she was beginning to feel about him. She only wished that she hadn't started off on the wrong foot with him.

She set out to win him over, acting more like her real self. She was polite and courteous and caring, but without the rough edges she'd had in the beginning. She still did the mending, despite his grumbling, and she made cushions for the sofa out of some cloth Harry had put away. But all her domestic actions only made things worse. Quinn glared at her openly now, and his lack of politeness raised even Harry's eyebrows.

Amanda had a sneaking hunch that it was attraction to her that was making him so ill humored. He didn't act at all like an experienced man, despite his marriage, and the way he looked at her was intense. If she could bring him out into the open, she thought, it might ease the tension a little.

She did her chores, including feeding the calves, worrying even more about the littlest one because he wasn't responding as well today as he had the day before. When Elliot came home, she refused to help him with the keyboard until he did his homework. With a rueful smile and a knowing glance at his dad, he went up to his room to get it over with.

Meanwhile, Harry went out to get more firewood and Amanda was left in the living room with Quinn watching an early newscast.

The news was, as usual, all bad. Quinn put out his cigarette half angrily, his dark eyes lingering on Amanda's soft face.

"Don't you miss the city?" he asked.

She smiled. "Sure. I miss the excitement and my friends. But it's nice here, too." She moved toward the big armchair he was sitting in, nervously contemplating her next move. "You don't mind all that much, do you? Having me around, I mean?"

He glared up at her. He was wearing a blue-checked flannel shirt, buttoned up to the throat, and the hard muscles of his chest strained against it. He looked twice as big as usual, his dark hair unruly on his broad forehead as he stared up into her eyes.

"I'm getting used to you, I guess," he said stiffly. "Just don't get too comfortable."

"You really don't want me here, do you?" she asked quietly.

He sighed angrily. "I don't like women," he muttered.

"I know." She sat down on the arm of his chair, facing him. "Why not?" she asked gently.

His body went taut at the proximity. She was too close. Too female. The scent of her got into his nostrils and made him shift restlessly in the chair. "It's none of your damned business why not," he said evasively. "Will you get up from there?"

She warmed at the tone of his voice. So she did disturb him! Amanda smiled gently as she leaned forward. "Are you sure you want me to?" she asked and suddenly threw caution to the wind and slid down into his lap, putting her soft mouth hungrily on his.

He stiffened. He jerked. His big hands bit into her arms so hard they bruised. But for just one long, sweet moment, his hard mouth gave in to hers and he gave her back the kiss, his lips rough and warm, the pressure bruising, and he groaned as if all his dreams had come true at once.

He tasted of smoke for the brief second that he allowed the kiss. Then he was all bristling indignation and cold fury. He slammed to his feet, taking her with him, and literally threw her away, so hard that she fell against and onto the sofa.

"Damn you," he ground out. His fists clenched at his sides. His big body vibrated with outrage. "You cheap little tart!"

She lay trembling, frightened of the violence in his now white face and blazing dark eyes. "I'm not," she defended feebly.

"Can't you live without it for a few days, or are you

desperate enough to try to seduce me?" he hissed. His eyes slid over her with icy contempt. "It won't work. I've told you already, I don't want something that any man can have! I don't want any part of you, least of all your overused body!"

She got to her feet on legs that threatened to give way under her, backing away from his anger. She couldn't even speak. Her father had been like that when he drank too much, white-faced, icy hot, totally out of control. And when he got that way, he hit. She cringed away from Quinn as he moved toward her and suddenly, she whirled and ran out of the room.

He checked his instinctive move to go after her. So she was scared, was she? He frowned, trying to understand why. He'd only spoken the truth; did she not like hearing what she was? The possibility that he'd been wrong, that she wasn't a cheap little tart, he wouldn't admit even to himself.

He sat back down and concentrated on the television without any real interest. When Elliot came downstairs, Quinn barely looked up.

"Where's Amanda going?" he asked his father.

Quinn raised an eyebrow. "What?"

"Where's Amanda going in such a rush?" Elliot asked again. "I saw her out the window, tramping through waist-deep snow. Doesn't she remember what you told her about old McNaber's traps? She's headed straight for them if she keeps on the way she's headed…Where are you going?"

Quinn was already on his feet and headed for the back door. He got into his shepherd's coat and hat without speaking, his face pale, his eyes blazing with mingled fear and anger.

"She was crying," Harry muttered, sparing him a glance. "I don't know what you said to her, but—"

"Shut up," Quinn said coldly. He stared the older man down and went out the back door and around the house, following in the wake Amanda's body had made. She was already out of sight, and those traps would be buried under several feet of snow. Bear traps, and she wouldn't see them until she felt them. The thought of that merciless metal biting her soft flesh didn't bear thinking about, and it would be his fault because he'd hurt her.

Several meters ahead, into the woods now, Amanda was cursing silently as she plowed through the snowdrifts, her black eyes fierce even through the tears. Damn Quinn Sutton, she panted. She hoped he got eaten by moths during the winter, she hoped his horse stood on his foot, she hoped the sled ran over him and packed him into the snow and nobody found him until spring. It was only a kiss, after all, and he'd kissed her back just for a few seconds.

She felt the tears burning coldly down her cheeks as they started again. Damn him. He hadn't had to make her feel like such an animal, just because she'd kissed him. She cared about him. She'd only wanted to get on a friendlier footing with him. But now she'd done it. He hated her for sure, she'd seen it in his eyes, in his face, when he'd called her those names. Cheap little tart, indeed! Well, Goody Two Shoes Sutton could just hold his breath until she kissed him again, so there!

She stopped to catch her breath and then plowed on. The cabin was somewhere down here. She'd stay in it even if she did freeze to death. She'd shack up with a grizzly bear before she'd spend one more night under Quinn

Sutton's roof. She frowned. Were there grizzly bears in this part of the country?

"Amanda, stop!"

She paused, wondering if she'd heard someone call her name, or if it had just been the wind. She was in a break of lodgepole pines now, and a cabin was just below in the valley. But it wasn't Mr. Durning's cabin. Could that be McNaber's...?

"Amanda!"

That was definitely her name. She glanced over her shoulder and saw the familiar shepherd's coat and dark worn Stetson atop that arrogant head.

"Eat snow, Goody Two Shoes!" she yelled back. "I'm going home!"

She started ahead, pushing hard now. But he had the edge, because he was walking in the path she'd made. He was bigger and faster, and he had twice her stamina. Before she got five more feet, he had her by the waist.

She fought him, kicking and hitting, but he simply wrapped both arms around her and held on until she finally ran out of strength.

"I hate you," she panted, shivering as the cold and the exertion got to her. "I hate you!"

"You'd hate me more if I hadn't stopped you," he said, breathing hard. "McNaber lives down there. He's got bear traps all over the place. Just a few more steps, and you'd have been up to your knees in them, you little fool! You can't even see them in snow this deep!"

"What would you care?" she groaned. "You don't want me around. I don't want to stay with you anymore. I'll take my chances at the cabin!"

"No, you won't, Amanda," he said. His embrace didn't

even loosen. He whipped her around, his big hands rough on her sleeves as he shook her. "You're coming back with me, if I have to carry you!"

She flinched, the violence in him frightening her. She swallowed, her lower lip trembling and pulled feebly against his hands.

"Let go of me," she whispered. Her voice shook, and she hated her own cowardice.

He scowled. She was paper white. Belatedly he realized what was wrong and his hands released her. She backed away as far as the snow would allow and stood like a young doe at bay, her eyes dark and frightened.

"Did he hit you?" he asked quietly.

She didn't have to ask who. She shivered. "Only when he drank," she said, her voice faltering. "But he always drank." She laughed bitterly. "Just...don't come any closer until you cool down, if you please."

He took a slow, steadying breath. "I'm sorry," he said, shocking her. "No, I mean it. I'm really sorry. I wouldn't have hit you, if that's what you're thinking. Only a coward would raise his hand to a woman," he said with cold conviction.

She wrapped her arms around herself and stood, just breathing, shivering in the cold.

"We'd better get back before you freeze," he said tautly. Her very defensiveness disarmed him. He felt guilty and protective all at once. He wanted to take her to his heart and comfort her, but even as he stepped toward her, she backed away. He hadn't imagined how much that would hurt until it happened. He stopped and stood where he was, raising his hands in an odd gesture of helplessness.

"I won't touch you," he promised. "Come on, honey. You can go first."

Tears filmed her dark eyes. It was the first endearment she'd ever heard from him and it touched her deeply. But she knew it was only casual. Her behavior had shocked him and he didn't know what to do. She let out a long breath.

Without a quip or comeback, she eased past him warily and started back the way they'd come. He followed her, giving thanks that he'd been in time, that she hadn't run afoul of old McNaber's traps. But now he'd really done it. He'd managed to make her afraid of him.

She went ahead of him into the house. Elliot and Harry took one look at her face and Quinn's and didn't ask a single question.

She sat at the supper table like a statue. She didn't speak, even when Elliot tried to bring her into the conversation. And afterward, she curled up in a chair in the living room and sat like a mouse watching television.

Quinn couldn't know the memories he'd brought back, the searing fear of her childhood. Her father had been a big man, and he was always violent when he drank. He was sorry afterward, sometimes he even cried when he saw the bruises he'd put on her. But it never stopped him. She'd run away because it was more than she could bear, and fortunately there'd been a place for runaways that took her in. She'd learned volumes about human kindness from those people. But the memories were bitter and Quinn's bridled violence had brought them sweeping in like storm clouds.

Elliot didn't ask her about music lessons. He excused

himself a half hour early and went up to bed. Harry had long since gone to his own room.

Quinn sat in his big chair, smoking his cigarette, but he started when Amanda put her feet on the floor and glanced warily at him.

"Don't go yet," he said quietly. "I want to talk to you."

"We don't have anything to say to each other," she said quietly. "I'm very sorry for what I did this afternoon. It was impulsive and stupid, and I promise I'll never do it again. If you can just put up with me until it thaws a little, you'll never have to see me again."

He sighed wearily. "Is that what you think I want?" he asked, searching her face.

"Of course it is," she replied simply. "You've hated having me here ever since I came."

"Maybe I have. I've got more reason to hate and distrust women than you'll ever know. But that isn't what I want to talk about," he said, averting his gaze from her wan face. He didn't like thinking about that kiss and how disturbing it had been. "I want to know why you thought I might hit you."

She dropped her eyes to her lap. "You're big, like my father," she said. "When he lost his temper, he always hit."

"I'm not your father," Quinn pointed out, his dark eyes narrowing. "And I've never hit anyone in a temper, except maybe another man from time to time when it was called for. I never raised my hand to Elliot's mother, although I felt like it a time or two, in all honesty. I never lifted a hand to her even when she told me she was pregnant with Elliot."

"Why should you have?" she asked absently. "He's your son."

He laughed coldly. "No, he isn't."

She stared at him openly. "Elliot isn't yours?" she asked softly.

He shook his head. "His mother was having an affair with a married man and she got caught out." He shrugged. "I was twenty-two and grass green and she mounted a campaign to marry me. I guess I was pretty much a sitting duck. She was beautiful and stacked and she had me eating out of her hand in no time. We got married and right after the ceremony, she told me what she'd done. She laughed at how clumsy I'd been during the courtship, how she'd had to steel herself not to be sick when I'd kissed her. She told me about Elliot's father and how much she loved him, then she dared me to tell people the truth about how easy it had been to make me marry her." He blew out a cloud of smoke, his eyes cold with memory. "She had me over a barrel. I was twice as proud back then as I am now. I couldn't bear to have the whole community laughing at me. So I stuck it out. Until Elliot was born, and she and his father took off for parts unknown for a weekend of love. Unfortunately for them, he wrecked the car in his haste to get to a motel and killed both of them outright."

"Does Elliot know?" she asked, her voice quiet as she glanced toward the staircase.

"Sure," he said. "I couldn't lie to him about it. But I took care of him from the time he was a baby, and I raised him. That makes me his father just as surely as if I'd put the seed he grew from into his mother's body. He's my son, and I'm his father. I love him."

She studied his hard face, seeing behind it to the pain he must have suffered. "You loved her, didn't you?"

"Calf love," he said. "She came up on my blind side and I needed somebody to love. I'd always been shy and clumsy around girls. I couldn't even get a date when I was in school because I was so rough edged. She paid me a lot of attention. I was lonely." His big shoulders shrugged. "Like I said, a sitting duck. She taught me some hard lessons about your sex," he added, his narrowed eyes on her face. "I've never forgotten them. And nobody's had a second chance at me."

Her breath came out as a sigh. "That's what you thought this afternoon, when I kissed you," she murmured, reddening at her own forwardness. "I'm sorry. I didn't realize you might think I was playing you for a sucker."

He frowned. "Why did you kiss me, Amanda?"

"Would you believe, because I wanted to?" she asked with a quiet smile. "You're a very attractive man, and something about you makes me weak in the knees. But you don't have to worry about me coming on to you again," she added, getting to her feet. "You teach a pretty tough lesson yourself. Good night, Mr. Sutton. I appreciate your telling me about Elliot. You needn't worry that I'll say anything to him or to anybody else. I don't carry tales, and I don't gossip."

She turned toward the staircase, and Quinn's dark eyes followed her. She had an elegance of carriage that touched him, full of pride and grace. He was sorry now that he'd slapped her down so hard with cruel words. He really hadn't meant to. He'd been afraid that she was going to let him down, that she was playing. It hadn't occurred to him that she found him attractive or that she'd kissed him because she'd really wanted to.

He'd made a bad mistake with Amanda. He'd hurt her and sent her running, and now he wished he could take back the things he'd said. She wasn't like any woman he'd ever been exposed to. She actually seemed unaware of her beauty, as if she didn't think much of it. Maybe he'd gotten it all wrong and she wasn't much more experienced than he was. He wished he could ask her. She disturbed him very much, and now he wondered if it wasn't mutual.

Amanda was lying in bed, crying. The day had been horrible, and she hated Quinn for the way he'd treated her. It wasn't until she remembered what he'd told her that she stopped crying and started thinking. He'd said that he'd never slept with Elliot's mother, and that he hadn't been able to get dates in high school. Presumably that meant that his only experience with women had been after Elliot's mother died. She frowned. There hadn't been many women, she was willing to bet. He seemed to know relatively nothing about her sex. She frowned. If he still hated women, how had he gotten any experience? Finally her mind grew tired of trying to work it out and she went to sleep.

AMANDA WAS UP helping Harry in the kitchen the next morning when Quinn came downstairs after a wild, erotic dream that left him sweating and swearing when he woke up. Amanda had figured largely in it, with her blond hair loose and down to her lower spine, his hands twined in it while he made love to her in the stillness of his own bedroom. The dream had been so vivid that he could almost see the pink perfection of her breasts through the bulky, white-knit sweater she was wearing, and he almost groaned as his eyes fell to the rise and fall of her chest under it.

She glanced at Quinn and actually flushed before she dragged her eyes back down to the pan of biscuits she was putting into the oven.

"I didn't know you could make biscuits," Quinn murmured.

"Harry taught me," she said evasively. Her eyes went back to him again and flitted away.

He frowned at that shy look until he realized why he was getting it. He usually kept his shirts buttoned up to his throat, but this morning he'd left it open halfway down his chest because he was still sweating from that dream. He pursed his lips and gave her a speculative stare. He wondered if it were possible that he disturbed her as much as she disturbed him. He was going to make it his business to find out before she left here. If for no other reason than to salve his bruised ego.

He went out behind Elliot, pausing in the doorway. "How's the calf?" he asked Amanda.

"He wasn't doing very well yesterday," she said with a sigh. "Maybe he's better this morning."

"I'll have a look at him before I go out." He glanced out at the snow. "Don't try to get back to the cabin again, will you? You can't get through McNaber's traps without knowing where they are."

He actually sounded worried. She studied his hard face quietly. That was nice. Unless, of course, he was only worried that she might get laid up and he'd have to put up with her for even longer.

"Is the snow ever going to stop?" she asked.

"Hard to say," he told her. "I've seen it worse than this even earlier in the year. But we'll manage, I suppose."

"I suppose." She glared at him.

He pulled on his coat and buttoned it, propping his hat over one eye. "In a temper this morning, are we?" he mused.

His eyes were actually twinkling. She shifted back against the counter, grateful that Harry had gone off to clean the bedrooms. "I'm not in a temper. Cheap little tarts don't have tempers."

One eyebrow went up. "I called you that, didn't I?" He let his eyes run slowly down her body. "You shouldn't have kissed me like that. I'm not used to aggressive women."

"Rest assured that I'll never attack you again, Goody Two Shoes."

He chuckled softly. "Won't you? Well, disappointment is a man's lot, I suppose."

Her eyes widened. She wasn't sure she'd even heard him. "You were horrible to me!"

"I guess I was." His dark eyes held hers, making little chills up and down her spine at the intensity of the gaze. "I thought you were playing games. You know, a little harmless fun at the hick's expense."

"I don't know how to play games with men," she said stiffly, "and nobody, anywhere, could call you a hick with a straight face. You're a very masculine man with a keen mind and an overworked sense of responsibility. I wouldn't make fun of you even if I could."

His dark eyes smiled into hers. "In that case, we might call a truce for the time being."

"Do you think you could stand being nice to me?" she asked sourly. "I mean, it would be a strain, I'm sure."

"I'm not a bad man," he pointed out. "I just don't know much about women, or hadn't that thought occurred?"

She searched his eyes. "No."

"We'll have to have a long talk about it one of these days." He pulled the hat down over his eyes. "I'll check on the calves for you."

"Thanks." She watched him go, her heart racing at the look in his eyes just before he closed the door. She was more nervous of him now than ever, but she didn't know what to do about it. She was hoping that the chinook would come before she had to start worrying too much. She was too confused to know what to do anymore.

CHAPTER FIVE

AMANDA FINISHED THE breakfast dishes before she went out to the barn. Quinn was still there, his dark eyes quiet on the smallest of the three calves. It didn't take a fortune teller to see that something was badly wrong. The small animal lay on its side, its dull, lackluster red-and-white coat showing its ribs, its eyes glazed and unseeing while it fought to breathe.

She knelt beside Quinn and he glanced at her with concern.

"You'd better go back in the house, honey," he said.

Her eyes slid over the small calf. She'd seen pets die over the years, and now she knew the signs. The calf was dying. Quinn knew it, too, and was trying to shield her.

That touched her, oddly, more than anything he'd said or done since she'd been on Ricochet. She looked up at him. "You're a nice man, Quinn Sutton," she said softly.

He drew in a slow breath. "When I'm not taking bites out of you, you mean?" he replied. "It hurts like hell when you back away from me. You'll never know how sorry I am for what happened yesterday."

One shock after another. At least it took her mind off the poor, laboring creature beside them. "I'm sorry, too," she said. "I shouldn't have been so…" She stopped, averting her eyes. "I don't know much about men, Quinn," she said finally. "I've spent my whole adult life backing away from involvement, emotional or physical. I know how to flirt, but not much more." She risked a glance at him, and relaxed when she saw his face. "My aunt is Mr. Durning's lover, you know. She's an artist. A little flighty, but nice. I've…never had a lover."

He nodded quietly. "I've been getting that idea since we wound up near McNaber's cabin yesterday. You reacted pretty violently for an experienced woman." He looked away from her. That vulnerability in her pretty face was working on him again. "Go inside now. I can deal with this."

"I'm not afraid of death," she returned. "I saw my mother die. It wasn't scary at all. She just closed her eyes."

His dark eyes met hers and locked. "My father went the same way." He looked back down at the calf. "It won't be long now."

She sat down in the hay beside him and slid her small hand into his big one. He held it for a long moment. Finally his voice broke the silence. "It's over. Go have a cup of coffee. I'll take care of him."

She hadn't meant to cry, but the calf had been so little and helpless. Quinn pulled her close, holding her with quiet comfort, while she cried. Then he wiped the tears away with his thumbs and smiled gently. "You'll do," he murmured, thinking that sensitivity and courage was a nice combination in a woman.

She was thinking the exact same thing about him. She managed a watery smile and with one last, pitying look at the calf, she went into the house.

Elliot would miss it, as she would, she thought. Even Quinn had seemed to care about it, because she saw him occasionally sitting by it, petting it, talking to it. He loved little things. It was evident in all the kittens and puppies around the place, and in the tender care he took of all his cattle and calves. And although Quinn cursed old man McNaber's traps, Elliot had told her that he stopped by every week to check on the dour old man and make sure he had enough chopped wood and supplies. For a taciturn iceman, he had a surprisingly warm center.

She told Harry what had happened and sniffed a little while she drank black coffee. "Is there anything I can do?" she asked.

He smiled. "You do enough," he murmured. "Nice to have some help around the place."

"Quinn hasn't exactly thought so," she said dryly.

"Oh, yes he has," he said firmly as he cleared away the dishes they'd eaten his homemade soup and corn bread in. "Quinn could have taken you to Mrs. Pearson down the mountain if he'd had a mind to. He doesn't have to let you stay here. Mrs. Pearson would be glad of the company." He glanced at her and grinned at her perplexed expression. "He's been watching you lately. Sees the way you sew up his shirts and make curtains and patch pillows. It's new to him, having a woman about. He has a hard time with change."

"Don't we all?" Amanda said softly, remembering how clear her own life had been until that tragic night. But it was nice to know that Quinn had been watching her. Certainly she'd been watching him. And this morning, everything seemed to have changed between them. "When will it thaw?" she asked, and now she was dreading it, not anticipating it. She didn't want to leave Ricochet. Or Quinn.

Harry shrugged. "Hard to tell. Days. Weeks. This is raw mountain country. Can't predict a chinook. Plenty think they can, though," he added, and proceeded to tell her about a Blackfoot who predicted the weather with jars of bear grease.

She was much calmer, but still sad when Quinn finally came back inside.

He spared her a glance before he shucked his coat, washed his hands and brawny forearms and dried them on a towel.

He didn't say anything to her, and Harry, sensing the atmosphere, made himself scarce after he'd poured two cups of coffee for them.

"Are you all right?" he asked her after a minute, staring down at her bent head.

"Sure." She forced a smile. "He was so little, Quinn." She stopped when her voice broke and lowered her eyes to the table. "I guess you think I'm a wimp."

"Not really." Without taking time to think about the consequences, his lean hands pulled her up by the arms, holding her in front of him so that her eyes were on a level with his deep blue, plaid flannel shirt. The sleeves were rolled up, and it was open at the throat, where thick, dark hair curled out of it. He looked and smelled fiercely masculine and Amanda's knees weakened at the unexpected proximity. His big hands bit into her soft flesh, and she wondered absently if he realized just how strong he was.

The feel of him so close was new and terribly exciting, especially since he'd reached for her for the first time. She didn't know what to expect, and her heart was going wild. She lowered her eyes to his throat. His pulse was

jumping and she stared at it curiously, only half aware of
his hold and the sudden increase of his breathing.

He was having hell just getting a breath. The scent
of her was in his nostrils, drowning him. Woman smell.
Sweet and warm. His teeth clenched. It was bad enough
having to look at her, but this close, she made his blood
run hot and wild as it hadn't since he was a young man.
He didn't know what he was doing, but the need for her
had haunted him for days. He wanted so badly to kiss her,
the way she'd kissed him the day before, but in a different
way. He wasn't quite sure how to go about it.

"You smell of flowers," he said roughly.

That was an interesting comment from a nonpoetic
man. She smiled a little to herself. "It's my shampoo,"
she murmured.

He drew in a steadying breath. "You don't wear your
hair down at all, do you?"

"Just at night," she replied, aware that his face was
closer than it had been, because she could feel his breath
on her forehead. He was so tall and overwhelming this
close. He made her feel tiny and very feminine.

"I'm sorry about the calf, Amanda," he said. "We lose
a few every winter. It's part of ranching."

The shock of her name on his lips made her lift her
head. She stared up at him curiously, searching his dark,
quiet eyes. "I suppose so. I shouldn't have gotten so upset,
though. I guess men don't react to things the way women
do."

"You don't know what kind of man I am," he replied.
His hands felt vaguely tremulous. He wondered if she
knew the effect she had on him. "As it happens, I get
attached to the damned things, too." He sighed heav-

ily. "Little things don't have much choice in this world. They're at the mercy of everything and everybody."

Her eyes softened as they searched his. He sounded different when he spoke that way. Vulnerable. Almost tender. And so alone.

"You aren't really afraid of me, are you?" he asked, as if the thought was actually painful.

She grimaced. "No. Of course not. I was ashamed of what I'd done, and a little nervous of the way you reacted to it, that's all. I know you wouldn't hurt me." She drew in a soft breath. "I know you resent having me here," she confessed. "I resented having to depend on you for shelter. But the snow will melt soon, and I'll leave."

"I thought you'd had lovers," he confessed quietly. "The way you acted…well, it just made all those suspicions worse. I took you at face value."

Amanda smiled. "It was all put-on. I don't even know why I did it. I guess I was trying to live down to your image of me."

He loved the sensation her sultry black eyes aroused in him. Unconsciously his hands tightened on her arms. "You haven't had a man, ever?" he asked huskily.

The odd shadow of dusky color along his cheekbones fascinated her. She wondered about the embarrassment asking the question had caused. "No. Not ever," she stammered.

"The way you look?" he asked, his eyes eloquent.

"What do you mean, the way I look?" she said, bristling.

"You know you're beautiful," he returned. His eyes darkened. "A woman who looks like you do could have her pick of men."

"Maybe," she agreed without conceit. "But I've never wanted a man in my life, to be dominated by a man. I've made my own way in the world. I'm a musician," she told him, because that didn't give away very much. "I support myself by playing a keyboard."

"Yes, Elliot told me. I've heard you play for him. You're good." He felt his heartbeat increasing as he looked at her. She smelled so good. He looked down at her mouth and remembered how it had felt for those few seconds when he'd given in to her playful kiss. Would she let him do it? He knew so little about those subtle messages women were supposed to send out when they wanted a man's lovemaking. He couldn't read Amanda's eyes. But her lips were parted and her breath was coming rather fast from between them. Her face was flushed, but that could have been from the cold.

She gazed up into his eyes and couldn't look away. He wasn't handsome. His face really seemed as if it had been chipped away from the side of the Rockies, all craggy angles and hard lines. His mouth was thin and faintly cruel looking. She wondered if it would feel as hard as it looked if he was in control, dominating her lips. It had been different when she'd kissed him….

"What are you thinking?" he asked huskily, because her eyes were quite frankly on his mouth.

"I…was wondering," she whispered hesitantly, "how hard your mouth would be if you kissed me."

His heart stopped and then began to slam against his chest. "Don't you know already?" he asked, his voice deeper, harsher. "You kissed me."

"Not…properly."

He wondered what she meant by properly. His wife had

only kissed him when she had to, and only in the very beginning of their courtship. She always pushed him away
and murmured something about mussing her makeup.
He couldn't remember one time when he'd kissed anyone with passion, or when he'd ever been kissed by anyone else like that.

His warm, rough hands let go of her arms and came up
to frame her soft oval face. His breath shuddered out of
his chest when she didn't protest as he bent his dark head.

"Show me what you mean...by properly," he whispered.

He had to know, she thought dizzily. But his lips
touched hers and she tasted the wind and the sun on
them. Her hands clenched the thick flannel shirt and she
resisted searching for buttons, because she wanted very
much to touch that thicket of black, curling hair that covered his broad chest. She went on her tiptoes and pushed
her mouth against his, the force of the action parting his
lips as well as her own, and she felt him stiffen and heard
him groan as their open mouths met.

She dropped back onto her feet, her wide, curious eyes
meeting his stormy ones.

"Like that?" he whispered gruffly, bending to repeat
the action with his own mouth. "I've never done it...with
my mouth open," he said, biting off the words against
her open lips.

She couldn't believe he'd said that. She couldn't believe, either, the sensations rippling down to her toes
when she gave in to the force of his ardor and let him kiss
her that way, his mouth rough and demanding as one big
hand slid to the back of her head to press her even closer.

A soft sound passed her lips, a faint moan, because

she couldn't get close enough to him. Her breasts were flattened against his hard chest, and she felt his heartbeat against them. But she wanted to be closer than that, enveloped, crushed to him.

"Did I hurt you?" he asked in a shaky whisper that touched her lips.

"What?" she whispered back dizzily.

"You made a sound."

Her eyes searched his, her own misty and half closed and rapt. "I moaned," she whispered. Her nails stroked him through the shirt and she liked the faint tautness of his body as he reacted to it. "I like being kissed like that." She rubbed her forehead against him, smelling soap and detergent and pure man. "Could we take your shirt off?" she whispered.

Her hands were driving him nuts, and he was wondering the same thing himself. But somewhere in the back of his mind he remembered that Harry was around, and that it might look compromising if he let her touch him that way. In fact, it might get compromising, because he felt his body harden in a way it hadn't since his marriage. And because it made him vulnerable and he didn't want her to feel it, he took her gently by the arms and moved her away from him with a muffled curse.

"Harry," he said, his breath coming deep and rough.

She colored. "Oh, yes." She moved back, her eyes a little wild.

"You don't have to look so threatened. I won't do it again," he said, misunderstanding her retreat. Had he frightened her again?

"Oh, it's not that. You didn't frighten me." She low-

ered her eyes to the floor. "I'm just wondering if you'll
think I'm easy...."

He scowled. "Easy?"

"I don't usually come on to men," she said softly. "And
I've never asked anybody to take his shirt off before."
She glanced up at him, fascinated by the expression on
his face. "Well, I haven't," she said belligerently. "And
you don't have to worry; I won't throw myself at you
anymore, either. I just got carried away in the heat of
the moment...."

His eyebrows arched. None of what she was saying
made sense. "Like you did yesterday?" he mused, liking
the color that came and went in her face. "I did accuse
you of throwing yourself at me," he said on a long sigh.

"Yes. You seem to think I'm some sort of liberated
sex maniac."

His lips curled involuntarily. "Are you?" he asked, and
sounded interested.

She stamped her foot. "Stop that. I don't want to stay
here anymore!"

"I'm not sure it's a good idea myself," he mused,
watching her eyes glitter with rage. God, she was pretty!
"I mean, if you tried to seduce me, things could get
sticky."

The red in her cheeks got darker. "I don't have any
plans to seduce you."

"Well, if you get any, you'd better tell me in advance,"
he said, pulling a cigarette from his shirt pocket. "Just so
I can be prepared to fight you off."

That dry drawl confused her. Suddenly he was a different man, full of male arrogance and amusement. Things
had shifted between them during that long, hard kiss. The

distance had shortened, and he was looking at her with an expression she couldn't quite understand.

"How did you get to the age you are without winding up in someone's bed?" Quinn asked then. He'd wondered at her shyness with him and then at the way she blushed all the time. He didn't know much about women, but he wanted to know everything about her.

Amanda wrapped her arms around herself and shrugged. When he lit his cigarette and still stood there waiting for an answer, she gave in and replied. "I couldn't give up control," she said simply. "All my life I'd been dominated and pushed around by my father. Giving in to a man seemed like throwing away my rights as a person. Especially giving in to a man in bed," she stammered, averting her gaze. "I don't think there's anyplace in the world where a man is more the master than in a bedroom, despite all the liberation and freedom of modern life."

"And you think that women should dominate there."

She looked up. "Well, not dominate." She hesitated. "But a woman shouldn't be used just because she's a woman."

His thin mouth curled slightly. "Neither should a man."

"I wasn't using you," she shot back.

"Did I accuse you?" he returned innocently.

She swallowed. "No, I guess not." She folded her arms over her breasts, wincing because the tips were hard and unexpectedly tender.

"That hardness means you feel desire," he said, grinning when she gaped and then glared at him. She made him feel about ten feet tall. "I read this book about sex," he continued. "It didn't make much sense to me at the time, but it's beginning to."

"I am not available as a living model for sex education!"

He shrugged. "Suit yourself. But it's a hell of a loss to my education."

"You don't need educating," she muttered. "You were married."

He nodded. "Sure I was." He pursed his lips and let his eyes run lazily over her body. "Except that she never wanted me, before or after I married her."

Amanda's lips parted. "Oh, Quinn," she said softly. "I'm sorry."

"So was I, at the time." He shook his head. "I used to wonder at first why she pulled back every time I kissed her. I guess she was suffering it until she could get me to put the ring on her finger. Up until then, I thought it was her scruples that kept me at arm's length. But she never had many morals." He stared at Amanda curiously, surprised at how easy it was to tell her things he'd never shared with another human being. "After I found out what she really was, I couldn't have cared less about sharing her bed."

"No, I don't suppose so," she agreed.

He lifted the cigarette to his lips and his eyes narrowed as he studied her. "Elliot's almost thirteen," he said. "He's been my whole life. I've taken care of him and done for him. He knows there's no blood tie between us, but I love him and he loves me. In all the important ways, I'm his father and he's my son."

"He loves you very much," she said with a smile. "He talks about you all the time."

"He's a good boy." He moved a little closer, noticing how she tensed when he came close. He liked that reaction a lot. It told him that she was aware of him, but shy and reticent. "You don't have men," he said softly. "Well, I don't have women."

"Not for...a few months?" she stammered, because she couldn't imagine that he was telling the truth.

He shrugged his powerful shoulders. "Well, not for a bit longer than that. Not much opportunity up here. And I can't go off and leave Elliot while I tomcat around town. It's been a bit longer than thirteen years."

"A bit?"

He looked down at her with a curious, mocking smile. "When I was a boy, I didn't know how to get girls. I was big and clumsy and shy, so it was the other boys who scored." He took another draw, a slightly jerky one, from his cigarette. "I still have the same problem around most women. It's not so much hatred as a lack of ability, and shyness. I don't know how to come on to a woman," he confessed with a faint smile.

Amanda felt as if the sun had just come out. She smiled back. "Don't you, really?" she asked softly. "I thought it was just that you found me lacking, or that I wasn't woman enough to interest you."

He could have laughed out loud at that assumption. "Is that why you called me Goody Two Shoes?" he asked pleasantly.

She laughed softly. "Well, that was sort of sour grapes." She lowered her eyes to his chest. "It hurt my feelings that you thought I didn't have any morals, when I'd never made one single move toward any other man in my whole life."

He felt warm all over from that shy confession. It took down the final brick in his wall of reserve. She wasn't like any woman he'd ever known. "I'm glad to know that. But you and I have more in common than a lack of technique," he said, hesitating.

"We do?" she asked. Her soft eyes held his. "What do you mean?"

He turned and deliberately put out his cigarette in the ashtray on the table beside them. He straightened and looked down at her speculatively for a few seconds before he went for broke. "Well, what I mean, Amanda," he replied finally, "is that you aren't the only virgin on the place."

CHAPTER SIX

"I DIDN'T HEAR THAT," Amanda said, because she knew she hadn't. Quinn Sutton couldn't have told her that he was a virgin.

"Yes, you did," he replied. "And it's not all that far-fetched. Old McNaber down the hill's never had a woman, and he's in his seventies. There are all sorts of reasons why men don't get experience. Morals, scruples, isolation, or even plain shyness. Just like women," he added with a meaningful look at Amanda. "I couldn't go to bed with somebody just to say I'd had sex. I'd have to care about her, want her, and I'd want her to care about me. There are idealistic people all over the world who never find that particular combination, so they stay celibate. And really, I think that people who sleep around indiscriminately are in the minority even in these liberated times. Only a fool takes that sort of risk with the health dangers what they are."

"Yes, I know." She watched him with fascinated eyes. "Haven't you ever…wanted to?" she asked.

"Well, that's the problem, you see," he replied, his dark eyes steady on her face.

"What is?"

"I have…wanted to. With you."

She leaned back against the counter, just to make sure she didn't fall down. "With me?"

"That first night you came here, when I was so sick, and your hair drifted down over my naked chest. I shivered, and you thought it was with fever," he mused. "It was a fever, all right, but it didn't have anything to do with the virus."

Her fingers clenched the counter. She'd wondered about his violent reaction at the time, but it seemed so unlikely that a cold man like Quinn Sutton would feel that way about a woman. He was human, she thought absently, watching him.

"That's why I've given you such a hard time," he confessed with narrowed, quiet eyes. "I don't know how to handle desire. I can't throw you over my shoulder and carry you upstairs, not with Elliot and Harry around, even if you were the kind of woman I thought at first you were. The fact that you're as innocent as I am only makes it more complicated."

She looked at him with new understanding, as fascinated by him as he seemed to be by her. He wasn't that bad looking, she mused. And he was terribly strong, and sexy in an earthy kind of way. She especially liked his eyes. They were much more expressive than that poker face.

"Fortunately for you, I'm kind of shy, too," she murmured.

"Except when you're asking men to take their clothes off," Quinn said, nodding.

Harry froze in the doorway with one foot lifted while Amanda gaped at him and turned red.

"Put your foot down and get busy," Quinn muttered irritably. "Why were you standing there?"

"I was getting educated." Harry chuckled. "I didn't know Amanda asked people to take their clothes off!"

"Only me," Quinn said, defending her. "And just my shirt. She's not a bad girl."

"Will you stop!" Amanda buried her face in her hands. "Go away!"

"I can't. I live here," Quinn pointed out. "Did I smell brandy on your breath?" he asked suddenly.

Harry grimaced even as Amanda's eyes widened. "Well, yes you do," he confessed. "She was upset and crying and all…"

"How much did you give her?" Quinn persisted.

"Only a few drops," Harry promised. "In her coffee, to calm her."

"Harry, how could you!" Amanda laughed. The coffee had tasted funny, but she'd been too upset to wonder why.

"Sorry," Harry murmured dryly. "But it seemed the thing to do."

"It backfired," Quinn murmured and actually smiled.

"You stop that!" Amanda told him. She sat down at the table. "I'm not tipsy. Harry, I'll peel those apples for the pie if I can have a knife."

"Let me get out of the room first, if you please," Quinn said, glancing at her dryly. "I saw her measuring my back for a place to put it."

"I almost never stab men with knives," she promised impishly.

He chuckled. He reached for his hat and slanted it over his brow, buttoning his old shepherd's coat because it was snowing outside again.

Amanda looked past him, the reason for all the upset coming back now as she calmed down. Her expression became sad.

"If you stay busy, you won't think about it so much," Quinn said quietly. "It's part of life, you know."

"I know." She managed a smile. "I'm fine. Despite Harry," she added with a chuckle, watching Harry squirm before he grinned back.

Quinn's dark eyes met hers warmly for longer than he meant, so that she blushed. He tore his eyes away finally, and went outside.

Harry didn't say anything, but his smile was speculative.

Elliot came home from school and persuaded Amanda to get out the keyboard and give him some more pointers. He admitted that he'd been bragging about her to his classmates and that she was a professional musician.

"Where do you play, Amanda?" Elliot asked curiously, and he stared at her with open puzzlement. "You look so familiar somehow."

She sat very still on the sofa and tried to stay calm. Elliot had already told her that he liked rock music and she knew Quinn had hidden his tapes. If there was a tape in his collection by Desperado, it would have her picture on the cover along with that of her group.

"Do I really look familiar?" she asked with a smile. "Maybe I just have that kind of face."

"Have you played with orchestras?" he persisted.

"No. Just by myself, sort of. In nightclubs," she improvised. Well, she had once sang in a nightclub, to fill in for a friend. "Mostly I do backup. You know, I play with groups for people who make tapes and records."

"Wow!" he exclaimed. "I guess you know a lot of famous singers and musicians?"

"A few," she agreed.

"Where do you work?"

"In New York City, in Nashville," she told him. "All over. Wherever I can find work."

He ran his fingers up and down the keyboard. "How did you ever wind up here?"

"I needed a rest," she said. "My aunt is…a friend of Mr. Durning. She asked him if I could borrow the cabin, and he said it was all right. I had to get away from work for a while."

"This doesn't bother you, does it? Teaching me to play, I mean?" he asked and looked concerned.

"No, Elliot, it doesn't bother me. I'm enjoying it." She ran a scale and taught it to him, then showed him the cadences of the chords that went with it.

"It's so complicated," he moaned.

"Of course it is. Music is an art form, and it's complex. But once you learn these basics, you can do anything with a chord. For instance…"

She played a tonic chord, then made an impromptu song from its subdominant and seventh chords and the second inversion of them. Elliot watched, fascinated.

"I guess you've studied for years," he said with a sigh.

"Yes, I have, and I'm still learning," she said. "But I love it more than anything. Music has been my whole life."

"No wonder you're so good at it."

She smiled. "Thanks, Elliot."

"Well, I'd better get my chores done before supper,"

he said, sighing. He handed Amanda the keyboard. "See you later."

She nodded. He went out. Harry was feeding the two calves that were still alive, so presumably he'd tell Elliot about the one that had died. Amanda hadn't had the heart to talk about it.

Her fingers ran over the keyboard lovingly and she began to play a song that her group had recorded two years back, a sad, dreamy ballad about hopeless love that had won them a Grammy. She sang it softly, her pure, sweet voice haunting in the silence of the room as she tried to sing for the first time in weeks.

"Elliot, for Pete's sake, turn that radio down, I'm on the telephone!" came a pleading voice from the back of the house.

She stopped immediately, flushing. She hadn't realized that Harry had come back inside. Thank God he hadn't seen her, or he might have asked some pertinent questions. She put the keyboard down and went to the kitchen, relieved that her singing voice was back to normal again.

Elliot was morose at the supper table. He'd heard about the calf and he'd been as depressed as Amanda had. Quinn didn't look all that happy himself. They all picked at the delicious chili Harry had whipped up; nobody had much of an appetite.

After they finished, Elliot did his homework while Amanda put the last stitches into a chair cover she was making for the living room. Quinn had gone off to do his paperwork and Harry was making bread for the next day.

It was a long, lazy night. Elliot went to bed at eight-thirty and not much later Harry went to his room.

Amanda wanted to wait for Quinn to come back, but

something in her was afraid of the new way he looked at her. He was much more a threat now than he had been before, because she was looking at him with new and interested eyes. She was drawn to him more than ever. But he didn't know who she really was, and she couldn't tell him. If she were persuaded into any kind of close relationship with him, it could lead to disaster.

So when Elliot went to bed, so did Amanda. She sat at the dresser and let down her long hair, brushing it with slow, lazy strokes, when there was a knock at the door.

She was afraid that it might be Quinn, and she hesitated. But surely he wouldn't make any advances toward her unless she showed that she wanted them. Of course he wouldn't.

She opened the door, but it wasn't Quinn. It was Elliot. And as he stared at her, wheels moved and gears clicked in his young mind. She was wearing a long granny gown in a deep beige, a shade that was too much like the color of the leather dress she wore onstage. With her hair loose and the color of the gown, Elliot made the connection he hadn't made the first time he saw her hair down.

"Yes?" she prompted, puzzled by the way he was looking at her. "Is something wrong, Elliot?"

"Uh, no," he stammered. "Uh, I forgot to say goodnight. Good night!" He grinned.

He turned, red faced, and beat a hasty retreat, but not to his own room. He went to his father's and searched quickly through the hidden tapes until he found the one he wanted. He held it up, staring blankly at the cover. There were four men who looked like vicious bikers surrounding a beautiful woman in buckskin with long, elegant, blond hair. The group was one of his favorites—

Desperado. And the woman was Mandy. Amanda. His Amanda. He caught his breath. Boy, would she be in for it if his dad found out who she was! He put the tape into his pocket, feeling guilty for taking it when Quinn had told him not to. But these were desperate circumstances. He had to protect Amanda until he could figure out how to tell her that he knew the truth. Meanwhile, having her in the same house with him was sheer undiluted heaven! Imagine, a singing star that famous in his house. If only he could tell the guys! But that was too risky, because it might get back to Dad. He sighed. Just his luck, to find a rare jewel and have to hide it to keep someone from stealing it. He closed the door to Quinn's bedroom and went quickly back to his own.

Amanda slept soundly, almost missing breakfast. Outside, the sky looked blue for the first time in days, and she noticed that the snow had stopped.

"Chinook's coming," Harry said with a grin. "I knew it would."

Quinn's dark eyes studied Amanda's face. "Well, it will be a few days before they get the power lines back up again," he muttered. "So don't get in an uproar about it."

"I'm not in an uproar," Harry returned with a frown. "I just thought it was nice that we'll be able to get off the mountain and lay in some more supplies. I'm getting tired of beef. I want a chicken."

"So do I!" Elliot said fervently. "Or bear, or beaver or moose, anything but beef!"

Quinn glared at both of them. "Beef pays the bills around here," he reminded them.

They looked so guilty that Amanda almost laughed out loud.

"I'm sorry, Dad," Elliot sighed. "I'll tell my stomach to shut up about it."

Quinn's hard face relaxed. "It's all right. I wouldn't mind a chicken stew, myself."

"That's the spirit," Elliot said. "What are we going to do today? It's Saturday," he pointed out. "No school."

"You could go out with me and help me feed cattle," Quinn said.

"I'll stay here and help Harry," Amanda said, too quickly.

Quinn's dark eyes searched hers. "Harry can manage by himself. You can come with me and Elliot."

"You'll enjoy it," Elliot assured her. "It's a lot of fun. The cattle see us and come running. Well, as well as they can run in several feet of snow," he amended.

It was fun, too. Amanda sat on the back of the sled with Elliot and helped push the bales of hay off. Quinn cut the strings so the cattle could get to the hay. They did come running, reminding Amanda so vividly of women at a sale that she laughed helplessly until the others had to be told why she was laughing.

They came back from the outing in a new kind of harmony, and for the first time, Amanda understood what it felt like to be part of a family. She looked at Quinn and wondered how it would be if she never had to leave here, if she could stay with him and Elliot and Harry forever.

But she couldn't, she told herself firmly. She had to remember that this was a vacation, with the real world just outside the door.

Elliot was allowed to stay up later on Saturday night, so they watched a science-fiction movie together while Quinn grumbled over paperwork. The next morning they

went to church on the sled, Amanda in the one skirt and
blouse she'd packed, trying not to look too conspicuous
as Quinn's few neighbors carefully scrutinized her.

When they got back home, she was all but shaking. She
felt uncomfortable living with him, as if she really was a
fallen woman now. He cornered her in the kitchen while
she was washing dishes to find out why she was so quiet.

"I didn't think about the way people would react if you
went with us this morning," he said quietly. "I wouldn't
have subjected you to that if I'd just thought."

"It's okay," she said, touched by his concern. "Really.
It was just a little uncomfortable."

He sighed, searching her face with narrowed eyes.
"Most people around here know how I feel about women,"
he said bluntly. "That was why you attracted so much attention. People get funny ideas about woman haters who
take in beautiful blondes."

"I'm not beautiful," she stammered shyly.

He stepped toward her, towering over her in his dress
slacks and good white shirt and sedate gray tie. He looked
handsome and strong and very masculine. She liked the
spicy cologne he wore. "You're beautiful, all right," he
murmured. His big hand touched her cheek, sliding down
it slowly, his thumb brushing with soft abrasion over her
full mouth.

Her breath caught as she looked up into his dark, soft
eyes. "Quinn?" she whispered.

He drew her hands out of the warm, soapy water, still
holding her gaze, and dried them on a dishcloth. Then he
guided them, first one, then the other, up to his shoulders.

"Hold me," he whispered as his hands smoothed over

her waist and brought her gently to him. "I want to kiss you."

She shivered from the sensuality in that soft whisper, lifting her face willingly.

He bent, brushing his mouth lazily over hers. "Isn't this how we did it before?" he breathed, parting his lips as they touched hers. "I like the way it feels to kiss you like this. My spine tingles."

"So…does mine." She slid her hands hesitantly into the thick, cool strands of hair at his nape and she went on tiptoe to give him better access to her mouth.

He accepted the invitation with quiet satisfaction, his mouth growing slowly rougher and hungrier as it fed on hers. He made a sound under his breath and all at once he bent, lifting her clear off the floor in a bearish embrace. His mouth bit hers, parting her lips, and she clung to him, moaning as the fever burned in her, too.

He let her go at once when Elliot called, "What?" from the living room. "Amanda, did you say something?"

"No… No, Elliot," she managed in a tone pitched a little higher than normal. Her answer appeared to satisfy him, because he didn't ask again. Harry was outside, but he probably wouldn't stay there long.

She looked up at Quinn, surprised by the intent stare he was giving her. He liked the way she looked, her face flushed, her mouth swollen from his kisses, her eyes wide and soft and faintly misty with emotion.

"I'd better get out of here," he said hesitantly.

"Yes." She touched her lips with her fingers and he watched the movement closely.

"Did I hurt your mouth?" he asked quietly.

She shook her head. "No. Oh, no, not at all," she said huskily.

Quinn nodded and sighed heavily. He smiled faintly and then turned and went back into the living room without another word.

It was a long afternoon, made longer by the strain Amanda felt being close to him. She found her eyes meeting his across the room and every time she flushed from the intensity of the look. Her body was hungry for him, and she imagined the reverse was equally true. He watched her openly now, with smoldering hunger in his eyes. They had a light supper and watched a little more television. But when Harry went to his room and Elliot called good-night and went up to bed, Amanda weakly stayed behind.

Quinn finished his cigarette with the air of a man who had all night, and then got up and reached for Amanda, lifting her into his arms.

"There's nothing to be afraid of," he said quietly, searching her wide, apprehensive eyes as he turned and carried her into his study and closed the door behind them.

It was a fiercely masculine room. The furniture was dark wood with leather seats, the remnants of more prosperous times. He sat down in a big leather armchair with Amanda in his lap.

"It's private here," he explained. His hand moved one of hers to his shirt and pressed it there, over the tie. "Even Elliot doesn't come in when the door's shut. Do you still want to take my shirt off?" he asked with a warm smile.

Amanda sighed. "Well, yes," she stammered. "I haven't done this sort of thing before...."

"Neither have I, honey," he murmured dryly. "I guess we'll learn it together, won't we?"

She smiled into his dark eyes. "That sounds nice." She lowered her eyes to the tie and frowned when she saw how it was knotted.

"Here, I'll do it." He whipped it off with the ease of long practice and unlooped the collar button. "Now. You do the rest," he said deeply, and looked like a man anticipating heaven.

Her fingers, so adept on a keyboard, fumbled like two left feet while she worried buttons out of buttonholes. He was heavily muscled, tanned skin under a mass of thick, curling black hair. She remembered how it had looked that first night she'd been here, and how her hands had longed to touch it. Odd, because she'd never cared what was under a man's shirt before.

She pressed her hands flat against him, fascinated by the quick thunder of his heartbeat under them. She looked up into dark, quiet eyes.

"Shy?" he murmured dryly.

"A little. I always used to run a mile when men got this close."

The smile faded. His big hand covered hers, pressing them closer against him. "Wasn't there ever anyone you wanted?"

She shook her head. "The men I'm used to aren't like you. They're mostly rounders with a line a mile long. Everything is just casual to them, like eating mints." She flushed a little. "Intimacy isn't a casual thing to me."

"Or to me." His chest rose and fell heavily. He touched her bright head. "Now will you take your hair down,

Amanda?" he asked gently. "I've dreamed about it for days."

Amanda smiled softly. "Have you, really? It's something of a nuisance to wash and dry, but I've gotten sort of used to it." She unbraided it and let it down, enchanted by Quinn's rapt fascination with it. His big hands tangled in it, as if he loved the feel of it. He brought his face down and kissed her neck through it, drawing her against his bare chest.

"It smells like flowers," he whispered.

"I washed it before church this morning," she replied. "Elliot loaned me his blow-dryer but it still took all of thirty minutes to get the dampness out." She relaxed with a sigh, nuzzling against his shoulder while her fingers tugged at the thick hair on his chest. "You feel furry. Like a bear," she murmured.

"You feel silky," he said against her hair. With his hand, Quinn tilted her face up to his and slid his mouth onto hers in the silent room. He groaned softly as her lips parted under his. His arms lifted and turned her, wrapped her up, so that her breasts were lying on his chest and her cheek was pressed against his shoulder by the force of the kiss.

He tasted of smoke and coffee, and if his mouth wasn't expert, it was certainly ardent. She loved kissing him. She curled her arms around his neck and turned a little more, hesitating when she felt the sudden stark arousal of his body.

Her eyes opened, looking straight into his, and she colored.

"I'm sorry," he murmured, starting to shift her, as if his physical reaction to her embarrassed him.

"No, Quinn," she said, resisting gently, holding his gaze as she relaxed into him, shivering a little. "There's nothing to apologize for. I…like knowing you want me," she whispered, lowering her eyes to his mouth. "It just takes a little getting used to. I've never let anyone hold me like this."

His chest swelled with that confession. His cheek rested on her hair as he settled into the chair and relaxed himself, taking her weight easily. "I'm glad about that," he said. "But it isn't just physical with me. I wanted you to know."

She smiled against his shoulder. "It isn't just physical with me, either." She touched his hard face, her fingers moving over his mouth, loving the feel of it, the smell of his body, the warmth and strength of it. "Isn't it incredible?" She laughed softly. "I mean, at our ages, to be so green…"

He laughed, too. It would have stung to have heard that from any other woman, but Amanda was different. "I've never minded less being inexperienced," he murmured.

"Oh, neither have I." She sighed contentedly.

His big hand smoothed over her shoulder and down her back to her waist and onto her rib cage. He wanted very much to run it over her soft breast, but that might be too much too soon, so he hesitated.

Amanda smiled to herself. She caught his fingers and, lifting her face to his eyes, deliberately pulled them onto her breast, her lips parting at the sensation that steely warmth imparted. The nipple hardened and she caught her breath as Quinn's thumb rubbed against it.

"Have you ever seen a woman…without her top on?"

she whispered, her long hair gloriously tangled around her face and shoulders.

"No," he replied softly. "Only in pictures." His dark eyes watched the softness his fingers were tracing. "I want to see you that way. I want to touch your skin... like this."

She drew his hand to the buttons of her blouse and lay quietly against him, watching his hard face as he loosened the buttons and pulled the fabric aside. The bra seemed to fascinate him. He frowned, trying to decide how it opened.

"It's a front catch," she whispered. She shifted a little, and found the catch. Her fingers trembled as she loosened it. Then, watching him, she carefully peeled it away from the high, taut throb of her breasts and watched him catch his breath.

"My God," he breathed reverently. He touched her with trembling fingers, his eyes on the deep mauve of her nipples against the soft pink thrust of flesh, his body taut with sudden aching longing. "My God, I've never seen anything so beautiful."

He made her feel incredibly feminine. She closed her eyes and arched back against his encircling arm, moaning softly.

"Kiss me...there," she whispered huskily, aching for his mouth.

"Amanda..." He bent, delighting in her femininity, the obvious rapt fascination of the first time in her actions so that even if he hadn't suspected her innocence he would have now. His lips brushed over the silky flesh, and his hands lifted her to him, arched her even more. She tasted of flower petals, softly trembling under his warm, ardent mouth, her breath jerking past her parted lips as she lay with her eyes closed, lost in him.

"It's so sweet, Quinn," she whispered brokenly.

His lips brushed up her body to her throat, her chin, and then they locked against her mouth. He turned her slowly, so that her soft breasts lay against the muted thunder of his hair-roughened chest. He felt her shiver before her arms slid around his neck and she deliberately pressed closer, drawing herself against him and moaning.

"Am I hurting you?" he asked huskily, his mouth poised just above hers, a faint tremor in his arms. "Amanda, am I hurting you?"

"No." She opened her eyes and they were like black pools, soft and deep and quiet. With her blond hair waving at her temples, her cheeks, her shoulders, she was so beautiful that Quinn's breath caught.

He sat just looking at her, indulging his hunger for the sight of her soft breasts, her lovely face. She lay quietly in his arms without a protest, barely breathing as the spell worked on them.

"I'll live on this the rest of my life," he said roughly, his voice deep and soft in the room, with only an occasional crackle from the burning fire in the potbellied stove to break the silence.

"So will I," she whispered. She reached up to his face, touching it in silence, adoring its strength. "We shouldn't have done this," she said miserably. "It will make it...so much more difficult, when I have to leave. The thaw...!"

His fingers pressed against her lips. "One day at a time," he said. "Even if you leave, you aren't getting away from me completely. I won't let go. Not ever."

Tears stung her eyes. The surplus of emotion sent them

streaming down her cheeks and Quinn caught his breath, brushing them away with his long fingers.

"Why?" he whispered.

"Nobody ever wanted to keep me before," she explained with a watery smile. "I've always felt like an extra person in the world."

He found that hard to imagine, as beautiful as she was. Perhaps her reticence made her of less value to sophisticated men, but not to him. He found her a pearl beyond price.

"You're not an extra person in my world," he replied. "You fit."

She sighed and nuzzled against him, closing her eyes as she drank in the exquisite pleasure of skin against skin, feeling his heart beat against her breasts. She shivered.

"Are you cold?" he asked.

"No. It's...so wonderful, feeling you like this," she whispered. "Quinn?"

He eased her back in his arm and watched her, understanding as she didn't seem to understand what was wrong.

His big, warm hand covered her breast, gently caressing it. "It's desire," he whispered softly. "You want me."

"Yes," she whispered.

"You can't have me. Not like this. Not in any honorable way." He sighed heavily and lifted her against him to hold her, very hard. "Now hold on, real tight. It will pass."

She shivered helplessly, drowning in the warmth of his body, in its heat against her breasts. But he was right. Slowly the ache began to ease away and her body stilled with a huge sigh.

"How do you know so much when you've…when you've never…?"

"I told you, I read a book. Several books." He chuckled, the laughter rippling over her sensitive breasts. "But, my God, reading was never like this!"

She laughed, too, and impishly bit his shoulder right through the cloth.

Then he shivered. "Don't," he said huskily.

She lifted her head, fascinated by the expression on his face. "Do you like it?" she asked hesitantly.

"Yes, I like it," he said with a rueful smile. "All too much." He gazed down at her bareness and his eyes darkened. "I like looking at your breasts, too, but I think we'd better stop this while we can."

He tugged the bra back around her with a grimace and hooked the complicated catch. He deftly buttoned her blouse up to her throat, his eyes twinkling as they met hers.

"Disappointed?" he murmured. "So am I. I have these dreams every night of pillowing you on your delicious hair while we make love until you cry out."

She could picture that, too, and her breath lodged in her throat as she searched his dark eyes. His body, bare and moving softly over hers on white sheets, his face above her…

She moaned.

"Oh, I want it, too," he whispered, touching his mouth with exquisite tenderness to hers. "You in my bed, your arms around me, the mattress moving under us." He lifted his head, breathing unsteadily. "I might have to hurt you a little at first," he said gruffly. "You understand?"

"Yes." She smoothed his shirt, absently drawing it back together and fastening the buttons with a sense of possession. "But only a little, and I could bear it for what would come afterward," she said, looking up. "Because you'd pleasure me then."

"My God, would I," he whispered. "Pleasure you until you were exhausted." He framed her face in his hands and kissed her gently. "Please go to bed, Amanda, before I double over and start screaming."

She smiled against his mouth and let him put her on her feet. She laughed when she swayed and he had to catch her.

"See what you do to me?" she mused. "Make me dizzy."

"Not half as dizzy as you make me." He smoothed down her long hair, his eyes adoring it. "Pretty little thing," he murmured.

"I'm glad you like me," she replied. "I'll do my best to stay this way for the next fifty years or so, with a few minor wrinkles."

"You'll be beautiful to me when you're an old lady. Good night."

She moved away from him with flattering reluctance, her dark eyes teasing his. "Are you sure you haven't done this before?" she asked with a narrow gaze. "You're awfully good at it for a beginner."

"That makes two of us," he returned dryly.

She liked the way he looked, with his hair mussed and his thin mouth swollen from her kisses, and his shirt disheveled. It made her feel a new kind of pride that she could disarrange him so nicely. After one long glance, she opened the door and went out.

"Lock your door," he whispered.

She laughed delightedly. "No, you lock yours the way you did the other night."

He shifted uncomfortably. "That was a low blow. I'm sorry."

"Oh, I was flattered," she corrected. "I've never felt so dangerous in all my life. I wish I had one of those long, black silk negligees…"

"Will you get out of here?" he asked pleasantly. "I think I did mention the urge to throw you on the floor and ravish you?"

"With Elliot right upstairs? Fie, sir, think of my reputation."

"I'm trying to, if you'll just go to bed!"

"Very well, if I must." She started up the staircase, her black eyes dancing as they met his. She tossed her hair back and smiled at him. "Good night, Quinn."

"Good night, Amanda. Sweet dreams."

"They'll be sweet from now on," she agreed. She turned reluctantly and went up the staircase. He watched her until she went into her room and closed the door.

It wasn't until she was in her own room that she realized just what she'd done.

She wasn't some nice domestic little thing who could fit into Quinn's world without any effort. She was Amanda Corrie Callaway, who belonged to a rock group with a worldwide reputation. On most streets in most cities, her face was instantly recognizable. How was Quinn going to take the knowledge of who she really was—

and the fact that she'd deceived him by leading him to think she was just a vacationing keyboard player? She groaned as she put on her gown. It didn't bear thinking about. From sweet heaven to nightmare in one hour was too much.

CHAPTER SEVEN

AMANDA HARDLY SLEPT from the combined shock of Quinn's ardor and her own guilt. How could she tell him the truth now? What could she say that would take away the sting of her deceit?

She dressed in jeans and the same button-up pink blouse she'd worn the night before and went down to breakfast.

Quinn looked up as she entered the room, his eyes warm and quiet.

"Good morning," she said brightly.

"Good morning yourself," Quinn murmured with a smile. "Sleep well?"

"Barely a wink," she said, sighing, her own eyes holding his.

He chuckled, averting his gaze before Elliot became suspicious. "Harry's out feeding your calves," he said, "and I'm on my way over to Eagle Pass to help one of my neighbors feed some stranded cattle. You'll have to stay with Elliot—it's teacher workday."

"I forgot," Elliot wailed, head in hands. "Can you imagine that I actually forgot? I could have slept until noon!"

"There, there," Amanda said, patting his shoulder. "Don't you want to learn some more chords?"

"Is that what you do?" Quinn asked curiously, because now every scrap of information he learned about her was precious. "You said you played a keyboard for a living. Do you teach music?"

"Not really," she said gently. "I play backup for various groups," she explained. "That rock music you hate…" she began uneasily.

"That's all right," Quinn replied, his face open and kind. "I was just trying to get a rise out of you. I don't mind it all that much, I guess. And playing backup isn't the same thing as putting on those god-awful costumes and singing suggestive lyrics. Well, I'm gone. Stay out of trouble, you two," he said as he got to his feet in the middle of Amanda's instinctive move to speak, to correct his assumption that all she did was play backup. She wanted to tell him the truth, but he winked at her and Elliot and got into his outdoor clothes before she could find a way to break the news. By the time her mind was working again, he was gone.

She sat back down, sighing. "Oh, Elliot, what a mess," she murmured, her chin in her hands.

"Is that what you call it?" he asked with a wicked smile. "Dad's actually grinning, and when he looked at you, you blushed. I'm not blind, you know. Do you like him, even if he isn't Mr. America?"

"Yes, I like him," she said with a shy smile, lowering her eyes. "He's a pretty special guy."

"I think so, myself. Eat your breakfast. I want to ask you about some new chords."

"Okay."

They were working on the keyboard when the sound of an approaching vehicle caught Amanda's attention.

Quinn hadn't driven anything motorized since the snow had gotten so high.

"That's odd," Elliot said, peering out the window curtain. "It's a four-wheel drive... Oh, boy." He glanced at Amanda. "You aren't gonna like this."

She lifted her eyebrows. "I'm not?" she asked, puzzled.

The knock at the back door had Harry moving toward it before Amanda and Elliot could. Harry opened it and looked up and up and up. He stood there staring while Elliot gaped at the grizzly-looking man who loomed over him in a black Western costume, complete with hat.

"I'm looking for Mandy Callaway," he boomed.

"Hank!"

Amanda ran to the big man without thinking, to be lifted high in the air while he chuckled and kissed her warmly on one cheek, his whiskers scratching.

"Hello, peanut!" he grinned. "What are you doing up here? The old trapper down the hill said you hadn't been in Durning's cabin since the heavy snow came."

"Mr. Sutton took me in and gave me a roof over my head. Put me down," she fussed, wiggling.

He put her back on her feet while Harry and Elliot still gaped.

"This is Hank," she said, holding his enormous hand as she turned to face the others. "He's a good friend, and a terrific musician, and I'd really appreciate it if you wouldn't tell Quinn he was here just yet. I'll tell him myself. Okay?"

"Sure," Harry murmured. He shook his head. "You for real, or do you have stilts in them boots?"

"I used to be a linebacker for the Dallas Cowboys." Hank grinned.

"That would explain it," Harry chuckled. "Your secret's safe with me, Amanda." He excused himself and went to do the washing.

"Me, too," Elliot said, grinning, "as long as I get Mr. Shoeman's autograph before he leaves."

Amanda let out a long breath, her eyes frightened as they met Elliot's.

"That's right," Elliot said. "I already knew you were Mandy Callaway. I've got a Desperado tape. I took it out of Dad's drawer and hid it as soon as I recognized you. You'll tell him when the time's right. Won't you?"

"Yes, I will, Elliot," she agreed. "I'd have done it already except that…well, things have gotten a little complicated."

"You can say that again." Elliot led the way into the living room, watching Hank sit gingerly on a sofa that he dwarfed. "I'll just go make sure that tape's hidden," he said, leaving them alone.

"Complicated, huh?" Hank said. "I hear this Sutton man's a real woman hater."

"He was until just recently." She folded her hands in her lap. "And he doesn't approve of rock music." She sighed and changed the subject. "What's up, Hank?"

"We've got a gig at Larry's Lodge," he said. "I know, you don't want to. Listen for a minute. It's to benefit cystic fibrosis, and a lot of other stars are going to be in town for it, including a few pretty well-known singers." He named some of them and Amanda whistled. "See what I mean? It's strictly charity, or I wouldn't have come up here bothering you. The boys and I want to do it." His dark eyes narrowed. "Are you up to it?"

"I don't know. I tried to sing here a couple of times,

and my voice seems to be good enough. No more lapses. But in front of a crowd…" She spread her hands. "I don't know, Hank."

"Here." He handed her three tickets to the benefit. "You think about it. If you can, come on up. Sutton might like the singers even if he doesn't care for our kind of music." He studied her. "You haven't told him, have you?"

She shook her head, smiling wistfully. "Haven't found the right way yet. If I leave it much longer, it may be too late."

"The girl's family sent you a letter," he said. "Thanking you for what you tried to do. They said you were her heroine…aw, now, Mandy, stop it!"

She collapsed in tears. He held her, rocking her, his face red with mingled embarrassment and guilt.

"Mandy, come on, stop that," he muttered. "It's all over and done with. You've got to get yourself together. You can't hide out here in the Tetons for the rest of your life."

"Can't I?" she wailed.

"No, you can't. Hiding isn't your style. You have to face the stage again, or you'll never get over it." He tilted her wet face. "Look, would you want somebody eating her guts out over you if you'd been Wendy that night? It wasn't your fault, damn it! It wasn't anybody's fault; it was an accident, pure and simple."

"If she hadn't been at the concert…"

"If, if, if," he said curtly. "You can't go back and change things to suit you. It was her time. At the concert, on a plane, in a car, however, it would still have been her time. Are you listening to me, Mandy?"

She dabbed her eyes with the hem of her blouse. "Yes, I'm listening."

"Come on, girl. Buck up. You can get over this if you set your mind to it. Me and the guys miss you, Mandy. It's not the same with just the four of us. People are scared of us when you aren't around."

That made her smile. "I guess they are. You do look scruffy, Hank," she murmured.

"You ought to see Johnson." He sighed. "He's let his beard go and he looks like a scrub brush. And Deke says he won't change clothes until you come back."

"Oh, my God," Amanda said, shuddering, "tell him I'll think hard about this concert, okay? You poor guys. Stay upwind of him."

"We're trying." He got up, smiling down at her. "Everything's okay. You can see the letter when you come to the lodge. It's real nice. Now stop beating yourself. Nobody else blames you. After all, babe, you risked your life trying to save her. Nobody's forgotten that, either."

She leaned against him for a minute, drawing on his strength. "Thanks, Hank."

"Anytime. Hey, kid, you still want that autograph?" he asked.

Elliot came back into the room with a pad and pen. "Do I!" he said, chuckling.

Hank scribbled his name and Desperado's curly-Q logo underneath. "There you go."

"He's a budding musician," Amanda said, putting an arm around Elliot. "I'm teaching him the keyboard. One of these days, if we can get around Quinn, we'll have him playing backup for me."

"You bet." Hank chuckled, and ruffled Elliot's red hair. "Keep at it. Mandy's the very best. If she teaches you, you're taught."

"Thanks, Mr. Shoeman."

"Just Hank. See you at the concert. So long, Mandy."

"So long, pal."

"What concert?" Elliot asked excitedly when Hank had driven away.

Amanda handed him the three tickets. "To a benefit in Jackson Hole. The group's going to play there. Maybe. If I can get up enough nerve to get back onstage again."

"What happened, Amanda?" he asked gently.

She searched his face, seeing compassion along with the curiosity, so she told him, fighting tears all the way.

"Gosh, no wonder you came up here to get away," Elliot said with more than his twelve years worth of wisdom. He shrugged. "But like he said, you have to go back someday. The longer you wait, the harder it's going to be."

"I know that," she groaned. "But Elliot, I…" She took a deep breath and looked down at the floor. "I love your father," she said, admitting it at last. "I love him very much, and the minute he finds out who I am, my life is over."

"Maybe not," he said. "You've got another week until the concert. Surely in all that time you can manage to tell him the truth. Can't you?"

"I hope so," she said with a sad smile. "You don't mind who I am, do you?" she asked worriedly.

"Don't be silly." He hugged her warmly. "I think you're super, keyboard or not."

She laughed and hugged him back. "Well, that's half the battle."

"Just out of curiosity," Harry asked from the doorway, "who was the bearded giant?"

"That was Hank Shoeman," Elliot told him. "He's

the drummer for Desperado. It's a rock group. And Amanda—"

"—plays backup for him," she volunteered, afraid to give too much away to Harry.

"Well, I'll be. He's a musician?" Harry shook his head. "Would have took him for a bank robber," he mumbled.

"Most people do, and you should see the rest of the group." She grinned. "Don't give me away, Harry, okay? I promise I'll tell Quinn, but I've got to do it the right way."

"I can see that," he agreed easily. "Be something of a shock to him to meet your friend after dark, I imagine."

"I imagine so," she said, chuckling. "Thanks, Harry."

"My pleasure. Desperado, huh? Suits it, if the rest of the group looks like he does."

"Worse," she said, and shuddered.

"Strains the mind, don't it?" Harry went off into the kitchen and Amanda got up after a minute to help him get lunch.

Quinn wasn't back until late that afternoon. Nobody mentioned Hank's visit, but Amanda was nervous and her manner was strained as she tried not to show her fears.

"What's wrong with you?" he asked gently during a lull in the evening while Elliot did homework and Harry washed up. "You don't seem like yourself tonight."

She moved close to him, her fingers idly touching the sleeve of his red flannel shirt. "It's thawing outside," she said, watching her fingers move on the fabric. "It won't be long before I'll be gone."

He sighed heavily. His fingers captured hers and held them. "I've been thinking about that. Do you really have to get back?"

She felt her heart jump. Whatever he was offering, she

wanted to say yes and let the future take care of itself. But she couldn't. She grimaced. "Yes, I have to get back," she said miserably. "I have commitments to people. Things I promised to do." Her fingers clenched his. "Quinn, I have to meet some people at Larry's Lodge in Jackson Hole next Friday night." She looked up. "It's at a concert and I have tickets. I know you don't like rock, but there's going to be all kinds of music." Her eyes searched his. "Would you go with me? Elliot can come, too. I…want you to see what I do for a living."

"You and your keyboard?" he mused gently.

"Sort of," she agreed, hoping she could find the nerve to tell him everything before next Friday night.

"Okay," he replied. "A friend of mine works there—I used to be with the Ski Patrol there, too. Sure, I'll go with you." The smile vanished, and his eyes glittered down at her. "I'll go damned near anywhere with you."

Amanda slid her arms around him and pressed close, shutting her eyes as she held on for dear life. "That goes double for me, mountain man," she said half under her breath.

He bent his head, searching for her soft mouth. She gave it to him without a protest, without a thought for the future, gave it to him with interest, with devotion, with ardor. Her lips opened invitingly, and she felt his hands on her hips with a sense of sweet inevitability, lifting her into intimate contact with the aroused contours of his body.

"Frightened?" he whispered unsteadily just over her mouth when he felt her stiffen involuntarily.

"Of you?" she whispered back. "Don't be absurd. Hold me any way you want. I adore you…!"

He actually groaned as his mouth pressed down hard

on hers. His arms contracted hungrily and he gave in to the pleasure of possession for one long moment.

Her eyes opened and she watched him, feeding on the slight contortion of his features, his heavy brows drawn over his crooked nose, his long, thick lashes on his cheek as he kissed her. She did adore him, she thought dizzily. Adored him, loved him, worshiped him. If only she could stay with him forever like this.

Quinn lifted his head and paused as he saw her watching him. He frowned slightly, then bent again. This time his eyes stayed open, too, and she went under as he deepened the kiss. Her eyes closed in self-defense and she moaned, letting him see the same vulnerability she'd seen in him. It was breathlessly sweet.

"This is an education," he said, laughing huskily, when he drew slightly away from her.

"Isn't it, though?" she murmured, moving his hands from her hips up to her waist and moving back a step from the blatant urgency of his body. "Elliot and Harry might come in," she whispered.

"I wouldn't mind," he said unexpectedly, searching her flushed face. "I'm not ashamed of what I feel for you, or embarrassed by it."

"This from a confirmed woman hater?" she asked with twinkling eyes.

"Well, not exactly confirmed anymore," he confessed. He lifted her by the waist and searched her eyes at point-blank range until she trembled from the intensity of the look. "I couldn't hate you if I tried, Amanda," he said quietly.

"Oh, I hope not," she said fervently, thinking ahead to when she would have to tell him the truth about herself.

He brushed a lazy kiss across her lips. "I think I'm getting the hang of this," he murmured.

"I think you are, too," she whispered. She slid her arms around his neck and put her warm mouth hungrily against his, sighing when he caught fire and answered the kiss with feverish abandon.

A slight, deliberate cough brought them apart, both staring blankly at the small redheaded intruder.

"Not that I mind," Elliot said, grinning, "but you're blocking the pan of brownies Harry made."

"You can think of brownies at a time like this?" Amanda groaned. "Elliot!"

"Listen, he can think of brownies with a fever of a hundred and two," Quinn told her, still holding her on a level with his eyes. "I've seen him get out of a sickbed to pinch a brownie from the kitchen."

"I like brownies, too," Amanda confessed with a warm smile, delighted that Quinn didn't seem to mind at all that Elliot had seen them in a compromising position. That made her feel lighter than air.

"Do you?" Quinn smiled and brushed his mouth gently against hers, mindless of Elliot's blatant interest, before he put her back on her feet. "Harry makes his from scratch, with real baker's chocolate. They're something special."

"I'll bet they are. Here. I'll get the saucers," she volunteered, still catching her breath.

Elliot looked like the cat with the canary as she dished up brownies. It very obviously didn't bother him that Amanda and his dad were beginning to notice each other.

"Isn't this cozy?" he remarked as they went back into

the living room and Amanda curled up on the sofa beside his dad, who never sat there.

"Cozy, indeed," Quinn murmured with a warm smile for Amanda.

She smiled back and laid her cheek against Quinn's broad chest while they watched television and ate brownies. She didn't move even when Harry joined them. And she knew she'd never been closer to heaven.

That night they were left discreetly alone, and she lay in Quinn's strong arms on the long leather couch in his office while wood burned with occasional hisses and sparks in the potbellied stove.

"I've had a raw deal with this place," he said eventually between kisses. "But it's good land, and I'm building a respectable herd of cattle. I can't offer you wealth or position, and we've got a ready-made family. But I can take care of you," he said solemnly, looking down into her soft eyes. "And you won't want for any of the essentials."

Her fingers touched his lean cheek hesitantly. "You don't know anything about me," she said. "When you know my background, you may not want me as much as you think you do." She put her fingers against his mouth. "You have to be sure."

"Damn it, I'm already sure," he muttered.

But was he? She was the first woman he'd ever been intimate with. Couldn't that blind him to her real suitability? What if it was just infatuation or desire? She was afraid to take a chance on his feelings, when she didn't really know what they were.

"Let's wait just a little while longer before we make any plans, Quinn. Okay?" she asked softly, turning in his hard arms so that her body was lying against his.

"Make love to me," she whispered, moving her mouth up to his. "Please…"

He gave in with a rough groan, gathering her to him, crushing her against his aroused body. He wanted her beyond rational thought. Maybe she had cold feet, but he didn't. He knew what he wanted, and Amanda was it.

His hands smoothed the blouse and bra away with growing expertise and he fought out of his shirt so that he could feel her soft skin against his. But it wasn't enough. He felt her tremble and knew that it was reflected in his own arms and legs. He moved against her with a new kind of sensuousness, lifting his head to hold her eyes while he levered her onto her back and eased over her, his legs between both of hers in their first real intimacy.

She caught her breath, but she didn't push him to try to get away.

"It's just that new for you, isn't it?" he whispered huskily as his hips moved lazily over hers and he groaned. "God, it burns me to…feel you like this."

"I know." She arched her back, loving his weight, loving the fierce maleness of his body. Her arms slid closer around him and she felt his mouth open on hers, his tongue softly searching as it slid inside, into an intimacy that made her moan. She began to tremble.

His lean hand slid under her, getting a firm grip, and he brought her suddenly into a shocking, shattering position that made her mindless with sudden need. She clutched him desperately, shuddering, her nails digging into him as the contact racked her like a jolt of raw electricity.

He pulled away from her without a word, shuddering as he lay on his back, trying to get hold of himself.

"I'm sorry," he whispered. "I didn't mean to let it go so far with us."

She was trembling, too, trying to breathe while great hot tears rolled down her cheeks. "Gosh, I wanted you," she whispered tearfully. "Wanted you so badly, Quinn!"

"As badly as I wanted you, honey," he said heavily. "We can't let things get that hot again. It was a close call. Closer than you realize."

"Oh, Quinn, couldn't we make love?" she asked softly, rolling over to look down into his tormented face. "Just once...?"

He framed his face in his hands and brought her closed eyes to his lips. "No. I won't compromise you."

She hit his big, hair-roughened chest. "Goody Two Shoes...!"

"Thank your lucky stars that I am," he chuckled. His eyes dropped to her bare breasts and lingered there before he caught the edges of her blouse and tugged them together. "You sex-crazed female, haven't you ever heard about pregnancy?"

"That condition where I get to have little Quinns?"

"Stop it, you're making it impossible for me," he said huskily. "Here, get up before I lose my mind."

She sat up with a grimace. "Spoilsport."

"Listen to you," he muttered, putting her back into her clothes with a wry grin. "I'll give you ten to one that you'd be yelling your head off if I started taking off your jeans."

She went red. "My jeans...!"

His eyebrows arched. "Amanda, would you like me to explain that book I read to you? The part about how men and women..."

She cleared her throat. "No, thanks, I think I've got the hang of it now," she murmured evasively.

"We might as well add a word about birth control," he added with a chuckle when he was buttoning up his own shirt. "You don't take the pill, I assume?"

She shook her head. The whole thing was getting to be really embarrassing!

"Well, that leaves prevention up to me," he explained. "And that would mean a trip into town to the drugstore, since I never indulged, I never needed to worry about prevention. *Now* do you get the picture?"

"Boy, do I get the picture." She grimaced, avoiding his knowing gaze.

"Good girl. That's why we aren't lying down anymore."

She sighed loudly. "I guess you don't want children."

"Sure I do. Elliot would love brothers and sisters, and I'm crazy about kids." He took her slender hands in his and smoothed them over with his thumbs. "But kids should be born inside marriage, not outside it. Don't you think so?"

She took a deep breath, and her dark eyes met his. "Yes."

"Then we'll spend a lot of time together until you have to meet your friends at this concert," he said softly. "And afterward, you and I will come in here again and I'll ask you a question."

"Oh, Quinn," she whispered with aching softness.

"Oh, Amanda," he murmured, smiling as his lips softly touched hers. "But right now, we go to bed. Separately. Quick!"

"Yes, sir, Mr. Sutton." She got up and let him lead her to the staircase.

"I'll get the lights," he said. "You go on up. In the morning after we get Elliot off to school you can come out with me, if you want to."

"I want to," she said simply. She could hardly bear to be parted from him even overnight. It was like an addiction, she thought as she went up the staircase. Now if only she could make it last until she had the nerve to tell Quinn the truth….

The next few days went by in a haze. The snow began to melt and the skies cleared as the long-awaited chinook blew in. In no time at all it was Friday night and Amanda was getting into what Elliot would recognize as her stage costume. She'd brought it, with her other things, from the Durning cabin. She put it on, staring at herself in the mirror. Her hair hung long and loose, in soft waves below her waist, in the beige leather dress with the buckskin boots that matched, she was the very picture of a sensuous woman. She left off the headband. There would be time for that if she could summon enough courage to get onstage. She still hadn't told Quinn. She hadn't had the heart to destroy the dream she'd been living. But tonight he'd know. And she'd know if they had a future. She took a deep breath and went downstairs.

CHAPTER EIGHT

AMANDA SAT IN the audience with Quinn and Elliot at a far table while the crowded hall rang with excited whispers. Elliot was tense, like Amanda, his eyes darting around nervously. Quinn was frowning. He hadn't been quite himself since Amanda came down the staircase in her leather dress and boots, looking expensive and faintly alien. He hadn't asked any questions, but he seemed as uptight as she felt.

Her eyes slid over him lovingly, taking in his dark suit. He looked out of place in fancy clothes. She missed the sight of him in denim and his old shepherd's coat, and wondered fleetingly if she'd ever get to see him that way again after tonight—if she'd ever lie in his arms on the big sofa and warm to his kisses while the fire burned in the stove. She almost groaned. Oh, Quinn, she thought, I love you.

Elliot looked uncomfortable in his blue suit. He was watching for the rest of Desperado while a well-known Las Vegas entertainer warmed up the crowd and sang his own famous theme song.

"What are you looking for, son?" Quinn asked.

Elliot shifted. "Nothing. I'm just seeing who I know."

Quinn's eyebrows arched. "How would you know anybody in this crowd?" he muttered, glancing around. "My

God, these are show people. Entertainers. Not people from our world."

That was a fact. But hearing it made Amanda heartsick. She reached out and put her hand over Quinn's.

"Your fingers are like ice," he said softly. He searched her worried eyes. "Are you okay, honey?"

The endearment made her warm all over. She smiled sadly and slid her fingers into his, looking down at the contrast between his callused, work-hardened hand and her soft, pale one. His was a strong hand, hers was artistic. But despite the differences, they fit together perfectly. She squeezed her fingers. "I'm fine," she said. "Quinn…"

"And now I want to introduce a familiar face," the Las Vegas performer's voice boomed. "Most of you know the genius of Desperado. The group has won countless awards for its topical, hard-hitting songs. Last year, Desperado was given a Grammy for 'Changes in the Wind,' and Hank Shoeman's song 'Outlaw Love' won him a country music award and a gold record. But their fame isn't the reason we're honoring them tonight."

To Amanda's surprise, he produced a gold plaque. "As some of you may remember, a little over a month ago, a teenage girl died at a Desperado concert. The group's lead singer leaped into the crowd, disregarding her own safety, and was very nearly trampled trying to protect the fan. Because of that tragedy, Desperado went into seclusion. We're proud to tell you tonight that they're back and they're in better form than ever. This plaque is a token of respect from the rest of us in the performing arts to a very special young woman whose compassion and selflessness have won the respect of all."

He looked out toward the audience where Amanda

sat frozen. "This is for you—Amanda Corrie Callaway. Will you come up and join the group, please? Come on, Mandy!"

She bit her lower lip. The plaque was a shock. The boys seemed to know about it, too, because they went to their instruments grinning and began to play the down-beat that Desperado was known for, the deep throbbing counter rhythm that was their trademark.

"Come on, babe!" Hank called out in his booming voice, he and Johnson and Deke and Jack looking much more like backwoods robbers than musicians with their huge bulk and outlaw gear.

Amanda glanced at Elliot's rapt, adoring face, and then looked at Quinn. He was frowning, his dark eyes search-ing the crowd. She said a silent goodbye as she got to her feet. She reached into her pocket for her headband and put it on her head. She couldn't look at him, but she felt his shocked stare as she walked down the room toward the stage, her steps bouncing as the rhythm got into her feet and her blood.

"Thank you," she said huskily, kissing the entertainer's cheek as she accepted the plaque. She moved in between Johnson and Deke, taking the microphone. She looked past Elliot's proud, adoring face to Quinn's. He seemed to be in a state of dark shock. "Thank you all. I've had a hard few weeks. But I'm okay now, and I'm looking forward to better times. God bless, people. This one is for a special man and a special boy, with all my love." She turned to Hank, nodded, and he began the throbbing drumbeat of "Love Singer."

It was a song that touched the heart, for all its mad beat. The words, in her soft, sultry, clear voice caught every ear in the room. She sang from the heart, with the heart, the words fierce with meaning as she sang them to Quinn. "Love you, never loved anybody but you, never leave me lonely, love...singer."

But Quinn didn't seem to be listening to the words. He got to his feet and jerked Elliot to his. He walked out in the middle of the song and never looked back once.

Amanda managed to finish, with every ounce of will-power she had keeping her onstage. She let the last few notes hang in the air and then she bowed to a standing ovation. By the time she and the band did an encore and she got out of the hall, the truck they'd come in was long gone. There was no note, no message. Quinn had said it all with his eloquent back when he walked out of the hall. He knew who she was now, and he wanted no part of her. He couldn't have said it more clearly if he'd written it in blood.

She kept hoping that he might reconsider. Even after she went backstage with the boys, she kept hoping for a phone call or a glimpse of Quinn. But nothing happened.

"I guess I'm going to need a place to stay," Amanda said with a rueful smile, her expression telling her group all they needed to know.

"He couldn't handle it, huh?" Hank asked quietly. "I'm sorry, babe. We've got a suite, there's plenty of room for one more. I'll go up and get your gear tomorrow."

"Thanks, Hank." She took a deep breath and clutched the plaque to her chest. "Where's the next gig?"

"That's my girl," he said gently, sliding a protective arm around her. "San Francisco's our next stop. The boys and I are taking a late bus tomorrow." He grimaced at her knowing smile. "Well, you know how I feel about airplanes."

"Chicken Little," she accused. "Well, I'm not going to sit on a bus all day. I'll take the first charter out and meet you guys at the hotel."

"Whatever turns you on," Hank chuckled. "Come on. Let's get out of here and get some rest."

"You did good, Amanda," Johnson said from behind her. "We were proud."

"You bet," Deke and Jack seconded.

She smiled at them all. "Thanks, group. I shocked myself, but at least I didn't go dry the way I did last time." Her heart was breaking in two, but she managed to hide it. Quinn, she moaned inwardly. Oh, Quinn, was I just an interlude, an infatuation?

She didn't sleep very much. The next morning Amanda watched Hank start out for Ricochet then went down to a breakfast that she didn't even eat while she waited for him to return.

He came back three hours later, looking ruffled.

"Did you get my things?" she asked when he came into the suite.

"I got them." He put her suitcase down on the floor. "Part at Sutton's place, part at the Durning cabin. Elliot sent you a note." He produced it.

"And...Quinn?"

"I never saw him," he replied tersely. "The boy and the old man were there. They didn't mention Sutton and I didn't ask. I wasn't feeling too keen on him at the time."

"Thanks, Hank."

He shrugged. "That's the breaks, kid. It would have

been a rough combination at best. You're a bright-lights girl."

"Am I?" she asked, thinking how easily she'd fit into Quinn's world. But she didn't push it. She sat down on the couch and opened Elliot's scribbled note.

Amanda,
I thought you were great. Dad didn't say anything all the way home and last night he went into his study and didn't come out until this morning. He went hunting, he said, but he didn't take any bullets. I hope you are okay. Write me when you can. I love you.
Your friend, Elliot.

She bit her lip to keep from crying. Dear Elliot. At least he still cared about her. But her fall from grace in Quinn's eyes had been final, she thought bitterly. He'd never forgive her for deceiving him. Or maybe it was just that he'd gotten over his brief infatuation with her when he found out who she really was. She didn't know what to do. She couldn't remember ever feeling so miserable. To have discovered something that precious, only to lose it forever. She folded Elliot's letter and put it into her purse. At least it would be something to remember from her brief taste of heaven.

For the rest of the day, the band and Jerry, the road manager, got the arrangements made for the San Francisco concert, and final travel plans were laid. The boys were to board the San Francisco bus the next morning. Amanda was to fly out on a special air charter that specialized in flights for business executives. They'd managed to fit her in at the last minute when a computer-company executive had canceled his flight.

"I wish you'd come with us," Hank said hesitantly. "I guess I'm overreacting and all, but I hate airplanes."

"I'll be fine," she told him firmly. "You and the boys have a nice trip and stop worrying about me. I'll be fine."

"If you say so," Hank mumbled.

"I do say so." She patted him on the shoulder. "Trust me."

He shrugged and left, but he didn't look any less worried. Amanda, who'd gotten used to his morose predictions, didn't pay them any mind.

She went to the suite and into her bedroom early that night. Her fingers dialed the number at Ricochet. She had to try one last time, she told herself. There was at least the hope that Quinn might care enough to listen to her explanation. She had to try.

The phone rang once, twice, and she held her breath, but on the third ring the receiver was lifted.

"Sutton," came a deep weary-sounding voice.

Her heart lifted. "Oh, Quinn," she burst out. "Quinn, please let me try to explain—"

"You don't have to explain anything to me, Amanda," he said stiffly. "I saw it all on the stage."

"I know it looks bad," she began.

"You lied to me," he said. "You let me think you were just a shy little innocent who played a keyboard, when you were some fancy big-time entertainer with a countrywide following."

"I knew you wouldn't want me if you knew who I was," she said miserably.

"You knew I'd see right through you if I knew," he

corrected, his voice growing angrier. "You played me for a fool."

"I didn't!"

"All of it was a lie. Nothing but a lie! Well, you can go back to your public, Miss Callaway, and your outlaw buddies, and make some more records or tapes or whatever the hell they are. I never wanted you in the first place except in bed, so it's no great loss to me." He was grimacing, and she couldn't see the agony in his eyes as he forced the words out. Now that he knew who and what she was, he didn't dare let himself weaken. He had to make her go back to her own life, and stay out of his. He had nothing to give her, nothing that could take the place of fame and fortune and the world at her feet. He'd never been more aware of his own inadequacies as he had been when he'd seen Amanda on that stage and heard the applause of the audience. It ranked as the worst waking nightmare of his life, putting her forever out of his reach.

"Quinn!" she moaned. "Quinn, you don't mean that!"

"I mean it," he said through his teeth. He closed his eyes. "Every word. Don't call here again, don't come by, don't write. You're a bad influence on Elliot now that he knows who you are. I don't want you. You've worn out your welcome at Ricochet." He hung up without another word.

Amanda stared at the telephone receiver as if it had sprouted wings. Slowly she put it back in the cradle just as the room splintered into wet crystal around her.

She put on her gown mechanically and got into bed, turning out the bedside light. She lay in the dark and Quinn's words echoed in her head with merciless coolness. *Bad influence. Don't want you. Worn out your welcome. Never wanted you anyway except in bed.*

She moaned and buried her face in her pillow. She didn't know how she was going to go on, with Quinn's cold contempt dogging her footsteps. He hated her now. He thought she'd been playing a game, enjoying herself while she made a fool out of him. The tears burned her eyes. How quickly it had all ended, how finally. She'd hoped to keep in touch with Elliot, but that wouldn't be possible anymore. She was a bad influence on Elliot, so he wouldn't be allowed to contact her. She sobbed her hurt into the cool linen. Somehow, being denied contact with Elliot was the last straw. She'd grown so fond of the boy during those days she'd spent at Ricochet, and he cared about her, too. Quinn was being unnecessarily harsh. But perhaps he was right, and it was for the best. Maybe she could learn to think that way eventually. Right now she had a concert to get to, a sold-out one from what the boys and Jerry had said. She couldn't let the fans down.

Amanda got up the next morning, looking and feeling as if it were the end of the world. The boys took her suitcase downstairs, not looking too closely at her face without makeup, her long hair arranged in a thick, haphazard bun. She was wearing a dark pantsuit with a cream-colored blouse, and she looked miserable.

"We'll see you in San Francisco," Jerry told her with a smile. "I have to go nursemaid these big, tough guys, so you make sure the pilot of your plane has all his marbles, okay?"

"I'll check him out myself," she promised. "Take care of yourselves, guys. I'll see you in California."

"Okay. Be good, babe," Hank called. He and the others

filed into the bus Jerry had chartered and Jerry hugged her impulsively and went in behind them.

She watched the bus pull away, feeling lost and alone, not for the first time. It was cold and snowy, but she hadn't wanted her coat. It was packed in her suitcase, and had already been put on the light aircraft. With a long sigh, she went back to the cab and sat disinterestedly in it as it wound over the snowy roads to the airport.

Fortunately the chinook had thawed the runways so that the planes were coming and going easily. She got out at the air charter service hangar and shook hands with the pilot.

"Don't worry, we're in great shape," he promised Amanda with a grin. "In fact, the mechanics just gave us another once-over to be sure. Nothing to worry about."

"Oh, I wasn't worried," she said absently and allowed herself to be shepherded inside. She slid into an empty aisle seat on the right side and buckled up. Usually she preferred to sit by the window, but today she wasn't in the mood for sight-seeing. One snow-covered mountain looked pretty much like another to her, and her heart wasn't in this flight or the gig that would follow it. She leaned back and closed her eyes.

It seemed to take forever for all the businessmen to get aboard. Fortunately there had been one more cancellation, so she had her seat and the window seat as well. She didn't feel like talking to anyone, and was hoping she wouldn't have to sit by some chatterbox all the way to California.

She listened to the engines rev up and made sure that her seat belt was properly fastened. They would be off as soon as the tower cleared them, the pilot announced.

Amanda sighed. She called a silent goodbye to Quinn Sutton, and Elliot and Harry, knowing that once this plane lifted off, she'd never see any of them again. She winced at the thought. Oh, Quinn, she moaned inwardly, why wouldn't you *listen?*

The plane got clearance and a minute later, it shot down the runway and lifted off. But it seemed oddly sluggish. Amanda was used to air travel, even to charter flights, and she opened her eyes and peered forward worriedly as she listened to the whine become a roar.

She was strapped in, but a groan from behind took her mind off the engine. The elderly man behind her was clutching his chest and groaning.

"What's wrong?" she asked the worried businessman in the seat beside the older man.

"Heart attack, I think." He grimaced. "What can we do?"

"I know a little CPR," she said. She unfastened her seat belt; so did the groaning man's seat companion. But just as they started to lay him on the floor, someone shouted something. Smoke began to pour out of the cockpit, and the pilot called for everyone to assume crash positions. Amanda turned, almost in slow motion. She could feel the force of gravity increase as the plane started down. The floor went out from under her and her last conscious thought was that she'd never see Quinn again....

Elliot was watching television without much interest, wishing that his father had listened when Amanda had phoned the night before. He couldn't believe that he was going to be forbidden to even speak to her again, but Quinn had insisted, his cold voice giving nothing away as he'd made Elliot promise to make no attempt to contact her.

It seemed so unfair, he thought. Amanda was no wild party girl, surely his father knew that? He sighed heavily and munched on another potato chip.

The movie he was watching was suddenly interrupted as the local station broke in with a news bulletin. Elliot listened for a minute, gasped and jumped up to get his father.

Quinn was in the office, not really concentrating on what he was doing, when Elliot burst in. The boy looked odd, his freckles standing out in an unnaturally pale face.

"Dad, you'd better come here," he said uneasily. "Quick!"

Quinn's first thought was that something had happened to Harry, but Elliot stopped in front of the television. Quinn frowned as his dark eyes watched the screen. They were showing the airport.

"What's this all—" he began, then stopped to listen.

"…plane went down about ten minutes ago, according to our best information," the man, probably the airport manager, was saying. "We've got helicopters flying in to look for the wreckage, but the wind is up, and the area the plane went down in is almost inaccessible by road."

"What plane?" Quinn asked absently.

"To repeat our earlier bulletin," the man on television seemed to oblige, "a private charter plane has been reported lost somewhere in the Grand Teton Mountains just out of Jackson Hole. One eyewitness interviewed by KWJC-TV newsman Bill Donovan stated that he saw flames shooting out of the cockpit of the twin-engine aircraft and that he watched it plummet into the mountains and vanish. Aboard the craft were prominent San Francisco businessmen Bob Doyle and Harry Brown, and the lead singer of the rock group Desperado, Mandy Callaway."

Quinn sat down in his chair hard enough to shake it. He knew his face was as white as Elliot's. In his mind, he could hear his own voice telling Mandy he didn't want her anymore, daring her to ever contact him again. Now she was dead, and he felt her loss as surely as if one of his arms had been severed from his body.

That was when he realized how desperately he loved her. When it was too late to take back the harsh words, to go after her and bring her home where she belonged. He thought of her soft body lying in the cold snow, and a sound broke from his throat. He'd sent her away because he loved her, not because he'd wanted to hurt her, but she wouldn't have known that. Her last memory of him would have been a painful, hateful one. She'd have died thinking he didn't care.

"I don't believe it," Elliot said huskily. He was shaking his head. "I just don't believe it. She was onstage Friday night, singing again—" His voice broke and he put his face in his hands.

Quinn couldn't bear it. He got up and went past a startled Harry and out the back door in his shirtsleeves, so upset that he didn't even feel the cold. His eyes went to the barn, where he'd watched Amanda feed the calves, and around the back where she'd run from him that snowy afternoon and he'd had to save her from McNaber's bear traps. His big fists clenched by his sides and he shuddered with the force of the grief he felt, his face contorting.

"Amanda!" He bit off the name.

A long time later, he was aware of someone standing nearby. He didn't turn because his face would have said too much.

"Elliot told me," Harry said hesitantly. He stuck his hands into his pockets. "They say where she is, they may not be able to get her out."

Quinn's teeth clenched. "I'll get her out," he said huskily. "I won't leave her out there in the cold." He swallowed. "Get my skis and my boots out of the storeroom, and my insulated ski suit out of the closet. I'm going to call the lodge and talk to Terry Meade."

"He manages Larry's Lodge, doesn't he?" Harry recalled.

"Yes. He can get a chopper to take me up."

"Good thing you've kept up your practice," Harry muttered. "Never thought you'd need the skis for something this awful, though."

"Neither did I." He turned and went back inside. He might have to give up Amanda forever, but he wasn't giving her up to that damned mountain. He'd get her out somehow.

He grabbed the phone, ignoring Elliot's questions, and called the lodge, asking for Terry Meade in a tone that got instant action.

"Quinn!" Terry exclaimed. "Just the man I need. Look, we've got a crash—"

"I know," Quinn said tightly. "I know the singer. Can you get me a topo map of the area and a chopper? I'll need a first-aid kit, too, and some flares—"

"No sooner said than done," Terry replied tersely. "Although I don't think that first-aid kit will be needed, Quinn, I'm sorry."

"Well, pack it anyway, will you?" He fought down nausea. "I'll be up there in less than thirty minutes."

"We'll be waiting."

Quinn got into the ski suit under Elliot's fascinated gaze.

"You don't usually wear that suit when we ski together," he told his father.

"We don't stay out that long," Quinn explained. "This suit is a relatively new innovation. It's such a tight weave that it keeps out moisture, but it's made in such a way that it allows sweat to get out. It's like having your own heater along."

"I like the boots, too," Elliot remarked. They were blue, and they had a knob on the heel that allowed them to be tightened to fit the skier's foot exactly. Boots had to fit tight to work properly. And the skis themselves were equally fascinating. They had special brakes that unlocked when the skier fell, which stopped the ski from sliding down the hill.

"Those sure are long skis," Elliot remarked as his father took precious time to apply hot wax to them.

"Longer than yours, for sure. They fit my height," Quinn said tersely. "And they're short compared to jumping skis."

"Did you ever jump, Dad, or did you just do downhill?"

"Giant slalom," he replied. "Strictly Alpine skiing. That's going to come in handy today."

Elliot sighed. "I don't guess you'll let me come along?"

"No chance. This is no place for you." His eyes darkened. "God knows what I'll find when I get to the plane."

Elliot bit his lower lip. "She's dead, isn't she, Dad?" he asked in a choked tone.

Quinn's expression closed. "You stay here with Harry, and don't tie up the telephone. I'll call home as soon as I know anything."

"Take care of yourself up there, okay?" Elliot murmured as Quinn picked up the skis and the rest of his equipment, including gloves and ski cap. "I don't say it a lot, but I love you, Dad."

"I love you, too, son." Quinn pulled him close and gave him a quick, rough hug. "I know what I'm doing. I'll be okay."

"Good luck," Harry said as Quinn went out the back door to get into his pickup truck.

"I'll need it," Quinn muttered. He waved, started the truck, and pulled out into the driveway.

Terry Meade was waiting with the Ski Patrol, the helicopter pilot, assorted law enforcement officials and the civil defense director and trying to field the news media gathered at Larry's Lodge.

"This is the area where we think they are," Terry said grimly, showing Quinn the map. "What you call Ironside peak, right? It's not in our patrol area, so we don't have anything to do with it officially. The helicopter tried and failed to get into the valley below it because of the wind. The trees are dense down there and visibility is limited by blowing snow. Our teams are going to start here," he pointed at various places on the map. "But this hill is a killer." He grinned at Quinn. "You cut your teeth on it when you were practicing for the Olympics all those years ago, and you've kept up your practice there. If anyone can ski it, you can."

"I'll get in. What then?"

"Send up a flare. I'm packing a cellular phone in with the other stuff you asked for. It's got a better range than our walkie-talkies. Everybody know what to do? Right. Let's go."

He led them out of the lodge. Quinn put on his goggles, tugged his ski cap over his head and thrust his hands into his gloves. He didn't even want to think about what he might have to look at if he was lucky enough to find the downed plane. He was having enough trouble living with what he'd said to Amanda the last time he'd talked to her.

He could still hear her voice, hear the hurt in it when he'd told her he didn't want her. Remembering that was like cutting open his heart. For her sake, he'd sent her away. He was a poor man. He had so little to offer such a famous, beautiful woman. At first, at the lodge, his pride had been cut to ribbons when he discovered who she was, and how she'd fooled him, how she'd deceived him. But her adoration had been real, and when his mind was functioning again, he realized that. He'd almost phoned her back, he'd even dialed the number. But her world was so different from his. He couldn't let her give up everything she'd worked all her life for, just to live in the middle of nowhere. She deserved so much more. He sighed wearily. If she died, the last conversation would haunt him until the day he died. He didn't think he could live with it. He didn't want to have to try. She had to be alive. Oh, dear God, she had to be!

CHAPTER NINE

THE SUN WAS bright, and Quinn felt its warmth on his face as the helicopter set him down at the top of the mountain peak where the plane had last been sighted.

He was alone in the world when the chopper lifted off again. He checked his bindings one last time, adjusted the lightweight backpack and stared down the long mountainside with his ski poles restless in his hands. This particular slope wasn't skied as a rule. It wasn't even connected with the resort, which meant that the Ski Patrol didn't come here, and that the usual rescue toboggan posted on most slopes wouldn't be in evidence. He was totally on his own until he could find the downed plane. And he knew that while he was searching this untamed area, the Ski Patrol would be out in force on the regular slopes looking for the aircraft.

He sighed heavily as he stared down at the rugged, untouched terrain, which would be a beginning skier's nightmare. Well, it was now or never. Amanda was down there somewhere. He had to find her. He couldn't leave her there in the cold snow for all eternity.

He pulled down his goggles, suppressed his feelings and shoved the ski poles deep as he propelled himself down the slope. The first couple of minutes were tricky as he had to allow for the slight added weight of the backpack. But it took scant time to adjust, to balance his weight on the skis to compensate.

The wind bit his face, the snow flew over his dark ski suit as he wound down the slopes, his skis throwing up powdered snow in his wake. It brought back memories of the days when he'd maneuvered through the giant slalom in Alpine skiing competition. He'd been in the top one percent of his class, a daredevil skier with cold nerve and expert control on the slopes. This mountain was a killer, but it was one he knew like the back of his hand. He'd trained on this peak back in his early days of competition, loving the danger of skiing a slope where no one else came. Even for the past ten years or so, he'd honed his skill here every chance he got.

Quinn smiled to himself, his body leaning into the turns, not too far, the cutting edge of his skis breaking his speed as he maneuvered over boulders, down the fall line, around trees and broken branches or over them, whichever seemed more expedient.

His dark eyes narrowed as he defeated the obstacles. At least, thank God, he was able to do something instead of going through hell sitting at home waiting for word. That in itself was a blessing, even if it ended in the tragedy everyone seemed to think it would. He couldn't bear to imagine Amanda dead. He had to think positively. There were people who walked away from airplane crashes. He had to believe that she could be one of them. He had to keep thinking that or go mad.

He'd hoped against hope that when he got near the bottom of the hill, under those tall pines and the deadly updrafts and downdrafts that had defeated the helicopter's reconnoitering, that he'd find the airplane. But it wasn't there. He turned his skis sideways and skidded to a stop, looking around him. Maybe the observer had gotten his sighting wrong. Maybe it was another peak, maybe it was miles away. He bit his lower lip raw, tasting the lip balm he'd applied before he came onto the slope. If anyone on that plane was alive, time was going to make the difference. He had to find it quickly, or Amanda wouldn't have a prayer if she'd managed to survive the initial impact.

He started downhill again, his heartbeat increasing as the worry began to eat at him. On an impulse, he shot across the fall line, parallel to it for a little while before he maneuvered back and went down again in lazy *S* patterns. Something caught his attention. A sound. Voices!

He stopped to listen, turning his head. There was wind, and the sound of pines touching. But beyond it was a voice, carrying in the silence of nature. Snow blanketed most sound, making graveyard peace out of the mountain's spring noises.

Quinn adjusted his weight on the skis and lifted his hands to his mouth, the ski poles dangling from his wrists. "Hello! Where are you?" he shouted, taking a chance that the vibration of his voice wouldn't dislodge snow above him and bring a sheet of it down on him.

"Help!" voices called back. "We're here! We're here!"

He followed the sound, praying that he wasn't following an echo. But no, there, below the trees, he saw a glint of metal in the lowering sun. The plane! Thank God, there were survivors! Now if only Amanda was one of them...

He went the rest of the way down. As he drew closer, he saw men standing near the almost intact wreckage of the aircraft. One had a bandage around his head, another was nursing what looked like a broken arm. He saw one woman, but she wasn't blond. On the ground were two still forms, covered with coats. Covered up.

Please, God, no, he thought blindly. He drew to a stop.

"I'm Sutton. How many dead?" he asked the man who'd called to him, a burly man in a gray suit and white shirt and tie.

"Two," the man replied. "I'm Jeff Coleman, and I sure am glad to see you." He shook hands with Quinn. "I'm the pilot. We had a fire in the cockpit and it was all I could do to set her down at all. God, I feel bad! For some reason, three of the passengers had their seat belts off when we hit." He shook his head. "No hope for two of them. The third's concussed and looks comatose."

Quinn felt himself shaking inside as he asked the question he had to ask. "There was a singer aboard," he said. "Amanda Callaway."

"Yeah." The pilot shook his head and Quinn wanted to die, he wanted to stop breathing right there… "She's the concussion."

Quinn knew his hand shook as he pushed his goggles up over the black ski cap. "Where is she?" he asked huskily.

The pilot didn't ask questions or argue. He led Quinn past the two bodies and the dazed businessmen who were standing or sitting on fabric they'd taken from the plane, trying to keep warm.

"She's here," the pilot told him, indicating a makeshift stretcher constructed of branches and pillows from the cabin, and coats that covered the still body.

"Amanda," Quinn managed unsteadily. He knelt beside her. Her hair was in a coiled bun on her head. Her face was alabaster white, her eyes closed, long black

lashes lying still on her cheekbones. Her mouth was as
pale as the rest of her face, and there was a bruise high
on her forehead at the right temple. He stripped off his
glove and felt the artery at her neck. Her heart was still
beating, but slowly and not very firmly. Unconscious.
Dying, perhaps. "Oh, God," he breathed.

He got to his feet and unloaded the backpack as the
pilot and two of the other men gathered around him.

"I've got a modular phone," Quinn said, "which I hope
to God will work." He punched buttons and waited, his
dark eyes narrowed, holding his breath.

It seemed to take forever. Then a voice, a recognizable
voice, came over the wire. "Hello."

"Terry!" Quinn called. "It's Sutton. I've found them."

"Thank God!" Terry replied. "Okay, give me your
position."

Quinn did, spreading out his laminated map to verify
it, and then gave the report on casualties.

"Only one unconscious?" Terry asked again.

"Only one," Quinn replied heavily.

"We'll have to airlift you out, but we can't do it until
the wind dies down. You understand, Quinn, the same
downdrafts and updrafts that kept the chopper out this
morning are going to keep it out now."

"Yes, I know, damn it," Quinn yelled. "But I've got to
get her to a hospital. She's failing already."

Terry sighed. "And there you are without a rescue toboggan. Listen, what if I get Larry Hale down there?"
he asked excitedly. "You know Larry; he was national
champ in downhill a few years back, and he's a senior
member of the Ski Patrol now. We could airdrop you the
toboggan and some supplies for the rest of the survivors

by plane. The two of you could tow her to a point accessible by chopper. Do you want to risk it, Quinn?"

"I don't know if she'll be alive in the morning, Terry," Quinn said somberly. "I'm more afraid to risk doing nothing than I am of towing her out. It's fairly level, if I remember right, all the way to the pass that leads from Caraway Ridge into Jackson Hole. The chopper might be able to fly down Jackson Hole and come in that way, without having to navigate the peaks. What do you think?"

"I think it's a good idea," Terry said. "If I remember right, they cleared that pass from the Ridge into Jackson Hole in the fall. It should still be accessible."

"No problem," Quinn said, his jaw grim. "If it isn't cleared, I'll clear it, by hand if necessary."

Terry chuckled softly. "Hale says he's already on the way. We'll get the plane up—hell of a pity he can't land where you are, but it's just too tricky. How about the other survivors?"

Quinn told him their conditions, along with the two bodies that would have to be airlifted out.

"Too bad," he replied. He paused for a minute to talk to somebody. "Listen, Quinn, if you can get the woman to Caraway Ridge, the chopper pilot thinks he can safely put down there. About the others, can they manage until morning if we drop the supplies?"

Quinn looked at the pilot. "Can you?"

"I ate snakes in Nam and Bill over there served in Antarctica." He grinned. "Between us, we can keep these pilgrims warm and even feed them. Sure, we'll be okay. Get that little lady out if you can."

"Amen," the man named Bill added, glancing at

Amanda's still form. "I've heard her sing. It would be a crime against art to let her die."

Quinn lifted the cellular phone to his ear. "They say they can manage, Terry. Are you sure you can get them out in the morning?"

"If we have to send the snowplow in through the valley or send in a squad of snowmobiles and a horse-drawn sled, you'd better believe we'll get them out. The Ski Patrol is already working out the details."

"Okay."

Quinn unloaded his backpack. He had flares and matches, packets of high protein dehydrated food, the first-aid kit and some cans of sterno.

"Paradise," the pilot said, looking at the stores. "With that, I can prepare a seven-course meal, build a bonfire and make a house. But those supplies they're going to drop will come in handy, just the same."

Quinn smiled in spite of himself. "Okay."

"We can sure use this first-aid kit, but I've already set a broken arm and patched a few cuts. Before I became a pilot, I worked in the medical corps."

"I had rescue training when I was in the Ski Patrol," Quinn replied. He grinned at the pilot. "But if I ever come down in a plane, I hope you're on it."

"Thanks. I hope none of us ever come down again." He glanced at the two bodies. "God, I'm sorry about them." He glanced at Amanda. "I hope she makes it."

Quinn's jaw hardened. "She's a fighter," he said. "Let's hope she cares enough to try." He alone knew how defeated she'd probably felt when she left the lodge. He'd inflicted some terrible damage with his coldness. Pride had forced him to send her away, to deny his own happiness. Once he knew how famous and wealthy she was in her own right, he hadn't felt that he had the right to ask her to give it all up to live with him and Elliot in the wilds of Wyoming. He'd been doing what he thought was best for her. Now he only wanted her to live.

He took a deep breath. "Watch for the plane and Hale, will you? I'm going to sit with her."

"Sure." The pilot gave him a long look that he didn't see before he went back to talk to the other survivors.

Quinn sat down beside Amanda, reaching for one cold little hand under the coats that covered her. It was going to be a rough ride for her, and she didn't need any more jarring. But if they waited until morning, without medical help, she could die. It was much riskier to do nothing than it was to risk moving her. And down here in the valley, the snow was deep and fairly level. It would be like Nordic skiing; cross-country skiing. With luck, it would feel like a nice lazy sleigh ride to her.

"Listen to me, honey," he said softly. "We've got a long way to go before we get you out of here and to a hospital. You're going to have to hold on for a long time." His hand tightened around hers, warming it. "I'll be right with you every step of the way. I won't leave you for a second. But you have to do your part, Amanda. You have to fight to stay alive. I hope that you still want to live. If you don't, there's something I need to tell you. I sent you away not because I hated you, Amanda, but because I loved you so much. I loved you enough to let you go back to the life you needed. You've got to stay alive so that I can tell you that," he added, stopping because his voice broke.

He looked away, getting control back breath by breath. He thought he felt her fingers move, but he couldn't be sure. "I'm going to get you out of here, honey, one way or the other, even if I have to walk out with you in my arms. Try to hold on, for me." He brought her hand to his mouth and kissed the palm hungrily. "Try to hold on, because if you die, so do I. I can't keep going unless you're somewhere in the world, even if I never see you again. Even if you hate me forever."

He swallowed hard and put down her hand. The sound of an airplane in the distance indicated that supplies were on the way. Quinn put Amanda's hand back under the cover and bent to brush his mouth against her cold, still one.

"I love you," he whispered roughly. "You've got to hold on until I can get you out of here."

He stood, his face like the stony crags above them, his eyes glittering as he joined the others.

The plane circled and seconds later, a white parachute appeared. Quinn held his breath as it descended, hoping against hope that the chute wouldn't hang up in the tall trees and that the toboggan would soft-land so that it was usable. A drop in this kind of wind was risky at best.

But luck was with them. The supplies and the sled made it in one piece. Quinn and the pilot and a couple of the sturdier survivors unfastened the chute and brought the contents back to the wreckage of the commuter plane. The sled was even equipped with blankets and a pillow and straps to keep Amanda secured.

Minutes later, the drone of a helicopter whispered on the wind, and not long after that, Hale started down the mountainside.

It took several minutes. Quinn saw the flash of rust that denoted the distinctive jacket and white waist pack of the Ski Patrol above, and when Hale came closer, he could see the gold cross on the right pocket of the jacket— a duplicate of the big one stenciled on the jacket's back. He smiled, remembering when he'd worn that same type of jacket during a brief stint as a ski patrolman. It was a special kind of occupation, and countless skiers owed their lives to those brave men and women. The National Ski Patrol had only existed since 1938. It was created by Charles Dole of Connecticut, after a skiing accident that took the life of one of his friends. Today, the Ski Patrol had over 10,000 members nationally, of whom ninety-eight percent were volunteers. They were the first on the slopes and the last off, patroling for dangerous areas and rescuing injured people. Quinn had once been part of that elite group and he still had the greatest respect for them.

Hale was the only color against the whiteness of the snow. The sun was out, and thank God it hadn't snowed all day. It had done enough of that last night.

Quinn's nerves were stretched. He hadn't had a cigarette since he'd arrived at the lodge, and he didn't dare have one now. Nicotine and caffeine tended to constrict blood vessels, and the cold was dangerous enough without giving it any help. Experienced skiers knew better than to stack the odds against themselves.

"Well, I made it." Hale grinned, getting his breath. "How are you, Quinn?" He extended a hand and Quinn shook it.

The man in the Ski Patrol jacket nodded to the others, accepted their thanks for the supplies he'd brought with him, which included a makeshift shelter and plenty of food and water and even a bottle of cognac. But he didn't waste time. "We'd better get moving if we hope to get Miss Callaway out of here by dark."

"She's over here," Quinn said. "God, I hate doing this," he added heavily when he and Hale were standing over the unconscious woman. "If there was any hope, any at all, that the chopper could get in here…"

"You can feel the wind for yourself," Hale replied, his eyes solemn. "We're the only chance she has. We'll get her to the chopper. Piece of cake," he added with a reassuring smile.

"I hope so," Quinn said somberly. He bent and nodded to Hale. They lifted her very gently onto the long sled containing the litter. It had handles on both ends, because it was designed to be towed. They attached the towlines, covered Amanda carefully and set out, with reassurances from the stranded survivors.

There was no time to talk. The track was fairly straightforward, but it worried Quinn, all the same, because there were crusts that jarred the woman on the litter. He towed, Hale guided, their rhythms matching perfectly as they made their way down the snow-covered valley. Around them, the wind sang through the tall firs and lodgepole pines, and Quinn thought about the old trappers and mountain men who must have come through this valley a hundred, two hundred years before. In those days of poor sanitation and even poorer medicine, Amanda wouldn't have stood a chance.

He forced himself not to look back. He had to concentrate on getting her to the Ridge. All that was important now, was that she get medical help while it could still do her some good. He hadn't come all this way to find her alive, only to lose her.

It seemed to take forever. Once Quinn was certain that they'd lost their way as they navigated through the narrow pass that led to the fifty-mile valley between the Grand Tetons and the Wind River Range, an area known as Jackson Hole. But he recognized landmarks as they went along, and eventually they wound their way around the trees and along the sparkling river until they reached the flats below Caraway Ridge.

Quinn and Hale were both breathing hard by now. They'd changed places several times, so that neither got too tired of towing the toboggan, and they were both in peak condition. But it was still a difficult thing to do.

They rested, and Quinn reached down to check Amanda's pulse. It was still there, and even seemed to be, incredibly, a little stronger than it had been. But she was pale and still and Quinn felt his spirits sink as he looked down at her.

"There it is," Hale called, sweeping his arm over the ridge. "The chopper."

"Now if only it can land," Quinn said quietly, and he began to pray.

The chopper came lower and lower, then it seemed to shoot up again and Quinn bit off a hard word. But the pilot corrected for the wind, which was dying down, and eased the helicopter toward the ground. It seemed to settle inch by inch until it landed safe. The pilot was out of it before the blades stopped.

"Let's get out of here," he called to the men. "If that wind catches up again, I wouldn't give us a chance in hell of getting out. It was a miracle that I even got in!"

Quinn released his bindings in a flash, leaving his skis and poles for Hale to carry, along with his own. He got one side of the stretcher while the pilot, fortunately no lightweight himself, got the other. They put the stretcher in the back of the broad helicopter, on the floor, and Quinn and Hale piled in—Hale in the passenger seat up front, Quinn behind with Amanda, carefully laying ski equipment beside her.

"Let's go!" the pilot called as he revved up the engine.

It was touch and go. The wind decided to play tag with them, and they almost went into a lodgepole pine on the way up. But the pilot was a tenacious man with good nerves. He eased down and then up, down and up until he caught the wind off guard and shot up out of the valley and over the mountain.

Quinn reached down and clasped Amanda's cold hand in his. Only a little longer, honey, he thought, watching her with his heart in his eyes. Only a little longer, for God's sake, hold on!

It was the longest ride of his entire life. He spared one thought for the people who'd stayed behind to give Amanda her chance and he prayed that they'd be rescued without any further injuries. Then his eyes settled on her pale face and stayed there until the helicopter landed on the hospital lawn.

The reporters, local, state and national, had gotten word of the rescue mission. They were waiting. Police kept them back just long enough for Amanda to be carried into the hospital, but Quinn and Hale were caught. Quinn volunteered Hale to give an account of the rescue and then he ducked out, leaving the other man to field the enthusiastic audience while he trailed quickly behind the men who'd taken Amanda into the emergency room.

He drank coffee and smoked cigarettes and glared at

walls for over an hour until someone came out to talk to him. Hale had to go back to the lodge, to help plan the rescue of the rest of the survivors, but he promised to keep in touch. After he'd gone, Quinn felt even more alone. But at last a doctor came into the waiting room, and approached him.

"Are you related to Miss Callaway?" the doctor asked with narrowed eyes.

Quinn knew that if he said no, he'd have to wait for news of her condition until he could find somebody who was related to her, and he had no idea how to find her aunt.

"I'm her fiancé," he said without moving a muscle in his face. "How is she?"

"Not good," the doctor, a small wiry man, said bluntly. "But I believe in miracles. We have her in intensive care, where she'll stay until she regains consciousness. She's badly concussed. I gather she hasn't regained consciousness since the crash?" Quinn shook his head. "That sleigh ride and helicopter lift didn't do any good, either," he added firmly, adding when he saw the expression on Quinn's tormented face, "but I can understand the necessity for it. Go get some sleep. Come back in the morning. We won't know anything until then. Maybe not until much later. Concussion is tricky. We can't predict the outcome, as much as we'd like to."

"I can't rest," Quinn said quietly. "I'll sit out here and drink coffee, if you don't mind. If this is as close to her as I can get, it'll have to do."

The doctor took a slow breath. "We keep spare beds in cases like this," he said. "I'll have one made up for you when you can't stay awake any longer." He smiled faintly. "Try to think positively. It isn't medical, exactly, but sometimes it works wonders. Prayer doesn't hurt, either."

"Thank you," Quinn said.

The doctor shrugged. "Wait until she wakes up. Good night."

Quinn watched him go and sighed. He didn't know what to do next. He phoned Terry at the lodge to see if Amanda's band had called. Someone named Jerry and a man called Hank had been phoning every few minutes, he was told. Quinn asked for a phone number and Terry gave it to him.

He dialed the area code. California, he figured as he waited for it to ring.

"Hello?"

"This is Quinn Sutton," he began.

"Yes, I recognize your voice. It's Hank here. How is she?"

"Concussion. Coma, I guess. She's in intensive care and she's still alive. That's about all I know."

There was a long pause. "I'd hoped for a little more than that."

"So had I," Quinn replied. He hesitated. "I'll phone you in the morning. The minute I know anything. Is there anybody we should notify...her aunt?"

"Her aunt is a scatterbrain and no help at all. Anyway, she's off with Blalock Durning in the Bahamas on one of those incommunicado islands. We couldn't reach her if we tried."

"Is there anybody else?" Quinn asked.

"Not that I know of." There was a brief pause. "I feel bad about the way things happened. I hate planes, you know. That's why the rest of us went by bus. We stopped here in some hick town to make sure Amanda got her plane, and Terry told us what happened. We got a motel room and we're waiting for a bus back to Jackson. It will probably be late tomorrow before we get there. We've already canceled the gig. We can't do it without Amanda."

"I'll book a room for you," Quinn said.

"Make it a suite," Hank replied, "and if you need anything, you know, anything, you just tell us."

"I've got plenty of cigarettes and the coffee machine's working. I'm fine."

"We'll see you when we get there. And Sutton—thanks. She really cares about you, you know?"

"I care about her," he said stiffly. "That's why I sent her away. My God, how could she give all that up to live on a mountain in Wyoming?"

"Amanda's not a city girl, though," Hank said slowly. "And she changed after those days she spent with you. Her heart wasn't with us anymore. She cried all last night…"

"Oh, God, don't," Quinn said.

"Sorry, man," Hank said quietly. "I'm really sorry, that's the last thing I should have said. Look, go smoke a cigarette. I think I'll tie one on royally and have the boys put me to bed. Tomorrow we'll talk. Take care."

"You, too."

Quinn hung up. He couldn't bear to think of Amanda crying because of what he'd done to her. He might lose her even yet, and he didn't know how he was going to go on living. He felt so alone.

He was out of change after he called the lodge and booked the suite for Hank and the others, but he still had to talk to Elliot and Harry. He dialed the operator and called collect. Elliot answered the phone immediately.

"How is she?" he asked quickly.

Quinn went over it again, feeling numb. "I wish I knew more," he concluded. "But that's all there is."

"She can't die," Elliot said miserably. "Dad, she just can't!"

"Say a prayer, son," he replied. "And don't let Harry teach you any bad habits while I'm gone."

"No, sir, I won't," Elliot said with a feeble attempt at humor. "You're going to stay, I guess?"

"I have to," Quinn said huskily. He hesitated. "I love her."

"So do I," Elliot said softly. "Bring her back when you come."

"If I can. If she'll even speak to me when she wakes up," Quinn said with a total lack of confidence.

"She will," Elliot told him. "You should have listened to some of those songs you thought were so horrible. One of hers won a Grammy. It was all about having to give up things we love to keep from hurting them. She always seemed to feel it when somebody was sad or hurt, you know. And she risked her own life trying to save that girl at the concert. She's not someone who thinks about getting even with people. She's got too much heart."

Quinn drew deeply from his cigarette. "I hope so, son," he said. "You get to bed. I'll call you tomorrow."

"Okay. Take care of yourself. Love you, Dad."

"Me, too, son," Quinn replied. He hung up. The waiting area was deserted now, and the hospital seemed to have gone to sleep. He sat down with his Styrofoam cup of black coffee and finished his cigarette. The room looked like he felt—empty.

CHAPTER TEN

IT WAS LATE morning when the nurse came to shake Quinn gently awake. Apparently around dawn he'd gone to sleep sitting up, with an empty coffee cup in his hand. He thought he'd never sleep at all.

He sat up, drowsy and disheveled. "How is Amanda?" he asked immediately.

The nurse, a young blonde, smiled at him. "She's awake and asking for you."

"Oh, thank God," he said heavily. He got quickly to his feet, still a little groggy, and followed her down to the intensive-care unit, where patients in tiny rooms were monitored from a central nurses' station and the hum and click and whir of life-supporting machinery filled the air. If she was asking for him, she must not hate him too much. That thought sustained him as he followed the nurse into one of the small cubicles where Amanda lay.

Amanda looked thinner than ever in the light, her face pinched, her eyes hollow, her lips chapped. They'd taken her hair down somewhere along the way and tied it back with a pink ribbon. She was propped up in bed, still with the IV in position, but she'd been taken off all the other machines.

She looked up and saw Quinn and all the weariness and pain went out of her face. She brightened, became beautiful despite her injuries, her eyes sparkling. Her last thought when she'd realized in the plane what was going to happen had been of Quinn. Her first thought when she'd regained consciousness had been of him. The pain, the grief of having him turn away from her was forgotten. He was here, now, and that meant he had to care about her.

"Oh, Quinn!" she whispered tearfully, and held out her arms.

He went to her without hesitation, ignoring the nurses, the aides, the whole world. His arms folded gently around her, careful of the tubes attached to her hand, and his head bent over hers, his cheek on her soft hair, his eyes closed as he shivered with reaction. She was alive. She was going to live. He felt as if he were going to choke to death on his own rush of feeling.

"My God," he whispered shakily. "I thought I'd lost you."

That was worth it all, she thought, dazed from the emotion in his voice, at the tremor in his powerful body as he held her. She clung to him, her slender arms around his neck, drowning in pleasure. She'd wondered if he hadn't sent her away in a misguided belief that it was for her own good. Now she was sure of it. He couldn't have looked that haggard, that terrible, unless she mattered very much to him. Her aching heart soared. "They said you brought me out."

"Hale and I did," he said huskily. He lifted his head, searching her bright eyes slowly. "It's been the longest night of my life. They said you might die."

"Oh, we Callaways are tough birds," she said, wiping away a tear. She was still weak and sore and her head-

SUTTON'S WAY

ache hadn't completely gone away. "You look terrible, my darling," she whispered on a choked laugh.

The endearment fired his blood. He had to take a deep breath before he could even speak. His fingers linked with hers. "I felt pretty terrible when we listened to the news report, especially when I remembered the things I said to you." He took a deep breath. "I didn't know if you'd hate me for the rest of your life, but even if you did, I couldn't just sit on my mountain and let other people look for you." His thumb gently stroked the back of her pale hand. "How do you feel, honey?"

"Pretty bad. But considering it all, I'll do. I'm sorry about the men who died. One of them was having a heart attack," she explained. "The other gentleman who was sitting with him alerted me. We both unfastened our seat belts to try and give CPR. Just after I got up, the plane started down," she said. "Quinn, do you believe in predestination?"

"You mean, that things happen the way they're meant to in spite of us?" He smiled. "I guess I do." His dark eyes slid over her face hungrily. "I'm so glad it wasn't your time, Amanda."

"So am I." She reached up and touched his thin mouth with just the tips of her fingers. "Where is it?" she asked with an impish smile as a sudden delicious thought occurred to her.

He frowned. "Where's what?"

"My engagement ring," she said. "And don't try to back out of it," she added firmly when he stood there looking shocked. "You told the doctor and the whole medical staff that I was your fiancée, and you're not ducking out of it now. You're going to marry me."

His eyebrows shot up. "I'm what?" he said blankly.

"You're going to marry me. Where's Hank? Has anybody phoned him?"

"I did. I was supposed to call him back." He checked his watch and grimaced. "I guess it's too late now. He and the band are on the way back here."

"Good. They're twice your size and at least as mean." Her eyes narrowed. "I'll tell them you seduced me. I could be pregnant." She nodded, thinking up lies fast while Quinn's face mirrored his stark astonishment. "That's right, I could."

"You could not," he said shortly. "I never...!"

"But you're going to," she said with a husky laugh. "Just wait until I get out of here and get you alone. I'll wrestle you down and start kissing you, and you'll never get away in time."

"Oh, God," he groaned, because he knew she was right. He couldn't resist her that way, it was part of the problem.

"So you'll have to marry me first," she continued. "Because I'm not that kind of girl. Not to mention that you aren't that kind of guy. Harry likes me and Elliot and I are already friends, and I could even get used to McNaber if he'll move those traps." She pursed her lips, thinking. "The concert tour is going to be a real drag, but once it's over, I'll retire from the stage and just make records and tapes and CDs with the guys. Maybe a video now and again. They'll like that, too. We're all basically shy and we don't like live shows. I'll compose songs. I can do that at the house, in between helping Harry with the cooking and looking after sick calves, and having babies," she added with a shy smile.

He wanted to sit down. He hadn't counted on this. All that had mattered at the time was getting her away from the wreckage and into a hospital where she could be cared for. He hadn't let himself think ahead. But she obviously had. His head spun with her plans.

"Listen, you're an entertainer," he began. His fingers curled around hers and he looked down at them with a hard, grim sigh. "Amanda, I'm a poor man. All I've got is a broken-down ranch in the middle of nowhere. You'd have a lot of hardships, because I won't live on your money. I've got a son, even if he isn't mine, and…"

She brought his hand to her cheek and held it there, nuzzling her cheek against it as she looked up at him with dark, soft, adoring eyes. "I love you," she whispered.

He faltered. His cheeks went ruddy as the words penetrated, touched him, excited him. Except for his mother and Elliot, nobody had ever said that to him before Amanda had. "Do you?" he asked huskily. "Still? Even after the way I walked off and left you there at the lodge that night? After what I said to you on the phone?" he added, because he'd had too much time to agonize over his behavior, even if it had been for what he thought was her own good.

"Even after that," she said gently. "With all my heart. I just want to live with you, Quinn. In the wilds of Wyoming, in a grass shack on some island, in a mansion in Beverly Hills—it would all be the same to me—as long as you loved me back and we could be together for the rest of our lives."

He felt a ripple of pure delight go through him. "Is that what you really want?" he asked, searching her dark eyes with his own.

"More than anything else in the world," she confessed. "That's why I couldn't tell you who and what I really was. I loved you so much, and I knew you wouldn't want me…" Her voice trailed off.

"I want you, all right," he said curtly. "I never stopped. Damn it, woman, I was trying to do what was best for you!"

"By turning me out in the cold and leaving me to starve to death for love?" she asked icily. "Thanks a bunch!"

He looked away uncomfortably. "It wasn't that way and you know it. I thought maybe it was the novelty. You know, a lonely man in the backwoods," he began.

"You thought I was having the time of my life playing you for a fool," she said. Her head was beginning to hurt, but she had to wrap it all up before she gave in and asked for some more medication. "Well, you listen to me, Quinn Sutton, I'm not the type to go around deliberately trying to hurt people. All I ever wanted was somebody to care about me—just me, not the pretty girl on the stage."

"Yes, I know that now," he replied. He brought her hand to his mouth and softly kissed the palm. The look on his face weakened her. "So you want a ring, do you? It will have to be something sensible. No flashy diamonds, even if I could give you something you'd need sunglasses to look at."

"I'll settle for the paper band on a King Edward cigar if you'll just marry me," she replied.

"I think I can do a little better than that," he murmured dryly. He bent over her, his lips hovering just above hers. "And no long engagement," he whispered.

"It takes three days, doesn't it?" she whispered back. "That *is* a long engagement. Get busy!"

He stifled a laugh as he brushed his hard mouth gently over her dry one. "Get well," he whispered. "I'll read some books real fast."

She colored when she realized what kind of books he was referring to, and then smiled under his tender kiss. "You do that," she breathed. "Oh, Quinn, get me out of here!"

"At the earliest possible minute," he promised.

The band showed up later in the day while Quinn was out buying an engagement ring for Amanda. He'd already called and laughingly told Elliot and Harry what she'd done to him, and was delighted with Elliot's pleasure in the news and Harry's teasing. He did buy her a diamond, even if it was a moderate one, and a gold band for each of them. It gave him the greatest kind of thrill to know that he was finally marrying for all the right reasons.

When he got back to the hospital, the rest of the survivors had been airlifted out and all but one of them had been treated and released. The news media had tried to get to Amanda, but the band arrived shortly after Quinn left and ran interference. Hank gave out a statement and stopped them. The road manager, as Quinn found out, had gone on to San Francisco to make arrangements for canceling the concert.

The boys were gathered around Amanda, who'd been moved into a nice private room. She was sitting up in bed, looking much better, and her laughing dark eyes met Quinn's the minute he came in the door.

"Hank brought a shotgun," she informed him. "And Deke and Johnson and Jack are going to help you down the aisle. Jerry's found a minister, and Hank's already arranged a blood test for you right down the hall. The license—"

"Is already applied for," Quinn said with a chuckle. "I did that myself. Hello, boys," he greeted them, shaking hands as he was introduced to the rest of the band. "And you can unload the shotgun. I'd planned to hold it on Amanda, if she tried to back out."

"Me, back out? Heaven forbid!" she exclaimed, smiling as Quinn bent to kiss her. "Where's my ring?" she whispered against his hard mouth. "I want it on, so these nurses won't make eyes at you. There's this gorgeous redhead…"

"I can't see past you, pretty thing," he murmured, his eyes soft and quiet in a still-gaunt face. "Here it is." Quinn produced it and slid it on her finger. He'd measured the size with a small piece of paper he'd wrapped around her finger, and he hoped that the method worked. He needn't have worried, because the ring was a perfect fit, and she acted as if it were the three-carat monster he'd wanted to get her. Her face lit up, like her pretty eyes, and she beamed as she showed it to the band.

"Did you sleep at all?" Hank asked him while the others gathered around Amanda.

"About an hour, I think," Quinn murmured dryly. "You?"

"I couldn't even get properly drunk," Hank said, sighing, "so the boys and I played cards until we caught the bus. We slept most of the way in. It was a long ride. From what I hear," he added with a level look, "you and that Hale fellow had an even longer one, bringing Amanda out of the mountains."

"You'll never know." Quinn looked past him to Amanda, his dark eyes full of remembered pain. "I had to decide whether or not to move her. I thought it was riskier to leave her there until the next morning. If we'd waited, we had no guarantee that the helicopter would have been able to land even then. She could have died. It's a miracle she didn't."

"Miracles come in all shapes and sizes," Hank mused, staring at her. "She's been ours. Without her, we'd never have gotten anywhere. But being on the road has worn her out. The boys and I were talking on the way back about cutting out personal appearances and concentrating on videos and albums. I think Amanda might like that. She'll have enough to do from now on, I imagine, taking care of you and your boy," he added with a grin. "Not to mention all those new brothers and sisters you'll be adding. I grew up on a ranch," he said surprisingly. "I have five brothers."

Quinn's eyebrows lifted. "Are they all runts like you?" he asked with a smile.

"I'm the runt," Hank corrected.

Quinn just shook his head.

AMANDA WAS RELEASED from the hospital two days later. Every conceivable test had been done, and fortunately there were no complications. The doctor had been cautiously optimistic at first, but her recovery was rapid—probably due, the doctor said with a smile, to her incentive. He gave Amanda away at the brief ceremony, held in the hospital's chapel just before she was discharged, and one of the nurses was her matron of honor. There were a record four best men; the band. But for all its brevity and informality, it was a ceremony that Amanda would never forget. The Methodist minister who performed it had a way with words, and Amanda and Quinn felt just as married as if they'd had the service performed in a huge church with a large crowd present.

The only mishap was that the press found out about the wedding, and Amanda and Quinn and the band were mobbed as they made their way out of the hospital afterward. The size of the band members made them keep well back. Hank gave them his best wildman glare while Jack whispered something about the bandleader becoming homicidal if he was pushed too far. They escaped in two separate cars. The driver of the one taking Quinn and Amanda to the lodge managed to get them there over back roads, so that nobody knew where they were.

Terry had given them the bridal suite, on the top floor of the lodge, and the view of the snowcapped mountains was exquisite. Amanda, still a little shaky and very nervous, stared out at them with mixed feelings.

"I don't know if I'll ever think of them as postcards again," she remarked to Quinn, who was trying to find places to put everything from their suitcase. He'd had to go to Ricochet for his suit and a change of clothing.

"What, the mountains?" he asked, smiling at her. "Well, it's not a bad thing to respect them. But airplanes don't crash that often, and when you're well enough, I'm going to teach you to ski."

She turned and looked at him for a long time. Her wedding outfit was an off-white, a very simple shirtwaist dress with a soft collar and no frills. But with her long hair around her shoulders and down to her waist, framed in the light coming through the window, she looked the picture of a bride. Quinn watched her back and sighed, his eyes lingering on the small sprig of lily of the valley she was wearing in her hair—a present from a member of the hospital staff.

"One of the nurses brought me a newspaper," Amanda said. "It told all about how you and Mr. Hale got me out." She hesitated. "They said that only a few men could ski that particular mountain without killing themselves."

"I've been skiing it for years," he said simply. He took off the dark jacket of his suit and loosened his tie with a long sigh. "I knew that the Ski Patrol would get you out, but they usually only work the lodge slopes—you know, the ones with normal ski runs. The peak the plane landed on was off the lodge property and out-of-the-way. It hadn't even been inspected. There are all sorts of dangers on slopes like that—fallen trees, boulders, stumps, debris, not to mention the threat of avalanche. The Ski Patrol marks dangerous runs where they work. They're the first out in the morning and the last off the slopes in the afternoon."

"You seem to know a lot about it," Amanda said.

"I used to be one of them," he replied with a grin. "In my younger days. It's pretty rewarding."

"There was a jacket Harry showed me," she frowned. "A rust-colored one with a big gold cross on the back..."

"My old patrol jacket." He chuckled. "I wouldn't part with it for the world. If I'd thought of it, I'd have worn it that day." His eyes darkened as he looked at her. "Thank God I knew that slope," he said huskily. "Because I'd bet money that you wouldn't have lasted on that mountain overnight."

"I was thinking about you when the plane went down," she confessed. "I wasn't sure that I'd ever see you again."

"Neither was I when I finally got to you." He took off his tie and threw it aside. His hand absently unfastened the top buttons of his white shirt as he moved toward her. "I was trying so hard to do the right thing," he murmured. "I didn't think I could give you what you needed, what you were used to."

"I'm used to you, Mr. Sutton," she murmured with a smile. Amanda slid her arms under his and around him, looking up at him with her whole heart in her dark eyes. "Bad temper, irritable scowl and all. Anything you can't give me, I don't want. Will that do?"

His broad chest rose and fell slowly. "I can't give you much. I've lost damned near everything."

"You have Elliot and Harry and me," she pointed out. "And some fat, healthy calves, and in a few years, Elliot will have a lot of little brothers and sisters to help him on the ranch."

A faint dusky color stained his high cheekbones. "Yes."

"Why, Mr. Sutton, honey, you aren't shy, are you?" she whispered dryly as she moved her hands back around to his shirt and finished unbuttoning it down his tanned, hair-roughened chest.

"Of course I'm shy," he muttered, heating up at the feel of her slender hands on his skin. He caught his breath and shuddered when she kissed him there. His big hands slid into her long, silky hair and brought her even closer. "I like that," he breathed roughly. "Oh, God, I love it!"

She drew back after a minute, her eyes sultry, drowsy.

"Wouldn't you like to do that to me?" she whispered. "I like it, too."

He fumbled with buttons until he had the dress out of the way and she was standing in nothing except a satin teddy. He'd never seen one before, except in movies, and he stared at her with his breath stuck somewhere in his chest. It was such a sexy garment low on her lace-covered breasts, nipped at her slender waist, hugging her full hips. Below it were her elegant silk-clad legs, although he didn't see anything holding up her hose.

"It's a teddy," she whispered. "If you want to slide it down," she added shyly, lowering her eyes to his pulsating chest, "I could step out of it."

He didn't know if he could do that and stay on his feet. The thought of Amanda unclothed made his knees weak. But he slid the straps down her arms and slowly, slowly, peeled it away from her firm, hard-tipped breasts, over her flat stomach, and then over the panty hose she was wearing. He caught them as well and eased the whole silky mass down to the floor.

She stepped out of it, so much in love with him that all her earlier shyness was evaporating. It was as new for him as it was for her, and that made it beautiful. A true act of love.

She let him look at her, fascinated by the awe in his hard face, in the eyes that went over her like an artist's brush, capturing every line, every soft curve before he even touched her.

"Amanda, you're the most beautiful creature I've ever seen," he said finally. "You look like a drawing of a fairy I saw in an old-time storybook...all gold and ivory."

She reached up and leaned close against him, shivering a little when her breasts touched his bare chest. The hair was faintly abrasive and very arousing. She moved involuntarily and gasped at the sensation.

"Do you want to help me?" he whispered as he stripped off his shirt and his hands went to his belt.

"I…" She hesitated, her nerve retreating suddenly at the intimacy of it. She grimaced. "Oh, Quinn, I'm such a coward!" She hid her face against his chest and felt his laughter.

"Well, you're not alone," he murmured. "I'm not exactly an exhibitionist myself. Look, why don't you get under the covers and close your eyes, and we'll pretend it's dark."

She looked up at him and laughed. "This is silly."

"Yes, I know." He sighed. "Well, honey, we're married. I guess it's time to face all the implications of sharing a bed."

He sat down, took off his boots and socks, stood to unbuckle his belt, holding her eyes, and slid the zip down. Everything came off, and seconds later, she saw for herself all the differences between men and women.

"You've gone scarlet, Mrs. Sutton," he observed.

"You aren't much whiter yourself, Mr. Sutton," she replied.

He laughed and reached for her and she felt him press against her. It was incredible, the feel of skin against skin, hair-rough flesh against silky softness. He bent and found her mouth and began to kiss her lazily, while his big, rough hands slid down her back and around to her hips. His mouth opened at the same time that his fingers pulled her thighs against his, and she felt for the first time the stark reality of arousal.

He felt her gasp and lifted his head, searching her flushed face. "That has to happen before anything else can," he whispered. "Don't be afraid. I think I know enough to make it easy for you."

"I love you, Quinn," she whispered back, forcing her taut muscles to relax, to give in to him. She leaned her body into his with a tiny shiver and lifted her mouth. "However it happens between us, it will be all right."

He searched her eyes and nodded. His mouth lowered to hers. He kissed her with exquisite tenderness while his hands found the softness of her breasts. Minutes later, his mouth traced them, covered the hard tips in a warm, moist suction that drew new sounds from her. He liked that, so he lifted her and put her on the big bed, and found other places to kiss her that made the sounds louder and more tormented.

The book had been very thorough and quite explicit, so he knew what to do in theory. Practice was very different. He hadn't known that women could lose control, too. That their bodies were so soft, or so strong. That their eyes grew wild and their faces contorted as the pleasure built in them, that they wept with it. Her pleasure became his only goal in the long, exquisite oblivion that followed.

By the time he moved over her, she was more than ready for him, she was desperate for him. He whispered to her, gently guided her body to his as he fought for control of his own raging need so that he could satisfy hers first.

There was one instant when she stiffened and tried to pull away, but he stopped then and looked down into her frightened eyes.

"It will only hurt for a few seconds," he whispered

huskily. "Link your hands in mine and hold on. I'll do it quickly."

"All…all right." She felt the strength in his hands and her eyes met his. She swallowed.

He pushed, hard. She moaned a little, but her body accepted him instantly and without any further difficulty.

Her eyes brightened. Her lips parted and she breathed quickly and began to smile. "It's gone," she whispered. "Quinn, I'm a woman now…."

"My woman," he whispered back. The darkness grew in his eyes. He bent to her mouth and captured it, held it as he began to move, his body dancing above hers, teaching it the rhythm. She followed where he led, gasping as the cadence increased, as the music began to grow in her mind and filtered through her arms and legs. She held on to him with the last of her strength, proud of his stamina, of the power in his body that was taking hers from reality and into a place she'd never dreamed existed.

She felt the first tremors begin, and work into her like fiery pins, holding her body in a painful arch as she felt the tension build. It grew to unbearable levels. Her head thrashed on the pillow and she wanted to push him away, to make him stop, because she didn't think she could live through what was happening to her. But just as she began to push him the tension broke and she fell, crying out, into a hot, wild satisfaction that convulsed her. Above her, Quinn saw it happen and finally gave in to the desperate fever of his own need. He drove for his own satisfaction and felt it take him, his voice breaking on Amanda's name as he went into the fiery depths with her.

Afterward, he started to draw away, but her arms went

around him and refused to let go. He felt her tears against his hot throat.

"Are you all right?" he asked huskily.

"I died," she whispered brokenly. Her arms contracted. "Don't go away, please don't. I don't want to let you go," she moaned.

He let his body relax, giving her his full weight. "I'll crush you, honey," he whispered in her ear.

"No, you won't." She sighed, feeling his body pulse with every heartbeat, feeling the dampness of his skin on her own, the glory of his flesh touching hers. "This is nice."

He laughed despite his exhaustion. "There's a new word for it," he murmured. He growled and bit her shoulder gently. "Wildcat," he whispered proudly. "You bit me. Do you remember? You bit me and dug your nails into my hips and screamed."

"So did you," she accused, flushing. "I'll have bruises on my thighs…"

"Little ones," he agreed. He lifted his head and searched her dark, quiet eyes. "I couldn't help that, at the last. I lost it. Really lost it. Are you as sated as I am?" he mused. "I feel like I've been walking around like half a person all my life, and I've just become whole."

"So do I." Her eyes searched his, and she lifted a lazy hand to trace his hard, thin lips. After a few seconds, she lifted her hips where they were still joined to his and watched his eyes kindle. She drew in a shaky breath and did it again, delighting in the sudden helpless response of his body.

"That's impossible," he joked. "The book said so."

Amanda pulled his mouth down to hers. "Damn the

book," she said and held on as he answered her hunger with his own.

They slept and finally woke just in time to go down to dinner. But since neither of them wanted to face having to get dressed, they had room service send up a tray. They drank champagne and ate thick steaks and went back to bed. Eventually they even slept.

The next morning, they set out for Ricochet, holding hands all the way home.

CHAPTER ELEVEN

ELLIOT AND HARRY were waiting at the door when Quinn brought Amanda home. There was a big wedding cake on the table that Harry had made, and a special present that Elliot had made Harry drive him to town in the sleigh to get—a new Desperado album with a picture of Amanda on the cover.

"What a present," Quinn murmured, smiling at Amanda over the beautiful photograph. "I guess I'll have to listen to it now, won't I?"

"I even got Hank Shoeman's autograph," Elliot enthused. "Finally I can tell the guys at school! I've been going nuts ever since I realized who Amanda was...."

"You knew?" Quinn burst out. "And you didn't tell me? So that's why that tape disappeared."

"You were looking for it?" Elliot echoed.

"Sure, just after we got home from the lodge that night I deserted Amanda," Quinn said with a rueful glance at her. "I was feeling pretty low. I just wanted to hear her voice, but the tape was missing."

"Sorry, Dad," Elliot said gently. "I'll never do it again, but I was afraid you'd toss her out if you knew she was a rock singer. She's really terrific, you know, and that song that won a Grammy was one of hers."

"Stop, you'll make me blush," Amanda groaned.

"I can do that," Quinn murmured dryly and the look he gave Amanda brought scarlet color into her hot cheeks.

"You were in the paper, Dad," Elliot continued excitedly. "And on the six o'clock news, too! They told all about your skiing days and the Olympic team. Dad, why didn't you keep going? They said you were one of the best giant slalom skiers this country ever produced, but that you quit with a place on the Olympic team in your pocket."

"It's a long story, Elliot," he replied.

"It was because of my mother, wasn't it?" the boy asked gravely.

"Well, you were on the way and I didn't feel right about deserting her at such a time."

"Even though she'd been so terrible to you?" he probed.

Quinn put his hands on his son's shoulders. "I'll tell you for a fact, Elliot, you were mine from the day I knew about your existence. I waited for you like a kid waiting for a Christmas present. I bought stuff and read books about babies and learned all the things I'd need to know to help your mother raise you. I'd figured, you see, that she might eventually decide that having you was pretty special. I'm sorry that she didn't."

"That's okay," Elliot said with a smile. "You did."

"You bet I did. And do."

"Since you like kids so much, you and Amanda might have a few of your own," Elliot decided. "I can help. Me and Harry can wash diapers and make formula..."

Amanda laughed delightedly. "Oh, you doll, you!" She hugged Elliot. "Would you really not mind other kids around?"

"Heck, no," Elliot said with genuine feeling. "All the other guys have little brothers and sisters. It gets sort of lonely, being the only one." He looked up at her admiringly. "And they'd be awful pretty, if some of them were girls."

She grinned. "Maybe we'll get lucky and have another redhead, too. My mother was redheaded. So was my grandmother. It runs in the family."

Elliot liked that, and said so.

"Hank Shoeman has a present for you, by the way," she told Elliot. "No, there's no use looking in the truck, he ordered it."

Elliot's eyes lit up. "What is it? An autographed photo of the group?"

"It's a keyboard," Amanda corrected gently, smiling at his awe. "A real one, a moog like I play when we do instrumentals."

"Oh, my gosh!" Elliot sat down. "I've died and gone to heaven. First I get a great new mother and now I get a moog. Maybe I'm real sick and have a high fever," he frowned, feeling his forehead.

"No, you're perfectly well," Quinn told him. "And I guess it's all right if you play some rock songs," he added with a grimace. "I got used to turnips, after all, that time when Harry refused to cook any more greens. I guess I can get used to loud music."

"I refused to cook greens because we had a blizzard and canned turnips was all I had," Harry reminded him, glowering. "Now that Amanda's here, we won't run out of beans and peas and such, because she'll remember to tell me we're out so I can get some more."

"I didn't forget to remind you," Quinn muttered.

"You did so," Elliot began. "I remember—"

"That's it, gang up on me," Quinn glowered at them.

"Don't you worry, sweet man, I'll protect you from ghastly turnips and peas and beans," she said with a quick glance at Harry and Elliot. "I like asparagus, so I'll make sure that's all we keep here. Don't you guys like asparagus?"

"Yes!" they chorused, having been the culprits who told Amanda once that Quinn hated asparagus above all food in the world.

Quinn groaned.

"And I'll make liver and onions every night," Amanda added. "We love that, don't we, gang?"

"We sure do!" they chorused again, because they knew it was the only meat Quinn wouldn't eat.

"I'll go live with McNaber," he threatened.

Amanda laughed and slid her arms around him. "Only if we get to come, too." She looked up at him. "It's all right. We all really hate asparagus and liver and onions."

"That's a fact, we do," Elliot replied. "Amanda, are you going to go on tour with the band?"

"No," she said quietly. "We'd all gotten tired of the pace. We're going to take a well-earned rest and concentrate on videos and albums."

"I've got this great idea for a video," Elliot volunteered.

She grinned. "Okay, tiger, you can share it with us when Hank and the others come for a visit."

His eyes lit up. "They're all coming? The whole group?"

"My aunt is marrying Mr. Durning," she told him, having found out that tidbit from Hank. "They're going to live in Hawaii, and the band has permission to use the cabin whenever they like. They've decided that if I like the mountains so much, there must be something special about them. Our next album is going to be built around a mountain theme."

"Wow." Elliot sighed. "Wait'll I tell the guys."

"You and the guys can be in the video," Amanda promised. "We'll find some way to fit you into a scene or two." She studied Harry. "We'll put Harry in, too."

"Oh, no, you won't!" he said. "I'll run away from home first."

"If you do, we'll starve to death." Amanda sighed. "I can't do cakes and roasts. We'll have to live on potatoes and fried eggs."

"Then you just make a movie star out of old Elliot and I'll stick around," he promised.

"Okay," Amanda said, "but what a loss to women everywhere. You'd have been super, Harry."

He grinned and went back to the kitchen to cook. Elliot eventually wandered off, too, and Quinn took Amanda into the study and closed the door.

They sat together in his big leather armchair, listening to the crackling of the fire in the potbellied stove.

"Remember the last time we were in here together?" he asked lazily between kisses.

"Indeed, I do," she murmured with a smile against his throat. "We almost didn't stop in time."

"I'm glad we did." He linked her fingers with his. "We had a very special first time. A real wedding night. That's marriage the way it was meant to be; a feast of first times."

She touched his cheek lightly and searched his dark

eyes. "I'm glad we waited, too. I wanted so much to go
to my husband untouched. I just want you to know that
it was worth the wait. I love you, really love you, you
know?" She sighed shakily. "That made it much more
than my first intimate experience."

He brought his mouth down gently on hers. "I felt just
that way about it," he breathed against her lips. "I never
asked if you wanted me to use anything…?"

"So I wouldn't get pregnant?" She smiled gently. "I
love kids."

"So do I." He eased back and pulled her cheek onto his
chest, smoothing her long, soft hair as he smiled down
into her eyes. "I never dreamed I'd find anyone like you.
I'd given up on women. On life, too, I guess. I've been
bitter and alone for such a long time, Amanda. I feel like
I was just feverish and dreaming it all."

"You aren't dreaming." She pulled him closer to her
and kissed him with warm, slow passion. "We're married
and I'm going to love you for the rest of my life, body and
soul. So don't get any ideas about trying to get away. I've
caught you fair and square and you're all mine."

He chuckled. "Really? If you've caught me, what are
you going to do with me?"

"Have I got an answer for that," she whispered with
a sultry smile. "You did lock the door, didn't you?" she
murmured, her voice husky as she lifted and turned so
that she was facing him, her knees beside him on the
chair. His heart began to race violently.

"Yes, I locked the door. What are you…Amanda!"

She smiled against his mouth while her hands worked
at fastenings. "That's my name, all right," she whispered.
She nipped his lower lip gently and laughed delightedly

when she felt him helping her. "Life is short. We'd better start living it right now."

"I couldn't possibly agree more," he whispered back, and his husky laugh mingled with hers in the tense silence of the room.

Beside them, the burning wood crackled and popped in the stove while the snow began to fall again outside the window. Amanda had started it, but almost immediately Quinn took control and she gave in with a warm laugh. She knew already that things were done Sutton's way around Ricochet. And this time, she didn't really mind at all.

* * * * *

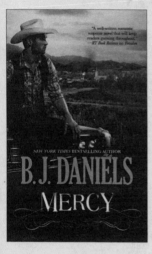

REQUEST YOUR FREE BOOKS!

2 FREE NOVELS
FROM THE ROMANCE COLLECTION
PLUS 2 FREE GIFTS!

YES! Please send me 2 FREE novels from the Romance Collection and my 2 FREE gifts (gifts are worth about $10). After receiving them, if I don't wish to receive any more books, I can return the shipping statement marked "cancel." If I don't cancel, I will receive 4 brand-new novels every month and be billed just $6.24 per book in the U.S. or $6.74 per book in Canada. That's a savings of at least 22% off the cover price. It's quite a bargain! Shipping and handling is just 50¢ per book in the U.S. and 75¢ per book in Canada.* I understand that accepting the 2 free books and gifts places me under no obligation to buy anything. I can always return a shipment and cancel at any time. Even if I never buy another book, the two free books and gifts are mine to keep forever.

194/394 MDN F4XY

Name	(PLEASE PRINT)	
Address		Apt. #
City	State/Prov.	Zip/Postal Code

Signature (if under 18, a parent or guardian must sign)

Mail to the **Harlequin® Reader Service:**
IN U.S.A.: P.O. Box 1867, Buffalo, NY 14240-1867
IN CANADA: P.O. Box 609, Fort Erie, Ontario L2A 5X3

Want to try two free books from another line?
Call 1-800-873-8635 or visit www.ReaderService.com.

* Terms and prices subject to change without notice. Prices do not include applicable taxes. Sales tax applicable in N.Y. Canadian residents will be charged applicable taxes. Offer not valid in Quebec. This offer is limited to one order per household. Not valid for current subscribers to the Romance Collection or the Romance/Suspense Collection. All orders subject to credit approval. Credit or debit balances in a customer's account(s) may be offset by any other outstanding balance owed by or to the customer. Please allow 4 to 6 weeks for delivery. Offer available while quantities last.

Your Privacy—The Harlequin® Reader Service is committed to protecting your privacy. Our Privacy Policy is available online at www.ReaderService.com or upon request from the Harlequin Reader Service.

We make a portion of our mailing list available to reputable third parties that offer products we believe may interest you. If you prefer that we not exchange your name with third parties, or if you wish to clarify or modify your communication preferences, please visit us at www.ReaderService.com/consumerchoice or write to us at Harlequin Reader Service Preference Service, P.O. Box 9062, Buffalo, NY 14269. Include your complete name and address.

ROM13R

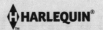
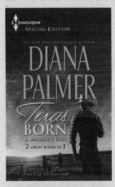

DIANA PALMER

77975	LONG, TALL TEXANS VOLUME 1:		
	CALHOUN & JUSTIN	___ $7.99 U.S.	___ $8.99 CAN.
77854	PROTECTOR	___ $7.99 U.S.	___ $8.99 CAN.
77762	COURAGEOUS	___ $7.99 U.S.	___ $9.99 CAN.
77727	NOELLE	___ $7.99 U.S.	___ $9.99 CAN.
77724	WYOMING BOLD	___ $7.99 U.S.	___ $8.99 CAN.
77666	MERCILESS	___ $7.99 U.S.	___ $9.99 CAN.
77633	LACY	___ $7.99 U.S.	___ $9.99 CAN.
77631	NORA	___ $7.99 U.S.	___ $9.99 CAN.
77570	DANGEROUS	___ $7.99 U.S.	___ $9.99 CAN.
77283	LAWMAN	___ $7.99 U.S.	___ $7.99 CAN.

(limited quantities available)

TOTAL AMOUNT	$_____
POSTAGE & HANDLING	$_____
($1.00 FOR 1 BOOK, 50¢ for each additional)	
APPLICABLE TAXES*	$_____
TOTAL PAYABLE	$_____

(check or money order—please do not send cash)

To order, complete this form and send it, along with a check or money order for the total above, payable to Harlequin HQN, to: **In the U.S.:** 3010 Walden Avenue, P.O. Box 9077, Buffalo, NY 14269-9077; **In Canada:** P.O. Box 636, Fort Erie, Ontario, L2A 5X3.

Name: _____
Address: _____ City: _____
State/Prov.: _____ Zip/Postal Code: _____
Account Number (if applicable): _____

075 CSAS

*New York residents remit applicable sales taxes.
*Canadian residents remit applicable GST and provincial taxes.

HARLEQUIN® HQN™
www.Harlequin.com

PHDP0914BL